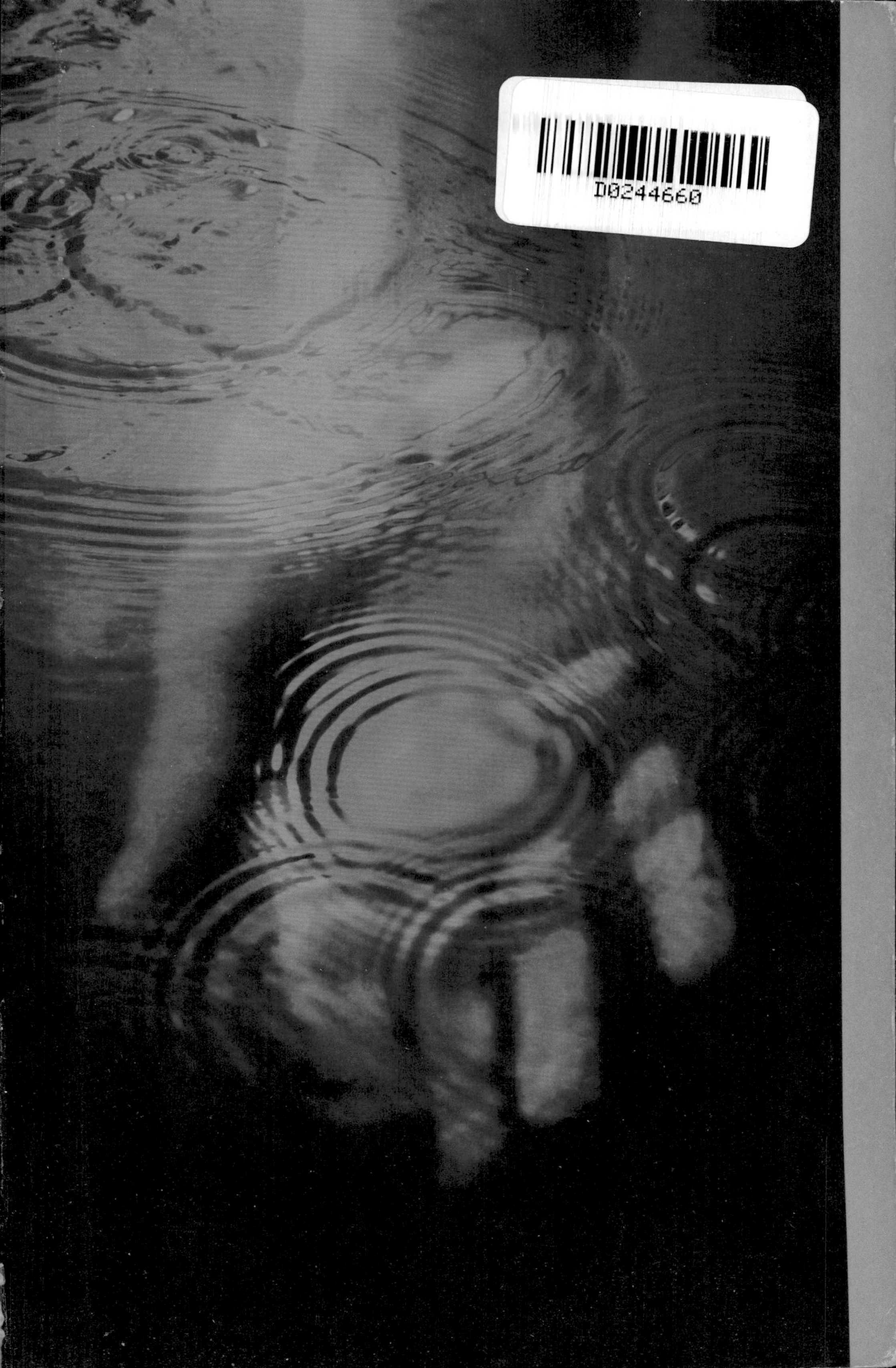

# THIS THING OF DARKNESS

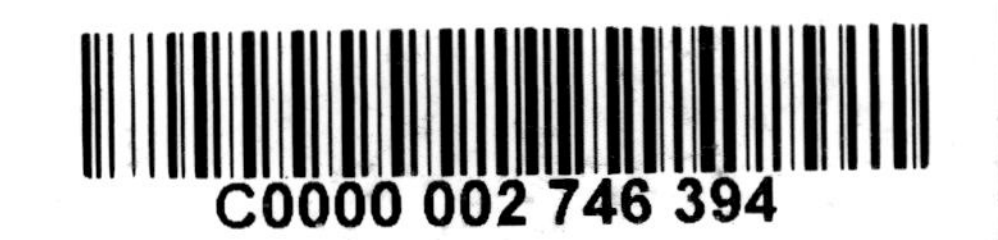

***Also by Harry Bingham***

*Fiction*

Talking to the Dead
Love Story, With Murders
The Strange Death of Fiona Griffiths

The Money Makers
Sweet Talking Money
The Sons of Adam
Glory Boys
The Lieutenant's Lover

*Non-Fiction*

This Little Britain
Stuff Matters
Getting Published
How to Write

# THIS THING OF DARKNESS

HARRY BINGHAM

First published in Great Britain in 2015 by Orion Books,
an imprint of The Orion Publishing Group Ltd
Carmelite House, 50 Victoria Embankment
London EC4Y 0DZ

An Hachette UK Company

1 3 5 7 9 10 8 6 4 2



A CIP catalogue record for this book is
available from the British Library.

ISBN (Trade Paperback) 978 1 4091 5271 2
ISBN (Ebook) 978 1 4091 5273 6

Typeset by Input Data Services Ltd, Bridgwater, Somerset

Printed and bound by CPI Group (UK) Ltd, Croydon, CR0 4YY

The Orion Publishing Group's policy is to use papers that
are natural, renewable and recyclable products and made
from wood grown in sustainable forests. The logging and
manufacturing processes are expected to conform to the
environmental regulations of the country of origin.

www.orionbooks.co.uk

To N, as always

You who are so beautiful
Have called my soul to wakefulness
The moon stands still.
A singing rib in my aching side
You shall abide.
Bright, arterial, true.

# 1

***March 2013***

Rain.

Or not rain, not really. More like a fine mist, a net of moisture. Hair speckles with it. The flanks of the heifers in the lower fields glisten with it. On ash and willow trees, the new buds at the end of each twig gleam with light. Even the spiky hawthorn catches the mood, softening into something almost delicate.

I'm on Gwyn's farm. I've been here three weeks. Iestyn, the labourer who does most of the heavier work around the place these days, is teaching me how to maintain a diesel engine.

'See that hose? It's getting knackered.'

He pokes at a bit of dirty tubing. The engine we're repairing belongs to a 1988 Massey Ferguson. One of its side panels is falling off and is held up with baling twine. The driver's door lies in the hedge behind us.

I agree with his verdict.

'It's a cooling hose, see? And because it's a diesel, you need good cooling.'

I don't say anything, but I expect my face somehow signifies the scope of my knowledge.

Iestyn – blue boiler suit, attractively curly brown hair and blue eyes – steps back. Rain beads on the rough cotton of his shoulders and sleeves.

'You got no spark plugs with a diesel. Ignition doesn't

happen because you're throwing a spark in. It happens because you compress your mixture, your fuel and air, compress it so hard that the temperature rises and – bang! ignition. It's a good system, but it runs very hot. If you don't cool it, you'll wreck your engine.'

He's a good teacher. Natural. Guides me back to the engine, shows where the cylinders are located. How the coolant reaches the parts it needs to reach. Gets me to remove the cooling hose and I see that it is, indeed, about to give way.

I replace the hose under his guidance. He explains the mysteries of the gasket, initiates me into the secrets of the oil filter. I'm clumsy to start with, but I realise I like this. Closing the wrench over a nut gummy with oil and grime. Getting it to loosen. Finding the gleam of clean metal amidst the filth. I change the oil filter and inspect the air filter.

We work for an hour and a half, then the rain starts to fall more insistently, the hills frown with cloud, and Gwyn shouts to us that lunch is ready. It's only eleven, but we've been up since five.

I don't know why I'm here.

Holiday, that's the official reason. Holiday, plus a period of study leave: I'm taking my OSPRE Part 1 exam shortly – a necessary step for advancement to sergeant – and in theory I'm here poring over the 1,300 pages of the various Blackstone's Policing Manuals, trying to figure out whether or not I need to be wearing uniform in order to prevent someone going to a rave and reminding myself of the precise age at which it becomes legal to supervise someone in the use of a crossbow. Somehow, though, I'm finding it hard to get concerned about rave-going archers. Not here, with ditches that need clearing and tractors that need fixing.

The truth is, things haven't been going well for me since my last big case. I broke off my engagement to Dave 'Buzz' Brydon, who has seemed to me, since then, to be the handsomest, kindest, strongest and most patient man I have ever met or am ever likely to meet. I simultaneously think that I was crazy to end things, yet find it hard to regret that I did so.

I have had no relationship since, nor the tiniest sniff of one.

I haven't had a single worthwhile case. One half-decent domestic assault. A kidnap which looked briefly interesting, then wilted. And that's it. Paperwork for various cases pushing their way through to prosecution. An involvement in the clean-up for Operation Tinker, my last good case, but nothing to get stuck into. Because I've been annoying, a fruit fly in search of fruit, DCI Jackson, the leader of my team in Major Crime, dropped a whole lot of cold-case files on my desk and told me to look through them. It's the sort of assignment I normally relish – an excuse to poke around on my own – but I'm having a hard time getting enthused.

Indeed, that sentence gets more truthful, the shorter it gets. I'm having a hard time, full stop. Since last October, my head has teetered on the edge of its own private darkness, not quite tipping over, but never really feeling safe. It's felt like my years at Cambridge. Death's yellow teeth in every shadow.

Not good.

The winter has been long, cold and unfriendly.

Various personal investigative projects of mine have made little progress.

The crime statistics are awful.

And I don't want to become a detective sergeant.

Gwyn serves last night's lamb with baked potatoes and a mountain of buttered kale. We eat as though famished.

Gwyn is my mother's older sister. Inherited the farm when their parents, my grandparents, both died, within nine months of each other. Agricultural accident in his case, a stroke in hers. Gwyn had been a veterinary nurse in Abergavenny, married to the manager of a local timber yard, but when she moved up the hill to take care of her mother and the farm, he stayed down in the valley with his two-by-fours and his pressure-treated fenceposts. The pair divorced, formally, four years later.

Gwyn is over sixty now. White-haired, blue-eyed, thin as a stick of hazel, and still as lithe as the whippets who used to crowd her kitchen floor. If I offered to move up here, learn how to run the farm, then, in due course, take over, I think she'd say yes.

To live up here, far from the city, in the blue light of these hills, watching them turn from green to gold, from gold back to green. And the years passing like falling leaves.

It might be better for me. It really might.

After lunch, I'm about to go out again with Iestyn, but Gwyn's natural toughness extends to me too. 'You're here to revise,' she tells me, 'not mend my gates.' She orders me up to my room.

From my upstairs window, I watch Gwyn and Iestyn set off for the upper fields. Two dark figures and a collie, joyful, in the bracken.

I don't revise.

With me from the office, I brought my cold-case files.

Most of them are dull. Boring when they were warm, more so now they're cold.

Only two cases strike me as having any real interest.

First, an accidental death, where the coroner's notes suggest just a scintilla of doubt. One rainy night eighteen months ago, a security guard, a couple of pints of beer inside him, fell off a clifftop on Gower. Probably just one of those things: cliffs and beer don't mix. But he knew that path well and a note on the autopsy report reads, *Injury to lower right parietal bone presumably inflicted by rock on descent. Impact site not conclusively located.*

It's not much to get excited about. The report confirms

that, yes, the security guard had fallen. Yes, the majority of his injuries – broken bones, gashes, bruises and the rest – were consistent with that fall. Nor was there any doubt about the injury that finished him: a blow to the back of his head which split his skull open and caused his brains to leak into the cloudy waters of Swansea Bay. But that one wound – *Injury to lower right parietal bone* – puzzled the pathologist enough that he saw fit to draw attention to it, no matter how quietly.

I look at the photos of the dead man's head.

Mostly, I'm just looking at a mashed skull. A skull which looks much as you'd expect it to when attached to a fourteen stone security guard who has toppled, tipsily, off a not-quite-vertical cliff. But there, on the upper right side of the skull, is a dent – possibly lethal, certainly dangerous – which suggests a blow from a heavy object with a roughly square cross-section. The line of the blow is quite straight. The angle of indentation just a few degrees off a perfect right angle.

It looks like the sort of mark you'd leave if you struck someone hard with a crowbar.

Suspicious? Or not suspicious?

It's hard to say. The entire wound is only about three-quarters of an inch long before it bleeds into other injuries altogether. And the cliff was thirty-five metres high – a hundred feet and more. Easily high enough for any number of interesting injuries to have accumulated on the way down.

What's more, the victim, Derek Moon, had a regular job, no money problems, was married, played football, had a young daughter. No record. Not quarrelsome, even when drunk.

I'm thinking not suspicious, but I like the skull photos and use one of them as my screensaver. Just that one injury, in extreme close-up. I find myself putting my finger out, as though laying it into the crevice of the head wound.

The case I like the most, however, doesn't even boast a corpse.

The file, a burglary, from 2009, only landed on my desk because, as Jackson put it, 'It's a bit quirky.' On the one hand, the burglary looks completely straightforward. A four-million-pound house – Plas Du – loses six lithographs (two Picassos, two Matisses, one each by Léger and Braque) plus a pair of silver Georgian candlesticks. Total value of the haul: about four hundred thousand pounds. You don't get ordinary burglars with that level of discrimination, so the thieves were almost certainly professional art-thieves, quite likely stealing on commission, and more than likely based in London or some place where poorly guarded Picassos are rather thicker on the ground than they are in the Vale of Glamorgan.

Not much to arouse the interest, then, except that Plas Du also boasted an oil painting by Robert Rauschenberg, a sculpture by Giacometti, a silk dress once worn by Marilyn Monroe, and various other bits and pieces. Total value: more than six million pounds. Those items were all on the ground or first floor and were left untouched. The stolen items disappeared from the topmost floor – the second storey – which was the only one unprotected by the security alarm system. The system was as high-spec as you'd expect, given the value of art in the house, and independent experts employed by the insurance company verified that the system had been switched on and operational at the time of attack.

Or rather: the *supposed* time of attack. There was no sign of forced entry to the property, save one. A second-floor window had been broken at the catch. The catch wasn't locked and entry would have been easy. Except that the window stood twenty-five feet or more above ground. The wall in which it was set was blank. The ground beneath was in the process of being reseeded and the bare earth was a fine tilth which would have taken any impression, had a ladder or some such been used. A large enough cherry-picker could have gained access, but it would need to have been an eight-wheeler, the engine would have needed to be in operation through the entire procedure, and there was a staff cottage within twenty-five yards of the site. The staff in question – two middle-aged, loyal-retainer types – swore blind they'd heard nothing.

The investigating officers at the time formed three broad theories about the burglary. Option one: Peter Pan and Tinker Bell flew twenty-five feet into the air, smashed a window and stole some artwork. Option Two: Plas Du staff stole the objects and broke the window as the clumsiest of all possible blinds. Option Three: the same as option two, except that in this version, the owner of the house, one Marianna Lockwood, stole the pictures for the insurance money.

Option one was ruled out as improbable. Option three was ruled out, as Lockwood was able to show liquid assets – cash and marketable securities – in excess of three million pounds and no one could quite figure out why someone that wealthy would want to commit serious fraud for such a small relative gain. So that left option two and, sure enough, staff at the house were investigated in minute depth, without yield.

So far, so *meh*. Most inside jobs aren't well organised. But some are. Sometimes thieves get away. That's just the way it is.

There are, however, two aspects of the case which intrigue me.

First, Marianna Lockwood is the ex-wife of a man named Galton Evans, who has been a personal investigative project of mine for some time. Any case that allows me to lift the carpet on his life, even if just a little, is one that I welcome.

And there is, second, a photo in the files which intrigues me. A photo of the broken window. Glass lying on the inside window sill and carpet. Evidence of a hammer blow from *outside*.

I call the forensics officer listed. He tells me, as though

talking to a simpleton, 'Crime scene analysis has to take context into account. If you see evidence of a blow struck from an impossible location, you have to interpret the evidence accordingly. And in any case, if a window is struck by a hard object, you often see two impacts. One when the glass is initially struck. Two, if the object is withdrawn so as to hit the remaining glass on exit.'

'In which case,' I say, 'you'd see two piles of glass. One inside, one outside.'

'Exactly.'

'And *was* there any glass outside?'

'No, but when we came the site was no longer forensically intact.' He blathers on, about how forensic conditions were imperfect, as they always are.

I hang up before I get too annoyed.

A text comes in from Rhiannon Watkins, a fierce DI whom I happen to like. She wants to know how my revision is going. I text back, FINE. GOING THROUGH THE MANUALS AGAIN NOW. IT'S BORING! FI.

Go outside to find Gwyn.

She's got a disintegrating shed at the end of her cow house, the place where sheep dip and glyphosate and fertiliser used to be kept. When Gwyn modernised her barns, those things were all rehoused and the shed is slowly collapsing back to the soil.

But it has windows. I say to Gwyn, 'Can I smash the windows, please?'

She says, 'Yes.'

I smash the windows.

Eight of them, with care. Using a hammer. A crowbar. A gloved fist. Photograph my work after each blow. Sweep away the glass before repeating my action. The hole made in the original window wasn't that huge, so with care I manage fourteen experiments.

On none of them do I get an exit scatter that looks like the photo in the case file.

I call the forensics guy again. 'Just checking, the window was single-glazed. Ordinary four millimetre glass? Nothing out of the ordinary.'

He checks things and, sighing theatrically, says, 'No. Nothing out of the ordinary.'

Views of the building show no overhanging trees, no obvious ways for Peter Pan to cheat.

There *is* a grand-looking porch in the middle of the house. I can just about see that you could get on top of the porch with a ladder, then pull the ladder up to gain access to the roof, then – maybe, somehow – pad up the roof to the ridge, and along the ridge to the gable end in which my precious window is housed.

But what then? Glide down on gossamer wings? Hammer a spike into the wall and abseil? Then hope that the spike is plucked away by a passing bird before it's noticed?

*Nothing out of the ordinary*, except that four hundred thousand pounds' worth of art somehow contrived to vanish.

Plas Du is a few miles in from the coast, near Llantwit.

Fifty miles. An hour and something, where the something varies with the density of traffic and the frequency of speed cameras.

I'm there in an hour and ten.

The house is as good as I'd hoped. Better.

The original detectives were perfectly correct: the window is impossible to reach. Set twenty-five foot up in a delightfully sheer wall. The masonry is dressed stone with only tiny gaps between each block. If someone had hammered a spike in anywhere, the scar would still be evident today. And there's no scar.

I take photos.

Call London. Reach a guy called Adrian Brattenbury, a

senior officer at SOCA, the Serious Organised Crime Agency. Beg a favour.

Because Brattenbury and I have been working together on Operation Tinker and because he still harbours a vague sense of guilt towards me – something to do with having let me be abducted by a bunch of homicidal gangsters – he's happy to help out. He promises quick results, and SOCA's quick is quicker than ours.

The rain is clearing from the mountains as I ascend towards Gwyn's farm. Light shines on floodwater. Pewter and tin.

Beyond Crickhowell, a rainbow stutters.

When I'm back, there's a new car in the yard. A silver-grey Audi A3. Not the newest, but clean. A city car, not rural.

In Gwyn's kitchen: Detective Sergeant Jane Alexander. Navy-blue suit. Cute shoes. Unfeasibly blond hair. She holds a china teacup and a grim expression.

'Fiona,' she says, standing. 'Study leave over. I'm sorry.'

# 2

'Fiona, you have detained an individual who is asking for an interpreter to help with a phone call. Under what circumstances can that request be refused and by whom?'

I don't answer.

Jackson leaves the silence long enough to allow my non-response to register, then tries again.

'A man is being prosecuted for arson, with insurance fraud as the suspected motive. His wife is believed to have knowledge of the alleged crime. No persons were present on the property at the time of the fire. Fiona, is the wife here a compellable witness?'

I'm pretty sure Jackson knows the answer to his question, so I stay shtum.

Rhiannon Watkins is sitting next to Jackson and has the peaceful demeanour of a barbarian army at the gates of Rome. She says, 'If an officer's behaviour has been deemed unsatisfactory, and has not been remedied by a first-stage disciplinary meeting, a second-stage disciplinary meeting will be held. What four things will the second-stage line manager do at that meeting?'

I've never yet had a second-stage meeting, though I've had plenty of first-stagers.

I say, 'Look, I know you want me to pass this exam.'

Jackson says, 'Yes, and we gave you study leave so you could revise for it. But it turns out your books never left your desk.'

He taps the pile of Blackstone's manuals in front of him. My manuals.

'I *have* read them,' I say. 'More than once.'

*More than once* is a good expression. What I mean is 'twice', except that I skipped through the boring bits and smoked quite a lot of cannabis and ignored anything that I thought I already knew. But for all Jackson knows, I've read the books a million times.

'Have you done the mock exam?'

I want to say yes, but I'm struggling to remember whether the damn thing came in a sealed wrapper or not. Because I can't remember, I stay mute and Jackson waves the exam at me. It *is* in a wrapper, the seal unbroken.

I wave my hands helplessly. He keeps asking questions whose answers he already knows.

Jackson resumes. 'The questions we just asked you are more straightforward than those you will face in the exam. You will have to answer 150 questions in the space of three hours. That's seventy-two seconds per question. The subject areas are incredibly broad-ranging. If it's in the books, it can feature in the exam. Do you understand?'

I don't nod exactly, but I do twitch.

'Most officers sitting the exam fail it. Not just in our force, but across the country. The pass mark is fifty-five per cent, but I know perfectly well you have the capacity to score better than that, and neither Rhiannon nor I will find it acceptable if you merely scrape a pass. We're looking for an outstanding score, and if you don't achieve one, I will ask you, in writing, why not. I am also going to place a note of this conversation on your record.'

It's not like Jackson to get all formal about these things. Normally, he just yells, looks like he's going to rip my head off, then somehow my head stays on and everything carries on much the same as before. I say 'yes sir,' but roll my eyes at the same time, which maybe diminishes the overall effect.

Watkins leans forward. Does her friendly voice at me.

'Fiona, we want you to become a sergeant because you have obvious aptitudes and we want to promote the best. But also, we need you to mature. As a police officer and as a person. And the standards we expect from a sergeant will be higher than those we've tolerated up till now.'

'Yes, ma'am.'

A phone call interrupts us. Jackson takes it. Watkins and I stare at the carpet. Jackson says things, but I don't listen, not really.

When he hangs up, he stares at me. 'Chicago. Ifor Dawes is getting overwhelmed by the volume of material coming in.'

Chicago: the codename given to a current rape inquiry. A woman, Kirsty Emmett, was abducted in Gabalfa. Blindfolded. Knocked around, fairly badly. She was raped, then deposited by the river down by the Tremorfa steelworks.

Ifor Dawes: a DC who's become a specialist exhibits officer, responsible for managing the collection, processing and storage of physical evidence gathered in the course of an investigation. In some inquiries, the number of individual bits of evidence – fibres, hairs, bodily fluid samples, pieces of rubbish – can run into the thousands. If Ifor says he's being overwhelmed, he's probably not inventing it.

That said, although I've done bits and pieces for both Ifor and his colleague, Laura Moffatt, I find the work so grimly tedious as to be life-threatening. And this particular rape inquiry is being headed by DI Owen Dunwoody who, in my unhumble opinion, is the stupidest officer of his rank in South Wales.

Jackson says what he says looking straight at me. But it wasn't a question, so I don't give him an answer.

Watkins, beside me, says, 'Fiona, a good officer might feel this was an opportunity to help.'

I say, 'I've got a whole stack of cases you asked me to look into. And an ongoing involvement with Tinker.'

Jackson says, 'A stack of *cold* cases. And Tinker will scrape along without you.'

I wave my hands again. What do they want from me? Either Jackson or Watkins, or the numpty Dunwoody, have the power to order me to help Ifor, if that's what they want. I can't see why I need to pretend to be keen to help out in my least-favourite role for my least-favourite DI.

Jackson and Watkins exchange a look.

A pause.

Sunlight gilds the carpet. Creeps slowly towards the wall.

Jackson: 'You'll help Ifor. You can report to him downstairs right now. Get further instructions from DI Dunwoody. When Owen decides he doesn't need you any more, he'll release you to your other duties. At that point, I'll ask Owen and Ifor to let me know in writing how, in their view, you have performed.'

Still not a question. I say nothing.

'Is that understood?'

'Yes, sir.' I don't say anything more and nor does anyone else, so I stand up. 'And I will pass the exam. I said I would.'

'With a score of seventy per cent or more please, Fiona,' says Jackson. 'We don't want good. We expect outstanding.' His voice is grimmer than usual. Unyielding.

'Yes, sir.'

I grapple with the door, trying to leave. Jackson says, 'Haven't you forgotten something?'

I look back. My books are still on his desk. I say, 'Oh,' retrieve them, then get the door open again. Stand there with my foot preventing the self-closing mechanism from doing its stuff.

'That burglary at Plas Du. The glass scatter. I had it analysed at SOCA. They were able to match the estimated surface area of the broken fragments against the size of the hole in the window.'

Jackson says nothing: his way of asking me to continue.

'Basically, the glass was all on the *inside* of the building and formed what their analyst called a "natural pattern". That is: it had fallen there, not been arranged.'

'So the blow was struck from outside?'

'Exactly. Yes, sir.'

Jackson stares at me. I stare at him. I don't know what Rhiannon Watkins is doing, but when she does a full-on stare, she usually burns holes in things.

It's Jackson who breaks the silence. 'Good. Then when you make sergeant, you can go and arrest Peter Pan.'

I give him one of my peachiest smiles. Him and Watkins, both. I think that's the first sensible thing either of them has said today.

'Yes, sir. Thank you. Thank you very much.'

# 3

Saturday. High winds, gusty and unstable.

I meet Brydon in a greasy spoon café near his parents' house in Pontypool: our first proper meeting since The Break Up. A trial day, an attempt to normalise.

Brydon is there before me. He's ordered a pot of tea for him, a cup of peppermint tea for me. A waitress in a black T-shirt takes our orders.

'The full breakfast,' Buzz says, closing the menu without really looking at it. Printed sheets encased in a padded leatherette wallet.

I hold the menu in front of me, staring at it but not really reading it.

'Why do they pad the menus? I mean, books aren't padded, are they?'

I think of other readable items which don't come with leatherette padding and start listing them. Marketing brochures. Theatre programmes. Phone directories. Clothing catalogues.

'Have you eaten?'

'No.'

This does feel weird. For me, certainly, but also I think for Buzz.

'How about sausage, egg and chips?' he suggests.

One of his roles in our relationship: trying to get me to eat normal, regular meals like a normal, regular human being.

'OK. Yes, that. I'll have that.'

'Sausage, egg and chips?' The waitress looks for my confirmation.

'Yes, but can I have it with bacon? And beans? And those things that come in triangles.'

I show her the shape of a triangle.

'Hash browns?'

'Yes. For the beans, I mean. I probably don't need the chips though,' I concede.

'You might as well have the full breakfast then.'

She goes through the contents of the full breakfast, which sounds quite like the thing I just said I wanted, but I already can't remember what I said and certainly can't imagine eating it, so add, 'Maybe you should bring chips as well, just in case,' which is logical to me, because chips are the one thing I can pretty much always eat some of, but I can see that my food-ordering technique isn't coming across as all that credible.

The waitress looks at Buzz checking, I think, that he'll underwrite this order. He commands her obedience with a nod, and she goes.

'Sorry. I'm still the same.'

'So I see.'

When I broke up with Buzz, I told him, in effect, that a man as sane as him needed a woman a good bit more sane than me. But I also tried to explain that the break-up was for my sake too. Buzz helped me first touch the soil of Planet Normal. Helped me breathe its atmosphere, understand its customs. Those were precious gifts, the most precious possible, yet I also came to see that, in Buzz's company, I could only ever be a resident alien. Travelling on faked papers. At constant risk of deportation.

If I am to become well – stably, reliably, confidently well – I had to take the risk of leaving Buzz's kind, protective custody.

Had to take the risk of living alone on this planet. Treading its soil without support.

One day, I hope I'll be well enough to contemplate a relationship again. Perhaps even marriage. But I need to do that without feeling giddily convinced that the whole enterprise is a sham that could be stripped from me at any time.

I need to become a sort-of-sane woman before I can become anyone's now-and-for-ever wife.

The breakfasts come, plus my side order of chips.

Buzz tucks in with gusto. I bite the end off a chip.

I say, 'How is your Using Computers To Destroy Policing As We Know It project coming along?'

Buzz had worked alongside me in Major Crime. Since he had done nothing wrong, not one thing, since the start of our relationship, and since I was the breaker not the breakee, it should by rights have been me who switched jobs to give him space. But since we both knew that I wouldn't cope anywhere other than Major Crime, he applied for, and secured, a transfer. He's now doing something with a boring acronym which involves using data-driven intelligence to target police resources.

Buzz starts to answer. I half listen, but there's something depressing about the relentless trend of the crime statistics and the way modern policing responds. I try to say the right things, but my heart's not in it.

'How about you?' asks Buzz.

I find a chip, a long one, and steal some of Buzz's ketchup.

'Boring, stupid crimes. Boring, stupid paperwork. Boring, stupid prosecutions.'

'That bad?'

'Worse.' I tell him about Ifor Dawes and Chicago and Owen Dunwoody.

Buzz laughs. 'You're going to be an exhibits officer? Bet you just love that.'

My mouth moves, but nothing comes out. I don't have the words to express how much I loathe the role. It's not even that I'm bad at it. I'm not. Truth is, if Ifor needed a temporary sidekick, they probably couldn't have found a more suitable helper. I'm fast and accurate at anything paperworky. My memory is excellent. I don't know a lot about forensic technicalities, but I know enough that I'm unlikely to cock anything up.

But, *Gott im Himmel*, the boredom!

'I'd honestly sooner spend time in prison,' I say with feeling.

Nor did it help matters that I was complaining loudly about Dunwoody in the canteen. Called him Owen Dunthinking and shared my thoughts about the extent to which he deserved his current position. I assumed I was in the clear because we'd just had news that protective coverings placed down at the crime scene might have failed, thereby compromising further forensic investigation. Any competent DI would have been down there like a shot, getting the problem sorted. Alas, Dunthinking decided it was more important to spoon a plateful of pie and mash into his face first and, as he was returning his tray, he managed to hear my full assessment of his abilities. He said nothing, but went pink with anger – pinker than usual – and his eyes were little raisins of hatred in the surrounding pudge.

I say something of this to Buzz, who says, 'Ah, yes, I did hear about that.'

I grimace. Not apologetically, just not very thrilled to know how widely my outburst has circulated. Dunthinking's nephew, Kyle Bransby – a part-time SOCO, a part-time instructor at the university sports centre, and in my never-humble view a full-time dickhead – told me with relish that Dunthinking 'is going to make this the biggest exhibits operation in force history. Months, it'll take. Months.' He leered at me, a wash of stained teeth and aniseed breath. That vision – and that threat – haunts me still.

I try to continue chatting with Buzz the way we normally would. But this isn't normal. Anything but. I break off and say, 'It *is* weird this, isn't it? It's not just me.'

'No, it's not just you.'

His smile tilts down to his plate, and I see that for all his Buzzishness, this is a man in pain.

Pain that I caused.

I'm tempted to say sorry – again – but instead say, 'I think it's the same for me. I think it hurts the same way.'

*I think*: with my crazy head, I can't always feel my feelings. They just get cotton-woolled away. But it all connects up. This long, dark winter. My restlessness. My gloom.

The awareness settles me. It's like I've been living with my own baffled version of this Buzzian pain, and now for the first time have a glimpse of it. A painful thing, yes, but also a true thing. A real one. It's like I've been carrying around a steel weight all winter without knowing it's there. Then someone shows me a glimpse of it – a metal edge, a dull sheen, the heft of something folded in cloth – and I feel a sense of relief. This pain, that weight: it all connects up.

'Oh, Buzzling,' I whisper.

He grimaces.

Sergeant Brydon isn't what you would call an emotionally complex man, but his methods for dealing with moments like these used to achieve consistently successful results. Those methods, however, would constitute a criminal act if carried out in a public place and we're trying to move on from all that anyway. So he sighs, and stands, and says, 'Let's make a move.'

I nod.

We go. I've eaten almost nothing.

One of our first dates was a day out at the seaside, and we've decided to reprise that, except that the weather then was all sunshine and white parasols. The weather now carries straight from the North Atlantic. Salt, grey, edged with spite.

We head for Gower, take one of the cliff paths. Grey rock, grey waves. When there's a break in the cloud cover, the volume of light feels overwhelming.

Mary Langton, one of my favourite corpses, had her ashes scattered over this bay. Brendan Rattigan, one of my least favourite, has his bones rattling somewhere in the tides beneath us.

'How drunk would you have to be to fall off?' I ask.

'What, here? Very drunk.'

'At night. Dark, but moderate visibility.'

'This is one of your cases?'

It is, I admit it. The accidental death.

Buzz is hurt, I think, that I can't let our first day since the break-up stand on its own, but I'm not entirely sorry about that. He always had this picture of me as someone capable of changing into the sort of woman he ought to marry. It's helpful for him to remember the cranky obsessive I actually am. It might make it easier to let me go.

'Who? What? Where?' he asks.

I give him the facts. We walk on five hundred yards to where the security guard fell.

The cliff stands at the eastern edge of a small, rocky bay. There are climbers – orange jackets, ropes, helmets – starting to work their way up the crags opposite. Standing where we are, we can see nothing of the cliff beneath our feet. There's just a short, tussocky slope, the soil bleaching into limestone. Then nothing. No middle distance. Just a long leap to a far horizon and the sound of waves breaking over rock.

A metal spike, corroded but still sound, stands a few yards below the path, just before the slope starts to tilt irreversibly into void. The path mostly doesn't come this close to the edge.

'Was it wet?'

'Yes, but not very. And he knew this path. He did night shifts at some telecoms construction site further on down the coast.' I point. 'He used to walk out sometimes, if his wife needed the car.'

'Any motive?'

'No.'

'Alcohol?'

'Two pints, drunk an hour or two before death.'

Buzz shrugs. 'Anyone can slip, I suppose. And once you start to fall . . .'

His sentence drops away, like the ground. We sit down, looking at the horizon, the waves that carry an edge of white at their crests.

I don't know what Buzz is thinking. I'm thinking of the man who died and that feeling I half understood in the café: that metal gleam, that weight of pain.

A couple of climbers walk past us on the path. Stuff jingling from their harnesses.

The first climber says, 'OK? Nice day.'

Buzz says whatever men say to each other.

I say, 'Is there rock climbing here? Underneath us?'

The climbers say yes, and start to argue about names.

'The cliffs have names?'

They show me a guidebook. Not only the cliffs, but each individual route up the cliff. The crag underneath us now has four routes – Critterling, Little Arrete, Idris Gawr, Crack and Slab. The climbers tell me the routes range from 'pretty simple' to 'well, if you fancy a challenge'.

Then they laugh.

Then they leave.

'Your boy was a climber, was he?'

For a moment, the tense confuses me. I don't know why Buzz is using the past tense, when the dead man's presence is so strong all around us. It feels like ignoring someone who's sitting right next to you.

So I sit there blinking, trying to feel the fence that separates dead from living, until I find the answer to Buzz's question. 'No, no. I don't think so anyway.'

'Does he have a name?'

'Derek Moon. Aged thirty-eight. Wife. One little girl.'

The man's presence still seems strong and I hang there between two worlds, until Buzz nudges me back towards his one, the land of the simply living.

We spend more time together. Walking. Pub lunch. Talking in a way that becomes less weird, as the day goes on.

But it's hard work and by three, we're both ready to finish. A success, more than not.

Buzz drives back into Cardiff. A sane man getting on with his life.

And me, what do I do? I've never really had a good answer to that question, but my legs take me, as I knew they would, back to that cliff, that fall.

A few hundred yards from the actual site, the slope eases enough that there's a way down to the sea, steep but manageable. I scramble down to the shoreline – waves foaming over rock – and traverse across to the cliff. The water is ankle-deep mostly, thigh-deep at worst. The exact depth, however, soon becomes immaterial, as I fall sideways and soak myself.

As I get closer to the cliff itself, the beach rises until it's clear of the foaming water. Rocks and sand, mixed. I stare upwards at the sweep of limestone. White, grey and ochre. Stippled with lichens.

Emptiness and the glitter of sea air. A long blue fall, that ends here, where I'm standing.

Boulders the size of bullocks.

Rocks the colour of tea.

I stare upwards trying to trace the line of descent. I don't know how you calculate these things other than by throwing crash dummies off the cliff. Except that if crash dummies bounce differently from humans, you wouldn't achieve much and there are rules – tedious, tedious rules – about throwing actual live humans off cliffs for the purposes of practical forensic study.

All the same, the big picture is clear. Once the guard had started his fall, he'd have encountered perhaps twenty or twenty-five feet of empty space, as he passed a long scooped-out overhang, then he'd have struck a fairly clean-looking slab as it rose to the overhang. A bit of rolling or bouncing on the slab, then he'd have been ejected by another change in slope and angle. He landed where I stand now, his skull impaled on a rock that angles sharply out of the sand like some sticklebacked Himalayan ridge.

Accidental death?

Maybe. Beer plus night plus cliffs equals an easy verdict.

But two pints in a fourteen stone man is hardly drunk. And he knew this path, knew its risks. The simplest conclusions aren't always the right ones.

A line of chalk marks dandles up the cliff. Up into the overhang and out of it. Marks left by passing climbers.

Although this whole coast is rocky and abrupt, the cliffs themselves are quite variable. Sometimes crags rise a hundred feet in a single swoop of limestone. Elsewhere, they're just a mass of broken rock and tussocky grass. None of the ground is easy, however, and the weather directly following the death was stormy and wet.

The crime scene investigation report commented, *Only a limited examination of the descent route was possible, owing to difficult access conditions and adverse weather conditions.* I can imagine it: a plump SOCO in a hi-vis jacket, dangling on a rope in a wicked sea-wind. Spray from the ocean and a storm blowing in. How much investigation would truly have taken place under those circumstances? And with accidental death already the only likely verdict?

*Injury to lower right parietal bone presumably inflicted by rock on descent.*

*Impact site not conclusively located.*

Was it not conclusively located because no one ever properly looked? Or because it wasn't there?

On a true murder inquiry, those sorts of questions never go unanswered. Officers and resources are flung at the problem until those little wrinkles get fully de-wrinked. But when you have an inquiry whose whole shape, from the outset, is tilting towards a verdict of Accidental Death, no one will authorise the expense involved to tease out those last little puzzles.

*Presumably inflicted.*

*Not conclusively.*

Evasive words. Snaky.

I stare up at the cliff, trying to imagine the line of flight, until I realise that the tide is still coming in, washing at sands that had been dry when I arrived.

I struggle back. I'm soaked already, but the parts that were thigh-deep before are waist-deep now and, when a bigger than normal wave comes in, I find myself lifted off the bottom and don't recover my footing until the backwash drops me.

But I make it back. Crawl up the slope I descended earlier and hurry back to my Alfa Romeo and the beauty of heated seats.

Putting my now-sodden boots in the back of the car, I notice that my Blackstone's Policing manuals are still sliding around in there. I'd put them there, intending to do some more revision at home one evening, but it seems like I might have forgotten to do that. Ah well.

I wish I'd brought some dry clothes with me. Or not have got the ones I'm wearing completely soaked. But I have to live with the person I am, not the one I might prefer to be.

I whack the heating up and shiver my way home.

The day ends. And I think I've got my murder.

# 4

That first day with Ifor. The dungeons of CID.

The exhibits rooms are downstairs in the basement. Each room is locked via a keypad to which only the relevant exhibits officer has the code. There are three exhibits rooms, of which only two are in general use. They're largish, but mostly taken up by racks of metal shelving. Boxes of evidence bags, latex gloves, desiccants, sticky labels. A drying machine, for use with any exhibits that need to be preserved dry.

The clutter, especially the shelving, dominates the room. Ifor's own desk seems huddled away somehow. Marginal. He has a chair, a desk, a lamp, a computer, a phone, a printer, a desk set with lots of biros, a spidery pot plant, a desk calendar, and a poster of sun shining on a waterfall.

My own table is like an afterthought to an afterthought. A bare table, on which a HOLMES terminal squats, the toad from a fairy tale.

He is a nice man, Ifor. Good at his job. Patient. Doesn't obviously dislike me. But he is slow. And repetitive. And keeps treating me like an apprentice wanting to learn at her master's feet.

'I'll go on down to Splott now. Pick up the next load.'

'Not Splott. Tremorfa.'

'Oh yes. My last job was in Splott. This one's in Tremorfa.'

'Yes, you said.'

Twice, in fact.

'And you'll get on with the cataloguing?'

'Yes.'

As we've already discussed.

'And you're sure you're OK with the labels?'

'Yes.'

Ifor looks at me like he can't quite credit me with that precocious degree of labelling skill. I can see he's about to ask me again, so I pre-empt him by typing up a label and sending it to the printer. The label says, 'I'm fine with the labels.' I stick it, still warm, to my forehead.

Ifor leans in to look, then laughs.

'You're very fast on the . . .' He gestures downwards. 'The . . .'

'Keyboard.'

'Yes.'

Ifor looks like he wants to continue this conversation, which I certainly don't. I say, 'I can touch-type. Eighty words a minute when I'm blitzing.' When that doesn't achieve an end to the discussion, I add, 'Which I'll start doing now.'

I sit at my little table and start work.

Ifor says, 'Good. OK. And you're all fine, so I'll go on down to the scene.'

He looks for the keys to his van, finds them in his pocket, leaves.

I start to catalogue exhibits.

*Item description.*
*Time and date of collection.*
*Location code of collection.*
*Cross-reference to pre-collection photographs (if any).*
*Notes on condition.*
*Name of forensics officer.*
*Time and date of pick-up from crime scene.*

*Officer in charge of transport.*
*Signature collected?*
*Signature scanned?*

A whole heap of further data covering any forensics activity. Signatures collected and scanned for each chain-of-custody movement. Further data on any additional transport and storage, right down to a location code for the position in the storeroom, so we can find the damn thing if we have to. More data each time a SOCO wants to take a second look at something or Dunthinking gets it into his head that he should show an interest in his own inquiry.

I don't object to any of this in principle. If we want to send someone to prison, it's not unreasonable to require that our forensics evidence be bullet-proof. That doesn't just mean we have to do the science correctly. It also means that we have to be able to prove that the evidence was collected where we said, when we said, and has been kept properly stored and free from interference ever since. If I ever face a serious charge, I'd want those guarantees for myself.

So the principle, I'm fine with. It's the practice that has me losing my mind.

I work for an hour. Then dive into the documents library and find a photo of the victim, Kirsty Emmett, that I like. One of her at the hospital. A close-up.

Someone has already cleaned her up. Removed mud and blood and grime. Made a basic attempt to comb the dirt and moss and dead leaves from her hair. But for all that, Emmett's face has the shocked eyes, the empty gaze of real crime. This is what we're investigating, I think. Those eyes. What happened to make them that way.

I use the photo as my new screensaver. Order the image from the print room, in the largest size they do.

I wonder if anyone thought to collect the soiled tissues

from the hospital waste system? Those things should be basic, but nurses don't think about evidence. Coppers sometimes forget about hospitals. I check the system. And no: no record of the material being collected.

That's not helpful, but nor is anything else. The victim was struck hard enough that she lost consciousness, she thinks, at points during her ordeal and her recollection is uncertain and scrambled. Her blindfold, crude as it was, meant she did not get a good view of her attacker and she evinces little confidence in the e-fit image she was coaxed to assemble. Her one confidently offered piece of testimony is that the van which deposited her was 'a large white van, not all that clean, with some markings.' Since that description fits half the vans in Cardiff – including almost the entire police fleet – it's not much to work with.

Nevertheless, I continue to do what is now my job.

Collecting data.

Checking data.

Entering data.

Any error, even a small one, could wreck this case.

Two hours in and I call the lab. Ask for half a dozen casts of the security guard's head wound. The lab had taken a master impression of the injury as part of the inquest process and I'm promised the casts by the end of the week.

Continue to work.

Location codes.

Reference numbers.

Check boxes.

Signing logs.

Three hours in and I have my first thought about self-harm. Wonder whether I could use the stapler to pin my hand to the desk. If I'd feel it, if I did.

Bad thoughts, dark thoughts.

I go outside for a cigarette. I used not to smoke much, not

tobacco at any rate, but I started smoking more last year and the habit lingers.

Jon Breakell, a DC and an occasional smoker too, is sheltering in the same insufficient doorway. He's had the wit to put on an outdoors jacket before leaving the office. I'm in a skirt and white shirt only. Sensible enough kit for data entry. Not good for a chilly outdoor smoke.

'Aren't you cold?' he asks, giving me a light.

'Jon, if a senior officer orders you to arrest someone, doesn't that imply an order to investigate first?'

'What are you talking about?'

'Are you free this afternoon? I mean, I need someone to accompany me to an interview. Jackson asked me to do it, but he didn't say who with.'

Jon shrugs. He quite likes me, or likes me enough. He's also chilled enough not to demand to know too much about Jackson's specific instructions. 'Sure, if you want.'

I shrug back. 'Boss's orders.'

When Jon pulls on his ciggy, my eyes are drawn to the glowing tip, the whitened ash. When I was in the mental hospital, at least half the patients had scars from self-inflicted cigarette burns. My craziness was normally more intense than that – self-harm never seemed particularly seductive – but I felt the edges of the impulse then. I feel it, more strongly, now.

I stub my cigarette out half-smoked. 'I'm frozen,' I say.

Jon looks at me. 'It *is* March.'

'Three o'clock? It won't take long.'

# 5

Plas Du. My second visit and first official one. The house looks sleeker than it did when I was here last. Lawns newly mown, beds dug over for the spring planting.

'Nice place,' says Breakell, as though contemplating a purchase.

'But poky,' I say. 'Where would you put the under butler?'

We park between a silver Mercedes and a glossy little Mini, all cream and white and chrome and edible.

Crunch over to the front door. Breakell wears a grey suit which he likes because, as he told me, 'It's washable. You just stick it in the machine.' He teams his suit with a white shirt, a strangely thin red tie and some black shoes which make a strange squeaky sound when he walks, like the exhalations of a tiny mouse.

At the door, Breakell pushes the bell, smooths his hair.

His ring is answered by a teenaged boy, sixteen or seventeen maybe. Blue T-shirt, jeans. A smirking look, but friendly. We say who we are and he says, 'Oh *yes*. Yes. Come on through. Real live detectives.'

Neither Jon nor I look much like Columbo, but we do at least look real. The boy – Lockwood's son, I assume – takes us through to a big, light-filled room. Cream carpet, soft suede sofas. A painting, which might be the Rauschenberg, hangs over a stone fireplace.

A slim woman – cropped trousers, leopard-print shoes,

loose green jumper – is talking on the phone. Holds a hand up to us, meaning wait. The boy vanishes. Jon and I hang around, looking at the Rauschenberg and try to see if we can see two million quid in it.

On a side table, there are some silver-framed family photos. The boy who opened the door to us is there. Ollie, I know from the police files. Also a girl, Francesca, a couple of years older than her brother. There are photos of the children at different ages, together and on their own. Some pictures of them with Lockwood. Some with her and Galton Evans, her ex. But though there are pictures of Ollie, Lockwood and Evans, there's nothing recent that includes Lockwood, Evans and Francesca. Maybe that's the result of some deliberate selection policy, but maybe not. You can read too much into things.

The woman finishes her call and approaches. '*Hi.* I'm Marianna. *Thank* you for coming out.'

There's something disconnected between her words and the rest of her. As it happens, I had to push to get an appointment, so if anyone should be thanking anyone it should be us to her. But her handshake is limp, absents itself too early, and her gaze gropes in the space behind my shoulder for someone who isn't there. I think she'd forgotten we were coming.

I introduce Jon and myself, and conclude, 'Would you prefer us to call you Mrs Lockwood? Or Marianna?'

Again that absent dart of the eyes, then, 'Oh, Marianna's fine. Look, someone should have told you. You didn't need to come out again about the pictures. They're here. We got them back.'

I don't think I actually say anything, but I see Jon's mouth fall open. Mine the same, I expect.

'They're *here*? How were they returned?'

'I'm not sure. The insurance company sorted it out.'

'May we see?'

We may.

Lockwood leads us upstairs. A sound of hoovering from behind a closed door. The top floor, the second floor, is lower-ceilinged, but it's light and somehow better proportioned. A cream-carpeted corridor leads down the centre of the house. On the left: two Picassos and a Matisse. On the right: the other Matisse, plus the Léger and the Braque. A console table, with a vase of silk flowers and a pair of silver candlesticks.

I look at the nearest picture – a Picasso etching – up close. I'm no expert, but it looks like the real deal to me. It has a pencil mark, *2/30*, indicating the print's number in the edition of thirty.

'You've had these authenticated?' I say.

'Oh, these are the ones we lost, all right.'

'I asked if you'd had them authenticated.'

'No. Not since they came back.'

'And the insurance money?'

'We returned it, of course. We got our pictures back.'

The window, through which Peter Pan once flew, stands at the end of the corridor. The drop, viewed from above, is as sheer as you could ask. The window has been repaired, of course, but the broken pane is still distinct from the others. Newer putty, brighter paint.

We go downstairs. Jon trails behind like a particularly low-rent groupie. I ask Lockwood to give us a moment. She clicks back to her Rauschenberg, leaving us in the cool black and white of the hall.

'Bish bosh,' says Jon. 'Another one bites the dust.'

'Yes.'

'Weird though.'

'Yes.'

There's a text on my phone from Ifor, wondering where I am.

A fair question.

I stand there not quite knowing what to do.

Jon says, 'Jackson does know we're here, doesn't he?'

I stare at him. Jon's fairly relaxed, but I don't think he'd regard 'Arrest Peter Pan' as a properly formulated Request for Action.

Jon says, 'Fi . . .?'

I'm about to agree with him. Bish bosh and head out of the door, out of Marianna Lockwood's life. But then I think of Ifor's underground cave. Those metal shelves. The latex gloves and evidence bags. That HOLMES terminal forever blinking.

And I can't go back there. Just can't. So I turn on my heel, leave Jon, head back to Lockwood and her Rauschenberg.

Once again, her smile is vague. Generically polite, but specifically absent.

I find myself saying, 'Mrs Lockwood, I've just considered the matter with my colleague, and we have a concern that an offence may have been committed under section 5(2) of the Criminal Law Act 1967, regarding the wasting of police time—'

'Oh for heaven's sake!'

'I'm going to have to ask you to accompany us to the police station in Cathays, where you will be interviewed under caution. You will not have to say anything, but it may harm your defence if you do not mention when questioned something which you later rely on in Court. Anything you do say may be given in evidence. Do you understand?'

'No, look, it's ridiculous.'

Because she said she didn't understand, I start to give her the caution in Welsh. Her right as a citizen of the principality. '*Does dim rhaid i chi ddweud dim byd, ond gall niweidio eich amddiffyniad os na fyddwch chi'n sôn—*'

'Yes, *OK*. I understand. When do you want to do this thing?'

She waves her hand, as though expecting a slim assistant to appear with an iPad and an appointment schedule.

No assistant, no iPad.

I tell her we're going now, and we do.

# 6

The next day. Tuesday.

I did interview Lockwood. Alone. Jon, coldly furious with me, checked the system, realised the entrepreneurial nature of our little excursion and flatly refused to have anything further to do with it.

All the same, I got what I wanted. Although she was lawyered up, there are times when that helps. I basically promised the lawyer, upfront, that if I got a truthful account of what happened, we would take no further action against his client. He told her to tell the full truth, and she, I think, complied.

Her story ran as follows. The pictures were stolen. Not by her. Not, in her opinion, by any member of her staff. She offered no explanation for how they were taken. The pictures were insured through an insurance company then owned by her then-husband. The company paid up in the regular way. Some months later, the now-divorced husband called up and said that his company had received an offer of the stolen work. If it was OK with her, he would go ahead and repurchase them. She said yes. A couple of weeks later, the pictures came back and she repaid the cash she'd received from the insurance company.

'That's it,' she said. 'That's literally all.'

I asked her if she would be OK with me making a further visit to the house, 'so we can potentially rule out any member of your staff.'

She said, yes, OK, she supposed so.

I finished the interview that night on a blast of positive feeling. Elation, excitement, something like that. The sort of mood which could have been quickly killed by a morning of data entry, but Ifor, bless him, is feeling headachey and reluctant to drive, so I get to spend my morning tootling up and down between Cathays, the crime scene and the lab in Bridgend. That still doesn't make me part of the investigation – my only job is to log and transport bagged-up evidence samples – but at least I get to see the crime scene, get a feel for the crime.

The bit of riverside where the poor woman was left is scrubby and unwelcoming. Weak soil, low trees and the first fistfuls of marram grass, spiky and tough. A bad place to find yourself, beaten and violated. Blood on your knees, your mouth, your arms, your thighs, and no way back to the life you once had. No way back to the person you once were.

I wonder if I'll ever meet the victim. If exhibits officers ever do.

I'm guessing no.

I wonder if Jackson will hear about my little escapade with Jon Breakell yesterday.

I'm guessing yes.

At one thirty, I'm done with my tootling around and I go to the print room to collect my picture of Kirsty Emmett.

It's a wonderful image. Emmett's shellshocked eyes and straggled hair, caught in blank inexpressive flash. I enter the dungeon with Emmett's picture in my hand, Ifor's stupid waterfall picture in my line of vision. And just stand there, gaping, gripped by a sudden uncertainty about whether I can manage this. Whether I can even get through the afternoon.

I ask Ifor where he's got to with the data entry, hoping he'd have solid progress to report, but he tells me he's been busy with SOCOs, or the lab. He's not quite clear, but either way not a lot has been done. We work solidly all afternoon.

Cataloguing.

Collecting data.

Checking data.

Entering data.

Ifor looks over my shoulder, watching me at the HOLMES terminal. His mouth moves, but says nothing.

*Exhibit code: LES-0903-122.*
*Exhibit description: Hair, suspected canine.*
*Collected: 18 March, 10.32.*
*Collecting officer: Kyle Bransby, SOCO.*
*Location: Layby, east side, code 10024.*
*Close-up photo(s): none.*
*Location photo(s): references LES-0903AM-100, LES-0903AM-102, LES-0903AM-104, LES-0903AM-108.*
*Bagged on site: Yes.*
*Log of collecting officer's signature: Yes.*
*Special evidence preservation techniques used: none required.*
*Notes on condition: None.*
*Transport from crime scene: 18 March, 15.41.*
*Transport officer: DC Ifor Dawes (EO).*
*Log of transport officer's signature: yes.*
*Exhibit transported to: EO storeroom, Cathays.*
*Index number: HSC-LES-0903-122.*
*Storage type: ambient.*
*Receipt confirmation: Yes.*

I say, 'We could get a really huge sound system in here. Play music really loud.'

Ifor says, 'I don't think so,' and queries one of my location photo references.

I call up the photo in question and he says, 'Oh yes.'

At three, I have a cigarette.

At four, I discover that if I press on the toes of my right foot hard with the heel of my left, I can cause myself enough pain that I notice it, even though I'm feeling spacey. I press as hard as I can until my leg gets tired. Then rest for fifteen minutes and do it again.

At five fifteen, I all but run from the building. Or would run, except that my foot is now quite painful and I have to try to keep my weight away from the toes, which isn't easy.

Drive out to the Pengam Road. Go the long way round so I can pass the site where Kirsty Emmett was dumped. The van in which she was raped: that would give us everything. Owner ID, forensics, everything. If we found the van, we'd close the case in a matter of days.

But no van.

Drive on to a warehouse-style building which houses an indoor climbing wall, its interior all looming plywood walls and coloured fibreglass holds. The walls bulge inwards as they rise, the perspective troubling.

There are a couple of dozen people here, perhaps. Teens and twenties for the most part. A guy with short ginger hair and one earring has his top off. He's attempting to climb a bit of abruptly sloping wall, but keeps falling off and muttering. His upper body looks like an anatomical drawing, sharply sculpted. A pattern of moving shadows.

A little café serves tea, coffee, basic hot food.

I get peppermint tea and an energy bar.

As I'm finding a seat, free of sweaty shoes, chalk, and climbing paraphernalia, a man bounds up to me. About my age. Six foot. Longish, blondish hair. A yellow T-shirt advertising some music thing and baggy shorts, the kind that has pockets on the thighs.

'Fiona, right? I'm Mike. Hold on, grab a seat, I'll join you.'

He bounds away. Gets a couple of bananas and a bottle of

water. On the way back, he has a few words with Ginger One-Earring Guy, then slots himself into the seat opposite me.

'Your first time here?'

'Yes.'

'Do you have gear? I can lend you some.'

There's a smell in the space that's mostly sweat, I suppose. A gym smell. I don't go to the gym often, but when I do, I tend to do the more girly things. Cross-training. Some low-intensity aerobic things. Very occasionally the kind of classes that only prove to me how unfit I am. The smell here is more masculine, less feminine, less cross-cut with shampoo and body lotions and scented conditioners. But there's also something outdoorsy about the smells here. Like rain on a wet sheepdog. Or that smell that tents get: damp socks and vegetation. Synthetic fabric under sunshine.

'Thanks,' I say. 'I'm fine.'

'You should try it, you know. One of those things, you don't know whether you like it till you try.'

I think, everything is like that, isn't it? Except that with me, I don't always know even after I've tried it.

I say, 'I think I've come to you with a stupid question.'

'Fire away. I can handle stupid.'

'I was going to ask you whether it's possible to climb a sheer wall. But looking at all this, I can see it isn't. You need holds.'

'Yes, true, but sometimes holds don't look like holds.'

Mike – Mike Haston – is the president of some Cardiff climbing club. This felt like a long shot before and a longer shot now I'm here. But I get out my iPad and show him photos of Plas Du.

'This is the wall. It's that window.'

He takes a look. Not just at one photo, but several. Zooming in when he needs to.

'OK. So what's the question?'

'Could you – could anyone here – climb that wall to the window?'

'Straight up, you mean? No. Not unless there's a lot more there than I can see.'

'There isn't.'

'Then no.'

I do my well-gosh-it-*was*-a-stupid-question face. One that gets plenty of use.

Mike says, 'And it has to be straight up, right?'

'What do you mean?'

'I mean, it would be OK to use the corner?'

'Yes.'

'Then yes. I mean, you never know until you're actually there. But the corner itself looks straightforward.'

He shows me what he means on one of the pictures. The stones – the quoins – which form the actual corner of the house project very slightly from the wall proper. An inch perhaps, no more, and all the joints chamfered in at about forty-five degrees. It's the kind of stonework you get on public buildings, or on Georgian mansions desperate to advertise their costliness.

'You could climb that?' I ask.

'*You* could probably climb it. I mean, not straight away, but spend a few sessions in here first, and . . .' He shrugs. 'It's mostly just body shape.'

'But that wouldn't get me to the window.'

'No, but then you've got this thing.' His finger traces the line of a cornice, or sill, that runs the width of the wall, meeting the very top of the window opening along the way. He tries to get the picture in super-close-up, but it just dissolves into pixels. 'You don't have any idea of the actual profile, do you? I mean, in the end, it depends on whether there's a real hold there or not.'

I don't know. I haven't thought to look. Nor any of my police colleagues, I'm betting.

I say, 'Mike, you know what would be incredibly helpful . . .?'

He's torn. Casts a longing look at the bit of overhanging wall, which his uni-earringed buddy has finally mastered.

'This house, whereabouts is it?'

I give the name of the village, adding, 'Just outside Llantwit.'

Mike hesitates, looks at his watch. It's still the right side of six o'clock. Mike calls his friend. 'Hey, Ginger Boy, what say we go and do some real climbing?'

Ginger Boy – Rhod, is how he introduces himself – assents reluctantly to Mike's plan, which is, I think, to take a look at Plas Du, then go on to a nearby sea cliff.

We're there by half-six. Daylight the colour of old washcloths, boiled and grey.

No one present, though I do knock first, the way we're meant to.

Rhod stands around by the corner of the house, looking grumpy. He's wearing baggy trousers and an oversized fleece, which makes him look underweight somehow, like those New Army recruits who were sent to the trenches in 1916. Sent to the trenches, then comprehensively slaughtered.

Rhod probably doesn't know he looks like cannon-fodder, though, and just spreads an old beach towel under the corner. Shoes and socks off. Slips on some stinky-looking rock shoes. Something about the stonework displeases him and he rubs at the lichen with an old toothbrush taken from a loop on his chalk bag.

Mike gets some luridly coloured foam mats from his car. Arranges them against a possible fall.

When Mike is ready, Rhod stops picking at the lichen and swings onto the corner. Toes on the horizontal chamfers, fingers round the vertical edge of the block on the wall proper. He hangs his body away from his fingers, as though hinged.

Then – I don't know – he simply pads up the wall. He doesn't move particularly fast. Checks holds before using them. He still doesn't like the bits of lichen and carries his toothbrush in his mouth, scraping away at the horizontals wherever they're more weathered. But the stone gets cleaner as it gets higher and his progress becomes more fluent.

It wouldn't even be true to say that he moves as though weightless. The opposite really: this whole game is a balance of weights and forces. But there's something sprung in the way he ascends, as though there's always a surplus of power, should he need it. Even the way he scrubs discontentedly at the chamfers is an advertisement of his confidence. The strength he keeps in reserve.

Two thirds of the way up, he asks Mike to adjust the matting, then climbs the last eight or ten feet to the cornice.

He examines it, in the sad light of a rainy spring. Makes no comment. Just adjusts his weight again, down-climbs a dozen feet or so, then jumps the short remaining distance to the mat.

'Nothing there. Not really. Like the stone has this little matchstick edge along the top, kind of Llanberis slate style, but . . .' He shrugs in a way which I interpret as meaning, 'Not enough to tempt me to out on it, and not enough to tempt anyone sane.'

From below, I can see the cornice has a kind of rounded bit, a bulge, that runs the full width of the wall. I ask about that, but Rhod just shakes his head, and says, 'No, it's nothing.'

As he's talking or, to be more precise, not talking, Mike swings up onto the wall. Same basic body posture, same rhythmical, controlled movement. He doesn't worry at the lichen, just climbs smoothly up the corner. He inspects the cornice and descends.

'OK. You've got this horizontal part about so big.' Mike holds his finger and thumb about four or five millimetres apart. 'If you had anything for the feet, or if the wall was more slabby, if it was lying at more of an angle, the hold might be enough to keep you on. As it is, though, there's just not enough there. If anything, you'd have to aid it.'

'*Aid* it?'

'Cheat, basically.'

He explains. I don't follow everything, but the gist is that the good old days were really the bad old days, and when climbers couldn't get up a particular route, they'd just invent some gizmos to help them do it, but these days nobody does that, except maybe in California, but then what are ethics really, when you think of sports climbing, after all?

My face expresses the degree to which I have understood him.

He says, 'Look, you can't climb out along there cleanly. But if you came with some skyhooks, you could do it, all right.'

'Skyhooks?' I ask, not sure if he's being serious. Then, when it's clear that he is, I ask if he can show me, but no, he doesn't have any skyhooks, no, climbers round here wouldn't typically have them or use them, and no, he can't think of anyone who would be able to demonstrate.

I would ask more, but all this time Rhod has been chucking stuff – mats, towel, boots, chalk bag – into the back of Mike's tatty-looking Mazda and looking pleadingly at his companion.

He says, 'We can still get something in on Witches Point, if we bomb it.'

Mike shoots him a look, to remind him that I'm a police officer with, no doubt, ferocious views on road safety, but I wave them off without making any arrests.

Rhod chalked up to make the climb, but Mike seemed happy to do without and in any case you could probably colour the chalk so it was more or less invisible against the stone.

Ollie appears from somewhere. Lockwood's son.

I say, 'Your mother's OK, is she?'

'She'll live.'

'Listen, your sister, Francesca. She was here on the night of the burglary, wasn't she?'

I know she was. Our files record all the names of all family and staff. Short statements from most of them.

Ollie says, 'Cesca? She's – she's in London now. Art student.' When my face reminds him that that is not an answer to my question, he adds, 'I think so, yes.'

'We might need to interview your dad too. I'm hoping not, but it's possible.'

He shrugs.

'You don't care?'

'Not particularly.'

I raise my eyebrows at that, nudging him to expand, but to start with he offers nothing. Just gazes out at the lawns. The dark topiary pillars. Clipped yew and regimental box. Then he says, 'Thing is, my dad's OK, but he *is* a bit of a dick.'

We laugh.

I think Ollie's summary rates somewhere between accurate and flattering. Ollie's dad, Galton Evans, made his money in agricultural insurance, then sold up and now passes his time screwing girls only a few years older than his son and dabbling in property and investment projects.

I don't really care about Evans's bedroom habits, but he's been a target of mine for two years now. I've watched him. Gathered data. Tried to find a route into the privacies of his life. Not because I've known anything bad about him directly, but because he was a close friend of a man called Brendan Rattigan, because Rattigan was an evil man, and because I have fair reason to believe that Evans knew about that evil and did nothing to stop it.

That's how they started, my little private investigations,

but they've deepened since. My second big case fingered a man called Idris Prothero – another of Rattigan's circle – and Prothero only escaped justice because the Crown Prosecution Service was too wimpy to bring a case in the face of political hostility. My most recent case of note also had some local rich guy at its heart, but I don't know who. I never got a name and I saw him only the once, a distant figure on a far-off hill. Evans knew Rattigan, knows Prothero, and – I'd bet my sweet little Alfa-Romeo, complete with petrol, road tax and dangly cardboard air-freshener – he also knows the man who was my target that dark morning.

I tell Ollie about Rhod and Mike. Their ease in climbing the corner.

Ollie looks up, says, 'Up there? Wow.'

'Do you have a ladder?'

He does. Finds a groundsman, or someone, to haul a ladder from an outbuilding. I climb it. The light, never great, is murkier now, but I'm able to view the cornice from above.

Mike was right. The actual horizontal part is very scanty. Five millimetres at the most, but this is eighteenth-century stone which has seen the weather of centuries. Some bits of that top edge look crisp and sound and certain. Other parts, not so much. A black lichen lines the crevice where the cornice meets the wall.

I come down and call Mike on his mobile.

'Fiona,' he says, 'hold a moment.' A pause, then, 'OK, you're on hands-free.'

'Are you *climbing*?'

'No, Rhod is. I'm belaying.'

'Quick then. If someone used a skyhook on that edge, what marks would you expect to see? I mean, assuming there was something there to take an impression.'

Mike's attention is mostly with his climbing partner, and there's a yelled conversation between them about some issue to do with the way the ropes are moving, or not moving. Then, hurriedly, 'Basically a skyhook is just a pointy metal hook. So if you're lucky you'll find a line of pointy metal hook marks.'

'And that climb – up the corner and along to the window – how hard is it? I mean, you and Rhod had crash mats underneath you, but would you have been happy to attempt the climb without protection? If there was four hundred grand at the end of it?'

Mike's attention absents itself, then returns. There's a booming noise in the background, which is, I realise, the sound of waves.

'Me, no. Rhod, maybe.' Then he corrects his answer to, 'Rhod, probably.'

I want to ask more, but there's a shout of 'Watch me!' and a sudden jingle of ropes and metal. The sound of something soft hitting something hard.

I say, 'Shit, Mike, are you OK? Is Rhod all right?'

There's a short pause. An ocean fretting against silence. Then, 'Yeah, fine. Look, can we finish this tomorrow?'

I say yes and hang up.

Go up the ladder again to see if I can see a line of pointy hook marks. I can't. Say thank you to Ollie and the groundsman.

Drive home, radio silent, still hearing the ocean roaring in my ears. And the sound of something soft hitting something hard.

# 7

Home, that place of uncertain welcome.

Magnolia walls and undrawn curtains. I open the fridge and say hello. Eat a tomato. Find some grapes and eat them.

I'd vaguely been intending to flip through my policing manuals again – my exam is tomorrow – but get diverted by an internet search for academic researchers in criminal forensics. Someone at the University of Kent is interested in lichens. I'm interested in lichens too. I whack off an email.

Smoke a joint. Have a bath.

Then, dammit, remember my exam, but it's raining, I'm in a dressing gown, and the manuals are still in the back of my car. I peer out at the rain and send my manuals some positive vibrations through the bedroom window. They vibrate positively back.

Those positive vibrations carry me through to what was once a spare room, now rather grandly renamed the ops room.

Computers. Lists. Photos. Data.

Lots of work. Not much product.

Fiddle around with a current interest of mine, Ned Davison. Once an accountant, now a general purpose 'business consultant', whatever that means.

Davison had a marginal relationship to my past assignment, Operation Tinker. I did what I could to rope him into the inquiry proper. Did enough that my boss at SOCA managed to pull some data on him. Data which shows him having done paid consultancy work for a dozen or more local businessmen in the period ending 2008. From January 2009, he channelled his activity through an offshore management company and his records basically dried up. He still pays tax, but our ability to see the fine grain of his income vanishes.

I've tried to find out more, but without joy. I know where he lives, what car he drives, where that car goes, who he sees, but the data reveals more or less nothing. For all I know, the guy is just a decently successful consultant, working hard, making a living.

I leave Davison. Turn to Francesca Evans.

Try finding her on Facebook. No joy. Try the same search a few different ways. Still nothing.

Then try Francesca Lockwood. Find her first go. She calls herself Cesca, but I know it's the right person, because she's a student of art and design at Central Saint Martins in London. Her friends include Ollie and her mother. Not her father.

Who changes her name to her mother's name following a family divorce? Someone who's pissed off at her father.

*Thing is,* Ollie tells me, *my dad's OK, but he* is *a bit of a dick.*

How much of a dick, Ollie? I want to ask. Just how much of a dick?

Go to bed. Sleep well.

In the morning, I sit my OSPRE exam. A hundred and fifty questions in three hours. Some I get right, some I get wrong. Jackson can yell at me if likes.

Phone Mike again, ask – properly – what happened last night on the phone and if Rhod is OK.

Mike, vaguely puzzled by the question, says, 'Yes, fine. He fell, that's all.'

I thought the point of climbing was about not falling, but I don't pursue the topic. Ask instead if Mike has ever climbed Critterling, the hardest of the four climbs on the cliff from which the security guard fell.

‘Critterling? No. Tried it once and kept lobbing off the crux. Love to try it again, though. It’s brilliant.’

I ask him for a favour and he’s happy to agree.

We ring off.

I can’t think of an excuse not to return to my dungeon, so I do.

When I enter the room, Ifor looks vaguely round and says, ‘Oh, hi . . .’ He gropes for my name.

‘Fiona,’ I say. ‘Fi, if you prefer.’

‘That’s right. Fiona.’

‘Are you OK?’

‘Oh yes. I’m fine. I’ve got a bit of a . . .’ He points at his head.

I get him some aspirin and send him off to make tea. When he’s gone, I look at his computer. He’s done almost nothing all morning. Twelve exhibits entered in the database, about half an hour’s work in total. The data entry is slipshod too. The data is clumsily duplicated from prior entries, or simply wrong.

I call Laura Moffatt, the senior exhibits officer, over from her dungeon, which stands a couple of doors down from ours. Show her the screen. Point out the errors.

I ask, ‘Is this normal? I’ve always found him to be—’

Laura agrees with her eyes, but at that point Ifor returns.

Laura says, ‘Ifor, how are you? Are you feeling all right?’

He says, ‘I’m feeling . . . I’m feeling . . .’

In his hands: two mugs. Coffee granules in his. A tea bag in mine. No water in either.

I reach for the phone and call for a patrol car.

Laura, speaking slowly, says, ‘Ifor. You’re not feeling well and we’re going to take you to hospital. Do you understand? To hospital.’

Moving his lips carefully, and with a lot of thought, Ifor says, ‘That’s right. I’m not feeling well.’

Two hours later and we know the worst.

Ifor has a brain tumour. Benign, but the size of a tangerine. Surgery has already begun. A full recovery is perfectly possible, but surgeons won't know until the operation is complete. In any case, recovery will take months, not weeks.

I have a sit down with Laura Moffatt, Owen Dunthinking and DCI Jackson.

We all say the right things. The personal ones, of course. Poor Ifor. So young. Shocking, really.

But the professional ones too. Where this leaves Chicago, our mounting pile of exhibits.

Six eyes looking at me.

Or eight, in fact, because the pair of eyes that matter aren't even in the room. Kirsty Emmett. That tangled hair, those empty eyes.

I say, in a tiny voice, 'I'd be happy to step in. Easier to keep going.'

There's a bit of further discussion. I don't participate. My gaze is on the floor. Grey carpet, running a little threadbare in places. I hoovered it once. Washed the skirting board.

Jackson tells Laura Moffatt to 'Keep an eye on this one. I want regular updates on her work. Speed, accuracy, attention to detail. All that.'

Laura assents, but is nice enough to add, 'From what I've seen, her work has been excellent so far. Really good.'

My mouth forms the words 'thank you,' but I don't think any sound comes out.

The one contribution I do make is to say, 'The one thing that we don't seem to have so far is anything from the hospital. Swabs, dressings, paper towels, that sort of thing. I'm worried that we've got them somewhere insecure or stored in a way that might compromise their evidential integrity.'

Jackson darts a glance at Dunthinking, whose pinkishness accelerates. Gathers in his cheekbones. Thickens in the shade of his gingery beard. He says, 'I'll need to look into that. I'll have to check where we've got to on that.'

He swallows once after speaking and drags a fingernail across his jaw.

Jackson's stare is as broad as the ocean, but he says nothing.

Dunthinking talks about his current strategy. He's looking for vehicles that were both in Gabalfa and on Rover Way in Tremorfa on the same day, and at roughly the correct times. Number-plate recognition cameras are fairly well positioned at both locations and, *mirabile dictu*, all working.

'There's a lot of work,' he says. 'Locate any suspect vehicles. Get them forensicated. Keep crunching through the data.'

He repeats himself. Stops where he shouldn't. Once again, Jackson says little or nothing.

When the meeting breaks up, I ask to stay behind. Want a private word.

Moffatt and Dunthinking leave. I'm alone with Jackson and Kirsty Emmett. Of the two presences, Emmett's seems the stronger.

Jackson says, 'Well done for getting Ifor to hospital.'

I nod. According to a registrar at the hospital, the tumour was pressing up against a major blood vessel. Ifor was no more than days, perhaps only hours, from a massive and probably lethal stroke.

'And thank you for volunteering just now. That was the right thing to do.'

Nod.

I say, 'I assume you heard about—'

'Your adventures at Plas Du. Yes, I did. And yes, you were totally out of line.'

His tone adds: 'And you're due one shitstorm of a bollocking, as well you know.'

'Sir?'

'Yes?'

'I don't know how much you know about – I don't know if you've ever looked at my HR file.'

'No. Should I?'

'No.' I realise I don't know how to say this. My file shows a two year gap in my CV. Years in which I was mostly in a mental hospital. Years I almost never discuss with anyone. So I skirt the topic. Stay safe. Say, 'I used to have problems. Not any more. None at all, really. Only – only my job is really important to me. Not just as a police officer, but as a detective.'

'We're not taking your job away, Fiona. You're still in CID.'

'I know. Sorry, sir, I know that. It's just . . .'

And I don't know what to say. Don't know how to tell him. Should I explain that I've wanted to crush the glowing tip of a cigarette against the pale skin inside my elbow? That I stood so hard on my own toes that two of them are crushed black, with nails that are turning purple? That the thought of going back down to the dungeon, to enter data, ferry exhibits, and stare pointlessly at Ifor's stupid waterfall poster in a room without windows, makes me actually shake inside? Long, violent, invisible shakes that are the precursors of something much worse.

I don't know what to say, so I don't say anything at all. Just sit there, mouth partly open, staring ahead.

'Fiona?'

'I'm an investigator. I need to investigate.' Because I know that Jackson wants to tell me that an exhibits officer is a vital part of any inquiry, because I know he wants to give me the senior officer crap which is every word of it true but still every word of it crap, I interrupt his interruption. 'I'm not saying I won't take over from Ifor. I will. And I'll do it right. I won't cock up. I won't piss you off. But I can't only do that. I mean, I *can't*. That's why I went to Plas Du. Why I pulled Lockwood in for interview. It wasn't because I thought the case required it. It was because *I* did. It's because I was struggling.'

I point to my head, in much the way that Ifor did with his. *Here*. This is the problem. His tumour, my craziness.

Jackson doesn't answer right away. One of the best things about him is his slowness. His silences.

He knows that some truths, the biggest ones, blossom best in emptiness.

And this is hard for him, I see that. When Jackson joined the force, policing was a more straightforward affair. The Police and Criminal Evidence Act didn't exist. Most coppers were men. The ones who weren't were called birds and had their bottoms pinched. Computers barely existed. DNA evidence hadn't been thought of.

And now? Jackson lives in a world where women police officers are called, simply, police officers. Where my five foot two inches is no barrier to recruitment or advancement. Where technology is rampant. Where attitudes to evidence handling, interrogation and much else are utterly different from the past.

I'm wearing a pleated blouse and grey woollen trousers. I'm looking at my knees and feeling Jackson's gaze hot on my face.

He says, 'Fiona, last year, I worked with you on an operation, during which—'

'I know.' I can't explain. Beyond a point, I just can't explain. Last year, I worked undercover. I worked full time as a payroll clerk, and part time as a cleaner. I was in constant danger, cut off from friends. My social life revolved largely round a homeless shelter. 'I found that easy, sir. I *liked* it. This won't make any sense to you, but I found that kind of life restful, almost.'

'And you're saying that working nine to five, in a warm room, doing an important job . . .'

Jackson trails off and I complete his thought. 'Working in safety, clerical work, seeing the same colleagues day after day, knowing that my tomorrow will look much like my yesterday? That's what I can't do. I wouldn't manage it.'

I don't say, 'wouldn't *survive* it,' though that feels like the truth. But I do realise that my finger is once again pointing at my head. Passing the blame, identifying the culprit.

The voice in my head wants to say, 'I'm not normal. I'm just not like other people.' But I don't say that. Not out loud. Don't disclose more of my craziness than I really have to.

A Jacksonian silence swells beneath us. Like one of those vast American deserts, all bleached sand and towering rock.

Sunlight on creosote bushes.

The sound of something small burrowing out of sight.

Then Jackson says, 'OK. So, you're happy to take over from Ifor. Do a proper job. But you want something else to run alongside. Something, I don't know, to keep you motivated. Keep you engaged.'

'That's it, sir, yes. Motivated and engaged.'

I almost laugh in relief. God! Here I am virtually telling Jackson that I'm a wacko. A crazy who half-belongs in hospital and he thinks I'm worried about a little ordinary boredom. The guy is so damn sane, he can't even imagine real craziness. I feel shaky with relief.

'You'll be busy enough with Chicago,' he says.

'That's OK. I don't mind working hard.'

'Tell me about it.'

He stares at me appraisingly. I wonder how I look through his eyes. A small young woman in a neat white blouse. But one who can't actually handle the kind of life that small, neatly bloused women are meant to lead.

'So. You've got a burglary at Plas Du. What else did I give you?'

It was a whole stack, in fact, but I only mention Derek Moon, the fallen security guard.

'That's a thin diet for you, isn't it?'

He means I normally like my cases fresher, bloodier. Corpsier.

'Yes, maybe, but with crime the way it is . . .'

Crime statistics: a favourite complaint of mine. The way crime always falls. The way each year brings fewer corpses, fewer Major Crimes for our dwindling team.

Jackson says, 'Fiona, falling crime is a good thing, remember? But look. Your priority, at all times, needs to be the EO job, OK? If Owen Dunwoody or Laura Moffatt tell me you're letting things slip, I will jump up and down on your head. Probably literally. But in any case, you won't have a job in CID afterwards. Is that clear?'

I nod. My submissive nod. The one that actually means I actually mean it.

'And no flying solo. No more interviewing people under caution when you haven't even bloody told me you wanted to visit the site.'

I do my nod again, but maybe not quite so submissive as the one before.

Jackson doesn't let that go. He says, sharply, 'Fiona?'

'Yes, sir. No flying solo.'

'OK.' And then he smiles and maybe I do too and then everything changes and there is light in the room again and I can stand up without wobbling and no longer feel the need to point upwards at my head.

'Your OSPRE exam. Did it go OK?'

'Made random guesses all the way through, sir.'

'Excellent.'

He wants to know when I hear the results. I'm not sure, but I think it's six weeks, something like that.

Then Jackson wants me gone. He'd quite like to do some real work, I think. But I have one last call on his patience.

'Lichens, sir. Do you have any interest in lichens at all?'

# 8

Lichens. Neglected but remarkable.

For one thing, they're not one organism, but two. All lichens are joint ventures that combine a fungus and an alga. The fungus does the rooty, mushroomy stuff. The algae do the photosynthesis part. A neat trick.

And they're tough little critters. A few years back, a Spanish scientist, don't ask me why, put some lichens on a spaceship and bounced them around in open space for a fortnight. Cosmic rays. Heat and cold. Total vacuum. Not great for the health, you'd imagine, but when they came back to Earth, they were just fine. All tickety-boo and ready to carry on lichening around.

There are drawbacks to this way of life, however. Most pertinently, lichens grow slowly. So slowly, indeed, they can be used to date the exposed surfaces of rocks. And if some remarkably adept burglar chose to go skyhooking his way across a narrow cornice near Llantwit in order to gain entry to a corridor full of minor Picassos, then the lichens will bear the imprint of that skyhookery for years, and perhaps even decades, afterwards.

My researcher from the University of Kent does indeed come to Plas Du. And finds that, sure enough, if you ignore the most recent growth – the stuff that has happened in the years since 2009 – the older lichens reveal a line of pointy metal hook marks running all the way from the corner to the window. The marks are so clear, we think we can even identify the brand of skyhooks.

The process takes two weeks. In academic-forensic terms, two weeks is blisteringly fast, but to me, down in the dungeons, the moment can't come soon enough. I chase Pam, the researcher, every day at least once, sometimes twice. But we get there. She gives me the confirmation I need. By phone and email, letter to follow.

'*Fab*,' I tell her. Tell her that she's my favourite ever lichenologist.

Go skipping into Jackson's office to tell him what I want to do next.

He laughs at me, but tells me to go ahead. 'You're to work with a grown-up, this time. Rhiannon, now. You and she get on all right, don't you? I'll get her to babysit.' He makes the call that makes it official. 'Tomorrow morning. She'll come and get you.'

I nod. 'Thank you.'

I don't go back to work though. I've booked today as a holiday. Only came in now to get the Plas Du thing moving forwards.

I've taken the day off to meet a friend. One I haven't seen, or not properly, for some time. I'm not sure exactly what gifts to bring, but decide on some beer, a packet of cigarettes, a cup of coffee in a stay-warm plastic mug and a bacon sandwich which I try to keep vaguely warm by leaving my coat on top of it.

Park at HM Prison Cardiff. The spaces are reserved for prison staff only, but I'm police, so I almost count. Check with the front desk for scheduled release time. Eleven o'clock, they say, but say it in a way that evades the question of whether anything will actually happen on schedule.

I say, 'Can you tell him to come and find me? I'm in the car park. A few routine questions.'

I'm parked up under the wall. The other cars in my row all have their noses pointing outwards, snouts toward Fitzalan Road and a glimpse of trees. My car faces in. Nothing to see but blocks of rough-hewn stone. Grey and brown and rust-red and a black so deep it shimmers blue in the shadow.

Play Classic FM until it annoys me. Radio 2 lasts no longer. Radio 4 is worse. A stupid drama about a stupid woman whose stupid life problems could, in my opinion, be solved by a good, hard slap.

Not that, as a police officer, I'm technically pro-slapping.

So I wait in silence, which is better. The zen of the prison yard.

Time does whatever it does near prisons. Flows fast on the street outside, thickens as it approaches these darkly rising walls. Minutes pass like flies struggling in syrup.

Penry appears at about twelve thirty. He moves slowly, like an old man blinded by sunlight.

I could help him, of course. Step out of my car. Toot my horn.

I do neither. Just stay at the wheel, watching him peer through the glare of windscreens.

He stops when he recognises me. Mouth wordless in the breeze. Shifts his face around till he finds something right for the occasion. Tough, male, but nevertheless a tough male face that balances on top of a sea of other feelings.

I lean across the passenger seat and flip the door open.

He stands in the opening. 'Jesus, Fi.'

I move my coat off the bacon sarnie and say, 'The coffee's cold. So is the sandwich.' Give him his gifts anyway.

He sits there on the seat, facing the wall, holding the beer, the coffee, the sandwich, the ciggies. His eyes are swimming.

After a bit, he says, 'Can I?' meaning the cigarettes.

I nod yes and we both light up. We wind the windows down, but the car fills with smoke anyway.

He says, 'I think that's the nicest thing anyone has ever done for me.' Looks straight ahead as he says it, because I don't think he'd trust his eyes if he looked at me, and Penry has this compulsively macho thing going, like he thinks his penis might fall off if he ever let up.

I say, 'Home?'

He nods.

I drive him home.

Penry: a former copper. A good one. Decorated for bravery. But took early retirement after an injury sustained in the course of duty. Felt his life go to pieces. Did some stupid things. Went to prison for them, not least because I did a lot to ensure he did. But we've become friends nevertheless. I've visited irregularly throughout his jail term and he once helped out on an inquiry of mine from the inside.

I park outside his house. It's been rented out for his stay inside, but has been empty the last six weeks.

I let Penry find his keys, get used to the idea of standing on the right side of a lock.

He opens up. Moves through the space, as alien to him now as the first explorer on Mars.

'It's cleaner than I thought,' he says. 'I thought the tenants would have trashed the place. Always assumed they would.'

He rests his hand on a radiator, which is somewhat warm. In the kitchen, he swings open the fridge door. There's milk there. Fresh milk. And butter, cheese, bacon, some orange juice. In the cupboard, fresh boxes of cereal, bread, tinned beans, a few bits and pieces. Beers.

His face turns to me, looking more pained than happy.

'I've been in when I can,' I say. 'Cleaning up and stuff.'

'You didn't have a . . .' he says, then remembers that I once burgled the place anyway, that I don't always need keys.

And then he just slumps down on a kitchen stool, face in hands. He cries silently, but his shoulders heave through his faded purple sweatshirt. I wonder if I'm meant to put my hands to him. Rest a hand on his neck, knead his shoulder muscles, something like that.

I don't. Just find a bottle opener, open a beer, push it his way. Go out to the car, get a joint from the boot.

When I come back in, he's stopped crying. He's halfway down his first bottle. He holds a second out to me.

'I don't drink,' I tell him. Show him my joint.

He laughs. I light up.

And then we sit there, in the cloister of his kitchen, him drinking, me smoking, and neither of us talking much.

I ask him what he'll do now.

'Security work of some kind, I suppose. Don't know if anyone will want to hire me, but being on the inside does give you a perspective. It does teach you stuff.'

'Ask Watkins for a reference,' I say. 'She might give you one.'

'Really?'

The inquiry where Penry helped me from the inside was one of Watkins's. She's got fierce views about bent coppers, but this particular bent copper showed a fair bit of heroism in helping us out that time.

'Worth a try.'

We chat. Him about prison, me about my cases. Plas Du and Dunthinking's damn Chicago.

He drinks another beer, then goes up to shower. Comes down in a different pair of jeans, a different top.

I've finished my joint and I'm getting bored.

I say, 'Brian, let's just say you were a copper again. Say you'd never been to prison, that none of that stuff had ever happened.'

'OK.'

'And let's say you were on a case. A serious one. Murder, rape, something like that. If you started to believe that the investigation, although properly conducted, would never result in a successful prosecution, would you do anything about it? I don't mean anything awful particularly, just – I don't know – entering premises without a warrant, tracking a car, stuff like that.'

'That stuff used to happen a lot. Half the time, it wasn't even all that clever. First time I worked on a big case, they had this suspect in custody, bastard was definitely guilty but saying nothing. When I came in the next morning, the guy had a fractured cheekbone and we had a full confession in writing.'

'Yes, but now. If it were you. And I'm not talking about hitting people.'

'Now? But look, I *have* been to prison. That stuff changes you.'

I leave it there.

Don't stay much longer. Drive out to Gower. To the churchyard where the security guard, Derek Moon, lies buried. A stone church with a low tower. Gravestones sloped against the wind. Grass shaggy in the spaces between.

Moon's grave is a good one. Simple carving. Welsh sandstone. Moss and lichens already claiming it. A deep fingernail's worth of growth already in the cleft of that M, the curl of the Os. Someone has left a clutch of daffodils here at the graveside. Out of water and with an elastic band pinching the stems.

I get a knife from my car – an ordinary kitchen knife, nothing special – and cut away the elastic band, take a couple of inches off the stems. Near the entrance to the churchyard, there's a little set of open shelves, holding a few plastic vases, some basic gardening bits and pieces. I take a vase, fill it from a water butt under the vestry roof. Settle the flowers properly back.

Take a photo. I've never seen Moon's actual corpse and that bothers me somehow, like a missing tooth.

As I'm doing this, I realise that I'm being watched from the other side of the graveyard wall by a girl in a red coat. Big eyes, serious mouth.

I say, 'Those flowers. Did you leave them?'

She doesn't nod exactly, but her face is more yes than no.

'They looked very nice, but they last a bit better in water. You can get vases from over there,' I tell her.

She nods.

'So they'll look nice for him,' I add and, as I do so, have this vision of Moon. Bearded beneath the soil. The blood on his scalp crusted over. Black as tar in the deeper-lying wounds. The dead man himself looking upwards, through the soil and the worms and the stones and the grass. Looking at the yellow daffodils and a silent girl in a scarlet coat.

When I get home, I find two missed calls. Penry's number, no message. I don't call back.

What I do do, however, is address a niggle that's been bothering me. Lockwood's divorce from Evans was clearly amicable enough, as amicable as these things ever are. Yet Francesca chose to change her name rather than stick with the one she was born with. And Ollie's first answer about his sister's presence in the house on the night of the burglary was a strange one. *She's in London now. Art student.* And there was something gap-toothed about Lockwood's photo collection, the one that contained no pictures of the daughter, Francesca, with her father.

The daughter has a car registered to her name. A Fiat Punto hatchback, forty thousand miles on the clock. I use the national number-plate recognition system to try and track times when Francesca Lockwood was in the same place as her father. Can't do it. That doesn't mean they never have been in the same place – there are trains and taxis and buses and friends' cars and a million other possibilities for interaction that I can't trace. But still. He has a car. So does she. Yet the two things have never been in the same place at the same time, not even around Christmas.

Another item for my to-do list, I fancy.

As I'm getting to bed later that evening, the phone goes again. I answer it.

'Brian,' I say.

'Fi.' His voice is slurred. Beery.

I imagine him standing upright, but leaning up against a wall. He has prison skin, too pale for the world.

I didn't call him, he called me, so I don't see any need to make conversation. Just sit on my bed listening to the crackle on the line until he gets to what he wants to say.

He says, 'Your question. About what to do if you thought an investigation was going nowhere.'

'Yes?'

'I didn't give you an answer. Not really.'

'So . . .?'

'Look, I think coppers need to obey rules, I really do. The rules aren't stupid, not most of them. But then, why become a copper at all? Why become a copper unless you want to deliver justice? And the rules don't always help. Usually, yes, but not always.'

That's still not an answer, I think, but I don't say so. Just sit listening to that crackle and thinking of Moon's churchyard at night.

Clay against the dead man's lips. Daffodils yellow against the wheeling stars.

Then Penry speaks again.

'This investigation of yours. The security guard. You think that investigation is going nowhere?'

'Maybe. Yes. Maybe.'

'And you want to do something about it? Take action outside the rules?'

'Maybe. Possibly. I'm not sure.'

A pause, a short one. Penry winding himself up to an actual answer.

'Fi, I think the justice comes first. It has to.'

'Yes. Thank you. I think so too.'

'But don't fuck up. You're still a police officer.'

'Yes.'

'And you don't want to end up like me. A copper *and* a convict.'

I say yes. Tell him thanks.

He says the same to me.

We don't hang up straight away. Just stay there, listening to the crackle. Then one of us says goodnight. Then the other one does too. And then we are alone, as alone as Derek Moon, but without the clay, the worms, the stars, the daffodils.

I think police rules matter and I'll try to abide by them. But the dead matter more. Their rules are sacred and they last for ever.

# 9

The next morning. Ten o'clock.

DI Watkins comes down to the exhibit rooms to get me. Knocks, because the entry system doesn't allow her to walk straight in.

I open the door. She looks around. Says, 'Christ!'

I look around too, sharing her joy.

'I made some changes.'

Turned off the overhead lights.

Got rid of Ifor's horrible waterfall poster. His loathsome pot plant.

Put up the picture of Kirsty Emmett. Also the one of Derek Moon's mashed skull. And also, because all inquiries are, for me, merely rivers that flow into the one great sea of investigation, other pictures too. A photo of Janet and April Mancini, the corpses that launched my CID career. Of Stacey Edwards, who was kind to Janet and who died the same way. Of Mary Langton: a photo of her head, the one I found, blackly dripping, in a barrel of old motor oil. Of Ali Al-Khalifi, a naughty boy who found himself chopped up and scattered across suburban Cardiff for his sins. Of Mark Mortimer, a man who would have had ethical issues with a roomful of bishops and died a suicide. Of Hayley Morgan, who died of starvation and rat poison, with plaster dust in her gums. Of Saj Kureishi, who died with his hands detached from his wrists, and a look of perplexity on his ash-grey face. Of Nia Lewis. A girl who died, tangled in nettles on a wet field margin, for almost no reason at all, except that I caused a scene and she was unlucky enough to witness it.

My photo gallery, my friends.

Watkins gapes and looks wonderingly at the space where Ifor's desk used to be.

'I got rid of it. It was annoying me.'

In its place now, a nest of cushions. Some borrowed from home. Others bought for the purpose. I've got two laptops. Also Ifor's old desktop, which I use mostly as a lampstand. A gizmo duct-taped to the ceiling that looks for the faint trace of a mobile phone signal and amplifies it, so I can use my own phone, even down here in the basement. The gizmo is an unlicensed transmitter and isn't actually legal, but I can hardly arrest myself and I don't think anyone else is about to do so. A catering size box of those oaty energy bars, a small kettle and a box of peppermint tea bags completes my domesticities.

The only regular furniture is the bare wooden table on which the HOLMES terminal toadily crouches.

I say, 'It's lovely, isn't it?'

Watkins chooses not to respond, but I'm genuinely proud of what I've accomplished. It's the first room I've ever really furnished. I mean, yes, I own a house and there is stuff in there which I purchased, but I only bought a sofa and put it in my living room because I know that's what people usually do with sofas and living rooms. Almost every choice I made, I made in order to bring myself closer to average. The whole place is beige and white and magnolia and chrome and so blandly inoffensive it's like a museum of my opposite.

Ifor's dungeon now pleases me in almost every detail. I even like the exhibit shelving stretching into darkness. The knowledge that amongst those hairs and drink cans and casts of footprints there might lurk the clue that clinches a prosecution. I like the intimacy of it all. The secrecy and excitement.

I stand there next to Watkins, almost absurdly house-proud. Bobbing up and down, awaiting compliments.

Watkins isn't the complimentary type, however. Her mouth moves, says nothing. A grim 'Let's go,' is all she manages.

So we do. Down to the Bay. Havannah Street. The sort of address that's meant to have us drooling with desire and envy.

No drool on me. None on Watkins.

We sign in, take a lift. A reception desk, then a corporate meeting room. Views out over the Bay.

We've not been here a minute before Watkins is smouldering with impatience.

'We could go and kick the door down,' I say.

'Fiona, the charge is wasting police time.'

'So we kick a door down. Waste a bit less.'

She unlooses a scowl at me, but it misses its target and goes through a couple of walls before burying itself in a secretary somewhere. What my eminent superior means is that wasting police time is a summary offence only. Triable in a magistrate's court, and then only with the consent of the Director of Public Prosecutions. The DPP is most unlikely to think that prosecuting basically law-abiding citizens for minor charges is a sensible use of resources. So whatever it is we're doing here will not lead to a conviction.

That's her logic, but I think it's flawed.

'Fossicking,' I say. 'We're fossicking.'

I'd like to tell her all about fossicking, but I can tell she's not interested, so I shut up and watch the boats.

A young secretary arrives shortly before Watkins detonates. She leads us down a hallway, taps at a door, steps back. We are admitted into The Presence.

The Presence, aka Galton Evans, is a somewhat portly fifty-two-year-old. Greying beard, round the mouth and chin only.

Short, slightly messy hair. Suede jacket, white open-necked shirt, desert boots. It's a look – the clothes, the hair, the sleekly furnished office – which is trying to say, as loudly and clearly as possible, 'I've got money and I don't for a second want that to go unnoticed, but I'm cool too. Uninhibited and spontaneous.'

There's an appraising way in which he runs his eye over me that adds, 'And sexually available too, by the way.' The sort of man who might touch his lower lip with his tongue and inadvertently call me 'babe'.

He spreads his hands and says, 'Ladies.'

Watkins – mid-fifties and no heterosexual man's idea of a good night out – says, 'Mr Evans, you know why we're here.'

'The amazing reappearing etchings.'

'Please tell us the whole story, starting with when you heard the pictures were gone.'

Evans shrugs a little. He's maintaining the pose, but he's not a stupid man and he thinks carefully before answering. 'I got a call from Marianna, my ex-wife, saying the pictures were gone. Those candlesticks too. Mustn't forget those.' He glances at me as he says the last bit. Wrinkles his eyes and offers a half-smile.

'You were still living with Mrs Lockwood?'

'No. Joint assets and all that, but the divorce hadn't yet come through.'

'And the pictures were insured with . . .?'

'With my own company. We were primarily agricultural – protecting barns and crops and that sort of thing – but we had a majority stake in a small household insurance operation. The pictures were insured through that.'

'So although Mrs Lockwood recovered money from the insurers, she was effectively recovering money from you?'

Evans's answer was sort of yes, but essentially no. I don't quite understand the intricacies, but various reinsurance arrangements moved most of the risk on elsewhere. I don't know why these things always have to be so complex.

Watkins summarises. 'OK. So you've lost the pictures. Your insurance company has paid up, but most of those costs are borne by third parties. Did you send a claims investigator to the scene?'

Evans laughs. 'No. This was my wife.'

'From whom you were separated.'

'Marianna wouldn't . . . She *liked* those pictures. She *bought* them. Why contrive a theft for . . .' He doesn't finish his sentence, just waves his hands, but his meaning was, 'for such a small sum of money?'

'She could have pretended to lose the pictures, claim the money, then rehang the pictures once it had all blown over.'

'Why? To get at me, you mean? She *did* get at me. Through the divorce courts. You think she'd have been happy to nick a couple of Picassos and leave it at that?' He likes that line and it relaxes him. He sits further back in his chair and his appraisal of my figure is now very frank. I'm reasonably smart today. Navy trousers, matching jacket, ivory top. Shoes with a bit of a heel. But it's hardly pulling-wear.

I keep my expression steady, stay professional.

Watkins says, 'Did you suspect your staff?'

'Marianna's staff, not mine. I did wonder, yes. But she said there was a break-in, so . . .'

'So you just paid up.'

'Following a police report, of course. The normal procedures.'

'But no claims investigation.'

'No.'

'And then . . .?'

'Look, I'm an insurance guy. We work with the police, of course. Pride ourselves on good relationships with our friends in law enforcement.' Smile. 'But our job is different from yours. We're here to make money.'

'Please just tell us what happened.'

'One of my colleagues in the claims department got a call. The caller said the pictures could be made available at a price. With larger claims, we have a procedure for handling these things. The matter goes to an independent security consultancy. They do whatever they need to do.'

He shrugs. Not an embarrassed one, just a practical one. I've not come across this sort of thing in the past, but the resale of high value goods to their original owners does go on. The owners get their goods back, and at much less than their true value. The thieves manage to unload their takings at prices much higher than they could get on the black market proper. These grey-market dealings aren't exactly lawful, but assuming that they're handled via vaguely respectable intermediaries, we tend to let any minor irregularities go.

'So you repurchased the pictures.'

'Not me. The company.'

'Your company repurchased the pictures.'

'A company in which I held a majority share, yes.'

We wander off into technicalities. Basically, having previously paid out £400,000 to Marianna Lockwood, the company now recovered the money from Lockwood, and paid a total of about £100,000 to the security company, some of which was presumably passed on to the thief.

'You can document all this?'

'*I* can't, no. But the company could.'

A company which has since been sold.

We take names, phone numbers. Start a small administrative avalanche, which will hurtle down the slope of this little investigation and land on my desk, a papery explosion.

Watkins's limited patience is fast expiring. 'Why were we not informed of all this at the time?'

Evans spreads a pudgy hand on his chest. '*Mea culpa.* Not quite *mea maxima culpa*' – he reminds us that he was in the process of a divorce and that any actions were taken by the company, not him directly – 'but we should have informed you. That would have been our standard practice. I'll write to John Gill, the current CEO, to investigate the matter. Find out what went on.'

Watkins stands. A battle tank dressed by Hobbs.

'In your view, was Mrs Lockwood behind the theft?'

'No, certainly not.'

'Any member of her staff?'

'I've no idea.'

'And your business interests now? Are you still in insurance?'

A longer answer there, but one that still amounts, essentially, to no. A couple of city-centre property developments. A private investment fund, run by 'a small group of us, quite active.'

'That fund. It invests in insurance companies?'

'Maybe. I mean, some small fraction of its portfolio maybe. But it's not a particular interest of ours, no.'

Watkins stands and does a thing with her jaw that I've seen few people do. She just champs, in an odd, almost rotary motion, rather like a sheep with grass. There's a kind of squat immobility to her as well, something that doesn't give a damn about how others see her. I like that in her. I like her directness, her ready aggression.

Because she stands, I do too. Evans follows suit.

Watkins tells Evans that he'll need to make a statement. That's my job: to record the statement and get it signed. Watkins calls for a car to take her back to Cathays. The secretary appears again, bringing Watkins's coat.

I'm standing by the window, for no reason except that I have to stand somewhere. Evans approaches. Stands next to and behind me, his hand warm on my back. He leans in close enough that the swell of his chest presses against my upper arm. With his free hand, he points out the sights.

Sights which, since I'm a Cardiff girl through and through, I know every bit as well as him.

I step backwards, but manage only to tread on his foot. One of those clumsy stumbles, where all my weight comes down on the point of my heel, and the heel itself catches him just where the metatarsals fan out into toes. His boots are soft suede, offering no protection.

He howls in pain.

Watkins whirls round, glaring.

'Gosh, sorry,' I say. 'Did I get your foot?' I make one of those ouchy expressions, which conveys a 'Yikes, that must have been painful' message with just a thin sifting of apology.

The secretary jumps into activity – paper tissues, an offer of skin cream – but before all that, I'm fairly sure I saw something else. One of those fleeting micro-expressions which spoke of something other than upset. She catches my eye and looks away, but with a movement at the corner of her mouth that could be like the first stirrings of a smile.

Watkins watches impassive. Then leaves.

I take Evans's statement, writing longhand. Eight pages. He initials each sheet and signs the final page. He still nurses his damaged foot and there is blood dotting his sock. The skin cream was not required.

I think: *What we have written is all true, and all lies.* And in the lies lurk corpses.

I stand up to leave. Say, 'Your investment club.'

'Fund. Investment fund.'

'I should probably just take its name, sir. I know DI Watkins will ask.'

He stares at me. Plucks his lower lip. Not with lechery any more, but dislike. He's angry not because I hurt him, but because I rejected him, his damp advances.

'Idris Gawr Investments LP,' he tells me.

'LP?'

'Limited Partnership, a Cayman Islands vehicle. Very, very naughty of me, I know, keeping my money away from the taxman, but very, very legal.'

'It's a good name,' I say. 'Well chosen.'

He stares at me with that look of dislike. There's a tuft of grey hair under his jaw, a patch which the razor missed. The patch makes him look goaty, old, disreputable.

'Oh?'

I shrug. Gather my things. 'I mean, Critterling would have been too obvious. And Crack and Slab would have been just plain weird.'

His hatred follows me as I leave. On the way out, I ask the secretary her name. Bronwen, she says. Bronwen Woodward. Nice to meet you, Bronwen, I tell her.

# 10

My pact with Jackson holds up.

I work like crazy on Chicago. The inquiry has so far collected over three thousand four hundred exhibits, all of which need to be bagged, labelled, referenced and catalogued. It's the sort of job for which Ifor would normally have assistance, but Laura Moffatt is flat out on a job of her own, and sickness, budget pressures and staff turnover means that there's less back-up available than there normally would be.

The truth is, I don't think Ifor could ever have handled the volume of work on Chicago as efficiently as me, and both Jackson and Laura Moffatt think the same. Plus, though it's not strictly part of my remit, I read every interview transcript, stay closely in touch with the investigation itself. For once, my ever-precarious CID account is in credit.

But I've other fish to fry and they're browning nicely.

The Saturday following our visit to Galton Evans, Mike Haston, the climber, went out to Critterling with ropes and three mates. Not Rhod but other, more pliable, climbers. I was there too, with a technician from the forensic lab to check our procedures. We roped off a thirty foot wide chunk of cliff, the chunk down which Moon fell. And Mike, with his friends, traced every inch of that sweep of rock. Took moulds of every projection, every place where Moon could have hit his head. The climbers did essentially the same job that the original SOCO attempted, except that these guys didn't regard a hundred-odd feet of vertical or overhanging rock as 'difficult access'. They thought of it as a playground. Working on fixed ropes, but moving like dancers.

After four hours' work, we had a complete collection of moulds. The cliff remade in negative. And none of them had that right-angled cross section. Or anything close. It was obvious, more or less, from that first day I was there with Buzz. Once the guard had fallen over the overhang – a fall through empty space – he would have struck the smoothly rising slab. And that slab is a thing of delicate beauty. It's rippled in places. There are little crystals poking out now and again. Two cracks of not much more than a finger's width. Mike tells me there are a couple of fossils visible, ammonites. But the thing is basically just one smooth sweep of limestone. No deep fissures. No blocks. No sharp protrusions. And once Moon hit, rolled and bounced down the slab, he'd have been ejected into space again, as the slope of the cliff moved away from him. The final impact site lies almost fifteen feet from the base of the cliff.

My forensic guy, Bryn, stashed his accumulating moulds in an old fruit crate stacked on the rocks below the high tide mark. The moulds smelled of warm plastic, but had the colour of old flesh. An alien autopsy.

And as those moulds accumulated, the facts looked increasingly beyond dispute. Derek Moon was struck by an object with a roughly right-angled cross section. No such object exists on the cliff, so the injury must have occurred before or after the fall.

After is ruled out – he came to rest on his back, the side of his head untouched by that final drop. So that only leaves before.

Which means murder.

The bureaucracy takes time, of course. Getting casts made. Getting a damn report from Bryn, who normally has the honour of being harried and hounded by detective inspectors at the very least and isn't thrilled at being harried and hounded by a mere detective constable, and a wee, female, exhibits-managing one at that. But I get there. Assemble what I need. And – exactly one month from my first visit to Moon's death-place – I'm ready. Arrange a meeting with Jackson and Watkins, my appointed babysitter. Present my treasure.

A written report, by me. Bryn's, over-cautious, forensic summary. The key documents from the original case files. And my collection of plaster shapes: lumps from the cliff, that crucial dent in Moon's head.

Jackson's desk is a-scatter with my booty.

I talk it through. Neat, swift, professional, precise.

Finish into silence and Jackson's stare.

Eventually: 'It's a stretch, Fiona.' His terse conclusion.

'No, *that's* a stretch,' I say, pointing to the two lumps of plaster of Paris that Jackson has in his hand. One, an image of Derek Moon's skull wound. Two, a cast of the 'best fit' piece of rock we could find from the collection we assembled. The piece of rock that most fits the lethal injury. The two things don't match at all. 'What you mean is, we don't have a motive. And that's true. We don't. Not yet.'

'Any quarrels? Personal grievances?' Watkins's question.

'No. None uncovered. I've checked the original inquiry files and transcripts. Everything seems to have been done right. No obvious holes.'

'Theft?'

Watkins's question and one that arrives dripping in disbelief. You do get people killed for trivialities – a pocketful of cash, a fancy phone – but only by accident, only where alcohol is involved, and never, ever on a lonely clifftop path a couple of miles from the nearest village.

I don't answer her directly. Just shake my head. 'One aspect of the case which wasn't explored at the time was his work life. He was working nights at a telecoms installation down towards Oxwich Bay. I've not pushed things too far yet' – a glance at Jackson, letting him know that his 'no flying solo' pennant still flies from my masthead – 'but I understand that there's some pretty fancy technology there. Worth millions, not thousands.'

'Fancy technology? In Oxwich Bay? You're joking.'

'No, sir. It's a major launching point for undersea cables. Telecoms between Britain and Ireland, Britain and North America. And I guess when the cables come ashore, they need equipment to sort out which data goes where.'

'Anything missing that you know of?'

'Nothing reported, no.'

I put a little emphasis on the word 'reported'. Meaning that without authority, I wouldn't even dream of investigating further.

Jackson half conceals a smile.

Watkins says, 'OK, Fiona. Then take a look. Keep me in the loop.'

'Yes, ma'am.'

Jackson says, 'And Peter Pan. Plas Du. Where are we with that?'

I look at Watkins. 'That interview with Galton Evans, ma'am. Did you believe a word he said?'

'I don't think he *lied*. But no. He knows a hell of a lot more than he bothered to share.'

Jackson stares at us, looking for clarification.

Watkins says, 'Evans – or his soon-to-be ex-wife – has some stuff nicked. Evans's company has insured it. The thief contacts Evans's guys and offers to cut a deal. Evans figures it's cheaper to buy it back and does whatever he needs to do. Maybe he knows the identity of the thief or maybe not, but he certainly isn't telling us all he knows. I suppose, if we really pushed, we might be able to make a handling case out of this.'

Handling stolen goods is a reasonably serious offence. If the property involved is worth more than a hundred grand and, in the words of the sentencing guidelines, if the offence 'bears the hallmarks of a professional commercial operation', any sentence is likely to exceed four years and could be as long as fourteen. That's a case well worth going after, except that Evans wasn't really a handler. He was a guy trying to get some stolen goods back, and on behalf of somebody else at that. No court is going to bang him up for that, and Watkins doesn't want to waste her time with slap-on-the-wrist offences.

Nor does Jackson. In an ordinary world, he'd end things there, but he's still conscious of our conversation about my need for something beyond Chicago's stony walls.

He says, 'Fiona . . .?'

'Yes. No point in trying to manufacture a case when there isn't really one there.'

'Good. So we're agreed—'

'But I did wonder if it might be worth looking around to see if this case connects to anything else. I mean, a guy capable of entering totally inaccessible second-floor windows is probably going to do something similar again. Why wouldn't he? Burglar alarms won't stop him, because people don't bother to protect against the impossible.'

Jackson looks at Watkins, who nods.

I look at my hands, and mumble, 'I mean, Chicago, obviously. That comes first. But I expect I could fit in a little extra.'

The grown-ups laugh at me, and tell me OK.

'I might need access to the PND.'

PND: the police national database. Almost unbelievably, it's only very recently that one regional police force has been able to access the data held by another, without physically faxing a request through. Since there are forty-three regional forces, since data requests are often difficult to frame, and

– not least – since everyone hates faxes, that old system was atrocious, a gift to criminals. These days, everything is much more twenty-first century and slick but, *oy vey*, the audit trails. The smart card authorisations, the accreditations, the picky little 'proper purpose' rules. It's enough to make a woman turn to crime.

Watkins says, 'Tell me what you need. Don't go crazy.'

I don't go crazy, but I do, fortunately, have a prepared authorisation form with me, carefully phrased so it looks suitably narrow but, with a little generosity of interpretation, has enough breadth to let me do anything that I want.

Watkins reads through it, adjusts a couple of phrases with a bristle of impatience, then signs it. Hands it back.

I accept her gift with a 'Thank you, ma'am,' and a glow of satisfaction. Whether she knows it or not, I have in my hands the keys to the vault.

The keys to the vault and a licence to hunt.

# 11

A licence to hunt, yet for ten days I find nothing. No targets. No leads. No new directions.

A chilly April tips into May. The weather stays cold. A winter refusing to accept the logic of our spinning globe.

I can't even, for a change, complain of my working conditions. One of the unexpected pleasures of my EO work is that almost nobody knows what I'm actually working on. Yes, when I'm bagging things up and ferrying stuff to the Bridgend lab and chasing SOCOs to reference their location photos properly, the work I do is public and visible. But all that takes no more than half my theoretical working hours and when my door is closed and locked and my HOLMES terminal is on and I'm sitting either there or nested amongst my cushions, laptops and energy bars, I find that I have far more time for my own researches than I ever used to have. And if I sometimes work late, all through the night at times, kipping for a couple of hours in my nest, then waking up for yet more peppermint-tea-fuelled work, I realise that nobody even notices. I've taken to keeping a few changes of clothes in my lair. Wet wipes, toothpaste and soap keep me roughly hygienic. I've not yet found a way to wash my hair without a shower, but it survives.

Yet for all that, I find nothing.

Thefts of high-end telecoms equipment: nothing.

Crimes associated with telecoms firms: nothing, or nothing of interest.

Patterns of suspicious behaviour involving anything telecoms related: nothing.

Open police intelligence campaigns with a telecoms link: nothing.

Even when I skip out of the police system and start to investigate public sources – telecom industry committees on fraud prevention, that sort of thing – I find nothing.

Plas Du: the same thing. I look for high-value thefts where goods have been returned. I find one or two things, but nothing that appears to connect. I search for any thefts reported by friends of Galton Evans. I check out his business and personal connections – investment partners, present and former colleagues, people he's holidayed with. I even check, name by name, fellow members of his golf club, his yachting club. The odd racehorse syndicate.

Nothing. The odd reported crime, of course. Contacts with the police. Names mentioned in the course of other investigations. But nothing that draws these stray ends together. Nothing where the dim lamps of inquiry glow hot and bright.

I check out Idris Gawr LP, of course.

Idris Gawr isn't a particularly unusual choice of name for a Welsh venture. Idris Gawr – Idris the Giant – was a king of Meirionnydd. According to legend, Idris was so large that he used the mountain of Cadair Idris in North Wales as an armchair from which to study the stars. In historical reality, he lived and reigned a long time. Fought the Irish and the English. Defeated by Oswald of Northumbria in 632 CE. Died by strangulation.

He's not our best-known king, nor is he the most obscure. If naming your investment vehicles after murdered medieval kings was your thing, then Idris Gawr would be as good as any, better than most.

I check for any public information on the company, but get almost nothing. The Cayman General Registry Office supplies me the names of three directors, all of whom are local lawyers. Brass plates and nothing else. Those plates might conceal Lady Innocence herself, a barefoot girl in a field of buttercups. Or they might conceal a river of blood, a chatter of corpses.

I think the latter, but can prove nothing.

Common sense would say give up. No regular police investigation would pursue these cold trails for anything like as long as I've already spent. On the other hand, there *was* a dent in Moon's skull, a dent not made by the cliff down which he fell. And what I said to DCI Jackson about Plas Du remains true. A thief capable of wafting his way up a sheer wall and in through a second-storey window is hardly likely to play that game just the once.

And then, too, there's something strange about Picassos that vanish and reappear. About a reputable insurance company that ignores its own procedures even when the case involves £400,000 worth of the boss's wife's art collection.

These things murmur of hidden depths. Indeed, the only reason why no one but me is excited by these things is that without a plausible motive for Moon's murder, it's hard for a police force to treat the death as suspicious – and as for Plas Du, it's hard for a senior officer to get excited about stolen goods that have unstolen themselves.

But I'm not a senior officer. I have neither their budgetary constraints nor their conviction targets, and however little I find on the police database, I can't shake the feeling that there are big things – dark and violent – playing out in the shadows beyond our view.

More hard work, done the regular way, would find those things, but my patience isn't unlimited. So, when police resources fail me, I rely on my own.

The first step is the easiest.

I call Penry. Ask how he's getting on with his job hunting.

'Got bugger all. Middle-aged ex-con. *I* wouldn't give me a job.'

'*I* might though. What are your rates?'

'Don't know. Is it legal?'

'Brian, if it was legal, I'd do it myself.'

He dithers around, not giving me a proper answer. Thinks he can't charge me, because he has this idea that he owes me something, even though it was me who put him behind bars. I tell him he's useless. And to come to dinner tonight, with a scale of fees in his pocket.

He says yes, to the first part anyway.

I don't want to get in a muddle over cooking, so I prepare sensibly, not ambitiously. Leave work early. Get plenty of beers. Do a one-pot chicken and lentil thing which is so simple that even I can't cock it up. I can't tell if it tastes nice, but I'm ninety per cent sure it doesn't taste terrible.

I'm ready by six thirty and Penry isn't due till eight.

I check some used-car websites, looking for a van. Find nothing suitable. Sign up to an email alert thing which will tell me if what I want comes up.

Six forty-two.

That still gives me time for the next thing, so I tootle off to do that too.

Bronwen Woodward, Evans's secretary.

She lives, the electoral roll tells me, in one of the streets off Sedgemoor Road, the other side of Eastern Avenue. It's a frosty evening. Stained glass in the door. Sea-mist wandering through the streetlights.

It's not Bronwen who answers the door, but an overweight forty-something woman. Blond hair, perm, carmine nails, a wheezing cough. I say, 'Is Bronwen in, by any chance?' She doesn't answer directly. Just appraises me, coughs, and shouts up behind her. 'Bronsferyoo.' Then nothing happens. She doesn't let me in. Stays leaning across the hallway, the sound of a TV and its blue light falling from the living room door. Heavy floral wallpaper. One of those thick red carpets that seems to trap time.

I have one of those weird out-of-body sensations, where it's hard to tell whether this moment has lasted a second or a century, where I wonder if there's some *open sesame* spell, some hidden spring, which has to be touched to unlock things, to let time flow again.

I don't find out. Bronwen comes to the turn of the stair, sees me, and her face changes two or three times before settling on something bland and cautious. The older woman, her mother I assume, vanishes back to the land of the blue TV.

Bronwen comes downstairs. She's still dressed in her work clothes. A dark woollen skirt and formal jumper. No shoes, just stockinged feet.

'Bronwen, hi. I'm Fiona, remember? From the—'

'Yes. Is it OK?'

'It's all fine, totally. Just, could I have a private word for a minute?'

I can. We go upstairs. There are boxes in the hall and on the stair landing. Not the sort of boxes that say 'All packed and ready to ship', but the sort which say, 'Random crap accumulates in this house and never gets tidied or sorted.' A plus-size lace camisole hangs on the frame of a bedroom door. A giant teddy sits on top of a box from whose torn corner there is a spillage of DVD cases, a hoover part, a canvas strap, and some kind of kitchen gadget not removed from its plastic packet.

Bronwen makes a silent face which says, I think, 'I know what you're thinking and I agree.'

Her room is the opposite of the house. Ordered and neat. The window slightly open and a smell of air freshener.

I sit on the bed, Bronwen on the only chair.

I say, 'Is it OK coming here? If it was easier, I could come and see you at work.'

'No, no, it's OK. Here's probably better.'

'Mr Evans. A difficult boss, I imagine.'

She makes a curious gesture before she answers. A sideways bat of her hand, accompanied by a movement of the head. She says, 'He's a character, that's true.'

'Sexual harassment is an offence. You don't have to report it, that's your choice, but if you want to, you can call me. I'll give you my direct line.'

'Thank you. It's OK. I've done four months. I just want to build my CV, then . . .' She wants to dismiss the subject, but I do write out my direct line – the one leading in to Ifor's dungeon – and my mobile number as well. Tear those out of my notebook and pass them over. 'It *is* an offence. The law *does* protect you.'

Her lips say 'thank you', though her voice says nothing.

We sit without talking. Then, simultaneously, we speak.

She says, 'Can I get you anything?'

I say, 'And look, there's something else.'

# 12

Penry arrives punctually at eight. He gives me a bunch of flowers. Roses, stock, gerbera, carnations. They look nice, and I say so.

He looks smart too, or smartish. Clean, ironed shirt. Jacket. I've a momentary worry that he thinks this is a date, even though there's a good twenty years between us. I never know how these signalling things are meant to work. Whether I've been sending funny signals or not reading the ones he's been sending me. But then he rescues me by mentioning a party he's going to on Friday night. 'Maybe get back in the game,' he says, meaning, I think, that I'm not the game.

Which is good.

I give him beer and my ninety-per-cent not-awful chicken.

To start with we eat in the kitchen, but that feels strange, so I say we should go and eat in the living room, plates on our laps.

That's better, but still not right. I try turning most of the lights off. Then sitting on the floor. Then playing music. Then not playing music.

Then realise that it's the fakery which is bothering me, and I go and get my stash of photos for Penry to look at. Shots of Moon's injuries mostly. But also that one of the daffodils on his grave. Some of Plas Du, and the impossible burglary.

Only when those things are strewn all over the floor do I feel relaxed.

I tell him about my crimes. The burglary at Plas Du. The security guard with a broken skull.

I want to talk about Moon's long leap over the cliff top. About the sticklebacked rock that split his head open. But I don't do that.

I want to tell him about the girl in the red coat, about the grave and the daffodils, but I don't do that either.

Penry looks at the photos, longer than most people do, but he looks at me too. A long, discerning, Penry-ish stare.

'You *do* have a burglary. You *don't* necessarily have a killer.'

'That's true.'

'And the artwork came back, right? There's nothing missing?'

'Which makes it stranger. That wants more investigation, not less.'

'Found any thefts like it?'

'No. But again: that's strange. Why we need to investigate.'

'Who's in charge?'

'Watkins.'

'Jackson supervising?'

'Yes.'

'Strong team.'

'Yes.'

'But you're not happy.'

'Not unhappy. I'm OK, actually. OK for me.'

'But something.'

Penry stares at me again. He has one of the skull injury photos on his lap. Not one of the best ones, but still fairly explicit, fairly graphic. I have one of those moments where I'm hanging between two worlds. Can't quite tell whether I'm in the land of the living looking at pictures of the dead, or in the land of the dead wondering how it feels to be alive.

I don't know what I do or say, or if I do or say anything.

Then Penry says, 'So why does anyone return four hundred thousand pounds' worth of artwork?'

I say, 'Exactly. Who does that?'

Penry's thoughts change tack. He picks up one of the Plas Du pictures. Holds it up beside the Mofatt skull injury one.

'You're saying these are connected?'

'I can't be sure.'

'But . . .?'

'OK, let's assume for now that Moon *was* murdered. I know we're not a hundred per cent on that, but just assume it.'

'All right.'

'Our hypothesis is that someone met Moon on that path. Demanded something, threatened, had a fight – whatever. In any case, the attacker hits Moon with a crowbar, causing that skull injury. Moon is now either dead or badly disabled.'

'Right.'

'But it can't look like the guy's just been hit. It has to look accidental. For that to work, we need two things. Two things minimum. One, the path has to come close to the edge. Two, the cliff needs to be high enough and steep enough that everyone will just *assume* that the fall killed him. It's got to be the kind of fall that simply eliminates any questions.'

'Fair enough.'

'And most of the coast isn't like that. Yes, it's high, steep and rocky. But sometimes the path is just twenty or thirty feet above the waves. Other times, it's high enough, but the cliffs aren't properly steep. They're not sheer. You'd have to start questioning whether a fall would be enough to kill a healthy, well-put-together guy. And as soon as you raised those questions, you'd start to look at the skull injury in more detail, which would mean the entire plot could start to unravel.'

'Go on.'

'Look, I've walked that path. Jackson hasn't. Watkins hasn't. And you can see the land up to the edge. You can see the sea. You can't actually see the cliffs. Not when you're standing on top of them. No one can see the cliffs, so how do you know where Moon has to "fall"? There's only one type of person who has an easy answer to that.'

'A climber,' says Penry in a whisper. 'The sort of person who knew how to break in at Plas Du.'

'Correct. Those guys aren't just familiar with these cliffs. They go there for a good day out.'

I have my left hand on a photo of Moon. Right hand on the daffodil photo. My stockinged feet in the litter of all the other pictures on the floor.

And I feel OK. I think there aren't really two different worlds, that that whole idea is just a fraud perpetrated by the living. I think we have just one world, a continuum, one populated by living and dead alike. I'm most at ease when I feel no barrier between the two. An easy movement to and fro.

Penry says, 'And the one real solid lead we have is that your boy Evans bullshitted you when you went to see him.'

'Bullshitted to a detective inspector, on a live inquiry, in a signed statement. Yes. That's a lot of hiding.'

'Yes.'

'And his investment company seems to be named after a climb at the place where Moon fell and died. I mean, maybe a coincidence, yes, but a funny one, if so.'

'Yes.'

Penry was a good copper once. He can be an idiot, of

course. A posturing, macho idiot. But those things don't bother me much and, anyway, I think we're through most of that by now. In any case, I can tell Penry feels what I do. That there's a withholding here, a mystery to be pierced.

He finishes his beer. Brains. That's the brand. A brewery founded by Samuel Arthur Brain in 1882 and a gift to punning publicans ever since.

I say, 'There's more in the kitchen,' and Penry goes to get another bottle. When he comes back he stays standing, surveying me, my mess of photos.

He says, 'So . . .?'

I tell him about Francesca Ottilie Lockwood.

Ollie's brother, Marianna's daughter, Galton Evans's lost girl.

The girl who hasn't seen her father for years now. Who shed her father's name. Whose brother says of their father that 'he's OK, but he *is* a bit of a dick.'

Penry looks disconcerted. Says, 'What would you be hoping to find?'

'Anything. I don't know. Maybe nothing. I just know we ought to look.'

'When?'

'Saturday?' It's Thursday today.

He stays standing. Drinking beer. Staring down at me and my room. He says, 'I think you're a very bad person.'

A compliment.

He finds a bit of paper in his jeans back pocket, and tosses it at me. His scale of fees, I presume.

But I don't care about that now. Just go to a drawer. Get out my set of pick locks. Ask if he knows how to use them. He says no.

I give him the picks and a few locks that I keep loose, for my own practice. I show him what to do. He starts out useless, but soon begins to get the hang of it. We go to my own front door and pick that. Go to my back door and pick that too.

I put everything – the picks, the spare locks – in a plastic bag.

Then ask if he knows anything about computers.

# 13

We do it.

Go to London. Penry goes up to Seven Sisters, the not-particularly-nice part of London where Cesca Lockwood has her flat. I head for King's Cross. Central Saint Martins, where she studies.

It's the first Saturday in May. Lockwood's Facebook account has already pinned her to this place and this date. She doesn't normally work Saturdays, but the school is running a fashion weekend event and the place is heaving.

Lockwood has a class in the morning, followed by an afternoon of 'projects/workshopping', and not enough time between the two for her to go home.

I've dressed vaguely younger than I am. A bit studenty. Black jeans, striped top, one of my sister Kay's discarded jackets. Earrings.

But I don't care, or not really. I'm not undercover exactly, just don't want to attract attention.

I hang around in the café to start with, hoping to spot Francesca but no joy. Then drift along to the lecture theatre – Marek Adam, 'On Drawing' – and take a seat at the side. No one challenges me, or particularly looks at me. The tutor, with an accent that drifts between Paris and Central Europe, says, 'In the battle of style and realism, we always have to be on the side of style.' He pronounces 'style' *stil*, and 'realism' *réalisme*.

He shows us drawings of women with waists as thin as a bobbin of cotton, but with belts that are to die for.

Cesca comes in a minute or two late. Long, dark hair. Complicated silver jewellery and a black wrap top. She has a whiff of the dancer about her. Simultaneously gifted and vulnerable. Breakable.

She sits next to a girl who I had already provisionally identified as her flatmate – say what you like about Facebook, but we burglars love it. The two girls exchange a few words, then turn their full attention to the lecture. Take notes on tablets, faces slightly illuminated by their screens.

I text Penry: OK TO GO. I'LL LET YOU KNOW IF ANYTHING CHANGES. Three minutes later, get one back. I'M IN.

Then – nothing. We listen to Adam talking about *stil*. Pure imagination. How the true *stil* must move and change. How it is 'hard, hard' to find the true *stil*.

Pictures of women come and go.

The lecture breaks up.

I position behind myself behind Lockwood and her flatmate. They, and most others, drift down to the café I was in earlier.

I get a tray. A salad. A smoothie. Also some yogurt-granola thing, which tastes like upmarket gravel.

I eat until I don't want any more. Sit too close to Lockwood. Stare a bit too much.

There's a vibration there. The sort of vibration I normally get off dead people. Simultaneously peaceful, and alluring, and dark, and for ever. One of those things that I find hard to get out of my head once it's there.

I'm not doing this well. My old undercover trainers would rate my current observation tactics at about zero out of ten. Too close, too obvious, too prolonged. *Target will burn the surveillance.*

I think I'm burned.

It doesn't matter though. I'm just scraping out the last of

my finely gravelled yogurt, when I get a text from Penry. ALL DONE. SEE YOU SOON.

I clear my tray, walk away from Lockwood's following look, go to meet Penry at a coffee shop just round from where I've parked my car.

He arrives on a whoop of adrenalin.

'Getting in, easy as anything. No one saw me. No CCTV. Neighbouring flat either empty or very quiet.'

'Good.'

'OK. Now. *Interesting*. Look at this.'

We download his pictures to my laptop.

Bank statements.

Penry directs me to an image, and I zoom in enough that the text clarifies. On 5th April, Lockwood's account received a payment of £4,000 direct from her father. On 9th April, the same amount of money left her account, paid over to an outfit calling itself the London Women's Health Network.

'They help women with rape, domestic abuse, stuff like that,' Penry tells me. 'I didn't photograph everything, but the same money came in and went out every month.'

The bank statements don't portray a woman with a vast income. Certainly more than the average student – her mother owns millions of pounds' worth of artwork, after all – but she doesn't appear to be someone for whom £4,000 is immaterial.

'What's the flat like?'

'Cruddy. I mean, *I've* lived in worse places, but then I didn't have four grand coming into my account every few weeks.'

'Did you get into her computer?'

'Yes. Loaded up your stuff, no problem.'

My stuff: some Trojan horse software which allows me to operate a computer remotely. The software wouldn't evade an expert audit, but how many people get their computers manually checked for stuff like that? The software was a present to me from a reasonably classy criminal, so I know it's good.

'Anything else?'

'Not really. She was drying clothes on the radiator, which I don't think you're meant to do. Some dope in a desk drawer. Little hippy-dippy Indian box. The sort of box which says, "Hello, I'm where students keep their ganja." But not a lot of it. She's not dealing.'

Our gazes, both of them, go back to the screen. Four grand coming in and going out, every month.

'Blood money,' says Penry. 'Blood money that she won't accept.'

I nod.

That's what it looks like, all right.

But whose blood? And why the money?

Penry looks at me. I look at him. Big questions. No answers.

And the stink around Galton Evans has just got stronger.

# 14

North London and cluttered streets.

Railway bridges in dark Victorian brick. A canal, oily and secretive. Plane trees behind iron railings and buddleia growing where it shouldn't. It's May but still feels like March. Wet pavements and evening on the prowl long before the afternoon is done.

Penry has already gone home, his job complete. My day isn't yet finished, but I'm through with burglary. My contact, Eliot Whillans, stirs his coffee with a wooden stirrer. Blue and white striped shirt, grey tweed jacket, mid-forties. There's something sad in his expression, I think, but his eyes have an activity which I like.

'How much do you know?' he asks.

'Absolutely nothing. Nada, zip, zilch.'

He laughs. 'OK, from the start then. Submarine cables, all you need to know.'

He tells me that there's nothing new about laying cables beneath the sea. The first successful cable was laid in 1851. The world was already wired up by the outbreak of the First World War. Two things shook the industry up from the late-eighties onwards. First, the invention of fibre optic. Second, the internet.

'These days,' Whillans tells me, 'an ordinary cable can shift tens of terabits a second. Ten million million bits of data. People think that when they call the US, or order something from a US-based website, they're going via satellite. That's not right, or almost never. Ninety-nine point something per cent of all traffic goes undersea. It's faster and more reliable.'

'And those cables are owned by?'

'Well, in the old days, consortiums of different telecoms companies. Splitting the cost, sharing the traffic. These days, you get completely independent operators too. So you might get an indie operator laying a marine cable then selling capacity to anyone who wants superfast connectivity.'

'So it's a speed thing? That's important, is it?'

'Very.' Whillans – a lecturer in telecommunications technology at Middlesex University – looks at me to check I want the details. I do, but only because I'm not sure what matters here and what doesn't.

'OK, you're up against general relativity here. Signals can't move faster than the speed of light and the Earth is round. Assuming that you're not about to dig a tunnel from London to New York, that means you have to find the shortest undersea route, then shift the data as efficiently as possible. In the past, you'd have been happy with eighty or ninety milliseconds. These days, the best cables manage sixty-five millisecs, and there are new operators aiming to cut that to the high-fifties, or even mid-fifties. Even in theory, it's not possible to do it faster than about forty milliseconds, so we're getting ever closer to the limit.'

I make a face. At least, I assume I do, because Whillans responds to what I'm thinking.

'Who cares, right?'

'Yes. Who the hell cares?'

All inquiries have their moments like these. That sense that an important truth is here, lurking somewhere in this coffee-scented steam, this pinboard wall flapping with student posters. A truth that might just jump up and settle if only I knew what to ask – and how to recognise it when it arrived.

'The finance industry, basically. Let's say you're trading foreign exchange and the price in London moves, then there'll be some tiny difference between the London price and the New York price for the exact same thing. So if your London office can get information to your New York office quicker than the next guy, you can snatch an advantage. Buy or sell before the price in New York has reacted. It's not even humans doing this any more. We're way too slow. Obsolete technology. It's computer versus computer now.'

Whillans tells me that a one millisecond speed advantage is reckoned to be worth as much as a hundred million dollars a year to a good-sized hedge fund. He tells me that a human trader looking at a screen is like an astronomer looking at the light from a distant star. 'The data might as well be fifty thousand years old. You're doing archaeology, basically.'

He talks more. He's helpful, but I feel lost all the same. A stranger in my own world. A relic.

Impulsively, and contrary to procedure, I pull up some pictures on my laptop. Derek Moon, the dead security guard. I don't show my picture of his skull injury – my favourite – or any of the photos of him alive. Instead, I show the pictures taken when he was found. Before his body was moved.

A man with his skull split open. Brains leaking. The sky reflected in his open eyes and fish nibbling at his feet.

No fibre optics here. No hedge funds. Just the oldest story in the world.

Salt, rock and a dead man's eyes.

'Derek Moon,' I say. 'Somebody killed him. Smashed his skull in then pushed him off a cliff. He worked as a security guard. The landing station at Oxwich Bay.'

Whillans's eyes are with the man.

'Jesus,' he says. 'Jesus.'

His reaction confuses me for a moment. I think he's reacting to some clue that he can see but I can't. I lean forward eagerly, before realising that his comment is one of shock. That what I see as beautiful, he sees as something else.

I fold the laptop.

The table is dark wood. Its varnish treacled with the spillings of a million cups of coffee, a thousand crumbled muffins.

I say, 'It wasn't one of those ordinary murders. Money. Sex. Argument with an ex. Nothing like that.'

Whillans exhales. 'Oxwich Bay? That's an older site, mostly. A big Anglo-Irish cable. I think there was a plan to lay one of the new high-speed transatlantic cables from there, but they changed plans. It's coming in at Brean, Highbridge, somewhere like that. Somerset, anyway.'

'If you wanted to steal stuff? Presumably there's some fancy kit around.'

'Yes, but . . .'

He explains his 'but', and his 'but' is a hell of a lot bigger than his 'yes'.

The kit at Oxwich Bay is now at least ten years old, a century or so in telecoms terms.

The stuff may be expensive, but it's not off-the-shelf. The higher end bits of kit are built to order, designed for the specific purpose in hand. 'If you stole a switch from Oxwich Bay and tried to plug it in on a different site, a different network architecture, you'd have nothing at all. It wouldn't work.'

And then too, the only plausible buyers for any stolen bits of kit are the telecoms giants themselves. 'No one else has a use for these things. And, look, I'm hardly a fan of British Telecom, but even I don't think they're into bumping off security guards for a bit of junky old switching equipment . . .'

His eyes are kind. They say sorry. Sorry for trashing your dipshit theory. Sorry that you are a museum piece adrift in a world you no longer understand.

We do our goodbyes somehow. I'm not sure how. I'm

feeling spacey and uncertain. A group of students has entered behind us, and I feel myself getting tangled up in their presence, as though I could easily step out of my life and into theirs, all long hair, padded coats and muttered intimacies. One of the girls is wearing a purple jumper and because I own a jumper quite like it, I have this idea that she must be me, some simpler, easier version of me, and I quite like that thought, except that it leaves me – me, the unjumpered one – without anchorage. No port in the storm.

That night I take the train back to Cardiff. An obsolete technology transporting obsolete humans to an obsolete city in a country that isn't really a country at all.

But the train does have an internet connection. It's not secure and I shouldn't use it to access the Police National Database, but sod that. Live fast, die young. I connect anyway and spend some time investigating the records of the Avon and Somerset Constabulary.

Telecom related crime – nothing, or nothing of interest.

Crimes whose description contains the term 'telecom' or 'undersea' or 'cable'. Nothing.

Ditto, except that I search on descriptions of victims instead of the crime itself. Nothing.

Frustrating.

Frustrating, but not altogether surprising. Although I haven't, until now, focused on Avon and Somerset specifically, I have, over the past couple of weeks done similar national searches that have revealed nothing. I can't help feeling that the information I need is here, it's just that I'm not asking in the right way.

As I thump my keyboard softly for inspiration, an email tinkles in.

From Bronwen Woodward. Her home account, not her work one.

Her email lists all outgoing and incoming calls made or

received by Galton Evans at his office, from the day I took Lockwood into Cathays to two days after the visit from me and Watkins. Easy, as she told me it would be: she handled all his calls anyway. The call log on her phone gave her everything she needed.

Her list of numbers means nothing to me yet, but I'm good with lists. If Galton Evans knows more about that Plas Du theft than he's told us – and he does, I'm certain – he'll have got on the phone to someone to compare notes. The low-key nature of our inquiry will even have helped. Marianna Lockwood has already, in effect, been cleared. Even our visit to Evans had the air of a tidy-up meeting. No cautions handed out. A lowly DC left on her own to record the statement. If we'd come in more heavy-handed, Evans might have felt impelled to disguise his tracks. As it is, I'm hoping that he'll have proved over-confident. That his calls will betray him.

I think they will.

I'm tempted to start right away, but a train is not the best place for that kind of research.

I stare back at my screen.

What are you hiding, Avon and Somerset Constabulary database? I wish I knew.

And then, and only because I've a memory that Whillans once spoke about marine cables, instead of undersea cables, I search for crimes or victims with the word 'marine' in their description.

A lot more comes up on that search – unsurprisingly, because Avon and Somerset has a long stretch of shoreline, including the whole Port of Bristol – but in amongst the crap – the dockside thefts, the industrial accidents – there's a gem.

A man, Ian Livesey, found dead in a Bristol apartment block. Two months ago. Hanged. Swinging from an internal balcony on a length of bedsheet. Livesey was an American, only recently arrived in the UK. His occupation was reported as *consultant marine engineer.*

The facts don't look helpful. Hanging is a common enough method of suicide but it's almost unknown as a method of murder, at any rate in Britain where there's no history of lynching. And then too, nothing was missing from the apartment, the door was locked from the inside, and there was no evidence of forced entry.

And yet, and yet, two curious facts pokes out of the pile.

First, Carolyn Sharma, the dead man's fiancée, was apparently the last person to speak to him. They had a normal type of conversation but it was ended, she claimed, by him saying, 'Hey, babe, that's weird. I'm sure I locked the door.' A pause. Then, 'Call you back.'

He never did.

And then also this.

All suicides in England and Wales are examined post-mortem by a pathologist. That examination is normally conducted fast, so the family can arrange burial, but in this case the family chose to invoke their right for a re-examination of the corpse, stating their strongly held view that suicide, in Livesey's case, was inconceivable. From what I can see from the available records, the family is in the course of repatriating the corpse to the United States for re-examination by a pathologist there.

Now it's true that grieving families do strange things. Denial, anger, depression, acceptance.

But the oddness of the family's request – the insistence of their refusal to believe in Livesey's suicide – impels me to truffle further.

LinkedIn, Google, Facebook. Specialist marine journals.

Truffle further, strike gold.

Livesey was an engineer, who started his career in the US

Marine Corps, and who came to develop a speciality in subsea surveys. He worked for a big undersea firm for a while, then set up on his own. At the time of his death, he was retained by an independent cable company currently in the process of laying cable from Highbridge in Somerset to Long Island in New York. The very same cable that had been going to emerge from the waters of Oxwich Bay.

One cable, two deaths. And my dipshit theory is suddenly alive again.

Alive, strange and darker than ever.

The Avon and Somerset records contain contact information for the fiancée, Carolyn Sharma.

My fingers hesitate. The train is a lit tube passing dark embankments.

*No flying solo, Fiona.*

*Keep me in the loop, Fiona.*

Outside, the fields are still English, but the train will soon enter the Severn Tunnel. *Twnnel Hafren.* When they were building it, in the late 1870s, they hit an underground water source, the 'Great Spring', which caused the tunnel to flood. The work was all but complete by that point and the whole thing, all four miles of it, the longest undersea tunnel in the world, was underwater. Doomed, you would think, a failed project, except that a diver descended that flooded shaft, traversed more than three hundred yards, and closed off a watertight door that would enable pumping works to begin.

I always think of that when I'm beneath the estuary. Think of the diver, Alexander Lambert. Swimming down into that place of total darkness and total submersion. Wearing a newly invented form of breathing equipment, which might work or might not.

The loneliest place in the world.

As we enter the tunnel, I write an email to Sharma. Send it as soon as we recover signal. The email is brief, formal, professional, but it explains who I am and indicates an interest in talking to her.

The train is barely leaving Newport, before my phone rings. An international call.

Total darkness and total submersion.

# 15

Ten days later.

I'm in a car with Watkins. I've worked hard. Hard enough on Chicago. Logging data. Checking data. Ferrying exhibits. Sitting in meetings with Dunthinking's pinky beard and trying not to scream.

The inquiry has got nowhere with the tracking-vehicles-observed-in-both-locations strategy and is now focusing only on white, or whitish, vans that were spotted on Rover Way in Tremorfa at roughly the right time. Dunthinking's plan is simply to locate and investigate every such vehicle looking either for ones that have been suspiciously well cleaned or for ones still bearing poor Kirsty Emmett's DNA.

It's not a ridiculous strategy, but it is vastly time-consuming. Rover Way isn't the main route into town, but if Eastern Avenue and Newport Road are congested, plenty of traffic will simply sidle southwards in the effort to escape the crush. We have, at present, 122 vehicles to check, and that's excluding over a dozen emergency services vehicles which theoretically fit the description. Now, combing through 122 vehicles to find a dangerous and violent rapist seems like a good investment of time and money, but each one of those vehicles will yield a whole heap more samples for me to file and deal with. We'll likely still be dealing with the deluge a full year away. A thought I find terrifying. A thought I almost literally cannot endure.

At one point, during one of Dunthinking's eternal briefing sessions, I said, 'Or, you know what, we could think about the other end. Gabalfa. We could actually look at vans local to *that* area.'

In public, Dunthinking said something terse and negative, cutting me off. In private, thereafter, he said, 'You will do *as* I ask, *when* I ask, and *how* I ask. You will *not* tell me how to run my inquiry. And you will also remember that I will be reporting, in writing, to DCI Jackson my impressions of your overall performance here. Do you understand, Constable?'

I did my humble-acquiescent stuff. Chockfull of yes-sirs, no-sirs and penitent gazes at the floor. But he wasn't fooled and stared after me with hatred even as I gathered my things to go back downstairs.

Go back downstairs and – me being me – redouble the work I'm doing elsewhere.

I make use of any crevice of time I can find. I've made a couple of field trips. Once by myself, a second time with Mike Haston. But not mostly that. Mostly, I've pulled data from the PND. Spoken to Carolyn Sharma by phone. Found out more about the undersea cable which yanked one man to his death on a Gower sea shore, hanged another by his neck in a Bristol apartment.

I've gone slower than I like, but I know that I'll have to be rigorous if I'm to persuade my bosses that there's anything here to investigate. And since this damn investigation is the only air-tube connecting me to the world beyond Chicago's gloomy depths, I can't afford to have it snipped.

I sleep in the office most nights. Work till my eyes are green and sore.

I think: *This investigation can get me out of here. A couple of honest-to-God murder victims will spring me from this jail.*

No one has yet said anything to suggest that, but my extra-curricular work has produced enough of substance that

Watkins, sceptical as she is, has agreed to accompany me down to Bristol to inspect the scene of the hanging, to talk again to the officers who investigated at the time.

On her lap, she has two files. The original inquiry data. My own additional researches. She's on the first of those now.

'Nothing missing. Nothing stolen,' she says.

'We don't know that.'

Watkins doesn't answer directly. Just holds up a letter from Customs & Excise. She doesn't hold it so that I can read it, but she knows that I'll know what it refers to. Because it so happens that the dead man, Livesey, had been pulled aside for a random luggage check when he entered the UK. Those things are always recorded so that any subsequent allegation of theft or malpractice can be settled by video evidence. Investigators at the time of the suicide checked the videotape of the luggage search against the items found in the apartment. There was nothing missing. The apartment itself was a corporate rental, and its fixtures and fittings tallied precisely with the contents. The letter from Customs and Excise is just some boring blah about how to access the video.

Watkins doesn't pursue the argument, just says, 'Access. The apartment was on the eighth floor. Locked from the inside. No sign of forced entry.'

I say, 'How hard do you think Avon and Somerset would have investigated? How hard would we have done? Or *you* even? Hanged man. Locked door. Nothing missing. That's a suicide. You throw a couple of DCs at it, get a report written up for the coroner. Move on.

'But then you find out that the guy's fiancée and his entire family says they've never seen the guy so positive about life. That she, the fiancée, spoke to him for half an hour the evening of his putative suicide. She said he grumbled about his flight over. Was trying to figure out his apartment's wi-fi connection. How are those the concerns of a man about to take his own life? And then, too, that weird ending. Like the guy's become aware of an intruder where no intruder could possibly be.

'Now you're going to say – and I agree – that fiancées can get this kind of thing wrong. They get it wrong because they have to. Emotionally, they can't accept the facts. Only, then you find out that the dead man was working on some engineering project where a second man has also died under strange circumstances.

'Two deaths. Both strange. Neither properly investigated. Same project.'

Truth is, we're rehashing old ground. If Watkins didn't accept the need for a second look at this, we wouldn't even now be heading for the Severn Bridge, heading for England.

The car thrums.

Uniformed driver.

The spires of the bridge rising as we approach.

Watkins makes a noise in her throat and says, 'Are you around a week on Sunday? Cal and I are having some friends over in the afternoon. If you . . . if you wanted to . . .'

She doesn't know what to do with her facial muscles at this point, tries a smile, feels uncomfortable and glowers fiercely instead.

One of the reasons I like Watkins: her social skills are even worse than mine, so I feel agile and accomplished in her company.

'That would be lovely, Rhiannon. I'd love that.'

I pluck a smile from my rose-garden of happiness and pass it over.

Watkins smiles – glares – shifts position. Gives me, rather abruptly, data on time and place, as if she were arranging a dawn raid on a property where armed resistance was to be expected.

Down at seat level, where the driver can't see, I squeeze her wrist till I feel her relax. I say, 'Plas Du. Peter Pan. I've made some progress there too. Do you want to look?'

I have a pile of paperwork with me. Three files and a four-page summary document. I typed up the summary last night and my eyes are still stinging with sleeplessness.

The first file is the investigation into Plas Du. The other two files are ones copied from other police force records, one from the Metropolitan Police, one from the Sussex Police.

Watkins takes the pile with curiosity, reads my summary with increasing interest, stares at me without saying anything, then turns to the files.

The car is silent. We enter England.

And my attention drifts from Plas Du and from dead engineers. It drifts to the place where it most truly belongs: to myself, my embattled head, my mysterious past.

When I was a teenage nutcase, not actually sure if I was alive or dead, one of the things that baffled me was the strangeness of my affliction. Cotard's Syndrome is almost always associated with early childhood trauma, but I had, I was certain, enjoyed the safest of all childhoods. Happy, safe, settled, secure.

And so I did, from the age of two or two and a half. But it turns out that my life before that point is a mystery. Not only to me, but to my mother and father, the parents who adopted me one sunny Sunday, when they came out of chapel to find me, little me, alone in their Jag, a camera round my neck and no earthly explanation as to who might have put me there. Who, and why. I know nothing about where I was in the first two years of my life, or who I was with, or what happened to me. I am, however, certain that those two years hold the clue to the whole, precarious mystery of my head.

I've sought to investigate that mystery, but with scant

reward. Yet I do have a clue. A hopeless one, perhaps, but it's what I've got.

Back in the mid-1980s, a man called Gareth Glyn, a town planner type, made some allegations about corruption in the city planning process. Those allegations were investigated without result. He lost his job – one of those quit-before-you're-fired things – and continued to work as a freelance planning consultant thereafter. In 2002, Glyn simply vanished from view. Walked out on his wife. No warning, no preamble, just here one day and gone the next.

So far, so blah. But, point one, a thoughtful ex-detective who worked in the Cardiff CID of the right era says that Glyn's claims probably had merit. That there probably was corruption and, if there was, then my father almost certainly had a hand in it.

Point two, the whole period in question – Glyn's allegations, the investigations, his departure – coincided almost precisely with my own strange arrival into the world. Six months after he left the council, I arrived, a little girl dropped from heaven, in the back of my father's Jag.

Point three, a few months before Glyn's disappearance, one of the national intelligence services – presumably MI5 – searched police sources for any data they had on Glyn. Those sources had nothing much, but the request itself was significant. Why the hell were they interested? And why so many years later?

And finally, point four, towards the end of last year, I placed some dodgy software on a superintendent's computer. Software that allowed me to inspect his data. To use his computer as though it were mine. Now, I know – naughty me, bad girl, mustn't go sabotaging the computers of senior officers – but I did use my access to see if Glyn was in witness protection.

Checked, and discovered this:

**Witness name (original):** Glyn, Gareth Huw
**Codename:** Eilmer
**Status:** Witness protection
**Date from:** 9 May, 2002
**Date ending:** Indefinite
**Security status:** No alerts
**Current location:** Not available (security clearance not sufficient)
**Current identity:** Not available (security clearance not sufficient)
**Supervising force:** Not available (security clearance not sufficient)
**Supervising officer:** Not available (security clearance not sufficient)

Like so much in this little investigation of mine, the answer was frustratingly elusive.

Elusive, but not barren. Because perhaps I've been told what I need to know. Perhaps those dead ends contain an opening wide enough for me to wriggle through.

But not now, not yet. Those things lie in my future. Bristol lies in my present.

One man hanged, another man fallen, and an undersea cable that leaves corpses wherever it touches shore.

# 16

The apartment looks just like the photos. They don't always, but this one does.

Bland. Hotelly. Tasteful in a beige sofa and chrome lamp sort of way.

Also empty. The corporate rental began the day of Livesey's arrival and had been due to run two months. Given that the coroner has yet to report and that police interest in the property only recently ended, no new tenant has yet moved in.

A straw-haired DC, about my age, is waiting for us outside.

'Luke Creamer,' he says, shaking hands with an enthusiasm that indicates he knows nothing of Watkins's reputation. He was one of the original investigators and nothing in his manner suggests that he's at all doubtful about the verdict he came to back in February.

We go up in a lift. Creamer ushers us along a corridor to a door. A modern composite thing. Cream painted. Solid lock. Solid door frame.

Watkins: 'The frame hasn't been touched?'

'No.'

'Not replaced, repainted?'

'No, only the lock.'

'The lock is new?'

'Yes. When we were called, the lock was locked from the inside. We had to drill it out – destroy it, basically. Then, I don't know, I guess the lettings agent got the thing replaced.'

'OK.'

Watkins inspects briefly then makes a gesture of angry impatience. Her way of saying, 'I say, Constable, would you be so good as to let us in?'

He does so.

Watkins glares at me. Says to Creamer, 'Other routes in?'

'None.'

'Fire exits?'

'This door, then emergency stairs.'

'Access from the roof?'

'Nothing. Not without cutting a hole.'

Watkins starts stomping round, checking the facts.

I make a call. The person I want was due here already, but he's been a bit held up. He'll be here in a couple of minutes.

The apartment is top floor, arranged over two levels. The living room is double height, with a gallery leading to the two bedrooms and bathrooms. Livesey was found hanged from the gallery, his feet only a foot or so from the floor. A side table kicked away – or pulled away – a couple of feet distant. A pair of large French doors open onto a balcony with a view over the city and the brown ocean beyond.

I ask, 'Has the apartment been cleaned?'

Creamer says, 'I don't think so. Do you want me to find out?'

I don't answer. I'm on my hands and knees on the floor beneath the gallery. Beneath the swing of the corpse.

Inspecting the carpet for stains. Find nothing much. A little bleaching where Livesey urinated, post-mortem. But I moisten my finger, touch the carpet around the crucial area, though avoiding the bleaching. Taste my finger. Nothing. Repeat the process a few times. Still nothing.

Then spot a blond wood and metal chair that's been shifted slightly from the kitchen area.

'That chair,' I ask. 'Has it been moved?'

Creamer is being called over to the balcony by Watkins and doesn't answer, but I don't care.

Go over to the chair. Feel around with my wet finger on the carpet. Find something crystalline. Taste it.

It's salt.

'Salt,' I say. 'I've got salt on the carpet.'

Watkins comes in from outside. She's saying something about access. I don't know what, because I'm not listening, but in any case I already know what she's going to tell me. The apartment sits over the top two floors of the block, and its balcony juts like a smoothly curving prow over everything below. There are no balconies to either side, nor any balcony directly below.

I'm examining the chair now. The metal arms. I ask, 'This chair? Did anyone check it over?'

Watkins is saying something else now. My attention isn't with her, but there's a ferocity in her look which is eloquent enough. She's pissed off, I think, because she's concluded, wrongly, that this is an obvious suicide and is angry with me at bringing her here. Doubly angry perhaps that a junior member of a neighbouring force should have to witness us blundering through the obvious.

A knock at the apartment door relieves me of the need to answer Watkins.

Creamer opens the door.

Mike is there. Loose brown shorts. Tatty shoes. T-shirt and fleece. Hair tied back with a not-very-clean green hair tie. A backpack worn on one shoulder only.

He says, 'Hi.'

I say, 'Ma'am, this is Mike Haston. An access consultant.'

Watkins's face flickers through various different shades of glower, trying to find the right one for the situation. 'You've retained a consultant?' is what she says.

'Working gratis,' I say brightly. 'A citizen volunteer.'

I give Mike my happy face to make up for the thunderbolts he's getting from Watkins.

He doesn't care much either way. Just unslings his backpack. Pulls out a couple of ropes.

The gallery is supported at its centre point by a steel pillar. Mike tests it briefly, then loops a rope round the pillar. Pulls the ends out to the balcony.

Watkins snaps, 'This is a crime scene.'

Meaning: ask permission before touching anything.

But also, I note, acknowledging that we need to treat the apartment as a place of possible murder, not just one of unfortunate suicide.

Mike stops doing what he's doing. Waiting for someone to explain to him exactly what he should be doing.

I say, 'Mike, it's fine. Just don't touch anything too much without checking first.'

To Watkins, I say, 'Ma'am, I've been out here with Mike already. To the foot of the building, not up here. And according to Mike, any competent climber could make the ascent. We're not sure about the balcony, because we've not had a chance to inspect it. But the first seven storeys of this building aren't impregnable. They're a walk in the park.'

Mike digs around in his pack. Gets out a small, flexible wire with a couple of spring-loaded cams on the end, and a simple release mechanism. I'd never seen one before Mike showed me. Watkins is equally baffled.

Mike tosses the device from hand to hand. Says, 'OK, this building is clad in preformed concrete panels. Those things are made in a factory somewhere, then just clipped into place. On this particular building, there's a gap about so big between the panels.' He holds his finger and thumb about a quarter of an inch apart. 'That's not enough to get a real grip, but plenty to get one of these boys inside. You slide it in like this.' He pulls the release mechanism and the cams fold up. 'Then pop it in and let go.' He lets go and the cams snap back. 'Any half-decent climber could go all the way using a couple of these.'

Watkins: 'These gadgets. They're legal?'

Mike: 'Every climbing shop in the country. They're for climbing, not burglary.'

Watkins: 'Even so. No. The time it would take to do all that. You'd be seen from below.'

Mike: 'It's after dark. You wait for an empty street. Allow maybe twenty seconds to get above the level of the streetlamps. Easy.'

And, though Mike doesn't say it, no one looks up. Why would they?

Watkins goes through the same calculation. Tries to find a face to accommodate the situation. She has difficulty settling on one, but the mood has shifted. We all watch in near silence as Mike sets up his ropes.

He ties off the one looped round the pillar. Snaps a karabiner onto the loop. The karabiner is level with the very lip of the balcony. Wind and traffic noise. The blue light of high places.

Mike starts to put on harness, chalk bag, rock boots. Says to Creamer, 'You might want to check the flat below. They might get a surprise otherwise.'

Creamer does a short double-take, then nods. Disappears.

Mike takes his other rope, clips it into the karabiner, and throws both ends over the balcony, where they vanish into space. He makes some adjustments till he's happy with his set-up. Creamer re-emerges. Tells us there's no one below us. That he's left a Police Action notice on their door, just in case.

The balcony floor is weathered timber. The balcony edge is glass and brushed steel. The air around us is sea air. Air from the Bristol Channel, the Irish Sea, the dark Atlantic. Up here, solid ground seems no more than a memory.

Mike looks at me.

I look at Watkins.

We're all as though hypnotised by the light, the situation. All of us, except Mike, for whom these things are ordinary.

Watkins nods. 'OK.' Adds, 'Thank you.' A Watkinsian first, I do believe.

Mike clips into his descent rope. Swings matter-of-factly over the balcony. Winks. And vanishes.

There's a moment where nothing at all happens. Time, freed by the wind and the height, does what it likes. Stretches out, curls up, takes new shapes, new dimensions. The three of us left on the balcony stand back from the edge, stare at the karabiner, the tensely swinging rope.

Watkins is the first to find her voice.

She says, 'Salt?'

I explain what I'm thinking. I conclude, 'You said in the car that nothing was missing, but we don't know that. We only know that nothing *physical* was taken. But Livesey was an engineer. Seabed surveys, that was his thing. If this was a murder and if it was motivated by theft, he only had one thing worth murdering for. And that was his data. His passwords. His access.'

Watkins takes this in. The karabiner on the balcony wall creaks against steel. There are sounds below us, but they filter only dimly upwards. Mike, a few feet away, is already in another world.

Watkins says to Creamer, 'That chair. Has it been forensicated?'

Creamer says, 'I'm not sure,' then changes tack and adds, 'But I don't think so. We wouldn't have . . .'

'Get onto it now.' To me: 'This second post-mortem. Where does that stand?'

'It's due to take place imminently. I asked Sharma, the fiancée, to hold off while we took a look back here. So we can instruct the pathologist, if need be. I don't know if they'll be able to find anything, but we can at least tell him what he needs to look for.'

Watkins nods.

The karabiner creaks.

Creamer is making a call from inside. Watkins and I are left in this blue silence. Listening to the karabiner, watching the ever-shifting rope.

Creamer rejoins us. 'SOCO on the way.' He pauses, then adds, 'Should I get a DI over?'

Watkins *is* a detective inspector, of course, but not from the local force. And if this is a crime scene, it's theirs, not ours.

Watkins says, 'Let's wait for . . .' She doesn't complete her sentence, but doesn't have to.

The karabiner, the rope, the light.

More time passes, perhaps only moments.

Then a hand, Mike's hand. A lunge upwards from below. Seeking the lip of the balcony, the little gap between the timber floor, the glass retaining wall.

The lunge misses. A pause. A second lunge, closer this time. Then a third. This time, Mike gets the grip he wants. He gets two hands on the lip, swings a toe up to the platform, levering it between wood and glass. Then his grinning face. Then he pulls himself in one fluid movement to the barrier itself. Steps over it, smiling, shaking the acid out of his arms, wiping chalk off on his shorts.

He's breathing hard, but happy.

Pulls his rock boots off. Bare feet. Sweatmarks on the wood.

Watkins stares. Creamer too. I probably do the same.

He laughs at us.

'OK. It's interesting. Really interesting.'

He explains. The balcony is supported by steel girders sticking straight out of the main frame of the building. In construction terms, there's no great weight in the balcony, so the girders are quite slim. 'Standard I-frame cross-section,' says Mike, 'so quite easy. Nice juggy handholds, and enough room to get a heel hook as well.'

A heel hook: a type of foothold.

Watkins: 'So it's possible to climb out on them?'

'I *did* climb out on them. I mean, yes, it's exposed. I'm roped up and a fall wasn't going to be a big deal. Doing it without ropes, though, that would be pretty bold.'

But if you're here to murder someone, then a certain recklessness is already baked in, I reckon. Say something to that effect.

'Yes, but hear me out. Someone *has* been out along there. There are five girders beneath the balcony. I checked them all. Four of them were untouched. The third one, the middle one, that has fingermarks all the way along it. I climbed the next one along, this one,' he says, tapping on the floor with his bare foot. Then, moving along the balcony to the centre and tapping again, 'This one here, that's the one your fingerprint guys will want to look at. That's your intruder right there.'

His words break some sort of tension. Creamer looks at Watkins, who nods.

Creamer goes into the apartment. Makes a call. He'll be alerting a duty officer. A suicide is being upgraded to murder. Their Major Crimes team will need to get working on this, just two months too late.

To Watkins and me, Mike says, 'But there's something else. Something troubling. Yes, the route up to the balcony is OK. Yes, the route out on the girders is OK. Not trivial, it's not something I'd personally want to attempt without protection, but there are plenty of climbers who solo that kind of thing for fun.'

The wind blows. The ropes still tap restlessly against the balcony.

I say, 'But . . .?'

'But then you've got that final move. From the girder up

and out to the lip of the balcony itself. It's insane. Like this wild, off-balance slap for a hold you can't see.'

Watkins: 'But you did it. We just saw you.'

'Yes. On my fifth attempt. The first two times, I was a mile away. Then I took a long rest on the rope, I sorted out my start position and tried again. Missed twice, then got it. But doing that move? Unroped and at night? You just watched me die four times over.'

Watkins and I exchange glances. It's a strange experience this. Tiptoeing round the body of someone else's expertise. Not knowing what to ask. Where the right questions lie.

I make an attempt. 'Mike, in layman's terms, how good are you? How good would a climber have to be?'

Mike pulls the elastic out of his hair. Lets it blow free. He tries to explain. As I understand his explanation, Mike himself is pretty good, a talented and committed hobbyist, but he's not remotely an elite-level climber. I ask about Rhod, say, 'Would he have made that move? Assume that he's got some strong motivation to do so.'

Mike says, 'In terms of grade, I'd place the move at about a bouldering V6 or V7. Don't even ask what that means, it's just a way of gauging the difficulty of a climb. I climb that kind of thing at the wall in Cardiff. Fall a few times, then figure it out, climb it clean. Rhod's better than me. His best bouldering grade is V9, maybe even V10. If he's on form, I guess he'd climb V6 on-sight ninety-something per cent of the time. Climb it clean, without a fall, that is. V7, I don't know, but it's well within his ability. And, of course, you can train for things. If you know you're going to be making a particular type of move, you can practise it. Train specifically for it. But still. Fuck.'

He laughs. Not a happy laugh. A release of tension one.

Watkins and I still have the tension, not the release.

Mike looks at us and says, 'If you've got someone who's

capable of camming his way up to the eighth floor, then climbing out along those girders, then who still has the fitness and confidence to make a Do-Not-Fall type of V7 move at the end of it, then that's one hell of a dangerous man.'

He points in at the apartment.

A penthouse flat. A hundred feet up. The front door locked from the inside. No skylight. No other means of entry. Impenetrable.

'If that place wasn't safe, then nowhere is. Nowhere.'

Weathered timber, glass and brushed steel.

A wind blowing straight from the Bristol Channel, the Irish Sea, the black Atlantic.

And a climber who can enter any building, anywhere. A climber who kills and an undersea cable whose touch is murder.

# 17

We do what we have to do.

The very next day, I fly out to Virginia. Long haul to Washington, then a rinky-dink regional jet to Norfolk, so small and cute I feel like I could gobble it up. The flight has just one stewardess, who has a huge American smile and calls me ma'am. When I struggle to get my bag in the overhead locker, she thrusts it up there for me with a competence that suggests she could probably bundle me up there as well if she had to.

I meet Carolyn Sharma, Livesey's fiancée. We meet in the lobby of my hotel, drink coffee – decaf, in my case. The hotel is nice. Cheap, of course – police budgets aren't designed to support long-haul travel – but nice. The lobby is black and white and a soft coffee-tinted cream. Fake colonial mouldings and potted palms. Sharma wears khaki shorts, boat shoes, and a blue linen shirt, the colour of the sky.

She says, 'Officer Griffiths, I want to say thanks so much for coming out here. We all appreciate it.'

I stare. Her face offers one thing, her words something different.

She wasn't like this on the phone, but then maybe no one ever has the same phone-self and real-self.

I say, 'Fiona. Or Fi.'

'Oh, OK, sure. Fiona. That's a lovely name.'

I think I'm a disappointment to Sharma. I think she wanted

someone older, or more senior, or at least more capable of growing a moustache and twirling a nightstick.

'I think you're right. I don't believe that Mr Livesey – that Ian – took his own life.'

'Oh, honey. Oh, hon.'

This time her words and face find synchrony. She's not young. Livesey wasn't. He was fifty-two, she's late-forties, and this was to have been a second marriage for them both.

But love lives in older faces too. Love and grief.

I address those things the only way I know how.

'Carolyn, I'm not able to speak for my police service. As a body, we haven't drawn any firm conclusions and won't do so until our investigation is complete. But if you want to know where I personally stand, I do not believe that Ian committed suicide. I believe he was murdered. And although it won't really lessen your hurt, it's my intention to find the person who killed him. Find him, arrest him, prosecute him, jail him. I have a good record. And I will make it happen.'

Sharma wants to produce another 'hon', or something, but her face, her brave face, has dissolved completely now. She's crying, silently but with tears that fall ceaselessly, abundantly, like grain at harvest, like mackerel in swarm.

Her hand keeps groping for her bag, but she's too much of a mess to find the catch. I take her bag from her, open it, find the tissues I imagine she's seeking, and pass them over.

She wipes at her face, catching the tears as they fall, but she might as well try to catch a river. A waiter comes over to see if he can help but, unless he has the power of resurrection, there's no job for him here. I put my hand on Sharma's bare knee and she covers my hand with hers, and we sit together that way, the still centre of a noisy world.

After a bit, her tears turn to juddering sobs broken only by a handful of *oh, hon*s, which rise like boulders above the swirling current.

When she gets her voice back, or something like it, she says words to the effect that Livesey was a lovely man, that he had only friends, no enemies, that no one could possibly have had a reason to kill him. I think she thinks that he was killed in one of those random ways. A failed burglary, someone looking to score enough cash to buy the next hit of drugs, that sort of thing. I tell her gently that that's not our thinking.

I get out the statement that she made for the Avon and Somerset Police, a statement which dwells only on the matter of Livesey's mental state. I don't tell her this, but it reads like any number of similar statements we take at the time of a loved one's suicide. The general gist: Yes, So-and-so has his/her issues, we all do, but I can't believe he/she would do something like this, it's just not possible. The evidential value of those statements is close to zero, but if the bereaved need us to take them, we do.

I ask her if she's OK to do this next bit, and she says yes. In a funny way, I think the process of an official interrogation and statement-taking is helpful to her. Like the way you sit up straighter in tailored clothes.

'Carolyn, are you happy for me to call you by your first name? I can call you Ms Sharma or ma'am, if you prefer.'

'Oh no, gosh, Carolyn's fine.'

'Carolyn, I'd like to record our interview, if I have your permission to do so.'

'Sure. Of course.'

I do the preliminaries. Confirm her identity, her relationship with the deceased, have her confirm that her previous statement is full and accurate.

She gives me what I need, at first leaning forward to talk, rather formally, into the recorder, then adjusting position and speaking more naturally, more fluently.

I ask about Livesey's work. If she was aware of the detail.

'No. It was complicated stuff. I knew he was doing this big

project but, you know, as for the details . . .' She tails off into a shrug.

'You were not aware of the detailed progress of his work?'

'No.'

'The results of his work were stored electronically. On his laptop and on a data server. Did you have access to those things? Did you share passwords, for example?'

'Gosh, hon, I never thought . . . No.'

I probe away. Had Livesey ever been threatened? Suffered from identity theft, or a phishing attack, lost a laptop, anything like that?

No, no and no.

Had any of his colleagues or collaborators been threatened or suffered thefts, especially of electronics?

Longer, more complex, answers, but still, in essence, no.

Had Livesey ever referred to the possibility of violence in relation to his work?

'No. No, never.'

Sharma's face looks anxious, as though she thinks there are answers that I want, that she ought to be able to give, that she can't supply. She looks upset, as if she's failing.

I say, 'Carolyn, you're doing fine. These answers are helpful, actually. Sometimes a "no" is more useful than a "yes".'

Because the voice recorder can't see it, I rub her knee again, then her arm. She cries again, briefly, then wipes her eyes. We've pretty much run through her tissues and the non-resurrecting waiter brings a wodge of paper towels with a hushed 'You're welcome.'

I round out the interview. Compile it into a statement. Get her to sign it. It's a big fat negative on all fronts, but what I said is true: sometimes negatives are helpful. Truth is, if the lethal actors in this investigation are based in America, our chances of catching them are slim to zero. The more negatives Sharma can give me, the better I like it.

The next day – a smiling blue morning, their May like the best of our July – we meet at the morgue. The pathologist, Vincent DiGiulian, works for the US Navy mostly, hardly a surprise in this town which is half sea and all port, home to the US Navy's Atlantic fleet and one of NATO's two strategic commands. But DiGiulian also runs a small private practice and he welcomes us to his facility, the Bellavista, which, though much smaller than those I've been used to, is well-equipped and immaculately kept.

He produces coffee for Sharma, water for me, and we sit at his office window, watching traffic move sedately on a six-lane boulevard. The tarmac is already warm and big trees shadow the central reservation, the broad verges on either side of the road.

I feel a long way from Cardiff.

DiGiulian tries to dissuade Sharma from being present at what follows, but she's paid for all this – the corpse repatriation, the re-examination – and she insists on seeing it through. A rite of passage. And perhaps the grimness is what she needs. A walk through the valley of the shadow of death. A last farewell.

She sips the last of her coffee, looks as pale as her well-tanned skin can manage, and says, 'I want to do this. Sorry, but I do.'

We change into scrubs, masks, boots. DiGiulian, already dressed, takes us through to the examination room itself. Livesey is there, covered with a pale cloth, almost phosphorescent under the lamps.

DiGiulian says, 'OK, I'm going to do this like it was the first time. No preconceptions about cause, or anything like that. I deliberately haven't read your report' – he nods at me, referring to the report put together by the Avon and Somerset pathologist – 'because I don't want to fill my head with anyone else's dumb ideas. I want to get dumb ideas all of my own, right?'

He goes on to explain that it can't truly be like the first time. Avon and Somerset were reasonably careful with their crime scene procedures – careful, that is, considering that suicide was the presumption right from the start. But they did, for example, take residue and fingernail samples from Livesey's hands. The data from those samples proved negative for anything interesting, but the very process of analysis means that Livesey's hands can no longer be regarded as forensically intact.

His hands, or indeed anything else.

Livesey was a strong, fit man in his youth and was still clearly so in middle age. But he'd be less strong and fit now, with a Y-shaped incision running from both shoulders to his sternum, then down to his crotch. A second vivid tear running ear-to-ear across the forehead. The English pathologist removed organs, including the brain, for weighing, tissue analysis and all the rest of it, then returned the organs to the corpse after he was done, sewing up his original incision.

But these things are done to mortuary standards, not surgical ones. A surgeon's tiny, careful stitches, the sort designed to minimise scarring, have no place here. Livesey is sewn up with coarse thread and big stitches. Half man, half crafting project.

Before opening the corpse, DiGiulian runs through the standard surface examination. Checking skin for hair samples, gunshot residues, any foreign objects. He finds little enough.

I say, 'Traces of salt found at the scene on the floor. Also, on his trouser leg. Right leg, upper thigh.'

Traces which weren't found until we re-examined the clothing. Avon and Somerset hadn't been sloppy exactly. Just that a full no-holds-barred examination is expensive. It's not done for every violent or unexpected death. It wasn't done here.

DiGiulian stares at me. He has big, sad, clever eyes. He says nothing. Just turns to the right thigh. Checks the skin under a variety of UV lights. Checks it under close magnification. Swabs the right thigh and puts the swab in a sterile beaker.

Because the whole exam is being recorded, he says out loud, to the recorder, 'White crystals found on upper right thigh, inside the leg, five, six inches below the genitals. Crystals appear consistent with ordinary household salt. Swab removed for further examination.'

None of us say anything.

Sharma is very still, her face almost frozen. To start with, DiGiulian was making great efforts to keep Livesey covered in every area bar the one he was working in, but the effort meant a constant twitching and tweaking of the sheet. As he gets ready to start on the internal exam, Sharma says – the first time she's spoken – 'Just remove the damned sheet.' DiGiulian shoots her a glance, but does as she asks.

Livesey's naked body with its vivid Y-shaped laceration suddenly seems like the biggest thing in the world. The biggest and the quietest.

DiGiulian slides a scalpel down the stitches so softly it seems like he's miming the action, not performing it for real, but the body falls open at his touch. Falls open more abruptly, more completely, than seems quite plausible. Partly because of a body brick placed under the corpse's chest. Mostly, though, because this is a dead body, where cut surfaces don't heal, where the insides are just a jumble of discarded organs.

Ian Livesey, the man who was to have been Carolyn Sharma's husband, is now a thing of grey-yellow flaps of skin. His fat and muscle is exposed like a side of meat in a pork butchery, half a bucketful of brown-purple slops held within.

I've seen this before and I love it every time. My version of a winter sunset, a bowl of flowers.

Sharma hasn't and presumably doesn't. She swallows, her breathing accelerates. Her hands wander through space, looking for anchor. I catch one of them and settle it on my knee. She resists at first, then relaxes.

The internal exam is long and without adventure. I'm not expecting anything much from it and all the work has already been done. But it's part of the rite, and DiGiulian does it all, speaking to his recorder as he goes. Sharma doesn't get comfortable with it all exactly, but the tedium itself has a kind of anaesthetising quality and after a while she squeezes my hand, and pulls away.

Even when DiGiulian peels Livesey's face down – literally rolling it down from the forehead, in order to get better access to the skull and the brain inside – Sharma is OK. I hear her gasp a little, but she remains upright, keeps her hands to herself.

To have your face rolled down over your eyes and not even to notice your blindness. That's dead, I think, as dead as it's possible to be.

Livesey's skull isn't empty. His brain was removed for weighing by the Avon pathologist, but was returned afterwards. DiGiulian repeats the extraction, weighing, and observation process now. Takes a little sample for laboratory analysis.

To have your brain removed not once but twice. And to move no muscle, to experience no flicker of thought or feeling as it happens. That's dead, that's very, very dead.

Three hours in and the exam draws to a close.

DiGiulian looks at me. I know what he's asking.

I say to Sharma, 'Carolyn, Dr DiGiulian and I want to examine that inner thigh area. The examination might be upsetting for you.'

I suggest she might want to leave it there. Reassure her she'll get all the information we uncover. I use my most professional police constable manner. Like I'm interviewing for a role in Family Liaison. But Sharma shakes her head with conviction. 'No. No. I want to see the whole thing.'

She's right. It's what she's here for. To discover the horror she will have to live with.

DiGiulian washes his hands again and, with fingertips still slightly damp, draws his index finger over the site on the inner thigh. Once, twice, three times.

Grimaces.

To me, he says, 'My skin's kinda hard, I don't know if . . .'

'Sure.'

I wash my hands. My skin is quite soft anyway, but the washing helps exfoliate a bit. Increases sensitivity. I stroke Livesey's thigh. The first time I think I have it. The second time I'm sure. 'Here,' I say. 'Entrance burn. Leathery texture. And is it maybe . . .?'

DiGiulian angles the light so it shines across the spot I'd marked with my finger.

To the recorder he says, 'Area noted as somewhat leathery to the touch is mildly depressed.'

His eyes and mine shift to a slight reddening of the skin about an inch from the depressed area. He readjusts the lamp, says, 'One inch from possible entrance marks, we note mildly elevated area, some reddening visible.'

He and I both look at the dead man's genitals, but if there are marks there, we won't find them without tissue removal and microscope analysis. The skin is just too uneven, the colouration too variable.

DiGiulian goes through the same thought process as I do, turns back to the thigh.

He takes some photos. Tries to feel the leathery patch. Can't. Says, 'My wife is always on at me to moisturise.' Takes some super-close-up photos of the inner thigh area under different lighting set-ups. Gets a couple of shots which shows the hard spot I'd found. Skin a little browner, a bit more crusted over.

'Sheezus.'

His face is grim, his eyes on Sharma.

'Listen, Carolyn, I've got some tidying up to do here . . .' He sends Sharma to wait outside, in a voice that does not admit refusal, then says to me, 'I did a couple of tours in Iraq. I've seen burns before, but nothing at all like this. Christ, there's hardly anything there.'

'Will you find anything subdermally?'

'Maybe, I don't know. It's not an area where I have any experience. But there'll be research on this kind of thing. I'll hit the books.'

'Thank you.'

'And hey, I don't know what kind of process you folks have, but I wouldn't want you to bust any balls over this. If I'd been that first pathologist . . .'

'Thanks, but there'll be no busted balls.'

He grins. Turns back to the cadaver.

I go out to find Sharma. Walk her out to a pizza place, with a view out over the glittering sea. Order food and water and a huge bowl of green salad and make her tell me about how she met Livesey, about their romance, about the plans they'd made. Make her tell me in detail and with feeling. Make her do all that before I tell her what flavour of horrible she now has to live with.

'What we were seeing there was an electrical burn. Very high voltage, very low current. The massive voltage causes the pain. The low current means there's pretty much nothing to see.'

These aren't things that you discover from ordinary British policing work. They weren't even things that DiGiulian, a military man, came across during his time in Iraq. But if you fool around on Wikipedia, you find what you need. Electric cattle prods were used as tools in human torture – simple, cheap, nasty – until the 1970s when various Latin American governments developed the picana. The picana worked on the same basic technique, except that voltages were increased to ten or twenty thousand volts and the current reduced to as little as a thousandth of an amp. It's assumed that contemporary devices now run to far higher voltages yet. Exactly how high nobody knows, because the folk who work with picanas don't generally seek publicity.

I knew none of this myself. Only found it out because I wanted to discover if there were ways to torture someone without leaving any marks that a SOCO or pathologist might find.

Suicide is a hard sort of horrible, but there are other sorts, and not necessarily kinder to those left behind.

Sharma's face is very still. Ashen beneath the tan. A face etched with the realisation of the final act in her lover's biography.

She says, 'The salt. That was because they . . .'

'Wanted to improve electrical conductivity, yes.'

Whoever applied the picana to Livesey preferred to avoid the whole business of dressing and undressing him. Too hard. Too difficult to achieve without possible struggle or errors in the re-dressing. So, instead, a little salty water on the trouser leg. Application of the picana. To the thigh certainly. To the genitals, probably.

Then death by hanging.

All that done in a locked, inaccessible room.

A room from which nothing was missing, nothing stolen.

The perfect crime, the perfect murder.

Sharma, I can see, is on the verge of tears again, but something steers her away from that place and, without any change in her tone, she asks, 'How bad was it? Please tell me the truth.'

'We don't know. Probably won't know, even after DiGiulian has completed his work. But if you want my guess, then I think not all that bad. Whoever attacked your fiancé did so because they wanted some information. I don't know what that information was or why it was needed. But from Ian's point of view, it was just work. Something to treat with care, but not worth dying for. My guess is he just gave them what they wanted. Why wouldn't he? He had bigger things to live for. Way bigger.'

Sharma nods. Says, 'Thank you, Fiona. Thank you.'

We say goodbye under the restaurant's little porch, hung with vines, thick blue shadows massing on the tiles. We hug.

I say, 'Hang in there, Carolyn.'

'Fiona, when DiGiulian is done, we're going to hold a funeral service. Very small. Just intimate friends and family. But we'll have a memorial service too and, look, I'm sure you won't want to come, but—'

'I do.'

I'm too abrupt. I've slightly shocked Sharma with the speed and force of my response. 'Sorry. I get too involved. I always do.' My finger, I notice, is pointing at my head again. 'They matter to me. Ian Livesey, you, your families.'

'I'll let you know when we've got the details sorted. If you can come . . .' She shrugs. A light one, which says it's nice if you come, OK if you don't.

'Thank you.'

She punches me, very softly, on my shoulder. 'Just get the bastard, Fiona. You just get that sonofabitch.'

I tell her I will.

I think I'm forgiven my lack of moustaches.

I have one more meeting that day, before heading back to the airport and my flight home.

The meeting is with one of Livesey's former colleagues. Stuart Lowe. A fellow engineer. One who stayed working for a big company, when Livesey struck out on his own.

We meet by the water, inevitably – everywhere in Norfolk

is by the water. You turn your back on the sea at one corner, drive away from it, leave it shining in your rear-view mirror like a golden penny, then two blocks later, your windscreen starts to fill again with dancing blue, the heave of another bridge.

Lowe's office is a squat brown block jammed between a car park and a quay. Lowe – fiftyish, outdoorsy, silver hair shaved down to a prickle – looks cut from the same cloth as Livesey. Maritime engineers, a breed apart. Lowe meets me in the lobby, gives me a handshake like some kind of shipboard clamp and asks me if I want to come up.

I do, but the docks have my interest first. The clutter of shipping. Steel hulls. Thick white and yellow paint. Company colours.

Lowe says, 'Sure.' Bounds along the dock, pointing to boats. 'The *Moonflower*. One of our main workhorses. Subsea construction. Oil industry mostly. See that crane there?' The boat he's pointing to has a low stern mounted by a chunky white crane and other handling equipment I can't understand. 'That little sweetheart operates in pretty much any kind of sea. Automatic movement compensation. If we need to launch an ROV or pick one up, we can do it in pretty much any sea state.'

'ROV?'

'Remote Operated Vehicle. Any construction work we do happens down there. You can use divers for inshore work, or sometimes on rigs, but any deep-sea stuff we do with ROVs. We can lay pipeline or cable. Trench it. Recover it. Mend it, even.'

He continues with his tour. Points out trenchers and ploughs. Cable carousels, able to hold two thousand tonnes of cable. The *Rakekniven*, a specialist vessel equipped to work in extreme latitudes, her hull thickened to resist ice.

'Not that our equipment is mostly here,' he tells me. 'If

it's in dock, it's not earning its keep. Any one time, we aim to have eighty or ninety per cent of it at sea.'

I understand almost none of what I'm being shown. But I like it, all of it. Like the blue, gull-dotted sky. The thick steel hulls. The friendly nursery-coloured paint. The creak of metal against dockside, the slap of water, the smell of brine. I like the sense that all these incomprehensible digital things still rely, when it comes to the point, on men sailing ships like these, operating cranes, handling equipment which you can still see, feel and kick.

When I've had my fill of the docks, we go up to Lowe's office. Cheap windows, cheap carpet, cheap fittings, wonderful view.

I say, 'Ian, you used to work with him?'

He says yes. Says all the things you say about an ex-colleague, whom you liked, whom you shared summer barbecues with, but who wasn't a deep, essential part of your life.

'He was good at his job?'

'Yes, sure. Very – very regular, capable guy.'

'Meaning, he was good at his job, but nothing outstanding? That plenty of people are just as good.' When Lowe hesitates, I add, 'I'm not family. I'm not going to pass your comments on. I just need to know.'

He grins. Says, 'Ian was a good surveyor, but nothing so special. When he quit this firm to set up on his own, I thought he was stepping away from the big time. I mean, we're a global outfit. The big, interesting projects tend to come our way because there just aren't that many firms who can do what we can do. When Ian left us, he went from working for Exxon to working for' – he waves his hands – 'I don't know. Port authorities needing to upgrade their harbour equipment. Coastguards needing chart updates.'

'You know what he was working on when he died?'

'Yeah. Big cable project.' He names the company,

Atlantic Cables. 'It surprised me, that. We normally expect to win assignments like that. Or if not us, one of our major competitors. But you know, what we expect, we don't always get.'

'And Ian was capable of handling something on that scale?'

'Oh sure. It's just a seabed survey. He wasn't pitching for the trenching work, nothing like that.'

'So he made a map . . .?'

'Yeah, picking up from the estuary out to the edge of the Irish Sea.'

This is news to me. 'He handled a *portion* of the route, that's all?'

'Yeah. They wanted to chop it up into segments. I don't know why.'

We discuss that a bit. The approach doesn't seem either so normal or so strange. I drop the topic and go back to what exactly Livesey was doing for his money.

'Right, sure. The product from his survey would have been a map and a route plan. He'd have been able to highlight any potential problem areas. Inshore, that might be wrecks or other obstructions. Deep sea, you have to think about seabed stability. Any sharp cliffs or trenches. Debris. Dumping grounds. Seabed composition if you want to bury the cable. That kind of thing. If he came across real problem areas, he could always bring in a highly equipped specialist like ourselves to deal with the issue.'

'Cables are buried? I thought they were just dropped out of the back of a boat.'

'Mostly, sure. But you're from Wales, right? Take a situation like the Bristol Channel. You have a lot of traffic, a lot of movement. Ships dropping anchor, for example. If you leave cable exposed in a place like that, you're pretty much asking for snags or breaks. So if the seabed type makes it an option, you'll probably choose to bury the cable. Keep it safe.'

Somewhere, audible through an open window, a wire taps against metal. A ship slips through a channel beyond us. From where I'm sitting, I can't actually see water, so it looks like a big ship is travelling smoothly down some city boulevard, gliding past offices and burger joints.

Nothing here feels real.

I say, 'I never met Ian in life, but I've just come from the autopsy. He looked fit. Strong.'

'Once a marine, always a marine.'

'Did he work out, do you know?'

'Yes, always. Running. Weights. Some kind of martial arts thing, I don't know what. I'm sure Carolyn could tell you.'

'No, it's fine. Just a passing thought.'

We talk some more. Lowe shows me some 3-D maps of the seabed. Coloured images, all strange peaks and inky troughs. The maps mean nothing to me.

I thank him for his time.

I need to leave for the airport soon but before I do, I find a bit of dockside where I can sit and watch the sea.

The air is warm. The sea inviting and blue. The concrete I'm sitting on still holds the day's heat. Trash washes up against the sea wall in front of me. Discarded packaging. A fast food carton. Some dirty polystyrene filmed with algae. A fishing float, or buoy, bright orange in the blue.

I think that the broad shape of the case is fairly clear. Who did what to whom and why. Not just the Livesey case, but the Plas Du one too. One of those things where we don't have remotely enough facts to go on. Not for a courtroom, of course. The basis for a confident investigative hypothesis, nothing more. But I don't have names, not meaningfully, and my guesses tend to run a long away ahead of my colleagues' own, more routine-focused, process. There's a lot of work yet to do, I see that.

Briefly, I find myself thinking, *I'd like to try to do this police-*

*style. Run the case in a way that means Jackson wouldn't kill me, even if he knew everything I got up to.* I don't quite know what to do with that thought. I'm not good at staying within police rules, or at least not when they start to conflict with the needs of the investigation. I also think: *Bronwen Woodward, Cesca Evans. Those things weren't very police-style.* Not that they were so bad, either. And they produced useful intelligence in both cases. So I don't reflect long, before I revise my early opinion to: *I'd like to try and do this police-fashion if I can. And if I can't, Jackson will just have to kill me.*

As it is, I think the case should be easy enough to bring home. A nice one to work on.

It's Thursday evening and I feel relaxed.

# 18

Fly home. Evening flight to Washington. Overnight to Heathrow. Coach back to Cardiff.

I don't sleep much on the flight. I've hardly ever flown long haul and can't get the hang of sleeping on my poky economy seat, so end up typing my notes instead. Jackson wants me in at two p.m. for an inquiry review, which should in theory give me ample time to get home, shower, change and blink myself into the right time zone. Alas, however, the coach hits traffic on the M4 – major accident up ahead – and we sit looking at an unremarkable bit of Wiltshire for two disconsolate hours. The coach has wi-fi, and I use it to check out my emails.

A few boring work things.

An email alert from one of my used-car websites. Cardiff University is selling off an old mini-van for £750, or nearest offer. I make a call to check things over, then buy it.

I think about calling Dunwoody. Telling him about my new van. Offering him a ride.

I look at Wiltshire a bit more. Try to sleep. Fail. Then the coach moves on again.

I get into the office fifteen minutes late, not showered, not changed and my brain still riding the jetstream somewhere between Chesapeake Bay and County Limerick.

Jackson glares at me, like multi-vehicle pile-ups are my fault. 'Nice trip?'

I don't know what answer he wants. Just sit down, say nothing.

We're in a big conference room on the top floor. Jackson presiding. Watkins next to him.

Along with our team, there's Creamer from Avon and Somerset. Also a DI, Bob Findlay. A female DS whose name I don't properly catch. Jackson introduces me as, 'DC Fiona Griffiths, our Acting Deputy Exhibits Officer.'

I don't know why he uses that title for me. It's not one he's ever shoved at me before. He's making a point, I assume, but I don't know what.

Findlay is running through developments at their end.

Fingerprints, first. The obvious hope. But it's good news, bad news, with the bad outweighing the good.

The good news is that the prints on that middle girder beneath the balcony were definitely made by a human hand. What's more, to judge from the extent to which airborne dirt and particulates had built up, the prints are of approximately the right vintage. Created neither days ago, nor years ago, at any rate.

Also, there's no possibility of them having been left by a window cleaner or anything of that sort. As Findlay – bluff, practical – commented, 'They were a bugger to get to, quite frankly. We had six men on it and even so we had to pull in some firemen with high access training.'

That's the good news. The bad news is that no usable prints were found for matching purposes. No big surprise that. Prints are delicate things. You can't always pick them up the day after, let alone two months later. And in any case, sweat – the key ingredient of most latent fingerprints – would have been carefully blotted away by a climber's use of chalk.

Findlay concludes, 'Needless to say, they were forensically aware when inside. We've found nothing. Probably wouldn't have done if we'd checked at the time. Entrance into the apartment from the balcony would have been easy enough. Door almost always unlocked, for obvious reasons, but easy to force if not.'

'So,' says Jackson. One of his big Jacksonian *sos*. 'So. Murder it is.'

'Yes. No question.'

Six sets of eyes track towards me. Six sets, plus Sharma's tear-brimmed pair, plus Livesey's puzzled pair. I last saw Livesey's when DiGiulian peeled his face down from his forehead, blue eyes startled by the descending dark.

'And torture,' I say. 'Not certain, but highly probable.'

I tell them about the faint traces of electrical burns on the inner thigh. Tell them what I know about the picana, its modern descendants. Watkins already knows some of this. For the others, I think it's new, at least in large part.

'The pathologist will confirm this?' Jackson's question.

'Yes and no.' I explain that DiGiulian is not, in fact, in any doubt about what he discovered, but there may be a gap between what he personally believes and what we can make stand up in court. 'If he can prove the existence of subdermal damage, we're OK. If not, I doubt if the indications are strong enough to make a more than circumstantial case.'

The eyes are still looking at me, so I say, 'I spoke to Ms Sharma. She was aware of no threats to Mr Livesey. No attempted thefts. Nothing of that sort. I'll distribute her statement as soon as I'm back at my desk.'

I'm still meeting a whole hillside of silence. Acres of tumbled stone and waving bracken. Sheep trails through the bilberries.

I say, 'I interviewed one of Livesey's ex-colleagues.' Mention the curious fact of a big project being awarded to a minor operator. 'I typed up my notes on the plane back. I'll distribute everything properly soon.'

Then I shut up.

Findlay's mouth moves, but no words come out.

The sheep still wander silently through the bilberries.

I don't know what to say.

Jackson helps me out. 'Fiona, I think what everybody is wondering is how come you knew that Ian Livesey had been tortured and murdered, when all the indications pointed to a common or garden suicide.'

'Oh, I see. No. I didn't know.'

More silence.

I can see I'm meant to say something further.

I say, 'Derek Moon. It started with him. He took a blow to the head that didn't come from his fall. Hence an assumption of murder. Nothing showed up on a regular investigation. Nothing in his personal life. No thefts of physical property. So it had to be something else. I didn't know what. But then Livesey popped up. Same cable, same project. Moon's death was carefully covered up. It seemed worth asking if Livesey's was too.'

'The salt,' says Watkins. 'You were looking for salt the very first minute you were in that apartment.'

I blink. Maybe it's my brain still staggering out of the sky. Looking for baggage control and trying to remember where it left my passport. But as far as I remember, successful investigation is a good quality in a detective. Even in an Acting Deputy Exhibits Officer.

'It was a long shot, maybe. But if you want to extract information, and if you happen to know your guy is an ex-Marine who keeps himself strong and fit, you would have to think that you might need some kind of physical coercion to extract the relevant information. That's easy enough if you're just planning to beat the crap out of someone. But they wanted this murder to look like suicide, so they had to find a way to inflict pain without leaving marks. I poked around a bit. The picana seems like the torturers' tool of choice for those circumstances. But obviously electricity doesn't conduct well through dry clothing, so . . .' I shrug. 'I don't know if your team has had time to look at that chair?'

Findlay drills me with his gaze. Then nods. 'Traces of duct tape adhesive. They cleaned it up pretty well. It looks like they wiped the chair down with surgical spirit, something like that. But there were a couple of recessed screwholes, hard to clean. We found something there.'

The discussion spools forward. I don't participate much. But the conclusion everyone comes to is, I think, the right one.

Somebody wanted information on the undersea cable. We don't know what or why, but have to assume that both Moon and Livesey had access to it.

Both men were killed. Livesey tortured and killed.

There's discussion about the specifics of the Livesey murder. We have most of the essentials already. The rest is either possible to guess or perhaps doesn't matter too much

It's clear that someone climbed into Livesey's apartment. The noise of that entry, presumably, is what alerted Livesey to the presence of an intruder. What prompted his, 'Hey, babe, that's weird.'

Livesey cut the call and stepped out to find the climber in his apartment. We presume that the climber was carrying a weapon, because Livesey was strong and capable and there were no signs of a struggle. We also presume that the torture required at least two men. Hard to manage otherwise. That implies that there was an armed climber, who threatened Livesey, and let an accomplice into the room.

Once there, the two men forced Livesey into a chair and taped him into it. Livesey was at gunpoint and had no option but to comply. He was probably also thinking that he just needed to give these guys whatever they came for and they'd leave him be. Logical thinking, but logic doesn't always win the day.

Anyway. They tortured him. Obtained the information they needed. Then tied Livesey by the neck and hanged him. Cut him out of the chair only once he was already dangling.

Restore the apartment, pretty much to how it was. The accomplice left in the normal way. The climber then locked the front door and descended by abseil.

The discussion meanders.

Creamer says, 'But why get a climber involved? Why not just arrive at the guy's door and blag your way in? Or fight if you have to?'

That's a fair question, but the general consensus – in which I share – is that although that strategy *probably* works, it would have been too risky to trust. If Livesey hadn't liked the look of the people he encountered at the door, he'd only have had to yell once – down a long corridor, with other apartments leading off it – and the whole murder-as-suicide plan would have been a bust.

Entering the apartment by stealth and surprising him at gunpoint in his own room would have eliminated the risk of public exposure to almost nothing.

Someone asks about the coroner's inquest on Livesey. Findlay wants to give the coroner access to our recent findings.

I say, 'Maybe not such a good idea. If we have an advantage here, it's that whoever we're pursuing has no idea that we've figured this out.'

More chat. Withholding information from a coroner's inquest is a big no-no. On the other hand, there are public interest exemptions which would permit us to hold back material. It seems to me that anything which increases our chances of arresting a murderer might well be in the public interest, but what do I know? I'm only an Acting Deputy Exhibits Officer.

Findlay says he can't withhold evidence from a coroner.

I want to thump my head against the table, but don't.

Nip out. Go to the loo. Make some peppermint tea. Go crazy: pick a big mug and use two teabags. This girl lives her life to the max.

Return to the meeting.

My entrance interrupts things. The conversation falls silent.

Watkins takes three manila folders. Drops them on the table in front of her with a papery thwack. They're the ones I handed to her in the car on the way to Bristol.

Jackson says, 'Fiona. Let's move to the next item on our agenda. Peter Pan. Plas Du.'

I say, 'He probably isn't really called Peter Pan.'

That's not a clever thing to say, but then Jackson's interrogation technique isn't always very clever either. If he'd wanted to ask a question, he needed to supply a main verb and a question mark. Those things, minimum.

'Are we to gather that you suspect a connection between the Plas Du burglary and the Livesey murder?'

'Um. Yes, I suppose so.'

'And these suspicions were aroused *when*, exactly?'

That word 'exactly' bothers me. There's an issue in philosophy about how you individuate things – how you figure out exactly when something stops being one thing and becomes another. It's the sort of question which sounds obvious, and probably is if you're dealing with stones or dogs or dinner plates. But *exactly* when did my suspicion come into being? I don't know. I don't think that has a clean answer.

Since I don't know what to say, I say nothing.

Jackson waits to see if I have more to offer. I don't. He says, 'OK. Let's try another one. I asked you to take a look at a number of cold cases. The burglary at Plas Du was one of them. Right?'

His question is still short of a main verb, but his question mark is as plain as a pikestaff, so I say, 'Yes, sir,' with perhaps more enthusiasm than the occasion quite warrants.

'You took a look at Plas Du. You took the view that, despite the obvious difficulties of the ascent, somebody might have climbed in through an inaccessible second-floor window. On subsequent investigation, you discovered that, yes, that's exactly what did happen. Right?'

'Right. Yes, sir.'

I'm not quite sure where this is going, so I try to make my answers big, bright and shiny.

'Now, Rhiannon here asked you to take a look to see if other recent thefts had followed a similar pattern. I think she was assuming you might take a look at recent high value art thefts or other unsolved thefts in the South Wales area. In actual fact, you took it into your head to look for thefts from fellow members of the British Insurance Association, specifically company executives serving on the BIA's Evolving Security Risks Committee and, more specifically still, that committee's Senior Working Group on Household and Small Business Security Threats.'

He stops. No question mark anywhere. Just a set of factual statements all of which he knows to be true. But I can see he needs me to say something, so I stick to my current strategy and say, 'Right. Exactly. Yes, sir. Spot on.'

There's a pause, a silence. No sheep, no bilberries, though. This silence is harder than that. Edgier.

Watkins takes over where Jackson left off.

She pushes the three folders I gave her out on the table in front of her. Taps the first and says, 'Marianna Lockwood and Plas Du. Six etchings, two candlesticks. Total value £400,000.'

Taps the second and says, 'John and Andrea Redhead. Lost various items of family jewellery from an luxury inner London apartment. Insured value, about £12,000.'

Taps the third and says, 'Eleanor Bentley, known as Nellie, reported a break-in at her holiday property in Sussex. Nothing stolen except for a giant teddy bear. Value, don't know, a hundred pounds, something like that. The matter was only reported to the police because a large curved plate glass window had been broken, and the replacement cost of the window went significantly over the insurance excess.

'Nellie Bentley, John Redhead and Galton Evans, Lockwood's former husband, all served on the insurance sub-committee that Dennis just mentioned.

'All three break-ins were effectively impossible. A twenty-five-foot sheer wall in the case of Plas Du. An exterior window on a thirteenth-floor apartment in the case of the Redheads. The Sussex property was a converted lighthouse, with the thief gaining access, apparently, from the very top of the building. Local police – different forces in each case – dismissed evidence of a break-in as totally implausible.'

She stares at me.

I stare back. Neither she nor Jackson seem to be wearing their interrogation knickers today. Lots of statements. All verifiably true. No questions.

She concludes. 'Marianna Lockwood, recently interviewed by Fiona here, reported that the stolen items had all been returned and the insurance money refunded. On further enquiry, it now turns out that the Redhead family jewellery was also recovered. Insurance money repaid. No report of the recovery made to the Metropolitan Police. It is not known whether Nellie Bentley recovered her teddy bear.'

I nod. Watkins's summary was characteristically terse, but correct, and missing no major facts. She's a very good officer, I think.

Jackson stares. Everyone stares.

I feel strange, but I didn't sleep overnight and I've just crossed half a dozen time zones twice in two days.

Jackson says, 'Fiona, is there anything you would like to add to the facts currently on the table?'

I say, 'Jet lag. I think I might have jet lag.'

His face tightens in a way that tells me my answer didn't quite hit the target, so I say, 'The cable outfit. They assigned the mapping to different surveyors, each one with their own segment of the route. That's not unheard of, apparently, but it's not standard either.'

'Noted.'

Jackson has a deep voice anyway, but when he's in certain moods it turns into one of those bass rumbles which you don't so much hear as feel through the soles of your feet. But when the rumble finishes the silence comes back, so I say, 'Those undersea cables. You know how long it takes to get a signal to America? About fifty-something milliseconds. The theoretical limit is around forty milliseconds. Speed of light and all that. You'd have to cut a tunnel through the earth to go much faster.'

I mime the action of digging a tunnel to help anyone whose comprehension isn't that great. On reflection, that probably doesn't include anyone in the room.

'Finance types. Hedge funds. They care about those things. I don't think anyone else does.'

Then I shut up.

Then there's a pause.

Then a Jacksonian rumble says, 'Thank you, Fiona. You've been very helpful.'

There is a discussion of what to do next. There'll be two separate investigations. One into Livesey's death, headed by Findlay, and to operate out of Bristol. The second into Moon's death, the Plas Du burglary and the apparently related thefts. That operation will be headed by Watkins, supervised by Jackson, and will operate out of Cardiff. Liaison officers on both forces to keep the inquiries closely connected.

Jackson says to Watkins, 'Codenames?'

'Yes, what haven't we used yet? *Where Eagles Dare*? "Eagles" would be good . . .'

'Or "Zorro". It's got to be "Zorro",' says Jackson. To Findlay, 'We're on Welsh films, or films with Welsh stars, anyway.'

That puzzles me. How does "Chicago" fit in? Then I think there might have been a film about the city, although why you would need a Welsh actor in that, I don't know.

I don't ask.

The meeting breaks up. Findlay talks to Watkins. Creamer mutters in annoyance, because he's lost his phone and can't call out. Then the Somerset deputation leaves, and Jackson and Watkins beckon me over.

Jackson says, 'I need you to stay working in Exhibits. Can't switch at this stage. But if you're not too much of a pest, Rhiannon will let you sit in on things when it makes sense.'

Sit in on things? *Sit in on things?* I produce two honest-to-God, prime-quality murder victims plus a string of burglaries, which are, admittedly, only burglaries and don't have any lovely, lovely corpses dancing in their wake, but are nevertheless pretty much gold-standard in their class – and Jackson tells me that I can *sit in on things*?

I don't know what to say. Or rather: I have a number of options, but all of them come thickened with more swearwords than Jackson is likely to relish.

I stand there gaping.

He says: 'If I could simply shift you, I would. But right now, we're short of exhibits officers, and Chicago needs you. OK?'

I think of asking him for a number. Like, is there some minimum quantity of corpses I have to produce before I'll be allowed out? You know: allowed out, to do my *actual* job, which involves *actual* investigation of *actual* murders?

Jackson says, 'Chicago is an important case and you're an important part of it. I'm not moving you.'

*Important*? I want to say. We have now three thousand

nine hundred exhibits and not a single useful lead. The hospital swabs were not secured and have long since been destroyed. The weather-coverings which collapsed, that time I was bad-mouthing Dunthinking in the canteen, did indeed compromise subsequent investigation. Dunthinking currently has his team forensicating every van that has ever rolled down Tremorfa's leafy avenues, but all his work has not provided one single interesting lead – and I'm damn sure he knows it.

And, as it happens, there's one damn van which Dunthinking has *not* chosen to forensicate and which is now my very own personal property: a fact which would, I'm pretty sure, turn Dunthinking's face pinker and angrier than I've ever yet seen it.

I would say these things, would even talk about my new van, except that the words which lie closest to my lips are a vigorous and expressive jumble of Anglo Saxon and Old High Dutch, and Jackson – though perfectly capable of a little Old English himself – doesn't always love it when I speak my mind.

So I stand there, useless, gawping, silent.

Watkins uses the silence to say, 'We'll run both parts of the inquiry – Moon and Plas Du – together. Briefings at eight thirty. I'll make sure you have access to the material.'

And that's it.

Jackson goes, holding the door for Watkins.

I'm left alone in an empty room.

I think I feel angry *and* upset. Those things and the fog of jet lag.

I stand there a while – breathing hard, feeling the press of my knuckles against the melamine table top – until I conclude that standing alone in an empty room does not constitute an effective protest.

Back at my desk, I call Ed Saunders, a friend now in the third incarnation of our relationship. In its first incarnation, he was my carer, a young clinical psychologist, right at the start of his career, who took care of me when I was a mad, angry, scarily endangered teenager. In the second incarnation – one that happened years later – he was my lover. We've settled now, I think, into the kind of friendship which will stand the test of time.

He answers, 'Fi! Hi. How are you?'

'Angry, definitely. Maybe also upset. Both things, I think.'

'Something bad?'

Yes, bad, I tell him. I keep producing corpses, proper triple-A-rated murder victims, and I keep getting stuffed back into Ifor's dungeon. 'It's like no one values a corpse any more,' I complain, 'and these are really, really good ones.'

Ed sympathises. Asks me if I'd like to meet up.

I would, yes.

I need reminding of the day of the week – it's Friday – so I ask about tomorrow. Ed says no, then maybe, then figures out a way to shuffle some stuff around and says yes.

We ring off.

Maybe it's about quantity, not quality. Maybe I just need to produce more and more corpses.

I call Mike.

Say, 'Mike, if Watkins asks you for help, can you tell her you're busy, except for weekends?'

'I'm not particularly busy,' he says. 'Anyway, my hours are totally flexible.' He works part time as an outdoors instructor at a place for learning disabled kids, and he's already told me that the real joy of his job is his ability to escape from it at short notice.

'I know,' I say snappishly, 'just don't say that.'

He agrees placidly. He's nice. Nicer than I am.

We ring off.

I bring up Penry's number, ready to call. My finger hovers over the call button.

Hovers and hesitates, dithers and delays.

*No flying solo, Fiona.*

*We need you to mature. As a police officer and as a person.*

I'm a good girl. I don't call. Just complete my notes. Distribute them. Add my contact details to the Project Zorro team list.

Maybe it's four corpses I need. Or five. I just think there should be some tangible target, so you can have something to work towards.

Home. Shower. Bed. Sleep.

# 19

Home, shower, bed. Those are the easy bits. The Just Be Normal template for every evening.

But then what?

My Saturday mornings are the hardest part of every week, harder still now that I'm not with Buzz. In a way, I'd prefer to spend the weekend working, particularly now that Zorro and whatever stupid name the Somerset police are giving their inquiry are opening up into something really worthwhile.

But I'm strict with myself. Since being sent down to Ifor's dungeon, I've been working ever longer hours in the effort to spring myself. In the two weeks leading up to my American trip, I was in the office every evening, often overnight, and working the weekends as well. Chicago swallowed pretty much all my normal working hours, so my various other projects stole whatever scraps of time were left over.

Those other projects kept me sane but, much as I love those long marathons of work, I do get lost in them. Start to slip the moorings which keep me tethered to this difficult planet.

So no work for me this fine morning. Instead: life – a more difficult proposition.

I get up at eight. Ask my fridge if it has any food for me. It offers me a plastic container of fruit that is only slightly fizzy. A yogurt with a use-by date that seems to have passed some time ago, but which seems fine. A cold sausage.

I take those things to the table and eat them. The fruit, the yogurt, the sausage.

Make some tea. Drink it.

Smoke a joint, not a particularly big one.

Cleaning. I should do some of that, I think. I don't normally like cleaning my house. I enjoy the feeling of the dust slowly settling, things returning to nature.

But this weekend my Just Be Normal rule will be my guide and lodestar. On my last big case, I worked undercover as an office cleaner, Fiona Grey. She became pretty good at her job. OK with hoovering and dusting and nothing less than a whirlwind in the bathrooms. So from time to time, I step back and let her do her stuff. Even went out and bought those yellow plastic buckets we used to use. Commercial cleaning fluids in five litre tubs.

This Saturday morning, I give that other Fiona her head. She scrubs, cleans, hoovers, wipes. Rooms dazzle at her touch. She does things that wouldn't even occur to me: running the hoover up the inside of the curtains, wiping condensation spots with vinegar as a precaution against mould.

She's blitzkrieg fast, but peaceful. She has a contentment I never quite manage. I let her get on with things, not intruding. Then, when she's done, she puts the cleaning stuff away and goes out into the garden so we can share a ciggy. We stand out there in the chill – two women, one body – and watch the smoke curl up towards the grey sky. We like the way that nobody tries to stop it.

And after a bit, Fiona Grey fizzles out. As though that part of me dwindles and the other part, the me-part, comes back strong.

I think about taking some exercise, but decide that thinking about it must be almost as good as doing it.

Have another conversation with my fridge. It tells me that

the milk is so sour it is forming islands. It shows me a packet of bacon with last year's date on it.

I throw everything out and go out to buy some groceries.

Come back. Put them away.

Pick up the phone to call Penry. Start to dial, but don't hit the call button. Just listen to the silence.

*No flying solo, Fiona.*

I think of those cables undersea. Snaking past the sunken clutter of the estuary floor, past the flatfish and the hagfish and the skates and the rays, down to the black waters beyond the continental shelf, where dark things move.

I replace the phone. My house crawls in its own silence. Beetles moving behind wood.

Moments like this, I miss Buzz with an intensity that is so physical, it almost takes my breath away. What's worse is that I have this vision of him, standing in his flat, feeling the same thing, in the same way.

I lean my forehead against the glass of the kitchen window. Feeling it cold and clear and empty against my skin.

It's not yet time to go round to Ed's house, so I spend a little time on naughty things. Enter Cesca Lockwood's computer. Read her emails. Steal her passwords. Facebook. Gmail. Instagram. Everything. Look for phone numbers. Inspect her documents and photos.

Find nothing obviously wonderful, but you don't always know what's golden when first you see it. When it's time to go over to Ed's house, I drive slow, not the idiot behind the wheel that I normally am.

He asks how I am. I tell him OK.

'Getting to grips with the single life again?'

'Maybe. Yes, maybe.'

'Have you been out on a date yet?'

'No.'

Ed is single too. Divorced, two kids, ones he only gets to

see every second weekend. He's had one or two fairly short-term girlfriends since the collapse of his marriage, but nothing major.

And I suddenly worry that Ed has been waiting for this. For me. To become available again. So that we can do as properly functioning adults what we tried to do too early, too young, too foolish.

I like Ed, but not like that. His silence troubles me.

I say, 'But I'm getting closer. There's a guy at the office I quite like. Not CID. But, you know. Nice. And I've been thinking I should start to do all that again.'

Ed nods, says something, starts kitchening around, the way he does.

He doesn't drop the conversation right there. Not straight away. He probes a bit more, but I adhere to my policy of careful indifference. An indifference which pretends not to have noticed that he is a boy and I am a girl and we once used to share a bed.

And then – I don't know. The moment passes. That ghost of a possibility in his mind snuffed out by the glassy impenetrability of my response.

Did I read things right? I can't tell. I'm not very good at these things. There's maybe a slight angry edge to the way Ed opens a bottle of wine, cracks eggs, shifts crockery. But I'm not sure. And any case, I can't go climbing into bed with someone, just because their feelings might be hurt if I didn't.

Things move on.

I sit on the kitchen counter as he works. He asks about my case and I tell him about my corpses. I ask about his work and he tells me about his nutcases.

When I talk about Ifor's dungeon and the problems I have in managing my head down there, he looks at me carefully. Steady blue eyes, with the wisdom of experience.

He doesn't tell me what he finds, though. Just makes an

omelette for us both. Welsh goats cheese and chives chopped in its middle. A green salad, mixed, dressed and served while the omelette goes golden. After a bit, I get off the counter. Go and stand at the stove so I can jiggle the pan now and again, pretending to be useful. When Ed comes over to check what I'm doing, I lean my head against his shoulder.

We stay like that a while. The omelette doing whatever it does. Me leaning on Ed. Him letting me lean, blue eyes grave above me, sentinels guarding a lonely sea.

When the moment is over, and the omelette divided between two plates, and I'm sitting down and finding my knife and fork and remembering that I need to try and eat like a human being, I say, 'Thanks, Ed,' and I sort of make it look like I mean the food, but he knows and I know and the whole world probably knows that the food is only the smallest and least important part of it.

He says, 'You're welcome,' and smiles at me, and I smile back, and we eat.

Two friends. Just friends. Sharing a meal.

# 20

Linton Hill. Sussex.

A chalk down, a sloping field, a kind of nose or headland poking out into the surrounding sea. Bentley's lighthouse commands views of the sea on either flank, captain of all it surveys.

The day is blustery, but more sunshine than cloud. The sea almost jaunty. White sailing ships nearer shore. Big ships on the horizon. Brute, industrial shapes rendered flat by distance.

Mike – a fully paid-up consultant now, £250 a day plus expenses – seems slow to get started. He walks slowly round the tower, feeling the masonry. The walls aren't vertical – they slope inwards as they rise – but they're steep enough to feel effectively sheer. A fifty-foot leap of stone, painted in broad candy stripes of red and white.

Mike completes a couple of circuits then walks back to get a better view of its upper parts, at one point getting a pair of binoculars from his car. I just sit with my back to the building, feeling the sun on my face.

Chicago has become even worse than I'd first realised. Most of the work that Ifor did early on has turned out to be wrong or incomplete or otherwise problematic. If Dunthinking had been doing his job properly, he'd have been onto those things hard and early, but as it was he handled it his own way: Dunthinkingly. I have to clean up the mess, but cleaning up the mess weeks after the event is a much more serious proposition than doing the same thing when everyone's memory is fresh and irregularities can be sorted out with a single phone call. A morning's work takes a week. A week's work takes longer than I can bear to think.

So I don't.

Don't think about Chicago, or about Zorro even. Just sit in the sunlight, feeling the breeze.

Mike's done inspecting.

Or rather: he's done inspecting the walls. He's now inspecting me.

'Why did you tell me to say I was busy during the week?'

'Because I'm going crazy at work. I wanted an excuse to get out. I knew I'd be the only one to volunteer for anything on Sunday.'

Mike considers that.

'You don't seem like a policewoman, you know.'

'What do I seem like?'

'Don't know. Just not police.'

Mike gets ready to climb and I help him lug some of his mats into place. The mats are for bouldering, Mike tells me: fierce, short problems, usually no more than twenty feet high. The lighthouse is much higher than that, and the upper portion of the climb would effectively have been unprotected, no matter how many mats an intruder cared to strew beneath.

Mike boots up, chalks his hands.

The masonry here is fairly coarse, the pointing corroded. All the same, actual holds or edges are few and far between, and look desperately thin into the bargain. Mike makes a couple of false starts, then tries again. This time he rises five, maybe six, feet from the ground before his foot pings from a toehold and he slides to the ground, grazing his palms and swearing softly.

'My bad. That was doable.'

He ascends again. Gets to the point he was at before. Positions his foot a little differently. Reaches up for a positive edge. Makes the move that beat him before. He climbs a further ten or twelve feet, moving with painful slowness. Each move, I think, looks tentative. Precarious. I'm expecting that sudden downward slide at any point. I keep worrying that the mats aren't positioned right. Keep nudging them tight against the wall with my foot.

Then Mike decides against further ascent. He's looking down, figuring out where his holds are, but some change in his body position shifts his balance in the wrong way and there's that sudden abrupt slippage. Skin rushing against stone. Mike hits the mats all right, but his limbs are flung out and the slope bounces him out and off the mats onto hard earth.

'Are you OK?'

Mike rolls upright, rubs an elbow, says, 'Fine. I'm fine.'

He gathers his breath. I stay leaning against the sunny wall.

A stolen teddy bear. Value one hundred pounds. The only item reported lost not to have been returned.

'OK,' Mike says, 'it's hard. Really hard. Crimpy and strenuous and some really thin holds. A tough route.'

'But possible? I mean, someone *could* do it?'

'Oh sure. *Has* done it. Definitely.'

I stare. Most forensic evidence – prints, residues, traces – are easily destroyed by exposure to the elements. I can't see how Mike can have found anything which could have survived, visible to the naked eye, for two years.

Mike laughs at my face. Pulls off a climbing boot and smears the toe into the white-painted stone. The boot is soft rubber and leaves a small black trace behind.

'There are boot marks all the way up. You don't always get them. It'll depend on things like foot placement and the exact type of move you're trying to make. But, well, you can see for yourself.'

He's right. Little dabs of black. Hard to see unless you're looking for them, and impossible to interpret unless you already know what to expect. The boot marks rise higher than Mike just climbed.

I take photos.

I say, 'Sorry, but I'm going to need to keep your boots. Our forensic boys will need them to distinguish your marks from the other ones.'

He says, 'Really?' and I say, 'Really,' and tell him to get a new pair on expenses. Put his shoes in an evidence bag. We'll need to resurvey the Bristol apartment for traces of boot rubber.

I suddenly remember Watkins's get-together. That was today. Sunday. I wonder if I upset her by volunteering for this trip? I'm thinking maybe yes. I send her a nice text. So sorry I can't be there, that kind of thing.

I wish I was a better human.

I wish we had food for the hungry and harmony between nations.

We drive to London.

A block of flats outside the Barbican. Thirteen floors above us: the apartment where the Redheads live.

This time, Mike hardly bothers to get out of the car. He just shrugs. Says, 'Easy.' It's a modern building. So consciously styled it might as well drench itself in hair mousse and wear aviator shades. The upper storeys boast some angled, louvred window screens which form what is, to Mike and his kind, essentially a ladder. The first couple of storeys lack that gimmick, but a couple of service shafts have been enclosed to form what look like a pair of pillars or buttresses standing a few feet apart from each other. Mike makes a star-shape with his body, one hand and one foot on each pillar, and shimmies his way up the first few feet to show me how easy it is. He doesn't even need his climbing boots, just his ordinary shoes.

He drops back to the ground, looks at his watch.

Six thirty. A long day.

I say, 'I'll call Watkins.'

Get her at home. Hear Cal's voice in the background, a clatter of pans. I tell Watkins what we've found. That the London building is easy. That the climb up the lighthouse looked desperate, but someone had, for certain, done it.

'You're sure, Fiona?'

'Yes.'

She pauses. Doesn't accept my 'yes' straight away. I text her my photos of the boot marks on the tower, but they're the kind of things that don't photograph well. What looked unmistakable in the light of day, looks murky and ambiguous on screen.

She continues to hesitate.

I say, 'They *are* withholding from us. There *are* two murders here.'

She says, 'I'll have to run this by Dennis. And Findlay.'

'Of course.' I wait to see if she has anything else to say, but there's nothing on the phone but the faint sounds of Cal cleaning up. I ask, 'How was your party? I'm sorry I couldn't make it.'

She says, 'It was fine.' Then more gently, 'It was really nice. I hope you can make it next time.'

I say whatever I'm meant to say, then, 'Where do you want me now? I'm in London at the moment.'

I hear her exhale. She knows what I want. Suspects me, rightly, of having engineered this timing.

'You're up to date on Chicago?' she asks.

'Yes. You can check with Laura, if you want.'

Again, that out-breath. That pause.

'OK. Stay where you are. Let's see this through.'

'Thank you, ma'am.'

'OK.'

Then she says nothing, and I say nothing, and I say, 'Is that all, ma'am?' and she says yes, and we hang up.

Mike raises his eyebrows at me. 'What's next? I'm hungry.'

We get food. A nearby pizza place. Mike eats like a girl. Gets a pizza, yes, but no dough balls, no garlic butter, no dressing on his salad. Diet Coke, no pudding. I try teasing him, but he shrugs. 'Secret of climbing. Train hard. Rest plenty. Don't eat.'

He asks again what's next. I shouldn't really tell him but I do. 'We kick down some doors and make people cry.'

Mike says, 'Cool.' Pauses. Then, 'Tonight, were you thinking we would sleep together?'

# 21

We don't sleep together, no. Just take neighbouring rooms in a nearby Premier Inn. Say a prim goodnight to each other as we separate.

Sleep comes to me in snatches only. Rags of cloud over a tattered moon. Then, at two o'clock, my mobile rings, the screen luminous and urgent in the sudden dark.

I answer it.

'Fiona?'

It's Carolyn Sharma.

I say yes. Tell her hi.

She tells me she can't stop thinking about the way Livesey died. 'I just wanted to talk to someone, hon. I hope it's OK.'

'Yes. More than OK. It's good.'

'Everyone here, they're real nice. Kind people, you know. But they keep wanting to take me out of myself. Take me somewhere nice, get me to laugh. All those things.'

'And you think that's all well and good, but you want to be allowed to grieve. That sometimes you might want something that isn't just sunshine.'

'Yes. Exactly that. Exactly,' she says, and pauses. Then, 'It's like I had all this great time with him, these memories. We were friends long before we started to date. Then he dies, and all I can think of is those burn marks on his thigh.'

I want to tell her that she's got that wrong. That the actual dying is only a passage, something you have to squeeze through. That when you come out, it's not like that any more. That actually being dead is wide and dark and silent and without end. In that place without walls, a few scorched genitals hardly figure.

I don't say that though. Instead, I say, 'Carolyn, tell me about when you first met. What you were wearing. What he was. What he smelled like. Everything.'

She does.

They met at a garden party. 'I was with my first husband, then. He was kind of an asshole, but I hadn't figured that out yet. But Ian? Oh, he was different. Real courteous. An officer and a gentleman, in that old-fashioned navy way. I was wearing this blue dress and . . .'

She goes on. I only partly listen. There's a teeny tiny kettle in my room and some tea bags. I pad across the room and make peppermint tea, even as she continues to recount her story, low-voiced in the darkness.

She seems nice, I guess. Livesey too. But my attention isn't really with her, or Livesey when alive. All I can think of is the dead man. The hanged man. The half man, half crafting project with his Y-shaped cut and a face folded over his eyes.

At one point, Sharma says, 'Oh, hon, what time is it with you? I wasn't thinking.'

I say, 'It's the middle of the night, but I like talking. Go on.'

She does, but not for long. Cries once, but not really.

I say, 'Carolyn, will you make me a promise? I want you to tell me the full story of your relationship. Start to finish. The bad things and sad things, as well as the good things. And I want you to call me whenever you feel like it. If that's stupid o'clock my time, I really don't care. I just want you to call me. I want you to say that you'll do that, but then I also want you to actually do it. And to go on doing it until you really, truly don't need to any more.'

'Oh, hon, you're sweet, you really don't have to.'

That makes me snappish. 'I *know* I don't have to. Of course I don't have to. So when I ask you to do it, I must really mean it.'

'Oh, OK, sure. All right. I'll call. I mean, if you're really . . . But yes. I'll call. Thank you, hon. I'd like that.' She also tells me that 'you English police must sure have a different way of working than ours do over here.'

There are a lot of possible answers to that, but all I say is, 'Welsh. I'm Welsh, not English.'

Before she hangs up, I say, 'And Carolyn? Can I ask a favour?' I ask her how well she knows Stuart Lowe.

Her answer: not brilliantly well, but well enough.

I say what I want and ask her to ask him. 'I just think it would be better coming from you. I can email stuff over and he can say yes, no or maybe.'

She sounds puzzled, but not in a bad way. 'Sure, hon, sure.'

We say good night.

It's three o'clock and my alarm is set for four fifteen. No point in trying to sleep again. So I arrange my pillows in a nest and use the time to think.

Think about Carolyn Sharma and the fact that she called through the night to talk to me.

Think about Livesey and Moon and that undersea cable.

About myself too. The secrets of my past, and a man with the codename Eilmer.

At four ten, I climb out of my nest. Have a shower and dress for action. Ready to kick down doors and make people cry.

# 22

A car collects us at quarter to five.

Metropolitan Police, BMW 3-series. A DI Dunne is in it, next to a driver who isn't introduced except as Jimmy. Dunne is a chubby soul, but powerful. He doesn't seem to think much of me or Mike, but maybe that's just part of the Met's standard issue arrogance. He eats a warm sausage roll from a paper bag and balances a styrofoam coffee cup between his thighs. Golden flakes of pastry shower down, a high-cholesterol snowfall.

The car glides through empty streets. The radio crackles.

Notting Hill. Holland Park.

Stucco houses. Something glossy about the whole area. A morning light, tipped with rose.

We gather on a road that encircles a church. A Gothic revival spire above us. Plane trees coming into leaf. And four cars, fluorescent orange and yellow against white, beneath. A knot of uniformed police officers, black-jacketed, smoking a pre-raid ciggy, the sweetest of the day.

Radios. Batons. Handcuffs.

A few early commuters stare.

Dunne fidgets, till he gets the confirmations he's been waiting for. 'Let's do it.'

Our little troop shakes itself back into its vehicles. The house we want is close by. A tall house at the head of a T-junction just off Ladbroke Grove. Our vehicles enter each bar of the T.

Stop in the middle of the road, lights lazily circling, blocking exits. The men in the fourth car will be entering the large communal gardens at the back of the house, securing exits from the rear.

When we're all in place – less than two minutes from leaving the church – Dunne raises a thumb and our three cars put their sirens on at the same time. Not for long, just a few whoops of policeishness released into the late-dawn morning. Just enough to rouse people from their beds. Just enough to get these lawyers and bankers, these prosperous one-percenters, aghast at the black-white-and-fluorescent intrusion into their comfortable pre-breakfast lives.

Dunne and a couple of beefy coppers hammer at the front door. A fourth guy has a megaphone at the ready. Mike and I are out of the car, stretching our legs, watching the show.

We're on delicate ground here, not that we show it. English law is fiercely against excessive use of police force. And the truth is, had we made a far more discreet appearance – two plain-clothes detectives in an unmarked car – we'd probably have achieved all we needed. But as any copper knows, the single most effective weapon in an interrogation is fear, especially fear shot through with tiredness. An arrival like ours generates both things in a way that a quieter arrival never could.

A man – pyjama bottoms, T-shirt, rumpled hair – comes to the door. A brief dialogue. Then he stands back, granting admittance.

I say to Mike, 'I'm up.'

Trot up to the house. A female PC, built like an oarswoman, comes with me. The person who answered the front door is Nellie Bentley's husband. He escorts me, Dunne and the PC upstairs. The house is four storeys, but has generous ceiling heights so it seems higher.

Family photos on the wall. Some artwork.

The husband says, 'Look, if you can just tell us what this is about . . .'

Dunne says, 'If we can just go upstairs please, sir.'

We get to the top floor.

Nellie Bentley is there. In her bedroom. Blue nightdress and a dressing gown. One of those sexy Agent Provocateur-y numbers that probably seems like a sensible fashion choice when you and your husband share the run of the top floor and a lot less sensible when there are three police officers in the room with you, two of them in uniform, the radio always crackling, and the sight of those batons and handcuffs the biggest things in your current universe.

Two children – six and eight, maybe, a boy and a girl – shelter terrified behind their mother. She keeps tweaking at the join of her silk gown, then reaches behind her to find her children's heads. The silk, the children's heads. Repetitively, to and fro.

Dunne says, 'Are you Eleanor Bentley, known as Nell or Nellie?'

'Yes.'

'We are here in connection with a murder investigation and we'd ask you to accompany us to the station for questioning.'

'Murder? I don't know—'

'Mrs Bentley, please don't say anything now as we will need to record your answers. You don't have to say anything, but be aware that it may harm your defence . . .'

He ripples on with the caution, one that he'll repeat when he's in front of a video recorder at the station. I like these moments. These incantations. Our Nicene Creed, our little liturgy.

Bentley cries, as she should. As the moment requires.

She wants to be with the kids. Comforts herself by comforting them.

Dunne says, 'I'm sure your husband can take care of the children. These officers will stay with you as you dress.'

The oarswoman PC and myself stay with Bentley. She flusters over clothes. Part of her thinks she'll be going straight on to work after all the nonsense is sorted out and her hand hovers over trim little suits and dark dresses. Another part decides to play it safe, and she goes for comfortable trousers, a warm jumper.

When Bentley goes to the bathroom, we stand outside with the door half open and I turn up the knob of the oarswoman's radio, so its mutter can be heard in the bathroom.

The funny thing – funny if you're us, not if you're Nellie Bentley – is that we aren't actually arresting her. Our requests, our politely phrased *pleases*, are meant completely literally. If she said, 'No, sorry, it's five thirty in the morning,' we'd have to decide whether to arrest her and, if so, for what. In practice, we'd most likely just arrange for her to come in for interview at a mutually convenient time, much as if she were making a dentist's appointment. But though we know that, she doesn't and she lives in a world where the coercive power of the state is alive, well and creaking the floorboards outside her bathroom door.

On the drive into Charing Cross, Bentley says, in a small white voice, 'What am I being charged with?'

Dunne: 'We haven't charged you with anything yet.'

'I get a lawyer, don't I? When do I get a lawyer?'

Dunne pauses for a few seconds. No reason for the pause, except to establish dominance. Remind her that he can do what he wants, when he wants. His gaze flicks out of the window, watching traffic, the movement of taxis. Then he tells her, briefly, she can call from the station.

She's silent a moment or two.

The car slides past Hyde Park Corner. Up the side of

Buckingham Palace, then down the Mall. Flagpoles lining the street. Geese honking in the park.

Looking down at her hands, Bentley says, 'I'll tell you everything, you know. There's really nothing. Really.'

# 23

Really nothing. In practice, everything.

In the spring, summer and early autumn of 2009, the various members of the BIA's Senior Working Group on Household and Small Business Security Threats experienced a series of improbable burglaries. Bentley. Redhead. Galton Evans. A couple of other break-ins, not reported to the police, because the items stolen were of trivial value and the damage inconsequential. There were eight members of the committee, five break-ins. Bentley's London home wasn't touched, her holiday home was. Galton Evans's Cardiff townhouse wasn't targeted, the country home he shared with Marianna Lockwood was.

The common thread to all the incidents was simply their improbability. Bentley's Holland Park home, for example, contained much more of value and was vastly easier to access than her Sussex lighthouse.

Which was the point.

In Bentley's words, spilled under interview at Charing Cross, her face pale, her voice low and fragile: 'We came into the BIA's offices for one of our regular meetings. Nothing special about it. Just a routine review. And there was all our stuff. Galton's etchings. John's wife's jewellery. The ribbon from my teddy bear. All there in a big pile on the table.

'Our meeting room was on the *tenth* floor. A *tenth*-floor

conference room with this bloody great hole in the window and the glass lying on the inside of the room.'

Along with the stolen goods, there was a note. The note, now in our hands, read as follows:

> Dear Insurance People,
>
> Here's your stuff back. As you may have noticed, I can enter any building, anywhere, any time. So far, I've avoided causing any real damage and – as you see – you haven't even lost your stuff. (Well, except for your teddy, Nellie, but it <u>is</u> rather big.)
>
> Still, I'm sure that as insurance execs, you'll have considered that someone with my talents could cause a lot of destruction. A fire in a bank's trading room. Lost artworks. Maybe an explosion here and there (only when a building is empty, of course.)
>
> Now I don't want to get nasty and I'm sure you don't want me to either. So why don't we compromise? You pay me £10,000,000 and I go away. Make the payment and you never hear from me again. Don't make the payment and I can promise you that I will inflict a minimum of £50,000,000 of damage in the month following your non-payment. Then £75,000,000 in the second month. And so on. Oh, and my fee would go up too. An extra £5,000,000 for every month you're in arrears.
>
> Does that sound like a deal? I hope so. Anyway, think about it. I'll be in touch. And please don't call the police. I wouldn't like that at all.
>
> Yours,
>
> 'The Stonemonkey'

The note was typed and printed out on ordinary paper, nothing special. The name, 'Stonemonkey', sounds like the sort of self-adulating name a serious climber might choose to give himself.

As for the threat itself, Bentley and her colleagues took it seriously. They couldn't do otherwise. Until now, they hadn't compared notes on their various break-ins. Why would they? Their meetings were strictly for business. But with their stolen goods on the table and a hole gaping in their tenth-floor window, they could hardly avoid the subject. Nor, indeed, could they avoid the conclusion that the Stonemonkey could do exactly as he claimed.

'When you think about it,' Bentley said, 'the entire structure of the security industry assumes that intruders are bound by the laws of gravity. When we advise clients on alarm systems, CCTV networks and all that, we concentrate on the ground floor and perhaps the floor above. Secure the lower levels, and the rest will take care of itself. But if you can just float in through a tenth floor window . . . no one in the country has security against that. No one.'

The committee also discussed the man's threat to cause tens of millions of pounds' worth of damage.

Bentley again, 'I mean, yes. A couple of Old Master paintings. That could be fifty million in a single pop. But that's not what disturbed us, not really. Truth is, a hit of fifty million, even a hundred million, is kind of routine in our industry. But what if the guy poured a few cans of petrol over a bank's trading floor? Or chucked anthrax in the air conditioning?

'Suppose he achieved, I don't know, a relatively small outage in a mid-sized investment bank, maybe something that took a day or two to fix. Our colleagues in the Financial Industry Risks team reckoned the costs of that kind of incident could easily run to a hundred million pounds. Maybe more. These finance industry types are merciless. If they know one of their competitors is struggling, they'll go in for the kill. Make trades that just rip that competitor apart. And if you up the ante – let's say the guy chooses to target one of the biggest banks, that he has access to explosive devices, or whatever –

you could easily, easily be looking at a billion pounds' worth of damage. He might not even *mean* to cause that much damage. But it's not something he'd be able to judge in advance, because it would depend on things he couldn't see, like a bank's particular trading position. He might aim to do fifty million pounds' worth of damage and end up costing us billions.'

All that day, Bentley and her colleagues discussed the threat. The insurance industry isn't, for good reasons, in the habit of succumbing to blackmail. On the other hand, spending a billion pounds or more on defending a point of principle seemed a little excessive. There was a risk, of course, that the first request for £10,000,000 wouldn't be the last, but given the sums involved it seemed worth taking the chance.

'And that's what we decided. To make the payment. We didn't know when he would contact us. Or how. Or which one of us he'd reach. But when he got in touch, we resolved to say yes.'

Redhead, in an interview room next to Bentley's, confirmed those details. His story was the same in all crucial respects.

Over in Cardiff, Galton Evans was being worked over by DI Watkins, an experience roughly comparable on the pleasure scale with undergoing a seven-day capture-and-interrogation exercise with the SAS. Evans did well, or thought he did, cleaving hard to his original statement, the one that ended, 'This statement is true to the best of my knowledge and belief,' with his name and his signature beneath.

By eleven in the morning, Watkins started to go gentle on him – like the others, he'd been picked up at five thirty – and he clearly started to think he'd done all he needed to do. Then Watkins played him the audio we'd recorded in Charing Cross. Bentley spilling everything. Redhead doing the same. Evans's statement being revealed as a hatful of lies and evasions.

I've watched the video of that moment. Watkins hitting the off button. Redhead's voice vanishing into nothing.

Evans swallowed once, tried to speak, then swallowed again. 'I was trying to prevent a crime,' he said eventually. 'We all were. Trying to prevent crime.'

Bentley and Redhead have both been released. They should have informed us of the Stonemonkey's blackmail threat at the time, but they had strong reasons not to do so, and a failure to inform the police of criminal acts is not in itself a crime.

Evans's case is different though. He lied, by way of a formal written statement, to an active police inquiry. His lies attempted to cover up a substantial crime and his actions were both premeditated and, as Watkins's interrogation that morning proved, persistent. Those things amount to a serious attempt to pervert the course of justice. Evans was charged before he left the station.

Neither Evans, nor Bentley, nor Redhead have anything to tell us about Livesey, about Moon, about undersea cables, about Oxwich Bay, or anything else. Ditto the various other members of the committee when we pulled them in too. Truth is, they all sounded puzzled when we asked.

According to Bentley, Redhead, and everyone else involved – including, finally, Evans – the Stonemonkey did indeed make his demand for payment. The demand came via an email from a recently created Hotmail address.

The BIA made payment of £10,000,000 to a Swiss bank account, which was listed with a number only, no name. Neither Bentley nor any of the others knew what happened thereafter, but we've found out that the money swiftly exited the Swiss account and moved on to Belize. We can't trace its movements from there.

We asked Bentley and the rest if any further blackmail demands were ever forthcoming. They said no.

We asked if they were aware of thefts or cases of criminal

damage where the Stonemonkey appeared to have been implicated. They said no.

We asked if there had been any other contacts between any of them, their companies, and the Stonemonkey. They said no.

In Bentley's words, 'He wanted a ten million pound payoff and we gave it to him. He stuck to his end of the bargain. And, look, we got it right. We helped prevent some very substantial crimes and saved ourselves money at the same time. The truth is, sorry, but I'd do it all again.'

# 24

The new information propels Zorro into a hive of busyness, but my role remains one of observation only. Watkins hands out assignments – reinterviews, CCTV analysis, number-plate tracking, forensic work – leaving not a crumb for me.

At each morning briefing, I watch the light sparkling over the ocean, then plunge back downstairs, into my world of Chicagoan darkness.

Data entry.

Data checking.

Data management.

The number of exhibits has levelled out at about four thousand two hundred. Because Dunthinking hasn't, despite his frenzy of ill-coordinated activity, managed to find a single actual lead, we have no idea which, if any, of those four thousand exhibits may strike the lethal blow in court, so we have to treat every damn one of them as sacred.

Which I do, no matter that I still want to push biros into my eyes.

Each week, I have a review session with Laura Moffatt. She is, I think, somewhat freaked by my room makeover and by my reputation, which has a certain whiff of wildness. I don't normally mind that, but I want Laura to leave me in peace. So, when I'm Chicagoing, I dress the way I think Laura would if she were my age. Not demure, exactly, but safe. Restrained. And each week, I create three folders for her. A 'Log of

Exhibits'. A 'Log of Movements'. And a 'Log of Forensic Activity'. Ifor kept similar documents – they're essential in our line of work – but he just kept them on computer and printed them off when and if he had to. I get mine printed and bound in the print room, with a red cover for the first document, green for the second, blue for the third, and each cover titled and dated.

I give Laura the bound logs, still warm from the binder, and sit with my hands either on the keyboard or on my lap as she reviews my work. On the table with the HOLMES terminal, I have a packet of digestive biscuits, a line-up of pens in different colours, and some hand lotion. I don't use any of those things, but it gives the table a tidy feel.

In the early days, she used to take individual exhibits and check I had dealt with them correctly. Back then, I used to answer her questions from memory – I have good recall for stuff like that – but I realised that Laura was unnerved by that ability, so now I just go to the data itself and review it on screen. As she's come to trust me, our sessions have become ever briefer and less formal.

Once she indicated my picture wall and said, 'I'm amazed you can work with all that staring down at you.'

I answered, primly, 'I think it's important to remember why we're here. Why it matters.'

There's one new addition in my picture gallery. A picture, a modern artist's impression, of Eilmer of Malmesbury, an eleventh-century monk who built himself a pair of wings and hurled himself off a tower at Malmesbury Abbey. A chronicler recorded that he flew for about a furlong – two hundred metres – but '*agitated by the violence of the wind and a current of air, as well as the consciousness of his rash attempt, he fell and broke both his legs, and was lame ever after. He used to relate as the cause of the failure that he had forgotten to provide himself with a tail.*'

I like that story. The crazy adventure of it. Its basic success: had anyone ever flown so far before? And most of all, I like its wistful conclusion, a lifetime of lameness and all for want of a tail.

Laura stares but says nothing.

Our session goes well, as they always do. And – Lord be praised – I do now get to work in peace and quiet. Hours and even days go by with no interruption, apart from the odd visit from Dunthinking, offers of tea from Laura, a hatful of phone enquiries from various people connected with the inquiry.

Better still, I've discovered that the drying machine in the corner of my room vents into the building's general waste air extraction system. If and when I feel the need, I put my head into the machine, pull the glass front down as far as it'll go and light up a joint, with the fan set to maximum. I don't even hide my joints. Just package them up in an evidence bag and leave them on the exhibits shelves with everything else. If anyone needs to enter, they have to knock. Which means that, except that my hair sometimes has a somewhat herbal perfume, I'm as safe from detection as I can reasonably expect, give that I'm in the heart of a busy police headquarters.

Carolyn Sharma does call me, at crazy hours of the night, but I like her calls. Look forward to them.

But still. Those things ameliorate the awfulness. They do not give me what I want, which is a release from Chicago and a proper role on Zorro.

Then, one day, the Thursday of the week following the raids, Jackson comes down to my basement. Watkins occupies the corridor behind. It's Jackson's first time down here. He takes in my nest of cushions, my photo wall. Says, 'This is nice.'

I agree wholeheartedly.

Unlike Watkins and Laura Moffatt – and indeed, anyone

else who has set foot in here – he examines the pictures up close.

'Mary Langton, yes. She's hard to forget, isn't she?' He's referring to her head, her blackly dripping head, that I recovered from a barrel of oil in what is still probably my best ever moment in CID. 'And Khalifi here. What was his name? Ali. A silly bastard, that one. And this pair, the Mancinis. Poor little devil,' he says, meaning the girl, April, who was six when she died. I have to help him remember the names of Stacey Edwards and Mark Mortimer, but he's right on the money with Hayley Morgan and Nia Lewis. Saj Kureishi, too. The pictures of Livesey and Moon he studies without speaking. I don't have a full-face picture of Moon up for some reason. Just various shots of the blows to his skull, his face an awkwardly obstructive intrusion to an otherwise tidy anatomical view.

The only pictures I have that aren't of corpses are the sketch of my flying monk and the daffodils on Moon's grave.

Once he's done he stares at me.

A Jacksonian silence. Wind moving over ice.

In the end, he just says, 'OK, lunch. You, me, Rhiannon.'

We walk to a restaurant on The Friary.

A nice day. A summer's day – or our own skittishly unreliable version of one anyway.

But I can't make sense of it. The continued existence of the outside world always weirds me out after long hours spent in my dungeon. It's as though I emerge from below with no particular belief that the season will be the same or even that the basic frame of place and time will have endured through my absence. I honestly think that if, after working eight hours in the basement, I stepped outside to find the cars and vans of 2013 Cardiff replaced by pedlars and horse-drawn carts, or hooded men riding by torchlight, or if I found that the city had somehow leaped forward into an age of jetpacks and hover-cars, I wouldn't really be surprised.

At the Boulevard de Nantes, Jackson flings out an arm to stop me from stepping straight out into the traffic. When it is safe to cross, he asks, 'The exhibits role. You enjoying that at all, or are you still finding it hard going?'

That is, I realise, a perfectly good question. An appropriate question from a boss to a subordinate, nicely pitched between the personal and the professional. But I can't find a tune in my head to match the one he's playing. I'm mostly just aware of the din of traffic, these sadly non-flying cars.

All I can find to say is, 'The exhibits thing. Yes. No, it's OK. I'm managing, anyway.' A response which crams every shade of answer into a few grammatically mangled words.

We get to the restaurant.

Glass and steel. A menu full of no doubt tempting and nutritionally satisfying choices. A waiter who does the things that waiters do.

I order a salad, because I know I like salads. Jackson has a burger, a fancy one. Watkins has fish of some sort. The grown-ups talk amongst themselves while I sip a sparkling water and try to remember who I am and where and when and why.

I get there, or near enough. Say, 'Sorry. I get absorbed in stuff, then it takes me time to . . .'

I wave my hands instead of finishing the sentence. To me, the gesture means, 'remember that we don't have jetpacks.' I don't know what it means to them.

Jackson says, 'OK. Well, Fiona. Congratulations.'

'Congratulations?'

For a moment, I don't know what he's talking about. Then remember that I had an email from the OSPRE people, which I didn't open because it looked boring.

'You passed,' Jackson tells me.

'Oh. Good.'

'Seventy-eight per cent. An excellent score. Really excellent. Congratulations.'

I make out that I'm delighted. I don't know if I am, though. Not really. I didn't want to take their damn exam in the first place.

Jackson wants to order three glasses of champagne, but I remind him that I don't drink, and he cancels the order with a frisson of annoyance.

Watkins congratulates me too. I say thank you, pretending to care, and they accept my thanks, pretending not to notice that I'm only pretending to care, and then, to our joint relief, Jackson changes the subject.

'Moon. Livesey. Evans. Plas Du.'

'Yes.'

'Question one. How the hell – no, no, correct that – how the *bloody* hell did you know to investigate the affairs of some totally obscure insurance committee? Just what exact process led you to that particular group of people?'

'The exact process? Um, shaking every tree I could find. The thing is, I knew he was lying to us, so I just went on digging.'

Watkins: 'How did you know he was lying? He was holding back, clearly, but that's not the same as actual lies.'

And we get into it all. My reasoning on the case so far. Why I was so sure that Evans was lying. The procedures that weren't followed. The artwork that wasn't authenticated. The clues that said Evans's story was basically a lie.

Explain these things and eat my salad, which tastes nice, except that it's like a car crash of fashionable health foods. Edamame beans and artichoke hearts. Pumpkin seeds and quinoa. It's like someone figured out which ingredients were most voguish among health-faddy urban professional types, then dumped the whole lot into a bowl. Lime juice, coriander leaves, done.

I look at Jackson's chips and wonder if he would mind if I stole one.

He says, 'OK. You decided Evans was concealing something and you decided to go down every possible path until you found what that thing was.'

'Yes, exactly that. Yes.'

And I explain my whole reasoning on the case so far. The evidence that persuaded me to look at the lichens at Plas Du. The reason why I thought Moon's death looked climbery. The absence of plausible motives, which made me wonder about the installation at Oxwich Bay. The process of widening enquiry that led me to Livesey and Bristol and the realisation, with Mike's help, that what looked impossible was in fact very doable.

Because I'm intent on sculpting my answer into the sort of thing that junior constables are meant to say to their wise, if grizzled, superiors, I also, without really noticing, steal and eat one of his chips.

'Sorry,' I say, when I do notice.

He ignores the theft and says, 'OK. So far, so good. Now, any ideas on why a climber who scams ten million quid from some insurance folk should have an interest in transatlantic telecoms?'

'No. I mean, I doubt if he knows anything at all about telecoms.'

'Any ideas on who he is?'

'No.'

'Anything linking this climber with, I don't know, the cable company? Any telecoms companies? Anyone in that line of business?'

'No.'

He asks some more questions along similar lines. I answer them honestly, but always in the negative. I do reiterate my strong suspicions regarding Galton Evans and Idris Gawr, but my actual evidence is, I'm aware, very scanty.

At the end of my little grilling, Jackson exchanges a look

with Watkins. I realise something about this lunch. The reason why they've taken me to a restaurant to have this conversation, instead of just summoning me upstairs.

No doubt the congratulations thing was part of it, the thwarted champagne. But it was also because they've learned that I have to be treated like a difficult witness in a murder case. Not a suspect precisely, but one whose openness and truthfulness cannot be taken for granted. This lunch, this fancy salad and the occasional stolen chip, is aimed at getting me to drop my defences, to be a better officer.

I share that general aim. I really do.

I say, 'I think it might help if we spoke to the cable people.'

Watkins: 'We agree. Are there particular lines of inquiry you think we should pursue?'

'Yes.' I explain where I think we should direct our questions.

'Anything else we should be thinking about?'

'Well, ma'am, I think it might be quite a good idea to arrest this climber.'

To my right, I can see Jackson smiling.

Watkins's face doesn't flicker. It just says, 'We've got one out-of-date Hotmail address. We've got some marks on a girder in Bristol, but nothing that gives us DNA or a fingerprint. No CCTV. No witness statements. No one who has ever seen or spoken to the individual. We can't track the money. We can't connect him to any other crimes. No police force has any intelligence to offer. We don't know the most basic things about him: age, nationality, anything. We don't actually even know that he's a "he".'

I try eating a bit more salad as she's speaking, but the thing seems suddenly very complicated, more complicated than I can manage. I look longingly at Jackson's little white bowl of chips. He says, 'Christ,' and shifts them over.

I take one and say, 'Obviously, it's full steam ahead on Chicago.'

A Jacksonian rumble echoes, 'Obviously.'

'And I wouldn't want to get in the way of the inquiry proper, but . . .'

'But?'

'I think I can find him, if you let me look.'

Jackson looks at me. I feel the red dot of Watkins's gaze on my forehead. They'll want to know more, of course. The *No flying solo, Fiona* rubric still applies, as it always will. But they're going to say yes. They can't do otherwise.

Even when I explain what's involved, they give me permission to go ahead. Better than that, they formalise things. Watkins allocates me a role as Research Officer on Zorro, the first designation that actually ties me into the inquiry proper.

'Thank you,' I say. 'Thank you.'

I feel almost breathless with relief.

'Part time, mind,' Jackson cautions. 'Chicago still comes first. The jumping up and down on your head bit still applies, OK?'

'OK,' I tell him. But I'm happy, almost shakily so, like a prisoner granted leave to appeal, like a parole applicant hearing the word, 'Yes.' If I were the crying sort, I think I'd rush to the Ladies, and do that whole teary, blinky, eye-patting, mascara-renewing thing that other, more ordinary, people do. As it is, I just blink and say, 'Thank you, thank you.'

'OK. Now, is there anything else we should know? Anything else at all?'

A truthful answer to that question would technically include a statement to the effect that Cesca Evans is receiving – and rejecting – the sum of £4,000 a month, paid to her by a father whose name she rejects and who, apparently, she never sees.

But technicalities aren't really my thing. Instead, I say, 'I think it might be a good idea to watch ships entering or leaving ports in Wales. Also Bristol. Ideally ports in the south-west and Ireland as well.'

'The *ports*?'

It's Jackson's question, but the same enquiry lights Watkins's face as well.

'Some ships have the capacity to lay, lift, and repair cable. Most don't. I think we should watch the ones that do.'

'Fiona—'

'The cable is part of this. No one's stealing survey data just for the fun of it.'

'Fiona, first things first. You and Rhiannon can go and talk to the cable people. We'll let you hunt for this climber boy. If and when there's evidence calling for further action, we'll take it. Until then, just cool it.'

That's stupid, I think. We have two dead people. What are they, if not evidence? But I don't protest and Jackson leads us back to the office.

When we get to the lifts, I start to look for the red lamps, meaning 'Down', while my elders and betters are looking for the pale blue of 'Up'. But Jackson has a second thought about something and points me up to his office with a bass grunt and a jab of his finger.

I go with him. He has door-open and door-closed meetings. I don't know which this is, but close the door anyway.

'Fiona. I've spoken to Laura. She tells me your work has been first class. Really excellent.'

I nod. Say thank you.

'And your exam. Seventy-eight per cent. Not quite the best score we've ever had, but it's right up there.'

I nod. I know what this is about now.

'There are four main areas covered by that exam. Crime. Evidence and Procedure. General Police Duties. And Road Policing.'

'Yes, sir.'

'The areas aren't completely distinct, so, for example, a

question on evidence might also demand knowledge that relates to general police duties. Do you follow me?'

'Yes, sir.'

'Nevertheless, the examiners sometimes break down the results for us by subject, so we can see the areas where officers might have strengths or weaknesses. An interesting exercise.'

I've run out of 'sir's, so I just nod along.

'Would you like to know your results?' He picks up a sheet of paper. 'Crime. You scored a hundred per cent. I've never seen that before. Evidence and Procedure, ninety-six per cent. Again, astonishing. Never seen anything close. General Police Duties, not quite so strong, but still: eighty-eight per cent takes some doing.'

He stops.

Looks at me.

I open my hands. What does he want? He told me to pass the exam and I've passed his damn exam. I really don't see that I've earned a bollocking. He was trying to give me champagne an hour or two ago.

'Road Policing. Twenty-eight questions. You scored exactly zero. No marks at all.'

'I don't like traffic policing. Sorry.'

'So you scored zero?'

'I just thought – if I ever get into trouble, if you ever decide to chuck me out of CID, I *might* be able to cope in uniform, but not in roads, I wouldn't stand a chance.'

'So you thought if you ballsed up that side of the exam completely enough, you'd be protected. The traffic department would never take someone who had performed that badly.'

I shrug. *I* wouldn't take me, not if I were a traffic cop.

Jackson drums briefly, then throws the paper away.

'OK, Fiona. I just needed to know.'

I stand up. I think that's the end of whatever this thing is. He nods dismissal.

But as I'm at his door, he stops me again.

'Of course, there might be a flaw in your plan. It's multiple choice, isn't it? So if you were just guessing at random, you'd have got a few questions right. And, see, a cynical mind like mine might think you knew all the answers perfectly well, just didn't put them down on paper. So, if I wanted to bust you down to Roads, I'd probably go ahead and do it anyway.'

I go down after that, but thoughtfully.

The whole Acting Deputy Exhibits Officer nonsense. This promotion to sergeant thing. I realise: Jackson actually needs me to do this. To do the grunt work, to get the promotion. It's his way of telling me that he needs me to be more than a gifted individual investigator. He's trying to make a police officer out of me. A proper one.

I have a strange moment of double vision. One half of me wants to be the officer Jackson wants me to become. The other half thinks I'll achieve that happy state at just about the time I get my first hover-car. The two visions co-exist for a brief moment, like when two soap bubbles join, but still exist as two things, not one.

Then the vision collapses. The bubbles burst.

I pick up the phone and make a call. My first act as Research Officer on Operation Zorro.

# 25

King Street, London. St James's Square. A flamingo's flap from Buckingham Palace.

A grand stucco-fronted townhouse. Window boxes and clipped topiary. A front door so glossily black it might have been stolen from the entrance to hell. I half expect it to be opened by a goat-legged gentleman with a tufted beard and an elegant tail, a low whiff of sulphur on the air behind.

No goat legs, no sulphur.

A receptionist buzzes us in. There's some messing about with signing in. I do nothing to help, but somebody gives me a plastic badge anyway. I put it in my pocket.

We sit and wait. Cream and blue sofas in a Regency stripe. A clock, antique or a good imitation, sits on a mantelpiece and ticks. The receptionist, who is tiny, sits at a large green-leather desk and looks at a computer screen. On the wall, there's a photo of a ship with a huge cable carousel at its stern.

White ship, blue waters.

Watkins stabs out emails on her phone.

Findlay and Creamer are here too. They talk together in low voices. A murmurous hush.

I stare at the receptionist, trying to decide if she's actually doing anything on the computer or just waiting for us to leave.

A young man, my age or a little younger, enters. Blue suit, pink shirt, dark tie, no tail.

'Four of you? Gosh. Do come up. Was your trip up all

right? Did you come by car? No? Quite right, parking's awful, isn't it?'

He leads us upstairs into a conference room, big Georgian windows overlooking the street. Mahogany table. Another clock.

There are three more business types in the room, employees of Atlantic Cables.

Coffees. Business cards.

The job titles are meaningless, at least to me. *Strategic Director, Projects*, says one. *Chief Investment Officer*, says another. The young navy blue suit guy is just *Charles Warren, Project Associate*, which I think is private-sector-speak for *Nobody*.

We coppers have no business cards, so we just give names and ranks, like captured servicemen.

James Harding, the strategic director, seems the most senior of this bunch. At any rate it's he who opens his hands and says, 'So. How can we help?'

Watkins gives him a brief background, concluding, 'In short, there have been two suspicious deaths in connection with your cable. We have evidence that your marine surveyor was murdered. We are currently also regarding the death of Derek Moon, your former security guard, as murder. We're looking for any information you can give us as to why these men were killed.'

For half an hour, thirty minutes ticked out in Regency elegance, Harding gives us fluff.

He deeply regrets any loss of life on the project. He never knew Mr Moon, but understood him to be widely liked by those staff who had met him. Mr Livesey had already done some very useful work. His death struck the whole firm as a tragic accident.

'Not an accident,' says Watkins. 'Murder.'

'I'd understood it was being treated as suicide.'

Findlay: 'It was. We obtained new evidence.'

'I'm very sorry to hear that. The family has already had our condolences, but . . .'

Watkins: 'Mr Harding, they don't need your condolences. They need your cooperation. Were you ever made aware of any threat to Mr Livesey's life?'

'No, certainly not.'

'Threats to other employees or contractors?'

'No, none.'

'Threats of a more general nature? Threats which, with hindsight, could have carried a suggestion of violence?'

'No.'

'Can you think of anyone with a motive to kill Mr Livesey?'

'No.'

'Or Mr Moon?'

'No.'

'Following Mr Moon's death, you shifted the cable's intended route from Oxwich Bay in Wales to Highbridge in Somerset. Why?'

Harding, careful now, picks his way through an answer. He says that additional survey data suggested that the Somerset route might be better than first thought. Also that new land-based telecoms investment in that area tilted the balance.

My job, and Creamer's, is to take notes. I hope Creamer is better than I am, because I keep forgetting to write, preferring to stare at the men opposite. Nice suits, nice shirts, nice manners. And somewhere close, a river running ankle-deep in blood.

I feel the presence of the dead men, Moon and Livesey, quite acutely at times like these. Too acutely, a constant pressure. It's like those no-pull dog harnesses, which twist the animal around if they start to pull on the lead. The stronger the investigative scent in the room, the more I feel tugged sideways. I know I have to close my eyes, make real contact with the dead, before I can shift my attention elsewhere.

So I do. Close my eyes. Think of that jagged Himalayan rock which split Moon's skull.

Think of Livesey, swinging from a gallery in a corporate rental.

Think of Sharma sitting, white-faced, by her dead beloved.

The process settles me, and though the dead men still seem more real than the rest, I'm better able to concentrate. Watkins glares a couple of times, but I don't care. I've got my deflector shields up.

When I tune back in, Watkins is saying, 'Mr Harding, are you telling me that Mr Moon's death made no difference to your decision to shift the route? We will take a formal written statement later and I should advise you we already have one person on a charge of perverting the course of justice.'

Her question forces Harding into a half-retraction of his earlier comments. This time, he says, 'There *was* new survey data, yes. And the new investment in Horndean made a difference. But I suppose we also thought . . . Look, you have to realise what we do. When we go live, we will offer the fastest cable across the Atlantic, bar none. That's our promise to our customers. We will be the fastest cable in operation, full stop. If we don't live up to that promise, we will either discount our charges by as much as ninety per cent or we will let customers walk away from their contract. If we're not the fastest, everything we've done here will be a waste of time.'

'So?'

'The installation which Derek Moon looked after contained some computer equipment. There was survey data there, including a route map. Not all of it, because we didn't have it then. Just the coastal part of the cable, the part which goes out into the Irish Sea. When Moon died, we felt obliged to reconsider our security arrangements. It struck us that we had been unwise to leave our route maps in a place where they were vulnerable to attack. So we switched the route for technical reasons, yes, but also a security concern.'

One of the things that makes Watkins effective as an interrogator is her lack of gradations. Her freedom from the normal human dance of acknowledgement and response.

'So you are correcting your previous answer?' she notes. 'You are stating that anyone with a desire to steal your route maps might have had a motivation to kill Mr Moon. Correct?'

Harding first of all tries to square his answers up. Make it sound like he was saying the same thing all along. Watkins's driving insistence soon obliges him to say, 'OK, well then, yes. OK. In theory. That's very theoretical.'

'Moon had the necessary keys or, I don't know, codes?'

'Yes, he would have done.'

'Those route maps. How much value was locked up in them? How much were they worth?'

Harding, happy at finding himself back on safer ground, gives a lengthy answer. I don't think he's flannelling, just trying to explain to us how his industry works.

In short: Atlantic Cables expect to spend around three hundred million dollars on laying their cable and commissioning it. The vast bulk of that money will be spent on the physical works itself. Buying cable. Laying it. Digging it in. Plugging it in at both ends. Making sure that all the computer stuff is working right. 'We've already started that work, working west to east, so the New York side of things is already done. The deep Atlantic part is in process now. Then we just hook up the British end and we're done. We'll be live in two months.'

Watkins asks about the mapping and Harding says, 'Yes, that's important. Those route maps are our intellectual property. Our best effort to find the shortest, fastest path across the ocean. Now I think we've done a pretty good job. We're satisfied that we're at the limits of current technology.

'But what if things change? Let's say, we've figured out the best route across ninety per cent or more of the ocean. Three thousand miles or so. But what if new survey data comes along which tells us that we've got the very last part wrong? Suppose there's a route which could take a millisecond, half a millisecond even, off our time? That millisecond would kill us. Somebody could just drop a copycat cable down for the ninety per cent that we've already figured out, make a tweak to our configuration on the final stage and *bang!* – our business has disappeared. That's what we can't let happen.'

He finishes speaking.

People shift in their seats, or I think they do. I feel Moon and Livesey so strongly now, I want to get up and look for them. It actually bothers me that we are in a clean, nicely lit room, with a shiny mahogany table and a clock ticking on the mantelpiece. I'd prefer to be at the graveside or, better still, with the corpses themselves. It would be harder for Harding to lie if there was a dead man leaking his brains out on the table.

I say, pen poised over my pad and with a bland, even simple, expression on my face, 'So, Mr Harding, what you are saying is that the loss of your route maps might have threatened your three hundred million dollar business?'

Harding doesn't like the question, but he's already impaled by Watkins's gaze, and he has nowhere to go, so he just says, 'Yes, correct.'

'And Derek Moon had access to some portion – some important portion – of those route maps. Correct?'

'Yes.'

'So Derek Moon probably didn't know it, but the future of your three hundred million dollar business lay partly in his hands. Correct?'

Harding's voice is croaky now, but he manages a 'Yes, correct.' I can feel more than see Findlay grinning to my right. Watkins doesn't grin, she just bulldozes. She rips into the next line of questioning without pause.

'You selected Ian Livesey for a portion of the survey only? He didn't handle the whole thing?'

'No. If you draw a north–south line from Llanelli in South Wales to Barnstaple in Devon, Livesey handled everything west of that, basically the ocean side of that line, until the edge of the continental shelf. We had a local Bristol firm handle the estuary itself. That's territory they already know very well. We had a large contractor handle the deep ocean. One further firm handled the shallow waters on the New York side.'

'Why? Why subdivide the assignment like that?'

Harding seeks to fudge the issue, but Watkins chews up people like him without even blunting her blades.

It's not long before Harding is saying, 'Yes, OK. Post-Moon, we had to consider security. We didn't think there was a leak. We weren't aware of one. We use *highly* encrypted data-storage techniques. Not even my colleagues here—'

'You are telling me that you divided the assignment so that no one contractor had access to *all* the data? That they couldn't leak it if they wanted to?'

'Correct.' Harding's voice is tired now. Beaten. He glances sideways at the Nobody in a blue suit, who gets up and fetches water. Harding starts to say, 'That wasn't the only reason. There were operational considerations—', but Watkins isn't interested.

'Ian Livesey was an unusual choice of contractor, wasn't he? A solo operator. Had to charter a boat, because he didn't own one. No previous experience in the Atlantic south of Ireland.'

Harding resists, but defeat is soon forthcoming. 'Yes, we thought a one-man band was going to be less leaky than a big firm. And Livesey was a tough guy. An ex-Marine. We thought he couldn't be bullied or bought.'

'And when you heard of his death?'

'We thought, poor guy. I liked him. Anyone who met him—'

'Don't patronise me, Mr Harding. When you heard of his death, it must have occurred to you that this was a repeat of the Moon situation.'

'The thought occurred to us, yes.'

'And occurred to you, specifically?'

'Yes.'

'And you shared that thought with the coroner?'

'No.'

'With the Avon and Somerset Constabulary? Or the South Wales Police?'

'No.'

'If not you, then any of your colleagues?'

'No.'

'So you personally and you collectively chose to withhold evidence from a police investigation into a violent death? Evidence that might have tipped that inquiry into taking seriously the possibility of murder?'

Harding doesn't answer. How can he? He just opens his hands. I think the gesture is partly admitting the charge. But partly also defending himself. It's a gesture which says, 'I'm a senior executive of, and shareholder in, a three-hundred-million-dollar company that uses some pretty fancy technology to service some pretty fancy clients. And you really expect me to run along to a bunch of provincial coppers every time our business hits a little roadbump?'

I arrange my face back into bland 'n' simple mode and, pen hovering over my pad, say, 'Sorry, Mr Harding, but Inspector Watkins will want me to have a full record of your answer. She asked, "Did you personally choose to withhold evidence from a police investigation?" Shall I put "Yes" for that?'

I look young for my age, or I'm told I do anyway, and it doesn't take much to tip my natural accent into a kind of comedy Welsh. The sort of slightly exaggerated sing-song that arouses smiles among London professional types. In any case, my version of Young Welsh Simpleton makes a good foil for Watkins's bruising directness.

Harding tries to answer, can't, nods, recovers his voice, says, 'Yes.'

'And your colleagues. You collectively as a firm. You chose to withhold evidence from a police investigation? I'll put "Yes" for that too, shall I?'

'Yes.'

'And you were and are aware that your evidence could have changed the course of a police inquiry into a violent death, a death which we are now treating as murder? Shall I put—'

'Yes. Yes. Yes, we got it wrong. I'm sorry.'

From that point on, we have them surrounded and they know it. Our guns on the hills, their little settlement defenceless below.

Watkins takes occupation. Findlay – enjoying the show – struts along behind.

'We'll need complete customer lists,' says Watkins. 'Everyone who's signed up with you. Everyone who's been approached. Everyone who's ever received technical data from you.'

'Our customer lists. Those are *very* commercially sensitive. They—'

Harding runs straight into Watkins's stare. Her jaw. The barrels of her guns. He says, 'Of course. Of course. We'll give you everything.'

And they do. Findlay and Watkins demand documents, get them, add more requests to an ever-swelling list. Creamer and I, the Project Associates of the policing world, trot wherever our elders and betters direct us.

We don't even know what information we're looking for. Don't even know that it lurks within these stuccoed walls, behind that glossy door. But the smell of blood is stronger now. Visceral and thick. We can feel it clotting on our hands and clothes, feel the stick of it gumming our hair, squelching inside our city shoes.

I feel those things easily anyway. Too easily. But I'm not the only one now. Death's dark wing hovers over our little company and Harding and his fellows are not loving the experience.

Watkins also homes in on the big unanswered question of the hour. Are there, in fact, any rival cable companies competing to build a superfast cable? Is there, in fact, a group of people who might, even now, be profiting from any stolen data?

Harding is emphatic in his response.

'No. Nobody.'

Watkins: 'How can you be sure?'

Harding's answer is long, but remains confident, even under interrogation. Basically, laying an Atlantic cable is a big deal. It involves too many people, too many contractors and specialisms, for it to remain quiet. 'We spent three years putting the operation together before we dropped so much as an inch of cable,' says Harding. 'And we must have talked to literally thousands of people in that time. Investors, clients, telecoms companies, a whole bunch of IT companies, marine engineers, surveyors, a whole bunch of sub-sea specialisms. You just can't keep that lot quiet. Not a chance. Not a chance in hell.'

Watkins doesn't respond directly, but she shoots me a glance and I know what she's thinking. She's thinking that the main reason Harding and his merry men didn't contact the police when Livesey died was that they believed they were past the danger point. They were about to complete their damn cable without a competitor in sight. They'd plotted their route, dropped most of their cable, encrypted their data, divided the assignment. Even if a would-be competitor had coerced Livesey to reveal what he knew, he only knew a tiny fraction of the whole. He knew too little to be worth worrying about.

So why call the police? That would just have introduced a headache they didn't need. Sure, they contemplated the possibility that their dear colleague had been murdered for his knowledge, but they thought, what the fuck, we've won this game anyway. Let's just go and make some money.

Nice guys.

Harding and his merry men. Nice guys.

We work all day, breaking into teams, collecting documents. Making arrangements for further documents to be sent to Cathays and Portishead, the Bristol HQ. We arrange for data sharing too. Our security procedures are, in fact, excellent and Harding's reservations about the ability of a bunch of provincial coppers to handle his data confidentially start to dissipate as we work with him on the detail.

In an upstairs room, Warren starts to print off customer lists.

I ask, 'What's your timing? When does the cable go live?'

He says, 'Everything will be laid by the end of June. The connection centres are both ready, so it should be pretty much plug and play. July's set aside for testing, sorting out any gremlins. We start to carry customer traffic in August.'

'Gremlins,' I say, huskily. 'You do expect some niggles, do you?'

Warren shrugs. 'Basically yes. Think of this as a giant IT project. You have to have a beta-phase before launch. That's when you want your cock-ups to happen.'

It's already the second week of June. If the bad guys are to make their play, they have, I reckon, about seven weeks in which to do it.

Seven weeks *at most.* A mere scrap of time in which to make my doing-things-police-style plan work out.

And how's that going, Griffiths? The whole by-the-book thing?

Warren hands me sheets still warm from the printer.

Client lists.

Investment banks. Hedge funds. Names I recognise and names I don't.

But one that I do. One that belches a little stink of greed, violence and theft.

Grim-faced, I take the lists down to Watkins, who is doing something horrible enough to Harding that his face is tense and pale.

'May I have a moment, ma'am? Sorry.'

She sprays us both with an omnipurpose glare and tells Harding to wait outside. A lovely touch that, I think: to order someone out of his own room because she wants privacy.

'Yes?'

I show her the customer lists. Ring the name that caught my eye.

Idris Gawr Investments LP.

'It's Galton Evans's investment fund, ma'am.'

'Is it now?'

'And the name,' I say, tapping it.

'Yes?'

'Idris Gawr. I mean, that's a perfectly ordinary choice for a Welsh company, in one way.'

'But?'

'The cliff where Derek Moon fell. It had four climbing routes going up it. The hardest and most famous is Critterling. The easiest and most popular is Crack and Slab. But there's another route, on the same cliff, Idris Gawr.'

Watkins doesn't say anything, but she breathes fire and kills small animals for fun. Her look now makes words redundant.

I add, 'Moon died in late September 2011. Idris Gawr Investments LP was formed in November of that same year.'

'That's circumstantial,' she murmurs.

'Yes, but the kind of circumstantial that never lies.'

'Do we know who else is an investor in that company?'

'No. I've looked. It's all offshore bullshit.'

Watkins normally rebukes me when I swear, but not now.

'Of course, he's a finance guy,' she says. 'Insurance. For all we know . . .'

'Yes, the others on that committee. Maybe their firms connect to this cable as well. More than possible. I can look, if you want, when we get back to Cardiff.'

'No. You're on Chicago. But yes, I'll get someone to look.'

That's a disappointment, but not a grievous one. I wanted to be in the thick of it, and here I am: so in the thick of it that my ankles feel claggy with blood.

I work hard all day, but do nip out a couple of times, once for a cigarette, once for a sandwich and something to drink. The sandwich shop is pretty fancy, so I end up walking out with a mango smoothie and a warm chicken, chorizo and butternut squash wrap. It's tasty and I think, *I should learn how to make a sandwich like this*, then remember that I'm an atrocious cook and dismiss the idea.

At five thirty that evening, we're winding up. I look for my phone and can't find it. Not in my bag. Not in reception. Not in the main meeting room or the desk that I've been using this afternoon.

I find Creamer.

'Luke, you lost your phone recently. You mentioned it at it that meeting in Cardiff.'

'Yes?'

'When? When did you lose it?'

'Oh, I've got a new one now. Insurance covered it, luckily.'

'When? Sorry, I need to know.'

Answer: a day or so after our trip to that Bristol apartment.

'And how was it lost? Was it stolen, or do you remember leaving it somewhere, on a train or anything like that?'

Answer: no, he didn't remember leaving it anywhere. Maybe it was stolen, maybe not.

I don't remember leaving my phone anywhere either. Thinking back, there was a little crush at the door to the sandwich shop. An ordinary city-centre jostle, but in that jostle, I think, there lurked a theft.

I borrow a phone and walk out onto the street.

My mam and dad hold a key to my house. So does Buzz. Penry doesn't, but I did teach him to pick my front door lock, so he's an option too..

Dad. Buzz. Penry.

There are objections to calling any one of them, but I light on Buzz as the least bad option.

Call him.

He answers. He's leaving work, going off to the gym.

I say, 'Buzz, I'm really sorry, can I ask a favour?'

'Probably. What's up?'

I tell him. Say I'm worried that someone is seeking to obtain data on a confidential inquiry. That I'm worried about the security of my home computer.

'Have you spoken to Watkins? She could get a couple of uniforms.'

I don't want that, no. Partly, I can't see Watkins authorising the effort. Two stolen phones: it's hardly compelling evidence. But partly also there's material in my house which I wouldn't want any formal police investigation to get close to.

I say that, adding that my phone has access to my emails. Also to my home wi-fi. And my home computer will have stored passwords that could give access to police files. A security no-no, of course, but plenty of my colleagues do the same.

A sigh.

A long, fat Buzzian sigh.

'OK, Fi, I'll get over there.' Asks if I fancy like a late supper.

I hesitate.

He says, 'We're friends, Fi. We can risk supper now and again.'

I say, 'Buzz, sorry, that would be lovely. I'd love to see you.'

And I would, except that the caverns of our loneliness yawn beneath us. I hope that Buzz meets someone soon, starts dating. I'll find that hard, but it'll feel better to know that he's OK, or I imagine it will anyway.

As for me: I don't know. I don't know what rescues me.

I hang up.

On the train home with Watkins, we sit opposite each other. Faces reflected in the glass. The world slides past us. A world of back gardens, closeboard fencing and trackside weeds.

Watkins settles a scarf at the side of her head, ready to snooze, but before she closes her eyes, she says, 'That was productive.'

I say, 'Yes.'

She used the correct policeish term, I suppose, but I don't think she spoke quite as she meant.

I add, 'And bloody good fun.'

She smiles. 'Yes, it was, wasn't it?'

Then sleeps.

And when the train slides underneath the River Severn, she's still sleeping so I can't tell her about Alexander Lambert and his flooded tunnel.

The loneliest place in the world. Total darkness and total submersion.

# 26

Home.

Front of the house: normal.

Open the door. All normal.

Put the hall light on.

Normal.

Not so normal: Buzz at the top of the stairs. Limping. Blood and water down the side of his face. Blood on his jeans. A grin hanging lopsidedly, like a broken door.

'I'm fine,' he says, 'I'm really fine.'

I rush upstairs, awash with emotions I can't name.

And he *is* fine, he really is. I tug Buzz into the bathroom, remembering the big male weight of him, the heft of his arms. I make him sit on the edge of the bath and dab at his face with water and face cleanser and cotton wool. Do a better job than he was doing or would have done, but the truth is there are only two cuts – on his lip and just under his ear – which have bled, and they're neither of them deep or serious. I clean them up, put sticking plaster on the cut by his ear, tell him that he's going to have some nasty bruises.

On my orders, Buzz drops his trousers so I can attend to the gash on his leg. As I kneel in front of him, he tells me what happened.

He came over more or less directly after I called. Let himself in. Removed my computer and router from the house. Put them in his car and drove far enough away that no casual searcher would be able to link his car to my house. Came back to get some supper ready. 'It was all quite clean and tidy,' he comments, with a note of impressed surprise.

Then he heard movement at the door. Assumed it was me. Opened up. There were two men, some shouting, a short fight. 'I hit one of them quite hard. I think there'll be some blood anyway. Then tried to get a piece of the other, but . . .' He shrugs. 'It was two against one.'

He has that simple male way of talking about violence, as though there's nothing more at stake than the outcome of a rugby match. You want the red team to win, but then the blue team gets a try, and what can you do, that's just how it is.

I'm still down on my knees with my water and cotton wool, but his leg is fine, really, and there's nothing much for me to do. I'm exquisitely aware that my head is just eighteen inches from Buzz's boxer shorts. He's semi-hard inside them, and I'd only need to reach out, to lean my head in, and we'd be back to where we were. In lust. In love. An inch away from starting all that again.

I want to do it. Really do. Feel a physical ache as I've not experienced for six months now.

But I don't do it, or don't quite. I just lean my head against the sink, leave a hand on his knee, and say, 'Oh, Buzz. Oh Buzzling. I'm sorry.'

Don't even know what I'm sorry for, but he strokes my shoulder and lets me lie there and I say, 'Did they hurt you? Do you feel OK?' and he says 'Fine, I'm really fine,' and then we just stay there some more. When I do lift my head, I see that 'semi-hard' is no longer accurate at all – nothing 'semi' about it now – but we both behave ourselves, and Buzz pulls his trousers back on, and the unyielding bathroom light watches us clamber back to responsible adulthood.

Buzz says, 'You'll want to phone Watkins?'
'Yes.'
'Right now, or . . .?'
'Shall we eat first? Give ourselves a break?'
He nods. Buzz In Slightly Less Than Professional Police Mode Shock. I tell him he must have taken quite a bang to his head. Standing on tiptoe, I kiss the side of that lovely head and send him out to recover my computer junk, while I go to the kitchen and see that Buzz has already got almost everything ready: cooked rice, fried some chicken, done something nice with tomatoes and courgette.
I fill two glasses with water and put them on the table.
Buzz comes back. We start to eat. Two mouthfuls in and he starts laughing at me. 'It's typical. Let DC Griffiths loose on a case and—'
I object. Creamer was actually the first target. On this occasion, I did absolutely nothing to provoke anyone. '*And* it wasn't me who got hit. *And*,' I say, hammering away my advantage, 'I haven't shot anyone or blown anything up. I've been good as gold.'
'*Yet*. You haven't blown anything up *yet*.'
We eat.
We drink.
We call Watkins.
Buzz finds some wine which he once gave me and which I'd forgotten I had. He opens it. Pours a proper glass for him, a pretend one for me.
Watkins arrives. Jeans and an old jumper. She looks less tired than on the train, maybe, but older. Hints of actual human fragility.
She says, 'Fiona, Cal brought me over. She's happy to wait in the car . . .'
But that's silly, so Cal comes in. Cal-short-for-Caroline, Watkins's extremely nice partner. Ringlety dark hair, slim

build, lovely coffee-coloured skin. Warm and wifely and protective.

Wine for everyone. Watkins summons a SOCO. Ditto an e-fit operator. She says, 'We'll just do a voice recording now, take a proper statement tomorrow. OK?'

More than OK. This is now Watkins In Very Slightly Less Than Hyper-Professional Police Mode, and that's beyond a shock, it's an earthquake.

Watkins quickly runs Buzz through what happened, and records his answers.

Cal and I go into the kitchen and find cheese and crackers and Cal tells me about a painting course she's doing. I tell her that Watkins – Rhiannon, as I still find it odd calling her – is about a million times happier since she's been with Cal. Cal glows with happiness. I ask if they're going to get married, and she says, 'I really want to. We're talking about it.'

A SOCO comes to swab for blood. No need to dust for fingerprints, because both intruders were wearing gloves.

The e-fit guy comes. The system is as good as it gets, but still only generates good results about twenty per cent of the time. But not much time has elapsed and Buzz's police training means that even as he was being punched, he'd have been mentally logging face shape, hairstyle, mouth formation and the rest.

He and the e-fit guy go to work, muttering over a laptop in the corner of my now-crowded living room.

Watkins – Cal sitting beside her on the arm of the chair, hand on the back of her neck – asks me what I think is going on.

I say, 'Atlantic Cables is clearly under some kind of attack. Moon first, then Livesey. A very sophisticated attack too. Invisible thefts. Murders all but undetectable.

'My guess is that the attackers kept some kind of watch

on the Livesey apartment. Either that, or they had some route into the Somerset Police inquiry. In any case, as long as that inquiry was trotting down the road to a suicide verdict, they just let things roll. As soon as Findlay started releasing new data to the coroner, however, they realised they were potentially compromised.

'They went after Creamer first, because it gave them unobtrusive entry into the Somerset-led inquiry. They'd have assumed that it was Somerset mostly driving things because Livesey's death was the one with the open coroner's inquiry. I guess they took Creamer's phone, looked at his email, broke into his home computer, took a good look. Then, I don't know, they were either just being thorough or they realised that the inquiry had its real centre in Cardiff, and they wanted to repeat the trick with me. Find a junior level copper. Take her phone, check her computer, steal some passwords, keep a watch on things.'

Watkins considers this. 'You didn't tell me you'd lost your phone.'

'I knew Creamer had lost his. That could have been coincidence. For all I know he's one of these people who's always losing their phones. But it seemed wise to play it safe.'

'We'll need to tell Findlay. Check home security for everyone on the project.'

'Yes.'

'And we'll get our IT guys to do whatever they need to do to increase security. Here and Bristol.'

Nod.

'Physical protection? Do you think we need to worry about that? They killed Livesey.'

That's true, but we're police officers and it's a much bigger deal to kill a police officer, not least because any police force will dedicate more or less unlimited resources to finding those that kill our kind.

I say, 'Nicking a phone is a lot different from killing someone. And anyway, the scale we're at now . . .'

Watkins nods at that. The Zorro briefings are attended by about a dozen officers, most of them only part time on the case, but all of them with access to the data. There'll be a similar number in Bristol and arranging round-the-clock protection for two dozen officers is well beyond the capacity of two mid-sized regional police forces.

I go on thinking Findlay was an idiot for sharing as much as he did with the coroner. In effect he was sending out a red and white stickered warning notice to criminals: TAKE CARE. COVER YOUR TRACKS. PLEASE INFILTRATE OUR INQUIRY.

I don't say that. I do say, 'I still think we should watch the ports. Sorry, but I do.'

Watkins performs a strange anatomical contortion, her version of a smile. 'It doesn't work like that, Fiona. To justify those sorts of costs, we have to have a specific inquiry-related objective. We can't just do things because they might be interesting.'

That's different from her usual type of answer. Not a snappish rejection of a subordinate's request, but the sort you give a capable detective sergeant, a second-in-command type. I realise again how determined Watkins and Jackson are to grow me into the kind of officer who is not a disgrace to her force. I'm slightly awed by their patience. Their determination to get me right.

The truly strange thing, though, is that their strategy seems to be working. In the past, I might well have launched into a less-than-entirely respectful explanation of why my elders and betters were completely wrong. I still think Watkins *is* wrong, of course. I haven't changed to that dramatic an extent. But for now, my only reaction is to wander across to the bookshelves by the TV. Fetch a copy of *The Sting* which I recorded from a late-night showing a few nights back.

'Have you seen it?' I say. 'You should watch it. It's really interesting.'

Cal says, 'Oh, Paul Newman. I love Paul Newman.'

Watkins thanks me, sort of, and yawns.

Buzz and the e-fit guy are done with their imaging work. Two men on screen, tough customers both. Buzz points to the guy on the left. Says, 'I'm pretty sure of him. The other one's a bit more sketchy. But he *was* stamping on my leg at the time, so . . .'

The SOCO has his swabs in labelled evidence bags. Waves them cheerfully. 'Should have something here,' he says.

Those damn bags will need to be handled by an exhibits officer, but not me, I'm happy to say. Procedure wouldn't allow me to be both sort-of victim of the attack and the person who handles exhibits, so these bags will end up on Laura's desk, not mine.

The SOCO goes. The e-fit guy goes.

Watkins and I look at the images. Thin eyes, hard faces. The kind that decorate Police Wanted notices in every country in the world.

Is one of these the Stonemonkey? We're both wondering the same thing, but it seems unlikely. Why use expensive labour, when cheap should have worked just fine?

Watkins does what she has to do to enter both pictures onto a national wanted list. On the security designation, she writes, 'Very dangerous. Proceed with extreme caution.' What they did to Buzz wasn't such a big deal. If one or both of these guys was present with Livesey, on the other hand . . .

Cal runs her fingers into Watkins's scalp and says, 'Home.'

Cal likes me, not least because she views me as her fairy godmother, the person who got Watkins out and dating. She gives me an extra big hug, as she always does, and tells me I should drop by more, as she always does. I realise that she means it too. That it's not just something she says. I find myself realising that I have one more friend than I knew I had.

A little triumph. Another yard or two of Planet Normal claimed for my own.

They go. *The Sting* DVD ended up in Cal's bag not Watkins's.

Just me and Buzz left.

I turn the overhead light off, leaving just a sidelamp still on.

In the old days, that would have been the signal for a march upstairs to the bedroom. Now, we linger in the living room. The same sofa, but opposite ends.

'Thanks for coming round tonight, Buzz. Sorry about what happened.'

'That's OK.' Shadows in his face. Shadows and lines. 'Listen, Fi, I wanted you to know – know it from me first – that I've started dating again. My first date, last Friday.'

'How was it?'

'OK. I'm seeing her again. I think she quite likes me.'

'Everyone likes you, Buzz. And the girls I know all fancy you.'

Which is at least eighty per cent true. Some girls don't do freckles, though, which seems a pity when they speckle so nice a face.

We sit in one of those mobile silences, which could go anywhere, do anything. I don't know what I'm feeling. Something warm and rapid flutters in my chest, but I can't interpret what that means.

He says, 'You're OK, are you?'

Meaning his date. Our break-up. My always wobbly head.

'I'm OK. Miss you all the time, but I'm OK.'

We dwell a little longer in that darkened silence. If Buzz took me in his arms now, kissed me, took me upstairs, I don't think I'd resist or have the willpower to say no. But he doesn't. I don't know if he even thinks about it.

Instead, he says, 'Penny. Penny Haskett. That's her name. Works at Napes Needles in town, the soft furnishings place.'

I stand up. Give him a sisterly kiss on the back of his head. 'Choose well, dear Buzz. You deserve the best.'

He goes, and I realise we've crossed a threshold, an important one. One which, between us, we've handled well. Another little triumph for me, another yard of Planet Normal.

In my hallway, there are some dabs of blood. I should clean them off now, before they're properly dried on, but I can't be bothered and anyway, I like them.

Livesey and Moon are with me now. Looking at the blood, these marks of violence.

The hanging corpse and the fallen one. Both men went aerial in their own ways. But this case isn't about the air, but about the sea. The murk of the Irish Sea, the dark Atlantic. That great salt boneyard.

I call Penry.

'Brian,' I say, 'I've got another assignment for you, if you want it. Nothing illegal, just time-consuming.'

'OK.'

'Ports, basically. Bristol, Newport, Cardiff, Barry, Swansea, Milford Haven.'

'OK . . .?'

I tell him what I want. What I'm looking for.

'Will you recognise it?'

'Me, no. But I know a man who will.'

There's a pause. A long one.

Then: 'Shouldn't you leave this to, you know, the actual police?'

'I *am* the actual police.'

'No, you're not. Not working like this.'

'I've tried. I honestly have.'

'And if we find a ship you're interested in . . .?'

'I present the evidence to my commanding officer,' I say primly.

'And then?'

'We get search warrants. Intercepts. We send in the fucking SAS.'

'Because a ship looks funny?'

'Because we have evidence of a ship adapted for criminal purposes.'

'Or adapted in some way that is totally innocent, only you wouldn't know what it was because you don't know the first thing about the shipping industry.'

'That's why we get a search warrant. We take a look and if we're wrong, we say very sorry, have a nice day.'

'Right. A magistrate is going to bloody love that argument.'

'Livesey *was* murdered *and* tortured and there *was* a ten-million-pound scam.'

Penry considers that. He was a decent enough copper in his day and he can compute the odds as well as I can. The more serious the crime, the lower the evidential threshold needed to secure our authorisations.

In the end, though, he comes down against me.

'No. Even then. You have to have *something*.'

He's probably right, but until you look, you don't know what you might find, so you have to look. The thing that worries me more is that Penry will be limited in what he can cover alone. And really, there are other ports to look at as well. Southampton, certainly. Maybe Falmouth. Dublin and Cork in Ireland. Maybe others. I'm not a shipping specialist. I don't know how these things work.

Penry senses that I'm not happy and he asks why. I tell him.

He says, 'I've got some mates in Dublin. I don't mind going out there. Get someone to take a look.'

'Would you? That would be brilliant.'

'In terms of . . . I'm sorry to ask, Fi, but I'll need petrol money. I'm near enough broke as it is.'

'Petrol money? I'll pay you. Time and expenses. Isn't that what we agreed?'

'This could take weeks.'

'I've got the money, Brian. It's not an issue.'

And it's true: on an assignment last year, some gangsters gave me sixty thousand pounds. They were planning to kill me as well – it wasn't all nicey-nicey – but they didn't kill me and I kept the money. If my friends and colleagues on the force knew I'd taken the cash, I'd have had to give it back, but they didn't and I haven't.

I don't say this, though, and Penry doesn't push. I guess he assumes that I get money from my father, which indeed I also do.

'Starting when, Fi? You're going to say right now, aren't you?'

'Yes please. I don't know their timetable.'

We chat another minute or two and I ring off.

I was standing in the hall while on the phone, so I could look at the blood marks on the wall.

Moon fallen. Livesey hanging.

And now Buzz, dear Buzz, attacked in my own home.

It occurs to me that if I can't persuade Watkins to take the shipping angle seriously, I'll end up doing something dangerous and stupid at the end of all this. That thought doesn't bother me particularly. What's dangerous for me isn't quite the same as what's dangerous for other people. Chicago, for example, all that data-entry work down in Ifor's dungeon, that's dangerous. It's come close to threatening my sanity. My life even. Biros in the eyes and dark steps leading down.

A little bit of fire and brimstone at the end of a good case, on the other hand: that never feels scary, or not really, not in the same way. Even if I'm scared, it's a knowledge that reminds me that I am alive, that I do have feelings, that I join together. Those things are golden. For me, they're golden.

This case has a nice feel to it now, and I feel calm.

This has been a wonderful end to a wonderful day.

# 27

Gwynedd. North Wales. Not a different part of the same country but, for we native Taffs, a strange and different land altogether. Different accents. Different hills. Different words.

Language researchers put the boundary of North Walian and South Walian somewhere near Tre Taliesin on the road between Machynlleth and Aberystwyth. Gogs to the north. Hwntws to the south.

I tell Mike this, make him hear the difference between *dodrefn* and *celfi*, *llaeth* and *llefrith*.

He's English, though, and doesn't care. Says, 'What's that anyway?'

'*Llaeth*? Milk.'

'So call it "milk".'

The road is twisty and wet with a splash of summer rain. I'm at the wheel, but since I'm a highly skilled police-trained driver, I can punch him on the arm without crashing. He says, 'Ow!' but he laughs and doesn't look as guilty as he ought to, so I don't think I hit him hard enough.

On the way down to Llanberis from Pen-y-Pass, Mike points to a bit of wet rock on the side of the valley. A broad open-book corner. Steep, like the angle of a castle wall.

'That's Dinas Cromlech,' he tells me. 'Forget all your crap about milk. If you want the beating heart of North Wales, it's there. Cenotaph Corner, Cemetery Gates, Left Wall, Right

Wall, Lord of the Flies.' His finger jabs at climbing routes I can't decipher.

I say, 'It looks really . . .'

'Yes?'

'Really . . . wet.'

He revenge-punches me and we head down to Llanberis.

We're met by Nat Brown. Fifties, bearded, blue-eyed. Powerful, but in a way that's more cuddly than scary. He looks at my car, a cute little Alfa Romeo, and says, 'Best go in mine.'

His: a beat-up Land Rover. The old sort. Series III or something like that. The kind of car that rattles like seven devils when in motion, but which is still capable of crossing the Sahara, or fording a river in flood, or – as now – driving almost vertically up the side of a Welsh mountain on a track built of loose scree scattered over rhyolite, blasted through with potholes, then overlaid with swags of sodden grass.

When the track levels off, we encounter an old stone cottage, whitewashed, a handful of barns and outbuildings off to one side.

Brown takes us inside. His wife, Val, makes tea in a big brown pot and puts out the kind of fruitcake which could stop a bullet.

We talk.

Brown is the 'Out and About' columnist for one of Britain's biggest climbing magazines. ('Which isn't saying much,' he says.) Mike has already promised me that Brown is the best connected climber on the British scene. Been everywhere. Knows everyone. Heard everything. We offered Brown a consultancy arrangement on the same basis as Mike's, but he refused. 'No one else ever pays me for anything, so I don't see why you should.'

I rehearse the facts of the cases which have brought us here. Not everything. I'm careful to keep the disclosure of nonpublic facts to a minimum. But still. A number of outrageous burglaries. Two deaths. One of the men tortured before he was killed.

Brown looks grim, but a good sort of grim. The sort that prefaces action.

He takes his tea, a wodge of cake and points at the door.

We go out.

Wind, rain and sunlight take turns to paint these mountains in their colours. One distant crag broods dark as coal, while another glitters with gold. Apart from a low stone wall around the cottage itself, the hill here is unfenced and sheep crop the mountain grass around our feet, hardly bothering to trot away as we approach.

We head for one of the larger outbuildings. Brown pushes at the door, then kicks it when it sticks.

Inside: a strange lamplit gloom. The entire interior has been cloaked in sheets of plywood, painted grey, then studded with holds. Not just the wall, but the ceiling too. There's a man – loose trousers, old T-shirt, climbing boots – moving upside-down on the ceiling as we enter. He reaches out for a hold, finds it, adjusts grip, then shifts his body along to follow. The guy's footwork is surprisingly delicate. Precise. Then a long reach for a bright orange hold that doesn't seem like much of a hold to me. The guy shoots out an arm. A do-or-die sort of move.

On this occasion, it's die. The guy reaches the hold, gets a grip of it, but his body is travelling too fast, too out of control, and he falls onto the blue matting that covers the entire floor.

On his back, looking up, the guy says, 'Damn.' Then, rolling over and groping for a water bottle, 'You're Fiona, right? The police person?'

I am, I say.

Brown introduces the guy on the floor. 'This is Joe. Joe Allen.'

We shake hands. Sweat and chalk on his. I don't know what on mine.

Mike has already told me about Allen. He's one of the country's top climbers, placed twenty-something in the world lead climbing rankings, but Mike also told me to ignore the rankings. 'Not everyone wants to compete. The real stuff happens on rock.'

At the back of the building, a projecting wall is covered by an old sheet. Brown pulls it away.

'This is it,' he tells us.

It: an inch-perfect reconstruction of that Bristol balcony. The reconstruction was built by a local Llanberis carpenter, under the eye of our own forensic guys and using measurements taken by a team of climbers, led by Mike, at the apartment itself.

The climb looks desperate to me. If I hadn't just seen a man crawling upside down on a ceiling, it wouldn't even have occurred to me that anyone could climb out under that thing, then make the move up and out to the edge of the balcony itself.

Allen – our guinea pig – just shrugs.

Sits on the matting under the 'balcony'. Chalks up.

Brown says, 'OK, this is seven storeys up. You've just used a couple of camming devices to crack-climb up. Jumaring, effectively. Then this. It's dark. You haven't practised. No top-rope inspection, nothing like that.'

Allen says, 'Sheez. OK.'

He positions himself under our mock-up and climbs out on the bits of timber that are standing in for those Bristol girders. His movements are light, limber. Unforced. I can see that, for him, this bit is easy.

Then he gets to the end of the girders. The part where Mike fell.

Allen says, 'Sweet.'

Thinks about it. Adjusts body position, then swings out looking for the edge of the 'balcony'. His first swing is for practice only, a sighting shot. But he keeps his body well in control, he's not at risk of falling. 'Big reach that,' he says, but gathers his concentration again, swings out, and this time does it for real, gets the hold, swings a foot up to join his hand on the ledge, then just drops to the floor, because he's done the hard part.

'Seven storeys up, huh?'

'Yes.'

'I'm saying V7, maybe the softer end of V7. Not too bad, anyway.'

Mike nods. That is, I think, what he said to us, though I don't understand these climbing grades, no matter how often Mike explains them.

Somewhere else in this cave, I can't tell where, there's a reconstruction of the hardest bit of the lighthouse climb too. Mike went back to the lighthouse, with Rhod and a team of two other climbers, plus some of our forensic guys, who were able to take casts of the relevant holds and ripples in the stone. Mike has already told me that the lighthouse climb is fearsome. 'There were sections there I couldn't get close to, not even on top-rope. Rhod was OK, but even he came away twenty or thirty times before he got the sequence.'

Brown shifts us down to the far end of the building, till we're standing under the biggest length of vertical wall in the room, about six metres at its highest. And now, I realise, I do see the reconstructed lighthouse, not because I recognise any of the holds, but because I recognise the colour of the casts made by our forensic lab. The casts are screwed to the wall, picking their way up in shades of white and grey. Again: an inch-perfect reconstruction of the real thing.

Allen chalks up. 'Wow. Looks really thin.'

'You're about thirty feet up,' says Mike. 'No rope.'

'Landing?'

'Yeah, landing's OK.'

'And I've got mats?'

'We assume so, as many as you want.'

I never really understand these climbing exchanges. Mike seems to think that falling forty or fifty feet onto a bouldering mat – a few inches of foam padding – is no big deal. Allen the same. In the car on the way up here, I tried arguing it out with Mike. He said, 'Yes, OK, no one wants to fall forty feet onto a bouldering mat, even a big pile of them. But there's a difference between a lethal fall and just a bad one. If you fall forty feet onto matting, you'll break an ankle, maybe a leg, but there's no way you should kill yourself.'

He told me about an activity called deep water soloing, where people climb sea cliffs without ropes. 'The grading system basically rates danger from S0 to S3. S0 means you have a nice clear drop into deep water and as long as you can swim, you'll be fine.'

'And S3?'

'Means the water beneath you is very shallow, so it's basically as dangerous as soloing above a big pile of rocks, except that this way you have the possibility of drowning as well as just breaking your neck.'

'And people do that?'

'Yes,' he says, and gives me one of those nutty, happy climber grins at the thought of it.

Allen blows the excess chalk off his hands, then starts to climb. Fairly slow. Moving with a considered, powerful grace. There's one point a third of the way up when he starts to make a move, then reconsiders and pulls back. A tiny adjustment of foot position, then he's in motion again. Climbs carefully up to the top, then slaps the very top of the wall and simply falls off, landing happily back on the mat.

'Blimey.'

Mike says, 'Rhod thought hard 7c, possibly 8a.'

Allen: 'Yeah, solid 8a, I'd say. Not 7c. That was the crux?'

'Yes. The rest was hard 7b, maybe 7c.'

I call for a translation. It's Brown who provides it.

'That route there. The lighthouse climb. To do that on-sight and without ropes – well, it's doable, clearly. But you're basically looking at an elite-level climber. Allen's standard, or near enough.'

He looks grim. Allen too. I look between their faces, trying to understand their reaction.

Brown says, 'There just aren't that many people in the country like that.' But there's still something in the room here – a flavour, a scent, an emotional reaction – which I can't understand and Brown gives me the answer to that too.

'This guy. The one who's killed your two people. I've probably climbed with him. Allen too.'

We go back to the main house. Sit around the farmhouse table. More tea, more cake, except that Mike and Allen go easy on the cake.

I get out my e-fits, hoping for but not expecting an easy win. Get nothing but blank stares. Then get my notebook out. Say, 'OK, top-level climbers. Whatever you've got..'

Brown and Allen start to disgorge names. They're not always immediately helpful. Allen, for example, names one climber as 'Scottie Boy McHeadjob,' and everyone laughs before Brown gives me the guy's name in a more normal way. Allen, of course, would technically be a suspect, except that I checked him out when Brown first suggested getting him involved. Allen sustained a serious leg fracture ten days before the Livesey murder and has only recently restarted climbing. I've seen the hospital records and spoken to the doctor so, short of a ridiculously broad conspiracy, he's clean.

We accumulate names, and with each name some further data too. Home town. Age. Whether in a relationship or not.

Climbing style and preferences. Competition wins. Main areas climbed in.

Some of the facts I just don't know how to use, or even make sense of. 'Real limestone nut. Masses of sport climbing in France and Spain. Nothing to speak of on grit. Big pussy when it comes to hard trad.' Then an argument over whether a particular route put up on Devon granite counted as hard or not.

I use my phone to record the whole conversation. Start off taking detailed notes, but my hand gets sore and I can't keep up anyway, so I just leave the phone running. I'll get somebody to transcribe everything later.

Two hours travel past us and through us and on to wherever discarded hours go to die.

More tea.

Val Brown comes in and asks if we're staying.

I'm going to say no – I've booked hotel rooms for me and Mike on police expenses – but her husband just says, 'Well, *I'm* not driving down,' and Allen shrugs, and Mike does too, and I say, 'That would be lovely, thank you,' though I'm not quite sure what exactly I'm saying yes to.

So we sit and talk, as hours ghost past us into night.

As we talk, Val cooks up a huge meal of belly pork, potatoes and cabbage, and I help, because my phone is still recording – on permanent charger now – and I'm personally contributing very little to the discussion.

At seven o'clock, we eat and talk. Beers for the men. Val and I drink water that's piped in from a spring on the hillside behind us.

It tastes of minerals and rock and moorgrass.

We've evolved, by now, a list of twenty-two names. Two women on the list, two German climbers who have spent a lot of time in the UK. Aside from that, our names are all British men aged between nineteen and their early thirties.

I want to turn to dates. We have a precise date for the Plas Du burglary and the Livesey killing, but only an approximate one for the lighthouse. I'm hoping that those things will help us whittle down names.

We overachieve. It so happens that Livesey died on the day of a big indoor climbing competition in Birmingham. At a stroke, twelve of the men on our list and both the women are struck off – they were competing and Brown himself was there as commentator. The event went on all afternoon and into the night so there was no plausible way one of them could have snuck off, zoomed down to Bristol for a spot of murder, then sped back for the grand finale.

Our other names start dropping quickly too. The climber called Scottie Boy McHeadjob was in the Karakoram, along with one of the two Germans from our list. Another guy was in Italy with a film crew watching him climb something heinous in the Dolomites. Two were in the Verdon in France. And so on.

I want to know whether any of these notional alibis can be proved. So, if Climber X is thought to be climbing in the Verdon Gorge, is there any actual evidence that he was indeed present on the days in question? I assume that our search will proceed pretty much as any police search like this proceeds: test every alibi until one cracks under the pressure.

But this is a new world to me. Mike explains that all the climbers on the list are professional or semi-professional. I ask what that means. Who pays climbers to do what they do? The answer, it turns out, is equipment manufacturers who compete to get the top names sporting their brands. The money is piffling by the standards of other elite sportsmen – Allen, arguably the best climber in the UK, reckons he earns about sixty grand a year – but the climbers we're looking at are the superstars of their own exclusive world. Bloggers write about them, equipment makers chase them for photos, magazines want interviews. And of course they all need other climbers to hold ropes, clean routes, and all the rest of it. They just don't live in a world where they could pretend to be in one place for the week and really be off torturing marine surveyors in Bristol.

The task is far bigger than we can hope to accomplish in an evening – there are a huge number of checks for us still to make – but I'm not feeling hopeful. Nor is Brown. Val has already gone off to have a bath. Mike and Allen go back to the bouldering cave for a late-night work out. They're making plans to go climbing together the next day.

I think Mike is a bit starstruck hanging out with Allen like this. He's like I would be if I got to work next to a real-life Sherlock Holmes. Puppyish and sappy.

The kitchen seems suddenly quiet. Brown sticks the kettle on for more tea. 'I'm terrible,' he says, 'Drink the stuff non-stop.'

He asks me more about the cases and I answer him in pictures. Moon with his skull split. Livesey dangling from his bedsheet.

Bring up the picture of Livesey's thigh, too. 'That brown spot there? You can hardly see it, but it's the mark of an electric burn. Very high voltage, very low current. It doesn't leave much of a mark, but . . .'

Brown says, 'Christ.'

I've noticed that people blaspheme when I show them my pictures, blaspheme rather than swear. I don't know why.

He says, 'This is your job, this sort of thing?'

'Yes. I love what I do.'

We go through more names. Dig around in Brown's notes. Climbing websites, blogs and forums.

One guy is looking suspicious. No climbing on the crucial dates. No injuries. We're just trying to sort out a possible sighting of him at a bouldering venue in the Austrian Alps, when Brown interrupts.

'Oh bollocks!'

'Bollocks?'

'He was getting married that weekend. I was in the bloody congregation.'

Another one bites the dust.

Neither of us have the heart to continue.

Brown leads me upstairs. Says, 'You're with Mike, are you?'

'Friends, that's all,' I say, not sure if we're even that. I mean: would we still see each other if I didn't have a case that needed him? I don't know.

Brown doesn't care. 'OK, he can have the bunkroom with Joe. You'll be in here.'

Here: a tiny room, with a wooden bed, a chest of drawers, a view out over a flank of mountain and nothing else. The place looks a bit like one of those old-fashioned youth hostels. The kind of friendliness you get from old wood and warm tea.

'Thank you. This is lovely.'

'We get a lot of people coming through here. Sometimes people ask. Sometimes they don't. Most of the buggers on that list have been here at least once.'

My stuff is still in the car in the valley, but Brown finds me a toothbrush and a clean towel. When he asks if I have everything I need, I tell him, 'Yes.'

# 28

To bed, but not to sleep.

Lie awake looking at the ceiling. The window open a crack, and only moon and mountain beyond.

Sheep champ. Hours pass.

Watkins thought we wouldn't be able to find our bad guy because we had no CCTV, no witness statements, but I never thought we'd get him from all that police stuff. To me, all along, the clue was in the crimes themselves. These climbs of his weren't just hard, they were exceptional. Finding the exception should have been easy.

*Should have.*

Stupid words, stupid thinking.

Back in Cardiff, Zorro is going exactly nowhere. Watkins is doing almost everything right. Reanalysis of all the cold-case stuff. Combing through the Atlantic Cables material. Some clever computer stuff aimed at seeing if we can locate the IP address of any machine that accessed Livesey's files in the hours following his death.

And, following the attack on Buzz, security has been stepped up too. The operation has been elevated to Top Secret. The only computers which can access the Zorro files are located in Cathays itself, or Portishead in Bristol. Those machines are secured by double passwords. Somebody from the IT department enters one password. An officer named on the Zorro operation list has to enter another. Even then, all movements in and out of the operation room are logged. All data movements are tracked. No data greater than ten kilobytes, or something like that, can be transferred anywhere, even to another police computer, without Watkins expressly authorising the movement.

They extracted DNA from the blood on my walls, but found no match on the system.

Buzz's e-fit pictures have been distributed, but the men concerned have not been identified.

Activity, yes. Product, no.

I swing my legs out of bed. I'm in T-shirt and knickers only. There's no heating on and the window is open.

Starlight and moonlight.

Grey cliffs and black hills.

Two dozen names and two dozen alibis.

An inaccessible room. An invisible murder.

A puzzle that looks impossible, except that we have two corpses and they're real enough.

Since I can't see myself sleeping, I pull on some trousers and go barefoot downstairs.

In the kitchen, a lamp burns. I put the kettle on to boil. Root around in a cupboard for herbal tea. Find an elderly packet of camomile, which I don't really like, but which will have to do.

The Brown's kitchen has a huge old range cooker with a flue that whiffles, a big beast snoring. I lean up against it, liking its warmth.

Livesey and Moon.

Moon and Livesey.

I assume that Livesey has been buried. Some Virginia churchyard, perhaps. White clapboard in the sunshine and a solitary bell. But that doesn't feel right, not for him, not for Livesey. If I could arrange his burial – and I'd have really liked to – I'd have done it out at sea. A wooden deck. A canvas sack. A heavy stone or iron weight. A few words offered to an absent God. Mourners bare-headed beneath the sun. Then a swift heave over the side. A splash, a spew of bubbles, then that long, unhurried, unimaginable descent.

That's how I'd have done it, and no stone to mark the place.

The kettle boils. I make tea.

Then the stairs creak and, from the door, Brown says, 'Couldn't sleep?'

He's in tartan pyjama trousers, no top. He has a chestful of hair, turning grey, but there's still plenty of power in those arms, those pecs.

I tell him no, I couldn't sleep. Ask if he wants tea.

'Yes – or no, actually, sod that, fancy a hot chocolate?'

I do, and say so.

He puts on a pan of milk to warm. Finds a carton of chocolate. Roots around in a hall drawer, muttering softly, then comes away with an old tin of rolling tobacco. 'Thought I had some somewhere.'

He makes the hot chocolate and I roll the ciggies.

We sit outside on the front step and drink and smoke. Brown has put a coat on over his bare chest. He's given me one of Val's coats and a pair of wellies.

The silver moonlight lends the pale upland grass a sheen which is almost like frost. The very highest hills have curls of old snow still gleaming from the hollows.

On the mountain facing us, a distant cliff gleams. A black diamond beneath the stars.

Brown jabs his cigarette towards it. 'That's Cloggy. Clogwyn d'ur Arddu. Three decades back, a young man, a kid really, wanders up to the cliff and decides he's going to climb the hardest line on it. Practises for three days. The fourth day he just goes for it. There's no protection to speak of. At about a hundred feet, there's a little bolt but only an eighth of an inch, and it's tied off with two millimetre rope – a bit of string, basically. After that, there's nothing at all. Nothing until you hit the top at a hundred and fifty feet.'

He doesn't finish. I nudge. 'And?'

'He either climbs it or he dies. But he didn't die, didn't fall. The result was Indian Face, maybe the hardest route in the world at the time. Even now, with standards a million times higher, it's only been climbed three times.'

I think of that, the boy under the cliff. That swaggering belief. But also the other thing. That thing, whatever it was, that impelled him to that place of risk and skill and extreme danger.

I say, 'That's him, isn't it? Our boy. We've been doing this all wrong.'

That's hardly me at my clearest, but Brown is nodding.

'Yes.'

I say, 'Some hyper-talented kid. New to the scene. Newish. Enough that he hasn't got onto your lists, your "Out and About"s. Most kids like that, they want to achieve their Indian Face. They want to do the climb that etches their name in history. But what if this one is messed up? Angry, fucked up, who knows what? He doesn't choose Indian Face, he chooses Nellie Bentley's lighthouse. He chooses the wall of Plas Du. Pockets ten million quid. The kind of money which dwarfs anything that a Joe Allen can earn, even with a whole career at the top of his sport.'

Brown has finished his cigarette, reaches vaguely to see if there's another, but there isn't and his hot chocolate has gone cold.

He throws the remains of his drink on the ground in front of him. A milky spill.

He says, 'Yes.'

That sounds like an ending, but we're both thinking the

same thing. That the story can't end there. Can't either begin or end in that place.

That kid, that unknown boy, didn't get to that level of skill in isolation. He had some kind of prehistory. Climbs and experience that took him to the necessary level of skill. He climbed Plas Du, Bentley's lighthouse and those other insurance-related climbs in 2009. If it took him a year to plan that campaign, there must still have been a record from 2008 and before. Some place where he left his mark: a too-talented kid, angry at the world, and with an extraordinary appetite for risk.

And even post-2009, the story doesn't stop. Back in September 2011, he was, quite likely, involved in the murder of Derek Moon on a Welsh clifftop. Then, in February of this year, he breaks in to a Bristol apartment via a climb which, if not as extraordinary as the one up Bentley's lighthouse, still required a highly capable climber in peak condition.

I remind Brown of the dates, the timings.

He nods. Gestures back into the house.

'He's there,' he says, meaning the archive. The mass of notes and emails from which Brown compiles his column. 'And if he's not in my stuff, then *somebody* has run across him. You can't hide the good 'uns. You know 'em when you see 'em.'

A thread of cloud, a long thin streamer, obscures the lower face of the moon. The world darkens. A couple of sheep graze up against the wall of Brown's bouldering room. Another, annoyed by their presence, moves away with a sudden trot of hooves.

Starlight and moonlight.

Grey cliffs and black hills.

We go inside and work until dawn.

# 29

Friday morning. Late.

Granary toast and scrambled eggs. Val Brown drinking coffee. Nat and I are on tea. No sign of Allen or Mike, who are both out on the crags somewhere. The end of the table is heaped with papers. My notes and Brown's.

No breakthroughs, but we realise two things. First, that the process will take time. Second, that it'll succeed. It'll get its man.

I'll need to talk it through with Watkins, but I think she'll agree. We need more resources. More manpower.

Brown offers to drive me down to the valley, so I can pick up my car for the drive back. I wonder vaguely if I should wait around for Mike since, theoretically, I'm his wheels home.

'Those buggers won't be back before dark,' says Brown. 'And if the weather stays good, your boy won't be leaving tonight anyway.'

So I accept his offer. Drive down off the mountain. Set off for Cardiff. From the heart of North Wales to the heart of the south. Not far as the crow flies. A hundred and twenty miles, if that. But the road lies through mountains all the way. Small roads, twisty roads. Towns and villages, clustering grey beneath the hills. The journey up took five hours, and it'll be no quicker back.

So I take my time. Go slow, because there's no other way.

At Beddgelert I stop at a café with free wi-fi and send a

long email to Watkins. Updating her, but also suggesting that we'll need more manpower. I say, *Can we talk about this on Monday? I doubt if I'll be in Cardiff this side of 5.30.* Get an email back almost straight away. *I'm out Mon & Tues. Prepare a draft plan. We'll discuss Weds.*

*Prepare a draft plan.* The sort of chore which might usually be given to a trusted detective sergeant. I go back to my car feeling all grown up. The glow of pride lasts about twenty minutes, during which time I don't break the speed limit even though there's nothing ahead of me and no speed cameras in sight.

Trawsfynydd, Dolgellau.

Llanbrynmair, Llanidloes.

Low hills, green valleys.

Grey farmhouses and sheep-studded fields.

Bridges.

Rivers flowing fast under alders. Trout-coloured water breaking over rocks.

Near Llanwrthwl, I stop for fuel.

As I pull away, I hear a knocking sound under my car, as though a fallen branch has got trapped. Behind me, a white van flashes. Someone inside is pointing down at the back of my car.

There's a layby just ahead and I pull over. The van follows. Half overlaps me, and I'm expecting a patronising male explanation of a problem which will, presumably, become completely clear as soon as I take a look beneath my car.

I get out. Bend down. Try to see under my car.

I don't get patronised. That's the good news.

The bad news is that the van's rear door opens up.

That, as I turn, a blanket descends over my head.

That someone grabs me from behind. Both arms round me, encircling my chest. Pinioning me.

I kick, of course. Thrash, kick, bite, struggle.

But all I get is mouthfuls of blanket. Some low grunts when one of my kicks hit target. But soon my legs are captured. Taped together. My arms too. The blanket is tied loosely round my neck. I'm tipped sideways into the van. Not thrown particularly hard or particularly gently. The doors close.

We move off.

I can't see anything at all and go skidding round the back of the van whenever it climbs a hill or turns a corner.

I am completely fucked and I didn't see it coming.

I am completely fucked and no one knows where I am.

# 30

We drive perhaps half an hour. The last part is quite up and down, which suggests that we're in the hills. But since everywhere round here is hilly, that narrows the possible range of locations down not at all.

The van stops.

I'm dragged out. Left on a concrete floor.

There's stuff happening around the van. Boxes being shifted around, something like that.

No one speaks to me. I try asking what the fuck is going on, but no one wants to tell me.

Then it's my turn to receive some attention. I feel someone removing the laces from my shoes, which are soft canvas trainers, useless for kicking. They check me for a belt, but I'm not wearing one. Pat down my jeans pockets. Remove my phone. Also watch, cards and money. A male hand glides, needlessly, between my thighs but, after one or two pervily intimate strokes, it moves away again. A hand goes up the back of my T-shirt. Finds my bra. Two or three snips with some scissors, then it's freed and extracted.

Belt, bra, laces. It's the same as when I was in prison briefly last year, except that these guys aren't secretly on my side.

I'm patted down one last time. The process is icky, but not extremely so. My breasts and bum are fondled about as much as most male airport security guards would fondle them if they thought they could get away with it.

Then someone cuts the tape on my legs. Loosens, or does something, to the tape on my arms. Then I'm tossed back in the van. The doors are locked and the van reverses a short distance, a few feet maybe. A little jolt as we hit something, but at slow speed. A minor bump.

Someone cuts the ignition.

Then nothing.

No movement. No speech. No sound.

I roll around, loosening my bonds. It's not hard getting my legs free. I have to thrutch around a little longer to free my arms but get there in the end too. Uncloak my eyes.

My little metal chamber is almost completely dark, but not quite. A bit of light filters through from the front. There's a partition of some sort in place. Plywood, cut to fit and held in place by screws, whose heads I can feel with my fingertip.

By touch as much as sight, I explore my cell. There's a six-pack of two-litre water bottles. Three bags of supermarket apples. Two big blocks of cheese. Paper napkins, a big pack of them, maybe a hundred in the pile. A black plastic bucket: my toilet, I assume. All that, plus the blanket. No cushion or pillow.

Unexpectedly, my cards, money and phone are here too. No battery in the phone, of course, but even so it's nice to have.

I believe that a young woman in my position is generally expected to comport herself by banging on the side of the van and calling for help. That, plus a little sobbing in frustration, followed by a glum acceptance of her lot. Since I can't see that shouting for help is likely to achieve much, and since sobbing is hardly a strong suit of mine, I leap straight to the end of that sequence and sit discontentedly on the floor, my back to the partition wall.

The doors opposite me are locked. I heard my captors do it. But even if they hadn't, I'd have very little hope of escape that way. The van was reversed up against something and even if I found a way to force the doors open, I think they'd open two inches onto a blank wall.

The floors, walls and ceiling are metal. I don't have a microtransmitter in the sole of my shoe. No laser cutter concealed in an ordinary silver earring. I don't have the kung-fu skills to tear through metal. Can't punch my way through the plywood behind me.

I assume that this attack follows the theft of my phone and the attack on Buzz. Given the precautions that we so carefully took thereafter, our operational data is now secure from pretty much any external assault. That means that, if there are things about the operation that someone really, really needs to know, it'll have to come from the brain of one of the Zorro team members.

A brain such as mine.

And, I note, remembering Livesey, that these are not people averse to a little forceful encouragement.

The biggest chink of light round the partition comes from above the front passenger seat. I soak a wodge of napkins in water and squish them into the little gap, above a screw.

I pull my phone apart. Break the casing. The break gives me a moderately sharp edge, but no point, and even the edge I have is plasticky and vulnerable. I think I could probably use it to inflict an injury that would be worse than a paper-cut, not quite as bad as catching your thumb on a staple.

I toss the thing aside.

I can't think of much more to do, so do nothing. I'm not hungry, so don't eat. Not thirsty, so don't drink.

For half an hour, I just lie down, half rolled in my blanket, listening to the van tick as it cools. Thinking everything through. My strategy for battle.

But there's only so much thinking a girl can handle. Action is better.

I stand up. Inspect my little wodge of wet napkin and the bit of plywood partition.

Plywood is strong when dry, weakens when wet. The cut edge has frayed. Only a very, very little, but little is all I need.

I put a fingernail to the edge of the ply and start to pick. The first small splinter peels splendidly away.

I work hard. Keeping the ply wet, scratching at its torn edge. I think there's a metal grille behind the ply and my fingernail won't scratch away the steel, but I don't care.

Start small, work upwards.

I stand and work in the dim metal light. Wondering what comes next. Wondering how bad this gets.

# 31

A few hours later, I get to find out.

I was abducted from Llanwrthwl at around two thirty. At this time of year, a few days from the summer solstice, the sun doesn't set until well after nine o'clock and light burns in the sky a good bit after that. Light is still coming from my chink when I hear steps approach the van. A driver's door opens. The van moves forwards a yard or two. Then the engine dies.

Steps at the back of the van, then the double doors are opened up.

If I were Lev, I'd probably have a solution to my current conundrum. Some lethally effective krav-maga manoeuvre. A whirlwind kick to the jaw, a jab to the eye. A man disabled, a weapon snatched.

I'm not Lev.

He's a man. Five foot nine or ten. Normally built. And a former Spetsnaz trainer, whose speciality lay in unarmed combat. A killing machine, with a soft spot for black tea and the music of Dmitri Shostakovich.

I'm me. Five foot two. A shade under fifty kilos. Not particularly fit. I'm not completely unskilled in one-to-one combat. I've trained, sporadically, with Lev for years now. But fighters my size depend on surprise and some kind of weaponry, even if it's only a hard-soled shoe. Short of bombarding my captors with apples, or trusting that one of them is lactose-intolerant enough to be disabled by cheese, I've no assault weapons to speak of.

I leave the apples alone. Have cheese, but choose not to use it.

My two captors – black boots, loose trousers, black T-shirts, fleeces, balaclavas – pull back the doors and stand well back. Well-trained. Cautious.

I don't cause any sort of drama. Do nothing to provoke violence. Just point through the doors and say, 'Should I come out?'

They nod a yes.

I step out. I'm a bit shaky. Maybe lack of food – I still haven't eaten – but mostly, I think, fear.

Fear is normally one of my good emotions, I note. One of the ones I can feel without much difficulty. But I've been used to moments when fear arrives in a kind of *ka-boom* of adrenalin. A sudden falling away. A freezing wash that laps right up into the fingertips and nerve endings.

This isn't like that. The whole scenario is too slo-mo, too studiedly ambiguous.

But, I think, what I have now – this shakiness, this clumsiness of movement – this is the same thing. Fear inhabiting me. No abrupt Viking-style invasion. Just this steady leaching of confidence. A slow betrayal.

The van is parked inside a stone barn. There's a bit of agricultural rubbish around, but nothing much. No animals. No feed or baled straw or farm machinery.

I was right that the van had been backed up against a wall. A thick, old stone affair. My prison looks depressingly complete.

There's a single overhead bulb. A wooden door in the side of the building looks as though it leads to some little office or other internal space. There are lights on there, anyway. A gleam of painted walls.

The end of the building has a big wooden double-door.

The sort which, when fully opened, could admit a tractor. There are glass panes at the top, but so clotted with dirt and cobwebs that I see nothing beyond a vague impression of evening sky. There's also a small regular-sized door inset in the larger one, for use by people when they don't want or need to open the big ones.

In the middle of the barn, under the bulb, there's a chair. Wooden IKEA-type thing. Arms.

The chair sits on a plastic tarpaulin. I don't know if IKEA sells tarpaulins but, whether they do or not, this wouldn't be a look they'd offer their home-furnishing clients.

My legs go weak.

Not a feint. Not a ploy. Not a Lev-ian prelude to some stellar bit of lethal improvisation.

My captors support me over to the chair.

I sit, shakily. Unresisting.

The men tape my arms to the chair arms. My legs to the legs.

Duct tape. Too strong for me to tear or stretch.

The men chat quietly between themselves as they work. Not Welsh accents, I think. London probably. But who cares? Not me.

The pair decide that my position directly under the bulb makes it hard to see my face. So one of them simply lifts me up, chair and all, holds me while his mate adjusts the tarpaulin, then settles me down again, ten feet back from where I'd been.

My fear has swollen now. It lurches inside me like a second body. I think I'm trembling, but can't tell whether that's only inside or whether it's visible outside too.

I really, really don't want to be here.

The men go away.

Stay away.

There's no tape over my mouth, no attempt to gag me.

I don't shout. If I'm free to do so, that must mean that

there's no point in it, so I stay quiet. The men are leaving me here to freak me out further, I realise. It helps a bit knowing that but I'm freaked enough anyway. I want to tell them that. *Guys, I'm already freaked enough. Honest. I'm really very, very freaked.*

After perhaps half an hour, one of the guys comes out with some stuff. A table. A laptop. One of those fifty metre reels of electric cable. A couple of speakers, small ones, shit ones. The sort that office stores sell for twenty quid. The guy hooks everything up. Checks it's all working OK. Twizzles the screen so it's facing me. The laptop has an inbuilt webcam and the guy fixes me in its little lens.

He leaves.

I sit there looking at myself on screen. A woman tied to a chair in an empty barn.

Nothing happens.

The light outside starts to grow bored waiting, and begins to fade.

Time plays around in the corner, in a little scurf of dirty straw.

I do test my arms and legs against their bindings – when I can, I like to comport myself broadly in line with the generally expected behaviour – but my bindings are plenty, plenty strong enough to keep me where I am.

Time and the light fade and die.

Then, I don't know how much later, the internal door opens again. One of the goons comes out.

'Showtime.'

He does something on the keyboard and a voice comes out of the speakers. It says this:

'Good evening, Fiona. As you'll have guessed, you're here because there's some information I want. I'd have been perfectly happy to acquire it by a simple inspection of your office systems, but your colleagues have rendered that approach a little difficult. So I'm going to ask you some questions. You're going to give me some answers. I'm going to check that the answers you're giving me are truthful and complete. If they are, you'll be free to go. If they are not, the consequences will be extremely unpleasant. Do you understand me?'

I doubt if his final question is anything more than rhetorical in nature, so I just reciprocate with a mumbled 'Fuck off,' a humble rhetorical flourish of my own.

There's something weird about the voice that comes out of the speakers. Partly that's because they're crappy little underpowered speakers trying to fill a barn. But it's something else too. Something not quite human. Not quite fluid.

The voice ignores my swearword. It just says, calmly, 'We'll begin simply. You will please give me your name.'

'You know what it is. I'm Fiona Griffiths and I'm a detective constable with the South Wales Police, working under the command of DI Watkins on Operation Zorro.'

'Zorro.' The voice has a kind of snick of contempt.

I say, 'It's a stupid name. I didn't choose it.'

'No, quite.'

So far, so expected. The theft of my phone and Creamer's, the attack on Buzz, all indicated that we possess information that the bad guys want. Accessing that knowledge was the only possible motive for my abduction. Data theft handled the good old-fashioned way.

But what information? What data?

Mostly, our inquiry is crowded with stacks of paper and empty dead ends. We have no names, no images, no prints. No DNA or likenesses that we can connect to anything. On the whole, I think I can divulge everything I know with reasonable confidence that I won't be disclosing anything that will imperil the inquiry. Even our investigation into the Stonemonkey's identity has little more to it than, 'We're looking for a really good climber.'

But it's not quite so simple.

I have no dangerous information, perhaps, but I do have some suspicions. Suspicions which, I've a nasty feeling, lie in the cold dead centre of the things that the Voice is most anxious to know. And how to hide them? To hide them when this setting and these goons and this tarpaulin suggest I'm going to be under extreme pressure to reveal all.

I don't know the answer to that question – or, to be more precise, I'm going to find out if my answers stand any hope of working.

The Voice starts out simple.

'When did you join the police?'

'When did you transfer to CID?'

'Who do you currently report to?'

'What is your role on the inquiry team?'

'If you are not full time on the team, what do your other roles currently involve?'

'Please list the members of the inquiry team and talk to me about the allocation of work and responsibilities.'

'Please tell me why you were in North Wales. Who were you seeing? What was the purpose of your enquiries?'

I answer all these questions accurately. When the Voice asks follow-up questions, or demands clarifications, I give them. I try to offer answers the way I would to Watkins when she's in fire-breathing mode: fast, accurately, concisely. Once or twice, the Voice congratulates me on my responses. Trying to build the sort of relationship that morphs into Stockholm Syndrome.

I don't think I'm very promising Stockholm material, but I don't say that.

We get through the generalities and start to move into specifics.

'A team from your inquiry recently visited the offices of

Atlantic Cables in London. Please tell me which officers were present.'

'And who was present from the company? Please give names and job functions.'

'What was the specific purpose of your visit?

'What questions were asked? What answers were given?'

'You say that a certain quantity of data and documents were removed from the company. Please tell me what documents were removed. Be as complete as you can.'

Curiously, those kind of questions just can't be asked or answered in a simple tell-me-or-I'll-hit-you format. I need to sketch out the limits of my knowledge: although I was present in London – and I say as much – I was one of a team of four, and we didn't each know what precisely the others were doing. The voice has to listen as I explain the way we worked, the way electronic data removal happens, as far as I understand it. Because some of this – the techie part – lies at the outer limits of my knowledge, I'm a bit blurry on many of my details. The Voice also doesn't seem to understand the nitty-gritty of this sort of thing, so he largely accepts my blurriness and we work collaboratively to try and shape a narrative.

I don't know how long the Atlantic Cables interrogation lasts, but he's thorough. Detailed and repetitive. Asking the same questions from different angles, comparing any micro-differences in my answers.

And new questions come all the time.

'You are treating the death of Ian Livesey as murder?'

'Correct.'

'Yet you originally treated it as suicide? Why the change?'

I explain about Plas Du and Moon. The recognition that there was someone out there who could access the inaccessible. The cable linking Moon and Livesey.

'That's all? Mere suspicion?'

'No.' I go through our investigations of the Bristol

apartment. The fingermarks on the girder beneath the balcony. The duct tape adhesive on the chair. The scorch marks on Livesey's inner thigh.

My voice trembles as I say that. Glues up. I have to ask for water. The goon goes to fetch it. Tips me back in my chair and lets me drink. Most of the water goes down my throat. Some goes on my top. Neither of us say anything, except that I notice I'm cold. I ask for a jumper. The goon just glances at the laptop. The Voice says, 'Fine.' The goon goes off to fetch something.

The Voice says, 'You're doing well. Do you remember the rules?'

'The rules?'

'What I said at the beginning. About how this works.'

'Yes, I remember.'

'Please tell me what you remember.'

I say, 'You interrogate me. I tell you everything. Then you reinterrogate me under torture. If I haven't fucked up, you release me. If I do fuck up, you kill me.'

The Voice says, 'You have the general drift, yes.'

You can't hear a thin smile in theory, except you kind of can. And I realise, all along I've been assuming that the Voice belongs to Galton Evans, but I don't think this *is* Galton Evans. There's something leering in Evans. Something too nakedly lecherous. His smiles are fleshy, not thin. This whole van 'n' barn set-up is hellishly scary, but it's been essentially devoid of sexual threat. Sexual titillation even. I just can't see Evans not wanting to stage an altogether more porno version of all this.

I decide to check. Say, 'I'm sorry about your foot.'

'My *foot*?'

'Yes. I'm sorry about your foot.'

A short pause. Then, 'I don't know what you're talking about.'

I say, 'Sorry. Not your foot. Galton's foot. Galton Evans.'

Another short pause. Then, 'I don't know who or what you are referring to.'

That last comment was purely formal. The required response in the context. But that earlier response – 'my *foot*?' – had real surprise in it.

I'm temporarily non-plussed. Like a thing I thought was certain gives way at my first real touch. A question to put away for later.

The goon comes with an oversize fleece. A zip-up thing, which he arranges over my shoulders and front. I'm still cold, but the fleece helps.

The goon leaves again. Aside from a brief glimpse when I was first abducted, I've seen neither man's face, their balaclavas always down. I don't even know that there are only two of them. Just assume it.

The questions continue.

About our investigation of the insurance committee.

Our interrogations of Bentley and the others.

Any leads we have on the Stonemonkey.

Any accumulated forensic evidence. Any CCTV pictures. Any e-fit images.

I do, of course, know a lot of the answers and my recall for these things is always good. On the other hand, I *have* been on the inquiry part-time only and that has placed limits on how much detail I have at my command. I say so too. 'You picked the wrong person. I'm junior and I'm part time. I'll give you what I have, but there's lots I just don't know.'

The Voice says, 'I accept that. Just make sure you tell me everything you do have.'

That threat – that promise – flickers over this whole thing. Be good: and they'll let me go. Be bad: and they'll kill me.

I believe the threat, but not the promise. There isn't, in theory, a crime worse than murder, but our life sentences don't usually mean a full life term. Most regular murderers in Britain have at least a shot at parole. A chance to see their last arthritic sunsets from a window without bars. A final glimpse of winter sunshine. But no Home Secretary likes releasing cop killers, which means that parole is seldom offered to those who have killed serving officers. Their lives are finished from the moment the handcuffs snap over their wrists. Bleep, bleep. Game over. Do not pass Go. Do not collect £200. These walls are now for ever.

All that says that the Voice and his merry men will be reluctant to kill me. Reluctant to commit that greatest of all crimes.

Except, except. These guys are already drenched in blood. Already at the point where returning were as tedious as go o'er. They're not, now, considering the magnitude of a possible sentence, merely fixed only on ensuring that we, the police, never catch up with them.

So I think they'll complete this little interrogation. Get what they need. Kill me. Dispose of my corpse. Dump my car a long way from this barn. And bet that the police would never be able to put the clues together.

And that bet would, I think, be a good one. I don't think we'd have enough to go on. A terrible crime, yes, but one that would never be prosecuted.

I am beginning to think it would be a good idea to get out of here soon.

But before then: more questions.

When the Voice wants a break, he takes one. Maybe five minutes. Once maybe more like an hour or two. The goons are never both visible at the same time. I assume they're doing turn and turn about now. Eight hours on, eight hours off. Something like that. They needed two to abduct me. Right now, a kitten could master me.

And as for me, no breaks. When the others leave, I'm just

left on my chair, facing my own image on screen. I'd try to get some sleep, but I can't do it. I'm far too cold now, and achey. Though I can shift my bum an inch or two, I can't stretch. My hands, I notice, are purple with restricted blood flow. Part purple, part white with cold.

*And the bad bit hasn't yet started*, I think. *The bad bit hasn't yet started.*

# 32

Dawn. Fogged and dim behind the cobwebbed windows.

The questions still come.

An endless flow. Precisely delivered. Without emotion. Even as I feel my own answers slur and get stupider, I note the Voice remains in complete command of his faculties.

And though the questions still pour, their nature has changed. They've broken up, turbulent and uneasy, like a sheet of smooth water hitting rock.

So, for example, the Voice might ask about the Stonemonkey at one point, then ask about Atlantic Cables customer lists in his very next question. I think he probably has a transcript of my earlier answers with him. I suspect him of flipping pages, leaping from one thing to another.

I do my best to keep up.

I make errors, of course. Errors and omissions. Ones he pounces on, and with sharpness. 'That's not correct. That's not consistent with your earlier response. Do you understand the consequence of lying?'

My head sags. I'm mostly not looking at the screen now, just down at my lap. I can feel the first flicker of hallucination playing beyond the rim of my vision, like a rugby game happening just out of sight.

I only vaguely hear my answers. 'Yes. Understand. Earlier response probably right. Was trying to say . . .' And I go on, trying to stitch together a fabric that will hold together under this assault.

And I haven't lied. Not once. Not by choice. But I also feel certain he hasn't yet asked the question that brought me here.

I feel exhausted. Wrung out. But not yet at the point of collapse.

That will come, of course, but we're not there yet.

Some time, a few hours after dawn, there's another change.

The Voice changes timbre, tone, intelligence.

This one is more literal. This one is definitely reading my answers off a document. He doesn't understand it too well. Whereas the earlier Voice never showed direct anger, this one makes repeated leaps into blunt aggression. 'Don't lie. You're lying. You know the consequences.' Those things, shouted.

I'm pretty sure that this 'Voice' belongs to one of the goons in the inner room. The first voice was, I assume, altered and disguised by some sound modification software. Disguised enough to stop me from identifying my interrogator in any later encounter. This new one mimics the approximate pitch and tone of the first one, but not all that closely. Not enough to fool me. And, in any case, the stream of questioning, the language used, feels quite different. This has become like one of those old-fashioned pre-PACE Act police interrogations. Thuggish, brutal, effective.

I do what I need to do.

Answer the questions. Sag under the threats.

Sleep flickers around me all the time, as though this whole thing is unscrolling in half dream.

At one point I ask for food and water. Get both. One and a half bananas. Another glass of water. I say I need to pee. The goon just shrugs and says, 'Then pee.'

I assume this phase of things lasts only as long as the Voice himself needs for rest. Say what you like, there are some things you just can't delegate. Extracting information. Directing torture. It's tough at the top.

Questions shout at me through the speakers.

I tell them what they want to hear.

Light shifts without sound.

My head weighs a million tonnes and my body is nowhere at all.

I do notice – or is this already psychosis? – that the smaller door set into the larger one shifts a little in the wind. I think, *They haven't even bothered to lock it. I could just walk right out of here.*

Useless thoughts.

They haven't bothered to lock the door, because I am completely powerless. I can't move an inch and they know it.

Questions.

Answers.

Threats.

The world balling up into a single cold ache. A ball of exhaustion.

Then the Voice, the proper one, returns.

I'm relieved actually. Everything else has been a prelude. Phase one. An overture.

What happens now is the real thing. My chance at safety. My chance to not fuck this whole thing up.

# 33

The Voice spends time – an hour maybe, I've no real idea – just going over old ground, waiting for the moment.

Then it comes. No fanfare of introduction. No golden comet piercing the darkness.

Just, 'You have said that no one at Atlantic Cables is under suspicion. Yes, they should have shared their suspicions in relation to Mr Moon and Mr Livesey much earlier than they did. But that's all. You claim to suspect them of no serious crime.'

'S'right. S'what I said.'

'Yet Livesey was murdered. You've said so repeatedly.'

'Murder yes. Torture first. Got proof.'

'So you suspect whom of the murder?'

'Stonemonkey.'

'His motive?'

'Money. Don't know.'

'Money? So who's paying him?'

'Don't know.'

'I didn't ask for your knowledge. I asked about your suspicions. Don't evade.'

'Sorry.'

'So?'

Pause. 'Sorry. Forgot question.'

'Who do you suspect of paying the climber?'

'Me suspect or inquiry suspect?'

'The inquiry. Who does the inquiry suspect?'

'Not sure. Puzzled. Maybe cable company. Maybe Atlantic Cables competitor.'

'That doesn't sound very focused. What's being done to narrow the field of enquiry?'

'Need evidence. Catch Stonemonkey. Ask him. Go from there.'

The Voice tests out these answers, the first time it's ventured onto this territory. I continue to answer as accurately as I can.

I wish it was someone else under this interrogation. Someone who could do less harm.

The Voice comes back to one of my earlier answers.

'You distinguished between your suspicions and those of your colleagues. You implied your suspicions run further than theirs.'

'Yes. Wild speculation. "Exactly what we expect from our officers,"' I add, quoting Jackson from about a million years back.

The Voice ignores my reference. Asks, 'And your suspicions are?'

'Evans. Galton Evans. Greasy little fucker.'

The Voice doesn't even pretend not to know who Galton Evans is this time. It just says, 'Evans. Why him?'

I explain about Plas Du and Idris Gawr Investments and Idris Gawr the rock climb. Mention the coincidences of names and timing. Mention that Idris Gawr was one of the names on the Atlantic Cables customer lists.

There's a pause as the Voice digests all that. He hasn't paused much before now. This is sacred territory for him, I feel it.

Then, 'That's nothing. A few coincidences. What is the real basis for your suspicion?'

'That. What I said.'

'Please don't hold back. The consequences for you will be

unpleasant. So, again, what is the real basis for your suspicion?'

He bashes away.

My answers, I think, stay reasonably consistent. He asks if we've sought to uncover the other investors in Idris Gawr. I tell him yes. Tell him of course. Say that we haven't been able to get past the Caymans' wall of secrecy. That we probably won't ever be able to.

He drills away at that. I don't know much of the detail and say so.

Then, the real question. The thing that all this, finally, is about.

'Let's suppose you are correct. Let's suppose that Galton Evans and the people behind Idris Gawr caused Moon and Livesey to be killed. Do you understand?'

'Yes. Not suppose. Prob'ly what happened.'

'OK, if you like. But *why*? What is Evans hoping to gain? Why kill a marine surveyor?'

'Maps. Steal data.'

'OK. So your murderer has stolen some data. So what? What does he do with it?'

'Don't know. Sell it. Competing cable. Whatever.'

'Don't be stupid. You said you had a tangible suspicion. Are you aware of a competing cable company?'

'No.'

'Are Atlantic Cables aware of a competitor?'

'No.'

'So who would buy the data?'

'Don't know.'

'Don't lie. Your answers make no sense. Why would Idris Gawr steal data for which there is no conceivable buyer?'

'Don't know. Find Stonemonkey. Ask him. Evidence. Bit by bit.'

'Tell me about your surveillance activities. What teams do you have in operation? What are they surveilling?'

'No teams. No surveillance. I don't know what you're talking about. I've not the slightest idea.'

He's asked the million-dollar question.

I've given him my million-dollar lie.

All that remains is to see if my lie holds up.

The Voice pummels away. Asking questions at random again. Questions picked from everything we've talked about.

He pushes me harder. More brutal now. Faster to threaten. Faster to get aggressive.

Tiredness starts to drag at me so strongly that I think I start to sleep between me finishing one answer and starting the next.

I'm given more food, more water.

A couple of times I'm woken by one of the goons slapping me.

Questions.

Answers.

Lies.

It's hardly disguised now, the Voice's interest in this matter of why. Why Livesey was murdered. What Idris Gawr hopes to gain. I block, repeat, defend.

Questions.

Answers.

Lies.

Then things change again. It's time for phase three. The make or break one. The one that will kill me or, just maybe, free me.

One of the goons brings out a black holdall and puts it on the table. Gets out a yellow thing. Briefcase-sized. A defibrillator, I think.

And a black thing. Neat, the way modern electronics is always neat, always small, always sleek.

I look at it. The whole world has been Appleified. I'm looking at the iPod of torture.

'Picana,' I say. 'Picana.'

The Voice does that soundless small smile of his. Says, 'That's right. And now we'll see if you've been telling the truth.'

# 34

The pain, when it comes, is extraordinary.

I'd been tempted into hoping that they'd misjudged their prisoner. That my weakness and exhaustion would somehow have carried me over the lip of fine sensation. And perhaps it has. Perhaps there is pain worse than this.

But I doubt it.

The picana's touch causes a kind of explosion outwards. As though my body were abruptly and explosively disassembled, before being regathered. Each new touch, a new explosion. My vision goes as well. Explodes into star-spangled blackness, before slowly and cautiously reassembling itself, like a colony of rooks after a winter storm.

The goon is careful, of course. The care of experience, no doubt.

Before he even starts on me, he spritzes me with a solution of brine. He doesn't soak me. It's all more considered than that. A little spritz on my thigh. Then the device's explosive touch. A squirt on my breast or neck or arm or belly and, again, a starburst of pain.

The questions too, of course. There's not much point in this exercise without those. So they fly at me still.

'Who is the Zorro team leader?'

'When did you join the CID?'

'What forensic evidence was gathered from the Bristol apartment?'

I don't even know what answers I give now. I don't even know if my words make any sense. If they're audible.

I have this out-of-body sensation, in which I see myself repeatedly flung to the floor. I see myself as a puppet that keeps falling apart and has to be physically pieced back together.

The feeling is a protective one. It's as though the pain is still there, but isn't particularly mine. Isn't particularly anyone's. Just a gruesome spectacle you have to sit through, like a movie chosen by the wrong sort of boyfriend.

I'm even aware that what I'm seeing can't really be happening. Although I would certainly fall out of my chair if I could, I can't. No matter how much my body leaps about in response to the shocks, I'm bound too tightly to shift the chair.

And mixed in with the questions is *the* question. The golden one. The one I can't answer.

'Why do you think Idris Gawr had Livesey killed? Why did they want that data? Who – if anyone – are you surveilling?'

I block, defend, scream and lie.

Watch from above as my body falls apart.

# 35

After a while, they've had enough. I'm cut out of my chair, taken back to the van. Only one escort this time, not two. If I was little threat before, I'm none at all now. The guy who carries me has the picana slapping against his thigh. If I became difficult, even briefly, he'd simply give me another zap.

Back in the van, it's the same routine, I think. Doors locked. Van reversed against the wall. But I don't know, not really. I'm asleep before I'm even in the van. Don't wake, not properly, even as my head hits the floor.

Sleep is instant and total.

I don't know how long they leave me. They're being cautious, I think. The defibrillator was proof of that. You take all this trouble to abduct yourself a nice helpful policewoman, the last thing you want is for her to go and die on you before you're ready. And torturing a big, strong guy like Ian Livesey is one thing. Applying the same techniques to me is new territory for them. I think they're uncertain how much punishment my little frame can handle.

So they leave me and I sleep.

Sleep – until the music starts. Rock music at massive volume. Speakers, big ones, planted right next to the van's metal side. Music so loud I can feel the walls and floor leap with the sound.

Music intercut with other things too. A snatch of silence.

Then a woman's scream. A howl of dogs. A witch's laugh. Back to the music again. A pumping beat that rocks the van.

It's like Guantanamo would have been had it gone unsoftened by Dick Cheney's loving mildness.

But I welcome the sound. I've been sleeping, when I should have been working.

I drag myself upright.

To the corner with the plywood. Work away. Keeping the wood wet. As wet as I can make it.

I swear and mumble at myself as I work. Swear to the rhythm of the music beating, the woman screaming. There's no coherence to my swearing. No coherence in me even.

The only thing that holds me together is a dim knowledge that I have to get that plywood gap opened out a little more. The thing I want I can touch, but can't get a grip on.

So the woman screams. The dogs howl. The music rocks the van. And I tear my fingers to shreds pulling at that damp and fraying plywood.

# 36

I'm interrupted by the van moving forward again. I might not even have noticed – I'm still crazed with sleeplessness – but I do notice falling over and hitting my head. When the van doors swing open, I'm lying on the floor, wide-eyed and bloody-fingered. A madwoman halfway, more than halfway, to disintegration.

The goon sees my ragged hands, the torn plywood. Grins at it. You can see it in his face, even. Good luck with *that*, darling. He thinks I don't know about the metal grille behind the plywood. He sees my staring eyes as a mark of madness, which of course they are.

He supports me as I limp over to the chair. He tapes me into it and we begin again.

Pain. Questions. Pain. Questions.

It doesn't work really. A waste of everyone's time. I'm too far gone to answer anything sensibly. At one point there's a question, I don't really understand what, but it had to do with what happens next. I realise afterwards that the Voice means 'What happens next on the inquiry?', a question he's already asked a million times. But I don't understand that. Not straight away. I just point at the goon, and say, 'Waste him. Escape. Then send you to prison.' A good answer, in fact. Concise and accurate. But someone starts laughing. Maybe the goon. Maybe me. I'm not sure. Anyway, there's this hysterical laughter in the barn. A laughter that continues even after the goon holds his picana against my side and gives me another jolt of that old Guantanamo magic.

Things go on for a bit.

I leave them all to it. Float upwards to the roof of the barn looking down. Think, *It's terrible what they're doing to that poor girl.* There's some dim suggestion in my head that that poor girl might be me, but that's not a thought I can make any sense of and I don't pursue it. After a while, I get bored watching things down below. Float off into my own world. Dissociated, avoidant, unreachable. My own strange superpower protecting me when most I need it.

At some stage, I don't know when, I hear the Voice say, 'This is stupid. She needs more sleep. Give her two hours, no music.'

There's a bit of discussion. The two hours is extended into three.

The goon helps me out of my chair and I limp back to the van, sagging on his arm.

Just before the doors are closed again, as I'm lying on the floor, twitching at my blanket, the goon's eyes flash again up to the little hole in the plywood, trying to figure out the angles. There are no angles, he thinks. There's a glimmer of goonish pity in his eyes.

'Sleep well,' he says, as the doors close.

# 37

Sleep well: the one thing I can absolutely not afford to do.

Not yet. Not while this whole thing hangs in the balance. I go back to work at the wooden wall.

I wasn't far off before and it's not long before I have what I want now. Two fingertips just grazing the beautiful, soft nylon of the passenger side safety belt. Grazing just enough for me to get purchase. I pluck and tweak and draw the belt through to my side of the partition wall. The belt and its buckle. Its lovely metal buckle.

Careful now, I reach around the floor of the van. Find my broken phone. Saw softly at the nylon strap. The phone is a rubbish tool and the strap is built to last.

But I've not got this far only to be thwarted now. So I saw away and, thread by silvery thread, the seat belt comes apart.

And, in time, I do it. Cut the final thread. The belt divides. The nylon slithers back into its lair, leaving the buckle in my hand. My own golden apple plucked from the garden of the Hesperides.

I stand astonished at my own giftedness.

I lie down on the van floor. Fool around a bit with paper wadding. Make a mess of the water bottles. Eat some cheese. Try to fix my next steps in my memory. I don't altogether trust my addled brain to react with the speed and vigour that it will need to.

And sleep. No reason not to now. No ability to resist anyway.

Sleep comes to me with a rush of darkness.

No dogs. No screams. No music. No nothing.

The deepest, blackest, most needed sleep of my life.

# 38

Sleep – not long enough.

I only know the van is moving, because something – one of the water bottles, I think – hits my head.

I press myself awake. Force wakefulness on my reluctant body.

The van stops.

The yank of a handbrake.

Footsteps.

The doors opening up.

I'm lying on my front. Sodden. Water everywhere. My blanket soaked. Me sprawled out, limbs a-jangle. I try to keep my breathing minimal. Invisible, if possible.

The goon says, 'Fuck.'

Grabs my ankles. Pulls me towards him. My legs slop over the edge of the floor. A strong hand rolls me over, wanting to look at my face.

As I want to look at his.

This is now. This is the moment. The occasion for which I have been training with Lev all these years.

Surprise and a weapon. Those precious advantages which balance out my multiple deficiencies. My lack of height, weight, strength and fitness.

I have the belt buckle in my hand. The plastic base against my palm, wadded in a sheaf of paper napkins. Between the fingers of my fist, the steel clasp shines out like a dagger. I take a moment to check my aim, then slam upwards. All my force. All my strength. Every ounce of will.

I aim for the eye, a pale well in the dark ski-mask.

Aim for the eye, and hit it. Part of the buckle hits his eyeball. The upper part, I think, hits the bone of his eye socket. There's a gush of blood, instant and abrupt. The goon says something too, a kind of groan of shock. He staggers back. Not far. Not too far. He exposes his throat and offers me a second chance.

I take it.

A second blow. Less powerful than the first, but better aimed. His throat this time. The cartilaginous shelf just above his Adam's apple. Drive the steel buckle hard and deep into his neck.

Jugular. Larynx. Windpipe. Most of what matters passes through that narrow space. It's one of Lev's favourite targets.

The goon offers up a little puff of surprise. A small, bewildered *Oh!*, like a six-year-old ballet dancer falling at her very first plié.

He is tottering on his feet, about to fall backwards. I grab his fleece and pull him headfirst next to me on the van floor. The picana bumps against his thigh. I unclip it.

The device is sweetly simple. There's a trigger. And a dial. When they used the damn thing on me, they had the dial set relatively low. I know that, because when they tried nudging it higher, I fainted and they had to set it low again after reviving me.

I'm not such a wuss. A little goonish fainting won't worry me. So I ramp the dial up to max. Jam the thing against the man's throat. Give him a good long jolt of the hard stuff. He convulses once, horribly, then doesn't move. I check his pockets. There's some cash and a bunch of keys. I take both.

Pull his balaclava up. Take a look at his face. The guy is definitely not the one that Buzz had a good look at. Could well be the other one, though. Probably is, from what I remember of Buzz's two e-fits.

But it's time to go. The man's legs are hanging from the back of the van and I bundle them inside. Climb out. Lock the doors. I'm shaky, blurry, but OK.

Crouch down where the vehicle body shelters me from view and release air from the tyre.

What next?

Two options really. One is to walk in on the other goon. He's probably sleeping, or eating yogurt with his fingers, or curled up with a porn movie. He's off duty now and he's hardly expecting me to come through the door, picana in my hand and the white flame of avenging fury in my heart. If I could get up close to him before he sees me, I'd back myself to do what's necessary. And if I did – if I succeeded – there's a fair old chance that we could crack this case right now. Trace that data connection. Track it right through the telecoms network to the Voice himself. Snare him by the wires of his own evasions.

I'd love to do that. I really would. But it's a bum option, all the same. I'm too weak, too foggy, to take the risk. It's all very well to play the avenging angel, but if the angel in question keels over, or is weak as a newborn puppy, or just needs to sit a while to get her strength back, the overall effect might fall a little flat.

So, reluctantly, I play it safe. I walk to the big doors at the end of the barn. Not straight there, even. Because I don't want to fall, I stick close to the wall, keeping one hand against it as I move. I do nothing in haste. Look well to each step. Rest if I need to, move when I can.

I have the bunch of keys in my hand, but the little door which looked unlocked *is* unlocked. A breath of good Welsh wind even rocks it open a little as I approach. I ease it open and step outside.

The barn stands on its own, by the shelter of a big oak. A rough farm track rises into the hill behind. The same track, unmetalled, descends to a valley where lights twinkle in the soft dusk.

And, sitting beneath the oak, her lovely little nose pointing eagerly downhill, is my Alfa-Romeo.

The sight surprises me, then doesn't. It makes sense, indeed. If my disappearance had been reported for any reason, my car would have been the first thing my colleagues would have looked for. Leaving it by the side of the road somewhere, or burning it out in a remote field, would have attracted precisely the curiosity they didn't want. So they just brought the car to a place they had already pre-screened for privacy. Nice, simple, elegant.

I stare down at the bunch of keys in my hand.

See my car key.

The little door bumps gently behind me and I close it properly. Settle it in its wobbly latch. The world lies all before me. Soft blue light, fading to violet and the first wash of a deep, star-scattered indigo blue. Somewhere beyond, in the clotted shadows of a little wood, a night bird calls goodnight to its fellows.

And with wandering steps and slow, I cross the little lane, step into my own dear car, start the engine, and let the clutch down. We purr gently down the hill to freedom.

# 39

I'm sensible, of course.

I'm a million hours short of sleep. OK for food and water, but still very shaky. Still echoing with shock.

So I play things safe. Drive for ten miles, maybe more. Little back roads. Lanes twisting through hazel hedges that rise higher than the car. Starlight and moonlight surprising me through the gaps. Farm gateways and whitewashed cottages.

Sleep starts to pull at me in deep, mountainous waves. A sleep I can no longer resist. Don't want to.

I think I fall asleep at the wheel, in fact. One of those micro-sleeps that's precursor to something huger. I'm only woken by the car passing over a cattle-grid, bars set into the road to keep sheep from leaving the mountain.

I stop the car. Wind my window down.

A starlit hill. The greeny smell of young bracken. Sheep luminous in the half-light. To my right, the hill margin stretches away. The going firm, the grass close-cropped. I drive off-road, following the contour. Drive far enough that my car can't be seen from the road, and even so I take the precaution of reversing far enough into a stand of hawthorn that I'm even further camouflaged.

I'm safe, I think.

Safe, safe, safe, safe.

Cut the lights. Shove my chair back.

And sleep.

Wonderful, beautiful, peace-giving sleep.

When I wake, it's dawn. I'm cold.

I ache a thousand million times more than I knew possible. Like I've run a double-marathon carrying a sackful of rocks. Or like my entire nervous system is still screeching from a few too many blasts of industrial-grade voltage.

But I'm in one piece. And the aches will pass.

I scrabble around in the back of my car. My bag – the one I took up to Llanberis – has been taken, but there's a fleece lying loose in the boot. I put it on. I keep a blanket there too. And chocolate. And the sweet joy of five home-rolled joints of the best Pentwyn marijuana.

Eat the chocolate. Smoke two joints. Curl up in the blanket. Sleep again.

When finally I wake, the skies are the blue of heaven, the air is golden, there are birds singing and sheep grazing, and I am still safe and still free and the bastards who wanted to snap me open and pour me out haven't snapped me or poured me, and I'm still here, still me.

The same as I was, only angrier.

What now?

Ordinary good sense says: get to a phone. Call Watkins. Call Jackson. Get the whole machinery of a rageful police force to start working for me.

But ordinary good sense doesn't always work for the very unordinary me. I may be physically intact, but that's not where the danger lies. The danger for me lies, as it always does, with my fragile and unreliable mind.

My own breakability actually helped me back in the barn. My ability to dissociate – to simply cut off from my body, my feelings, my self – gave me some protection back there. A shelter from the storm.

But now? I can feel the ghosts of those agonies swooshing

around me now, plucking at my mental intactness. The one thing I can't do – the one thing I *mustn't* do – is touch those memories too closely. A police investigation would require me to make statements, answer questions, identify locations. To do all the things that will most endanger my recovery. Even now, thinking through my next steps, I have a joint in my mouth. I'm only able to think these things through as clearly as this because I'm seeing them through a fog of cannabis smoke.

I drive randomly to the nearest town I can find.

Rhayader.

Try to find a battery for my phone. Can't. So just buy a new one. A pay-as-you-go cheapie. Say to the guy who sells it to me, 'Can you tell me what day it is? What day of the week, I mean?'

He says, 'Monday. It's Monday.' Looks at me as though I'm strange.

I'm not strange, I want to tell him. You try spending the weekend under torture. See how you feel.

My hair feels horrible, but there's not much to be done with it. My jeans and top are sweaty and disgusting. Urine-stained too: at some point, I don't know when, I must have peed myself.

I find a shop that sells clothes. Buy some. Wear them. Throw my old ones away. Buy shoes too. The old ones were fairly new. They only really needed laces, but I don't want to keep anything that was there with me in that place.

Buy some food. Eat it.

Buy water. Drink it.

Buy painkillers. Chew up double the recommended dose.

Text Bev in the office. Say, FEELING REALLY ILL TODAY. CAN YOU LET PEOPLE KNOW? HOPEFULLY IN SOON. FXX.

Call Lev.

Normally, I only ever text him. That gives him the option

of when or whether to respond. But this isn't normal. He doesn't pick up, but five minutes later he calls me.

'Fiona?'

'Lev, hi.' I tell him briefly – very briefly – what happened.

'Person is dead?' He means the guy I zapped in the throat.

'I don't know. Really don't care.'

'And the other? You want to get?'

'No. I don't care about him either.'

I tell him what I do want: to get clean, not to go home, to feel safe.

Tell him what I don't want: to talk about it. To remember it, even.

I say, 'I don't know what to do. I've had three joints in six hours and it's still too close. If I start to think about it, I begin to fall apart.'

He says, 'Three joint is not enough. You are where?'

'Rhayader.'

'Rhayader?'

'It's the gateway to the Elan Valley, Lev,' I tell him. 'Across the river from Llansantffraid Cwmdauddwr. Why the fuck does it matter where I am?'

'This place. Is near Birmingham?'

'Kind of, yes. A couple of hours maybe.'

'So. You come to Birmingham.' He gives me directions. Not to where he's staying, exactly. He wouldn't do that, not over the phone. Just tells me roughly where to come – Dudley – and what to do when I get there.

'OK. Lev, thanks.'

'Is fine. No problem. And smoke more, yes? Also chocolate.'

I do as he says. Buy more chocolate. Take the road back north again to Llanidloes, before turning off to Newtown and Welshpool. By the time I get to Caersws, I have another joint in my mouth. By the time I cross the border into England, I have my fifth and final joint almost smoked. On the outskirts of Dudley, I see a white van on whose dirty rear someone has finger-written the words, 'Please clean me,' and I giggle so much that I have to pull over. I laugh until my sides ache, then eat another bar of chocolate and three more aspirin.

Lev meets me at a crossroads in town. I stop the car when I've got to the place he told me to go to. Then, two minutes later, I see Lev – khaki anorak, black T-shirt, jeans – cross the road towards me. He doesn't say hello particularly, just tells me where to go. I drive another minute or two, then we stop. A street of two-storey houses, mostly modern, mostly run-down. The road ends in a wasteland of lock-up garages and the rear view of some industrial workshops.

I park where Lev tells me to, outside a cream-painted house, with a sheet of graffitied chipboard for a door.

'Is here,' says Lev.

The door is held by a crude wooden catch. No lock.

Lev opens the door for me – there are no hinges, so he has to lift it – and I step inside.

I knew that Lev didn't have a permanent home in Britain or, I think, anywhere. Mostly he sleeps in his car or on the floors of friends' houses. But when he isn't doing those things, and isn't abroad, he uses squats.

But knowing that and being here: two different things.

The downstairs room is lightless. The doors and windows have been boarded up front and rear. There's a poor quality kitchen in place – white formica doors loose on their hinges, chipboard surfaces bubbling and splitting with damp – but I already know there's no water in the tap, no power in the sockets.

Lev says nothing. Just points me upstairs.

Upstairs: two bedrooms, one bathroom, nothing else. Bare boards. No furniture. No heating. No bathroom fittings, even. Lev has taken over the larger of the two bedrooms. A military-looking roll of bedding, neatly furled. A ten-litre jerrycan of water. A wash bowl. A primus stove and basic cooking equipment, all clean, all tidy. A black bag, of clothes I presume. A small box of food. The front window was boarded, but Lev has removed the boards and they stand leaning against the wall.

Light enters the room in silence. Leaves again the same way.

I don't say anything.

Don't even step into the room, not really. Just stand there in the doorway.

I am not what you would call a girly girl. I don't have a particular relationship with pink. Don't revere handbags or hoard shoes. I don't love to dress up, or bake, or follow faddy diets, or learn new ways to decorate my home. On the other hand, I *have* just spent the weekend being tortured in a barn near Rhayader and I was, I admit it, wanting something a bit homelier than this.

Lev stands behind me seeing the room through my eyes. Perhaps he was secretly expecting me to be thrilled. Perhaps he is thinking dark thoughts about decadent Western girls, our need for luxury.

He says nothing. Not straight away. We just stand there in the pale light. Even the tiniest sounds echo among these hard surfaces, so a single creak of a floorboard rolls around the room, like a pea in a shoebox.

Then Lev says, 'Is not suitable.'

That was halfway between a question and a statement, but I let it be a statement.

Lev says, 'We go somewhere else.'

I drive where Lev tells me to go. To a leafy street in Edgbaston this time. Lev says, 'Wait here,' and I do, and he goes up to a front door and opens it. He was remarkably fast, but he wasn't using a key. He goes inside for two or three minutes, then comes out again.

'Is good,' he tells me. 'You will like.'

I do.

It's a lovely golden palace of a house. A basement kitchen, all pale wood and slinky gadgets and drawers that slide shut with a glossily expensive whisper of satisfaction. And upstairs, a living room with deep cream sofas, and thick carpets, and clocks that tick, and a giant telly, and books, and art, and picture lights. And, one floor up, bedrooms that just ask you to lie down and sleep and a bathroom so crammed with scented luxuries that it could instantly convert me to the very girliest of girly girls.

'Thank you, Lev,' I tell him. 'Thank you.'

'One disadvantage,' he warns, holding up a bag of hash. 'We have to smoke outside.'

The house, I assume, belongs to one of Lev's women, one of his ladies in lycra. Those women come to krav maga as being more exciting than yoga, but they stick with it – some of them – because sex with an ex-Spetsnaz guy makes for better spa-room bragging than boring old sex with the tennis instructor. I don't know where the woman of the house is now, but nor do I care. When Lev needs me to leave, he'll tell me.

We sit in the garden and light up.

I'm stoned already, but soon I'm stonier. I don't giggle much on pot, not these days, but there's a rippling of something like laughter beneath the relaxation.

A tree above us is crammed with flowers and it takes me a long time to get there, but eventually I do. Point to the tree and say to Lev, 'Magnolia. It's a magnolia.'

I have a bath. Long and hot and with a squidge of every nice-looking smell I can find. There are brown dots on my thighs, belly, arms, breasts, upper chest, neck and sides. More visible than anything we found on Livesey, but I have softer skin and bruise easily. Also, I lived longer.

I don't look at my dots. They feel tender to the touch, but the tenderness of a mild bruise, nothing worse.

I put on knickers, bra and T-shirt, then a thick towelling robe over the top. Come out of that palace of luxury smelling like the sultan's favourite concubine.

We smoke another joint, or Lev does. I'm feeling too giddy to smoke much. Lev has been out shopping. He's got a pile of microwave meals and some DVDs.

We eat macaroni cheese (Lev), chicken tikka masala (me) and watch a chick-flick. I don't follow the story particularly well, but there are people in wedding dresses and everyone has nice hair.

I fall asleep before I find out what happens to the woman in the wedding dress.

Wake up in the bedroom upstairs. I'm not wearing my robe any more, which means Lev must have taken it off, which means he's seen the little brown dots, which means they have a reality they were beginning to lose.

I go downstairs – upset, shaky – roll another joint and smoke it. It's night now, but the magnolia flowers are a cloud of angel wings above my head.

Somewhere, out of view, a raggedy puppet keeps falling off her chair in an almost empty barn. I try to stay away from that thought. Try to stay with the angel wings and the cannabis.

Aspirin. Bed. Sleep.

Lev and I spend the next day smoking, watching romcoms, and eating random food. Lev watches the movies with great intensity. In the middle of one of them, he points a fork at the telly and says, 'You have been?'

'To America? Yes.'

'It is like this?'

We're watching a scene where a woman in a white skirt and yellow top is running through a wood, while a man who travels through time is talking to a nine-year-old girl in a golden meadow.

I say, 'Kind of, yes.'

That evening, I travel to Cardiff. See Watkins. Not at the office, but at her home.

Cal opens the door to me. Is ringlety and smiley and rich in food-related offers. I say I just want to speak to Rhiannon.

And do. Cal banishes herself to the kitchen. I sit with Watkins in their lamplit living room.

Say, 'On the way back from Llanberis, I was abducted. The same men that attacked Brydon, I think. They hadn't been able to get access to our data systems – you did a good job there, ma'am – and they wanted to know how far our investigation had run.'

'Jesus, Fiona. You say you were abducted. What did they—'

'I told them everything. Our work with Atlantic Cables. Our thoughts about the Stonemonkey. Everything.'

'Doesn't matter. It's not like—'

'I know. I'm not apologising. And as you say, it's not like we have a single tangible lead. Not one. But there was one area they kept on coming back to. It was, I'm certain, the key issue for them.'

I tell Watkins about the Voice's concern with possible surveillance activity. With this matter of motive. Why anyone would want to steal data when there was no conceivable buyer.

'What did you say?'

'Nothing. I lied. I told them we had no idea.'

'We *don't* have any idea.'

'Except we do. You know what I think. You know I think we need to investigate the shipping. I thought that before, and I think it doubly now. They thought we might have surveillance teams already operating. That means there is *something* we need to be surveilling.'

I also tell her about the Voice. That my interrogation

proceeded electronically. That the data exists somewhere, if we can find it.

'Fiona, when they abducted you, what else did they do?'

I can't answer that. My face shows I can't.

Watkins doesn't push at the question but she puts her hand to my top. Lifts it. Looks at my belly. The brown dots. She wants to look elsewhere, but my face won't let her. She drops her hand.

Says, 'We need to get you into the office. Do this properly.'

'I can't do that. Sorry. I can't. Can't talk about it. Can't think about it. Definitely can't get all official about it. I'm sorry, Rhiannon, but this is between you and me. It was hard even coming here.'

'OK.'

'And I'm going to need time off work. I don't even know how much.'

'OK.'

'And please, no official anything. No crime report, nothing like that. I couldn't manage it.'

'Can I talk to Dennis?'

'Yes. Him, yes. But the same basis. A private thing between you and him.'

'OK. Take as much time as you want.'

I nod. Should say thank you, I suppose, except that when you're covered in the marks of torture, you sort of expect a modern boss to ease up on all that sick-note malarkey.

'The Stonemonkey,' I say. 'We can find him. I wrote you a memo. Nat Brown will be helpful. Mike Haston too. Use them.'

She nods.

'And the shipping. If we can.'

She says, carefully, 'We need to proceed on the basis of evidence. At the moment, we have nothing.'

I whisper, 'Hardly nothing.'

I mean the question they kept pushing at me. That question, and these injuries. These brown dots that cluster like starlings.

Watkins says, 'I'll do what I can. I'll speak to Dennis.'

I smile. A sort of smile. Lopsided and underpowered. I feel more than hear Cal peeping in from the kitchen, then closing the door again when she sees us still at it.

Watkins whispers, 'At least they let you go. At least they did that.'

I want to say, 'It wasn't quite like that,' but the words just stay jammed somewhere between my larynx and my tonsils. Lodged sideways, like a seatbelt buckle embedded in cartilage. Like a steel clasp buried in a mash of blood vessels and major airways.

I say, 'I need to go.'

'OK.' Her face moves in the lamplit dimness. She had feelings for me once. A stupid, impulsive infatuation which I stupidly helped provoke. She's happy with Cal now. Those feelings for me lie safely in the past, but that doesn't mean that their mark doesn't still remain. She has something like tears in her eyes, I think.

I say, 'We didn't do anything wrong. None of us. We did nothing wrong.'

Watkins's eyes say thanks. But she'll be tough on herself. Reanalyse her decisions, and do it with the same pitilessness that makes her such a demanding officer to work under. But still. I spoke the truth. I don't think anyone could have predicted this – and even if she had, what could she have done? She, or any of us? If bad guys want to snatch junior coppers from remote country roads, nothing we do will stop them doing just that.

'Look after yourself, Fiona.'

'I will.'

# 40

Will – and do.

Return to Edgbaston. Live in a stew of dope and microwave food and romcoms. Have baths that last for two hours. Use every scented thing I can find.

Throw all my clothes away. The new ones, that I bought in Rhayader. Buy myself new-new stuff from chain shops in the Bullring shopping centre. Mango, Gap, Oasis, Zara. I buy things that are practical and things that really aren't. Buy nothing, though, that is short-sleeved or cropped or that might ride up to show an inch of thigh. I wear long-sleeved pyjamas in bed and avoid myself in the mirror.

My brown dots start to fade.

The first day or two, Lev is there all the time. Then he starts to disappear for ever longer stretches. I don't think there's anything he has to do particularly. He lives on nothing. His martial arts teaching is sporadic at best. I think he just prefers his squat to this palace and needs to spend time there.

The dope, though, I keep that up. That and the romcoms.

Although I've smoked cannabis for as long as I've been in recovery from Cotard's, I've never been one for bingeing. Don't like the fog, the excess. Yet the more I smoke, the more that barn recedes. When I try to find it in my mind – something I don't even attempt for the first few days – I discover that I can hardly find it. It's not even that I've lost my recall. It's more that I recollect all those things – the van, the chair, the questions, the pain – like something from a story, half-forgotten. And there are so many other stories in my head now. Women in white skirts and golden meadows. Bridesmaids searching for dresses. A girl taking a boy to a Celine Dion concert when it was meant to be something to do with sport.

And in the end, everything fuses. Like some weird movie where the heroine is tortured in a barn, then escapes to a world of taffeta dresses and silver lakes and implausibly handsome men. A movie so long and tangled that you get to the end barely able to remember what happened at the start.

Before too long, I feel that old investigative itch starting up again. It's not that I'm ready to abandon the cannabis – I'm not – or that I've given up on the romcoms (I haven't). Just that, in between times, I'm ready for something else. So I fire up a computer. Find out what's been happening.

Penry has been taking loads of photos of ships. He's covering everything from Bristol to Milford Haven. As good as his word, he has a mate of his taking pictures of the shipping in Dublin, and also Cork.

Thousands of pictures of hundreds of boats.

Iron and rust and machinery and waves. A world I don't understand.

I fiddle around on Dropbox and find a way to send the pictures to Stuart Lowe without burning out the internet. Get a note back from Lowe saying he'll take a look. The note is terse, but the promise seems genuine.

Good enough.

On the Stonemonkey, Watkins has been at her Watkinsian best. She's put together a decent team on the research. Headed by the sleeky blonde Jane Alexander, a capable, if not always imaginative DS. Three full-time team members: Jon Breakell, Essylt Jones, a new recruit, and Pete Pritchard, a uniformed constable over from Bristol and a reasonably keen amateur climber.

Jane's group – with support from a specialist web team in London – have identified around 150 climbing blogs, plus a whole heap of e-zines, magazines, climbing clubs and forums. They're starting to scour those things for anything suggestive of the guy we're looking for.

I think of Brown's comment, 'You can't hide the good 'uns. You know 'em when you see 'em.' If he's right, then Jane's accumulating pile of data holds our answers. A rubble heap, containing jewels.

That's good. Rigorous police work, properly conducted. But I also remember what I kept repeating to the Voice. My feeble summary of our inquiry's next steps. *Don't know. Find Stonemonkey. Ask him. Evidence.*

If we find the Stonemonkey and he tells us nothing, what then? We have the hands that murdered Livesey, but nothing else. Evans in prison, but on a trivial charge. The Voice untouched, unknown, out of reach.

An outcome I could not accept.

Time passes.

Lev checks in most days. Checks I'm maintaining my dope-and-romcom diet. He sometimes stays long enough for a joint and some microwave yukkery, but my present comforts don't suit his spartan tastes. He never, now, stays for long. He doesn't say much directly, but I sense he thinks I'm doing OK. Healing up.

Good enough.

On my sixth day in the house, I feel strong enough to attempt a search I've been putting off for too long.

Eilmer. My favourite flying monk.

When I accessed the data on Gareth Glyn's witness protection programme, I got virtually nothing. *Security clearance not sufficient*. Except that the case had an odd codename: Eilmer.

Odd enough that I checked it out on Wikipedia and found only one possible reference: to Eilmer of Malmesbury, the monk who flew.

Now just maybe whoever came up with that codename was a keen student of medieval aviators and wanted to tag all his projects with suitable monikers. But more likely not. More likely, the only people who know about Eilmer are those who have reason to think about Malmesbury when coming up with codenames. And since the codename itself is only visible to fairly senior police and intelligence officers, no one would have thought it necessary to avoid any glimmer of connection to the target. Which all goes to suggest that the little bird I'm seeking perches somewhere close to Malmesbury's stony walls.

Then there's the question of what cover Glyn now uses.

The answer: I don't know, but I doubt that people ever really reinvent themselves, that they inevitably migrate back to whatever they truly were in the first place. And if Gareth Glyn – a somewhat obsessive planning officer of only medium ability, intelligence and ambition – were forcibly transplanted to some other clime, would he not head back to the only thing he actually knew and was competent at? The answer, I think, is yes.

So: I search for planning officers on Malmesbury town council. Nix, nothing.

Then planning consultants and town planners. Get nowhere.

Run similar searches on towns and villages within thirty miles of Malmesbury.

Nothing.

Extend the range to fifty miles, but without confidence.

Nothing.

I think laterally. Extend my search. Not planning exactly, but closely related. And before too long – bingo! – I light on a Gareth Pollitt, a Malmesbury resident, with a small business in architectural drawings. Mr Pollitt has almost no online record. No Facebook page, no home blog, no professional memberships. I only come across him because he took out a paid ad in one of those little local advertiser booklets, that happened to release an online version.

I can't find a photo. No biographical detail. No entry on the electoral roll.

Those omissions are good. Very good.

I make a call. Reach 'Pollitt'. He speaks in an accent which is Cardiff born and bred. A native Taff.

I'm so pleased, I want to blow kisses down the phone.

I don't, of course. Instead I tell Pollitt that I'm building an extension and need drawings. Could he help?

He says yes, but starts to ask questions that I hadn't properly prepared for. What floor area? What kind of glazing? Any change in levels between the main house and the extension? I'm awkward to begin with, but then find my stride and start to build myself an extension. Give myself underfloor heating, and a roof lantern, and French windows with an arch above and a new terrace beyond, in York stone and herringbone brick.

'There's a Japanese maple, though. We'll need to build around that,' I caution him.

Pollitt, who sounds sour, says, 'I suppose we'd better meet.'

I say yes, but don't make a date.

Not yet. The barn still feels too close. I want more padding before I re-enter the world I had before.

Spend two more days in a fury of dope and movies. Then, on Tuesday, just eleven days from when I was taken, I borrow some sports things from the woman whose house this is and go out for a run. I'm rubbish, of course. My stew of cannabis and junk food hasn't helped my never-remarkable fitness. I run a mile, then jog another half-mile, then get a stitch and walk back.

But I'm done, I realise. This chicken is cooked.

I text Lev, GOING BACK TO CARDIFF NOW. THANKS. VISIT ANY TIME. FXX.

Clean the house. Wash anything that needs washing. Think about replacing the bathroom toiletries, but decide to leave them be.

I'm OK, I think. Injured but OK. When I undress now, my brown dots are barely visible. I have to search to find anything.

That evening, I ring Watkins. Tell her I'm coming back.

This coming Sunday, it will be the end of June. The Atlantic Cables line testing starts on Monday. And my *do-this-police-style* plan is looking calamitously far short of coming to fruition.

# 41

Wednesday.

Morning run. Shower. Breakfast.

My run is crap, but I'm two per cent less useless than I was before. I think, *I should really get fitter*, something I've thought often enough in the past, but this time the thought might actually preface action.

It's strange being home again – blood stains still a-glimmer on my hall wallpaper – but not a bad strange. It's nice being back.

Go into the office. Check in with Watkins.

She grips me fiercely, but in a way that is meant to be nice, then drags me straight through to Jackson's office. He gives me one of his shaggy-browed stares. Goes to the door and kicks it shut.

'Fiona.'

That's not even a statement, it's a name, and the rules say you don't have to yap every time someone correctly identifies you.

I say nothing.

'Welcome back. If you *are* back.'

'Um, I think so.'

'Anything you'd like to tell me? On the record, I mean. As a police officer.'

I shake my head slowly at that. No, no, I don't feel ready for all that. Maybe never will.

Jackson waits till his stare vanishes into pointlessness. 'OK, and off the record?'

I tell him what I told Watkins. That I was abducted. Pressed for information. Divulged everything, except my particular suspicions about the attacker's motives.

Jackson says, 'Rhiannon told me that she saw . . . some marks. I won't ask you about those. You tell me *what* you want, *when* you want, and *if* you want. But two things. One, we have as much support as you could possibly need. If you want someone to talk to, a psychologist or whatever, any of that, you just tell me. There's a guy in London who's worked with . . . these sort of issues. He might be good, he might be crap, but if you want to see him, you just say. All right?'

Nod.

'And two, we were pretty bloody focused on this inquiry before, but we're ten times as focused now. I've spoken to the chief' – he means the chief constable – 'and told him that I want there to be no limits to the resources I can chuck at this thing. Not that there *have* been limits so far, but just in case. I've given no reason for my request.'

I nod thanks. Can't speak. Not really. It's frightening being here, but OK.

Jackson does some more silent staring. Shows off his versatility in the field.

Then pulls out a file and passes it over.

'This came to us from Dyfed-Powys. There's a DNA correlation and we always exchange information when we have that sort of thing.'

I flip the pages. It's a police report from the force that covers mid-Wales.

A report that deals with an incident logged in a mountainside barn outside Abbeycwmhir. In the hills above Rhayader.

A burned-out van. A dead man inside. The man's body was badly burned but enough remained for a pathologist to determine that the probable cause of death was a succession of blows to the back of the head. His DNA matched one of the bloodstains left in my hall.

I try to speak.

Nothing comes out.

Try again.

Say, 'Those head injuries. That wasn't me.'

Jackson: 'Fiona, I wouldn't give a flying fuck if you had battered the man to death, then brought Jesus Christ and a retinue of his fucking angels down from heaven to bring him back to life, so you could kill him all over again. And I will, happily, put those sentiments on the record any time the situation requires.'

Me, huskily: 'Thank you.'

A pause while I wonder where my voice has gone to.

Then me again: 'I *did* disable him. Hurt him quite badly. Maybe it was a punishment thing.'

Jackson: 'You said to Rhiannon there were two men, correct? You think the other guy saw his buddy had messed up? This was his way of cleaning up?'

I shrug. Or maybe nod. Those blows to the back of the head mean I must have left the man alive. I hadn't been sure before. As to what came later, I guess Jackson's suggestion is approximately correct.

Leaning over me, Jackson flips through the file to the boring stuff at the back.

Telecommunications and Data Analysis. The sort of thing I normally chomp through, but not this time. It just looks like a lot of words.

Jackson: 'More crap. Basically, we can track a heavy use of mobile broadband – very unusual in that area – to the local mast. Some, not all, of that traffic was automatically captured and stored. But it was very heavily encrypted and – don't ask me how this stuff works – things were routed abroad through a billion different servers so we don't have a bloody clue who was on the other end of that line.'

I nod.

Disappointing, but as expected.

'Dyfed-Powys have asked the folks at GCHQ to do what they can. But if you encrypt things right, you beat the code-breakers every time. We'll just need to see.'

Nod.

I'd bet every marijuana plant I own that these guys know how to encrypt things right.

When I next become aware of anything, I see that the room is silent and Jackson and Watkins are both looking at me.

Jackson: 'Fiona, I need to ask. Are Dyfed-Powys likely to find your DNA on the scene? If the answer's yes, that's no problem, but it would help to know.'

It's a good question. My DNA would have been all over that van – blood, sweat, piss, you name it – but apart from that there was just the chair with the tarpaulin beneath. Take those two things away. Wipe down the door, maybe the walls, and you'd have a perfectly clean crime scene. No evidence I was ever there. That's why they burned the van: the one item they'd never have been able to clean.

Me: 'Don't think so.'

I get the words out, but that place has come closer again. That barn. That chair. That long first evening, where I sat alone, watching my face on screen, waiting for what was to come.

Gusts of something wash around and through me.

It was to avoid all this that I spent all that time in stoned-out luxury in that Edgbaston palace. I don't want to answer Jackson's questions. Don't want to step any closer to the things that happened in that place.

Jackson stares at me. Watkins too, but Jackson is doing the heavy lifting.

He says, 'Constable, I'm not sure you're fit for duty.'

'I think I need to work. Part time even. It might help.'

I give him my I'll-be-good face. It's one he's seen often enough before, usually just after he's ripped my head off for some offence or other.

To Watkins, Jackson says, 'Rhiannon, can you use this one? It's OK to say no.'

'Yes. Jane Alexander's got a group researching this climber. Fiona could help with that.'

'OK. But if you see her cracking up, you send her straight home.'

Watkins says yes, and Jackson looks at me to see if we've got a deal.

We have. I do my submissive nod. The one that promises good behaviour.

Jackson says, 'Anything else?'

My mouth moves. I'm not sure if words come out, but I think they both know what I'm trying to ask.

Watkins says, 'We've placed a watch on Cardiff Docks. Also Swansea, Barry, everywhere in our area.'

That means not Newport. Not Milford Haven. Not Bristol. Nowhere else in the south-west.

It's a start, I suppose, just not a very good one.

Watkins says, 'If we get any additional evidence – anything we can use to justify the request – we'll get other forces involved. At the moment . . .'

She trails off. Her meaning, I think, is roughly: 'We've put a watch on the ports in our own jurisdiction because you've been tortured in the line of duty and for some reason you've got a bee in your bonnet about all this, so we want to make you feel happy. As for actually taking you seriously, that'll have to wait for – you know – *evidence*.'

I don't say anything.

Jackson uses the silence to give me a bunch of stapled sheets. The title page says:

**TORTURE SURVIVORS' HANDBOOK.**
Information on Support and Resources for
Torture Survivors in the UK.

'This thing is mostly aimed at people coming here from abroad. But you should read it. And use it.'

I hold the book in my hands.

I say, 'They got the apostrophe in the right place. That's good.'

'Yes.'

I sit there holding the book, not looking at it.

Jackson says, 'Chicago. We were recruiting for a new exhibits officer anyway. But because we weren't sure exactly when you might be returning, we pushed that process forward a bit. Got a new guy. Somebody Nadin.'

'Trefor,' says Watkins. 'Trefor Nadin. Did the job over in Gwent. Knows his stuff.'

'So I'm . . . I'm done?'

I can't believe it. Feel almost shaky with gratitude. If I'd known all along that being tortured was all it took . . .

Jackson says, 'Yes, you're done. And you did a decent job, when we needed you to do it. Thank you.'

I shrug, as though I'm the sort of officer who regularly receives those compliments. I do wonder, vaguely, if Nadin is likely to find the ash from my joints in his drying machine, but I think I'll be OK.

'Sir?'

'Yes?'

'Chicago.'

'Yes?'

'I believe I'm right in thinking that the case has no useful leads. Lots of good work, but no actual leads?'

Jackson nods.

'It's just that during the course of my work, I noticed a couple of coincidences.'

Jackson nods telling me to go on. He doesn't know what I'm about to say.

'Well, my understanding is that perhaps the only tangible lead we have is that the victim, Kirsty Emmett, thinks she was deposited by a white van. A good-sized white van. She lost consciousness during her ordeal, so we can't be sure that she didn't switch vehicles at some point, but we're pretty sure she started in a van, and ended in a van. Just not necessarily the same one.'

'Go on.' That bass rumble, which is vibration as much as sound.

'And we've checked more than a hundred such vans, without result. No DNA match. No fibre match. No van that looks suspiciously clean. We've still got some results to come back from the lab. There are a number of vehicles we're still chasing. But no one is feeling particularly hopeful. The inquiry team has also failed to identify any vehicles that were both in Gabalfa and in Tremorfa at approximately the right dates.'

Jackson nods. His eyes are shaded, but glittering.

'Now, I don't have anything like proof, but I do have some questions.'

'For example?'

'Well, for example, DI Dunwoody knows perfectly well that his nephew is an instructor at the university sports centre, just outside Gabalfa. Knows perfectly well that the centre runs a fleet of vans. And of course the nephew in question, Kyle Bransby, works here as a SOCO. Works with Ifor Dawes a lot of the time.

'Now I'd presume that Bransby knew that Ifor was going down to Splott a lot of the time. I mean, a SOCO and an exhibits officer work together all the time. But Ifor's journey down to Splott would take him so close to Tremorfa that it would be totally unremarkable if we saw Ifor's van cropping up on Rover Way at the kind of time indicated by Emmett. What's more, Bransby had presumably observed Ifor's recent forgetfulness. Although Ifor may not have been driving his van in a particular place at a particular time, he wouldn't necessarily remember one way or the other.'

Jackson: 'And *was* Ifor's van present at the relevant time?'

'Yes. Yes, it was. But of course, we can't meaningfully forensicate the van, because any traces of Emmett's DNA could have found their way there via a spilled evidence bag, for example. And any traces of Kyle Bransby's DNA would be accounted for by his presence as a SOCO. In effect, the evidence could be hidden in plain view. Left in the only place where it would have no value in a court of law.'

Jackson – slowly, cautiously: 'And that's your hypothesis?'

'Not a hypothesis really, sir. A possibility.'

'The possibility being that Bransby used a college van to abduct a victim local to him there, in Gabalfa? He rapes her. Transfers her to a different van – Ifor's – and dumps her. He gets access to Ifor's van – well, we don't know how exactly . . .'

'And Ifor was,' I say, 'visibly forgetful about car keys and the like.'

'OK. Then Bransby dumps Emmett. Returns the van. Makes sure he's on the crime scene team, so his DNA is, legitimately, all over the place. I mean, yes, he'd have been suited up, but if we'd found his DNA, we'd have put that down to sloppiness, nothing else.'

I nod. 'Yes.'

Jackson stares at me. 'And you didn't say any of this before now, no matter that you hate it down there, because . . .?'

'Well, the inquiry *was* doing some necessary and useful work. Work which could have found a bad guy who wasn't

Bransby. Two, if Bransby *was* our perpetrator, then any court case would be stronger for having successfully ruled out so many other possibilities.'

'And three?'

I hadn't said anything about three, but maybe my face is suggesting something, or maybe Jackson is already thinking along the same lines as me.

'And three, because there may be two crimes here, not one.'

'Yes. Yes, indeed there may.'

He stares at me.

Over the years, Jackson has yelled at me plenty. Probably more at me than any other member of his team. Proper, old-fashioned, Welsh bollockings. Lungs trained on the hilltops and rugby fields. Language born of the pithead and the parade ground. An eisteddfod of rebuke. And I've always assumed – anyone would – that this was Jackson properly angry. That the shouting was how he showed it.

I now think I got that wrong. I mean, yes, when he's yelling at me, he's probably not secretly humming 'Mr Blue Sky' in his head. But I think how he is now – silent, glittering, emphatic, compressed – is how he is when he's really angry. When his jumping up and down on someone's head thing might actually happen.

Jackson, dangerously controlled: 'Do you know whether DI Dunwoody has made any effort to check those university vehicles?'

'No.' Jackson's eyes push a question at me, and I correct my answer. 'I mean, yes, I do know, and no, he hasn't.'

Jackson, in a whisper: 'And in any case, Bransby is a crime scene specialist. If he can't clean a van, then no one can.'

'True. But then there's a bizarrely well-cleaned vehicle to deal with. You might even expect that Bransby – if he were the perpetrator – might let a few weeks go by then seek to persuade the college authorities that the vehicle is faulty and needs to be sold or scrapped. Anything to remove it from possible investigation.'

Jackson, so quiet now I can hardly hear him: 'And has the college been selling off any such vehicles, Fiona?'

'Yes.'

'Do you know where those vehicles are now? Who the new owners are?'

'Vehi*cle*, sir. It was just the one. As for the new owner, you're looking at her.'

Jackson falls silent, but his eyes retain that dangerous intensity. I can feel Watkins's gaze, blowtorch-like, on my neck.

Jackson: 'Fiona, if you wouldn't mind, I'd ask you to give Rhiannon here access to that van. Rhiannon, if you would arrange the necessary analysis, I'd be most grateful. There will be no need to mention anything of this to Mr Bransby or Inspector Dunwoody.'

We nod. Make the necessary arrangements.

Watkins says, with some kindness in her voice, 'Is there anything else?'

'Not really. Just – well, Kirsty Emmett was blindfolded. She could see very little. But I presume she could smell. You might want to ask her if she remembers the smell of aniseed. Bransby favours a particular type of chewing gum.'

'That's a question we'd normally ask at first interview. Are you sure—'

'I've read the transcripts. The question was not asked.'

'And it was DI Dunwoody who led that interview?'

'Yes.'

'Thank you.'

And that's it.

We're done.

I'm assigned part-time to Jane Alexander's research effort. Jane says she wants me to review the work her team has already done. That's good policing – a way to avoid groupthink – but it's also an indication that she's not finding what she's looking for.

I accept a mountain of data from her and promise to start work.

She doesn't ask where I've been. Nor does anyone else. Partly, that's because I'm not the wheel at the centre of anyone's universe. Mostly, it's that Chicago has kept me well concealed from ordinary office life, so no one's really noticed anything different.

I sit at my desk, feeling strange.

An unthreatening sunlight falls across a peaceable carpet.

People who know me walk past, say hi, mean well.

No one is taping me to a chair.

No one is using me as a poor-quality electrical conductor.

*Constable, I'm not sure you're fit for duty.* Him and me, both.

I phone Penry. Tell him he doesn't need to bother with the Cardiff docks, or anything else in our area. Ask him to keep going with everything else.

He tells me to come over one evening. 'I'll cook,' he says. I say yes, OK.

See my friend Bev, who talks to me about a new diet and fitness thing she's just starting.

I tell her I'm starting one too. Have just started, in fact.

'You, Fiona? Dieting?'

I persuade her that I'm for real, and she tells me that she's trying to swim regularly down at the International Pool on the Bay. We agree to go swimming together that evening. I phone Ed Saunders, who lives in Penarth just a few minutes on from the pool. Invite myself round to dinner. He sounds keen, welcoming.

The world is strange.

No one is throwing me in a van.

I'm not ripping at wet plywood with ragged hands.

Lev isn't here, jabbing his fork at the telly.

I make peppermint tea and eat lunch at my desk. I wonder what Jackson will do to Dunwoody. I think that if he does go properly apeshit – if he does actually jump on Dunwoody's head – then I should get to watch. I mean, if not me, then who?

I dispose of my mozzarella and rocket sandwich. Turn my attention to Jane Alexander's documents.

Ninety-five names have been harvested so far. Of those, twenty-eight have been discarded as Not of Interest. Thirteen are deemed to be of Possible Interest. There are no names of Definite Interest.

I follow my sandwich with a plastic pot of chunked fruit that I eat with my fingers. If colleagues stop to chat, I find I'm able to conduct a vaguely normal conversation.

I feel OK. I feel OK.

I've survived and I feel OK.

I think: *If this police-style thing doesn't work out, maybe I don't have to do anything about it. Maybe I work hard, within police rules, and if we catch the criminals we do, and if we don't we don't.*

That is a possible course of action. Theoretically, I mean, that is possible.

# 42

Swimming with Bev is surprisingly brilliant.

We swim up and down and encourage each other lots. Afterwards, we sit in a chirpily colourful cafe and drink vegetable smoothies and Bev talks about her diet and whether her arms and thighs have got any thinner.

I listen to her with intensity, discuss her questions with earnestness, then agree with whatever she said in the first place.

Look at *my* thighs. Wonder if they've got thinner.

We agree to make our swimming trip a regular thing, Tuesdays and Thursdays.

Then Penarth. Ed's house.

I arrive with a bunch of flowers, nice ones not garage ones. Give him a friend-kiss, warm but not intimate. He has something lovely on the stove. A bottle of red wine open, and half a glass already poured. We chat a bit. This and that, nothing much.

I don't talk about the barn at all. Just skirt around any topic that comes close to that subject. I tell Ed about my swimming trip with Bev. We talk about work.

My corpses, his nutcases.

Ed normally sees through me when I'm not being authentic – a favourite word of his – but his attention isn't fully with me. He chops herbs and wields oil, but he's too slick in the kitchen for those things to be the cause of his distraction.

I don't care. We can be distracted and fake together, that's fine with me. Then, when he's done with his herbs and his chopping, he tops up his glass and says, with just the faintest rose-blush of embarrassment, 'Look, could I ask you a favour?'

The favour is that Ed, good old Ed, is about to launch out into internet dating. He wants me to look over his draft profile, help choose pictures.

Whatever felt crooked in the atmosphere before, that little bit askew, feels straightened out by his request. For all my inadequacies, I'm one of Ed's closest friends and probably his closest female friend. I respond at once. Busy myself with the duties and responsibilities of my new role. Help choose pictures. Comb out the text of his pitch. He's got four different websites in mind, and wants me to help choose one of them. We study the sites. Laugh at some of the pitches on offer. Pick out guys and girls that we think look hot. When we get hungry, Ed brings his stew – some rich, tomatoey, Italian thing – over to the computer desk and we eat and work at the same time.

I'm struck, actually, by how buff Ed looks in his pictures. He does some windsurfing from time to time, and there's one of him, ankle deep in water, wetsuited up, looking to his left and laughing, with wind and salt spray ruffling his hair. He looks attractive. More than attractive, in fact. He looks hot.

I say, 'That one's a keeper, definitely. You look like a hottie.'

When I say that, I feel his eyes shift back from the screen to me. I feel the odd interrogation of his gaze. Its ambiguity.

I remain as steady, unruffled as I was that night with Buzz, the night he told me that he'd started dating again. It's not even that I've thought these issues through. Would I, a somewhat nutty late-twenties woman, do well to seek some kind of a relationship with a (surprisingly buff) mid-thirties guy who, for reasons that I don't understand and can't explain, quite likes me, certainly as a friend but just possibly (or have I got this totally wrong?) as a romantic partner?

I've just no idea how I'd answer that, or answer any of the multiple questions locked away in its interstices. But in a way, that uncertainty *is* my answer. I'm still too messed up to make sensible choices. Buzz was a wonderful choice. My landing permit for Planet Normal. But, now that I have my feet temporarily set on this difficult planet, I need to choose carefully. Make a forever choice for my forever future.

I can't do that until my head is more settled and my head, at the moment, is a-crawl with beetles and thoughts I can't bear to touch.

So, for now, I just blink forward, study the screen and keep my voice blandly normal. If there's any question in Ed's glance, I bat it away with peaceable indifference.

Ed pours himself more wine. Drinks it with a little edge of anger or aggression.

The thing – whatever it was – passes.

We pick two websites, ditch the others. Select photos. Write text. Pick out some possible women for Ed to 'like'.

It feels good. Ed needs a proper relationship, I can see that. He's been available before, but not determined. Not strategic. This venture of his feels like he's at last taking the dating game seriously again. He got into his first marriage way too early – he had his first child when he was only twenty-two – and this feels like a mature attempt to refashion a life for himself.

I think of him and Buzz, two thirty-something men pushing down the slipway into the estuary that, with only a breath of good fortune, will open out into the placid seas of Forever Married Life.

I wish them both well.

We go on working. Laugh quite a lot. Ed drinks too much.

He looks a bit like a younger, more suit-and-tie version of Matthew McConaughey and I slip in a photo of the actor to the group that we upload. Ed calls me an idiot when he notices, but he likes the compliment.

A good evening.

Good for Ed, good for me.

When we hug goodbye, I don't feel that ambiguity any more, and think perhaps it was never there in the first place.

Ed closes the door, leaving him enclosed in the golden lamplight of his little hall. Me outside in the sea breeze and the blowing trees.

I walk to my car. Blip it open. Get in. Do nothing.

When I close my eyes, I see all those website women. An endless sun-swept parade of them. Blond-haired and brown. Long hair and laughing eyes. Bare shouldered on a foreign shore.

And Ed with them. The multiple Eds of those photos. In close-up. In a wetsuit. As Matthew McConaughey. Ed clean-shaven, Ed with some windsurfer's stubble.

I feel something. An emotion that wriggles out of reach.

I try holding up words to the shape.

*Lonely. Jealous. Confused. Happy. Horny.*

The words and the shape don't match. I think there aren't enough words.

Emotions flicker out of sight. Silver mackerel in a dark grey sea, uncatchable.

And when I check my emails last thing before bed, I have one from Stuart Lowe.

He's been looking at Penry's photos.

Most of them he's dismissed, but there's one of a ship in Milford Haven that he's singled out. A stern trawler. The *Isobel Baker*. The ship docked in Milford Haven yesterday. Unloaded a regular catch, caught after a couple of successful spells in the Irish sea.

Lowe's email says,

Gantry appears to have been adapted for non-standard load. Trawl winches look unusual for a ship this size – but certainly suitable for a load-bearing umbilical system. Can you get better photos? Superstructure if poss. Also close-ups of stern, especially gantry A-frame and any new cabling/control equipment. Also ramp and any on-deck fixings, particularly if recent, please. Thanks, Stuart.

I stare at Penry's photos. They look completely unremarkable to me. But then that's why I recruited Lowe, because he knows what to look for.

I shoot him a thank you note. Say we'll get more photos.

Call Penry. 'Brian, I think we've got it.' Tell him which boat, which port. He says he'll get onto it tomorrow. We ring off.

Silence swelling in a dark house.

Streetlights on outside, but nothing but the greenly glowing oven clock inside.

Silence and darkness and bloodstains in the hall.

I call Penry back.

'Brian?'

'Fi.'

'Be careful.'

'I will.'

'No. You don't understand. Be incredibly careful. More careful than you've been in your life. You *cannot* be seen. I can't tell you everything, but you have to believe that these people are extremely dangerous. They kill. They torture. And they are very, very close to making a lot of money.'

'OK.'

'You don't have to do this. You owe me nothing. You do not owe me this.'

'OK.'

I don't know what else to say. I think I should tell him not to head back to that port. But I think if I did that, he'd go there anyway.

He reads my mind, or close enough.

He says, 'If I don't go, if I don't take these photos, you'd go anyway, wouldn't you? You'd do it yourself.'

I hadn't quite got as far as thinking about that, but I know he's right and say so.

'Well then.'

'It's not the same. This is personal. For me, this is personal.'

Penry doesn't say anything straight away. For some reason, nothing I can explain, I'm suddenly sure that he's standing like me in a dark house. Silent inside and lit only by streetlights filtering in from the night.

Two people. Standing in darkness. Holding phones until the silence creaks with the waiting.

Then Penry says, 'I used to be a copper. And I fucked up. And I went to jail. And now I want to do something that makes me feel like the first part of my life, the policing one, wasn't a waste of time. That it wasn't just some kind of act. You're not the only one who gets to do stupid things because they're personal.'

I smile at that.

Smiling on the phone: not a brilliant telecommunication technique, but it works for me. A smile glimmering through the darkness.

We tell each other goodnight.

Hang up.

Listen to silence, as blood stains glimmer in the half-light.

Sleep.

# 43

The next day. Thursday.

A review meeting to go over the work that Jane Alexander and her team have been doing. Watkins leads. Alexander seconds. Plus me, Jon, Essylt, Pete Pritchard and Mike.

From what I've read of the group's work so far, there's been nothing wrong with the intensity or breadth of its research. But still. Those things should mean we have a fistful of promising leads, active investigations already under way. And instead? Nothing.

Alexander's best prospects are climbers who aren't quite good enough. Or not quite bold enough. Or whose current lifestyles (mature geography student at the University of Edinburgh, living in a shared house with three other students) aren't exactly typical of the just-scammed-ten-million-pounds set.

No names. No leads. No progress.

We're doing something wrong.

We riffle again through our names. Our best possibles. Jane Alexander seems nervous. Worried that she's been sloppy. I've a feeling she didn't sleep much last night. Her normal sleek perfection now a matter of concealer and under-eye creams as much as the standard issue Alexandrian flawlessness.

But I don't think she's done anything sloppy.

Nor, for all her air of fuming ferocity, does Watkins.

During a break in our meeting, I say as much. Tell her,

'Jane, you've done a really good job here. It's amazing how much you've managed to get done in a short time.'

She says, 'Oh, do you really think so?', flashes me a grateful look and hurtles off to get coffee.

I make myself peppermint tea in the kitchenette and, as I wait for the kettle, call Warren at Atlantic Cables. Ask him how the project is going.

A few connection niggles, he tells me, nothing major. Onshore testing starts on schedule next week, Monday 1st July. 'Then the full line tests right after that. Middle of July if all goes well. Basic tests first. Then speed tests. Signal quality, that sort of thing. We start to handle client traffic from mid-August, but on a mirror basis only. Basically replicating their existing data transfer and matching the two flows to make sure we're not losing data. Proper live traffic from September.'

'And what if something weird happens? What if there's a line break or something like that?'

'Oh, well, that sort of thing does happen. We assume 0.5 faults per thousand kilometres of cable per year – and we've got more than five thousand kilometres of line. But we can find those things right away these days. Just flash a signal down the line. Watch the reflection come back. We can locate any break to within a few metres. Just get a ship out to repair it and *boof!*, we're motoring.'

I say thank you.

Make tea.

Let the steam wash my face, a pale green scented cloud.

As I'm steaming, I see Dunthinking walk past. No bootprints on the side of his head. No look of terror.

Bransby has not been arrested, or even interrogated.

I don't know what's going on.

I call Whillans, the telecoms guy. I say, 'Eliot, if I wanted to mess about with someone else's telecoms line – a brand new line, transatlantic – what would be the best time to do it?'

He laughs. 'Like the Atlantic Cables line, right? A line like that?'

I acknowledge as much. Tell him what the testing schedule looks like. Tell him what I think is about to happen.

He says, 'You're going to need the full line to be operational and carrying enough traffic that you've got something to work with. Not too glitchy, but at the same time you're hardly going to mind if there's a little genuine noise to confuse things. If you were asking me to arrange the thing, I'd probably wait till the basic line tests were completed, then get started. The whole job should only take a day or so. A few hours even.'

I say thanks.

Cut the line.

On Whillans's cheerful account, our bad guys have the last part of July to do what they want. Any earlier, and the line might be too glitchy to give reliable feedback. Too late, and they risk the line being open for business, no longer in beta.

We've got maybe three weeks to catch these guys red-handed. A three-week window that closes with every passing day.

The thought makes me feel sickish. Empty.

I hope Penry gets his photos.

I hope the *Isobel Baker* is the right ship.

I hope that Stuart Lowe gives us the kind of report that even my beloved bosses and the yet-more-dearly-beloved magistrates of South Wales can't help but accept.

And then, more even than these other things, I hope that Watkins, and Jackson, and everyone right up to the Home Secretary herself authorises the use of helicopters and gunboats and a whole squadron of special forces to go and rip that ship apart. Rip it apart, until they find what they need: the evidence that will close this case.

The things I hope for I don't always get.

I go back to the Stonemonkey meeting.

More paper. More questions. More long, complicated, unsatisfactory answers.

It's Mike who sees it first. He's standing at the window, his back to the room. With his ragged blond hair in its dirty green hair elastic, he looks a bit like the caveman version of Jane Alexander. What she might become if civilisation collapsed.

Mike says, 'He's not here, that's the thing.'

Watkins doesn't understand him at first.

Gesturing at the mass of data, she says, angrily, 'It's *precisely* to discover if he's here that—'

Mike says, 'No, what I mean is he's not *here*.' He gestures at the window. A view out over Bute Park. Green trees tossing in the wind. The weather is clear for the moment, but there are squalls heading towards us from the west.

Frown-lines written in cloud. The fish-scale gleam of rain.

Watkins says nothing.

I say, 'Mike, we're pretty sure he's British. His blackmail letter was written in perfect English. And why scam British insurers if you're really French, or whatever? Why not just scam your own insurers?'

Mike turns and answers me direct.

'Oh, I'm not saying he's not British. Just – you don't reach elite standards these days without a lot of sport climbing.'

Sport climbing: he means climbers working on routes that have been protected by steel bolts drilled every two or three metres. The alternative – trad climbing – means making use of whatever natural protection a cliff does or doesn't offer.

'I know. We know that. We're already prioritising those type of people.'

Mike shakes his head. 'No we're not. We're acting like typical Brits. One of our young climbers goes over to France. Spends a winter there climbing on bolted rock. Comes back here in spring. Does some hard routes on gritstone or up in North Wales and everyone says this guy is the Next Big Thing.

But the fact is that southern Europe has all the sun. And their rock is bolted, almost all of it. Here, you can't even drill a bolt without some big theological discussion of whether you've just insulted the gods of the mountains.'

This has been a theme of Mike's. One I've heard before, except that now I think maybe I haven't *heard*-heard him.

In summary, Mike's argument comes down to this: Brits are mad. Our best climbers climb on damp mountain rock without drilling bolts in it first. Their hardest climbs are terrifying do-or-die affairs, the kind of thing no self-respecting French, Spanish or German climber would think of attempting. On 'traditional' – that is, potentially lethal – routes, British climbers are among the best in the world.

Yet that excellence is bought at a cost. The cost is that you can't push yourself to the very limits, because if you do, you will wind up dead. And our terrible weather means that our climbers don't even get to climb as often as their competitors in southern Europe. With the result that – in terms of strength, fitness, and sheer damn standards of difficulty – British climbers are outranked by those of pretty much every other major climbing nation in Europe. On ordinary, safe, bolted rock, British climbers are little more than mediocre.

Mike shuts up.

Watkins's stare swivels from him, to Jane, to me.

I interpret: 'Mike is saying that our guy is a Brit who bases himself abroad. The reason we haven't yet come across him – in those "Out and About" columns, the blogs, all the rest of it – is that our guy has hardly touched the British scene. He's got the strength and fitness of those top French or Spanish climbers, but combines that with an all-British insanity when it comes to risk. We've been doing everything right, except for one thing. We've been looking in Britain, when we need to look overseas.'

There are quite often moments like this in an investigation.

When you look at the same data from a different angle and all of a sudden that new view looks entirely compelling. Ungainsayable.

Even Watkins feels it. She does that rotary champing thing with her jaw that she, and no one else in the world, does.

Then, 'OK. We look abroad. Mike, which countries do we need to prioritise? France clearly. Also Spain . . .'

The investigation revolves on a sixpence. Heads inexorably off on its new course.

I tune out. Watkins will do what she needs to do.

When the meeting breaks for lunch, I say to Watkins, 'Ma'am, I'll take the afternoon off, if I may.'

She nods. Happy that my needs are so modest. But her attention is elsewhere, as it should be.

The Stonemonkey.

European fitness married to British insanity.

A torturer and a killer, who belongs behind bars of good Welsh steel.

# 44

Leave the office. Find my car.

A few minutes later, I'm out of Cardiff, heading east.

Leaving Wales, entering England. The Severn Bridge a pale green arch through the heavens and Duffy on the sound system, yelling her little Celtic heart out, as seagulls ride the air above.

*I'm doing OK, I'm doing OK.*

That whole idea of doing this police-style or not at all: I think that could work. It could really work.

That's possibly the first time I've had that thought since joining CID. It feels nice, the notion that I might not have to put life and limb on the line. That I could simply live a life more ordinary. Let Watkins and Jackson and the Home Secretary decide what to do with the *Isobel Baker*. That is, in theory, a possible way to do things. Other people, I understand, do it all the time.

Bristol.

Hullavington.

Malmesbury.

A hilltop town. One of the oldest fortified towns in England. Created by a charter from King Alfred in 880. A hilltop fort centuries before that. The two branches of the Avon curling below. A natural castle.

If the town is a castle, Glyn's house is one of its less-lovely outbuildings. A down-at-heel semi, in a row of down-at-heel semis. I ring his doorbell. Smell moss and damp timber. A drain that isn't discharging right.

Glyn – 'Pollitt' – comes to the door. Clean shirt. Oatmeal cardigan. Grey trousers worn with the kind of shoes that are halfway to slippers.

He lets me in. Takes me through to his 'lounge'. Thick pile carpet and a flame-effect gas fire.

He sits me down. Says, 'So. Your extension.' His Cardiff accent feels stronger face to face than on the phone.

I say, 'I'm not building an extension.'

I say, 'You're Gareth Glyn. In witness protection now, but that's who you were. I'm Fiona Griffiths. Tom Griffiths's daughter.'

He doesn't say anything. Not straight away. Looks at me with sad eyes. The eyes of a spaniel left too long in kennels.

He picks food from between two molars with a long fingernail. 'I suppose this had to come.'

He makes tea. I lean on the kitchen doorframe as he makes it. Neither of us say much. There's a dog bed in the corner, but no dog.

Glyn comes back through with the tea. Teacups and saucers. But his hands have a tremor and the cups jiggle and shake on their china bases.

He's scared, I see that. I don't particularly want to frighten him but I do want information.

I say, 'I just want to know what happened. Tell me what happened and I'll get out of your life.'

He says nothing.

I say, 'February 1985. You claimed that municipal planning decisions were being rigged. That there was corruption. I believe you. I'm sure there was. If you say my father was involved, I'd believe that too.'

He says nothing.

'I've spoken to DCI Yorath and he told me you were on to

something. I've spoken to your wife. I know you were taken into witness protection.'

Still nothing, but the silence has elongated now, stretching out till it's too thin to hold.

I wait.

For some reason, I don't know why, I think that Glyn's dog is dead. The bed in the kitchen just a keepsake.

I don't say anything.

And eventually, Glyn says, 'You saw Delia?'

'Yes.'

'How is she?'

'She's having a rough time. She found it hard, your leaving like that.'

I'm putting it mildly. When I saw her, Glyn's wife, Delia, had the angry, injured look of the slightly mad. A house that badly needed a clean and tidy. Hair that needed washing. And clothes that weren't quite right: a too-short flowery dress worn with bright red tights and heavy black shoes.

I don't judge her for any of that. I've been to those places myself. Those places and worse. But I don't know how Glyn would react if I told him the full truth, so I hold back.

'She was always having a rough time.'

The bitter comment of a husband who chose to leave. But his eyes are watery and distant, and sometimes a bad marriage is better than no marriage at all.

More silence.

I say, 'I'm sorry about your dog.'

The kitchen: there was no water bowl. No dog bowl. And nowhere else in this little house for those things to be.

Glyn says nothing, but his eyes are full. He wipes them with a handkerchief, taken from the sleeve of his cardigan.

'Your father was on the fucking take,' he tells me. 'They all were. Councillors. The whole redevelopment company. The property developers.'

'Go on.'

'Look, I'd be the first to say that the old Tiger Bay was a shithole. It *was.* But it's how you phase the development. Which pieces of land get built on first. Who gets to do what parts. So, if you're given a slice of prime waterfront – the place where you're going to get the big hotels, the luxury flats – you're going to make a killing. Fifty yards back from the water. Same area, but no view of the Bay, and the profits aren't there. I mean, yes, you'll make money, but not on the same scale, nothing like.'

'So the big developers, the corrupt ones, decided in advance what bits they wanted, then approached the key councillors with handfuls of cash? Rigged the whole thing in advance.'

'Yes, exactly.'

'And where did my dad come in?'

'Where *didn't* he come in?' Glyn spits.

I don't answer, but I want more than that and Glyn, I now know, wants to talk. Unless I mess up, this hummingbird is going to sing.

He wipes his mouth and proves me right. 'Look, you don't get gentleman's agreements in these things. What if one of the councillors took the cash, then didn't vote the way they said? Or what if two developers got into a fight about who got what? Remember that this was Tiger Bay. Your father's stamping ground. His domain. Nothing happened there without his permission. The councillors and the developers divvied up who did what. Your dad provided the muscle.'

*The muscle.*

Violence.

How much violence, I've never really known, but the thought makes me shift uncomfortably, slippery in my own skin.

For some reason, I remember the barn. When I was taped

to the chair, alone in the silence. In those long hours before the questions started. When time fooled around in the straw and light died in the cobwebbed windows.

How dark did my father's past get? I don't know. Yorath and his fellow detectives didn't know. Only my dad and his very closest associates, Uncle Em and people like that, only they would have known.

Increasingly spacey, I ask for names, dates, specifics.

Glyn doesn't have much. Most of his suspicions arose from coincidences of timing. Minor oddities in the planning process which don't signify much to me, but which told him, an insider, that things were being rigged. Where Delia, his wife, was rambling, obsessive and muddled, I would say Glyn is simply obsessive. That, and probably correct. The one absolutely clinching piece of evidence he brings to bear is a conversation overheard in a corridor of the planning department's offices. A promise that a certain permission will be given, even though an appeal had yet to be heard. There was an activist, a Tina Jewell, who was successfully arousing local opposition, but the planner in question 'promised' – Glyn's word – that she would be 'sorted'.

'And?' I ask.

Silence floats in the air. The ghost of a dog. How many other ghosts, I can't say, but too many. The room feels stifling.

'She was sorted all right. Killed. That's when I . . . that's when . . .'

Glyn doesn't finish his sentence, but I think I can guess his meaning. He snapped. His whistle-blowing wasn't an act of courage exactly. It was a failure of nerve by a man who didn't know how to handle the environment he found himself working in.

'Who killed her?'

He shrugs.

I try again. 'OK, who was the developer? Who profited?'

'Look it up. Who had the waterfront? Who made the cash? They were all in on it.'

He has the exhausted face of a man who has spilled his all. The way my face must have looked after that first long night of interrogation. The way it looked before the bad stuff started.

Bad things, dark things, pluck at my awareness.

Ravens snatching at roadkill.

My head wobbles. Loses its bearings. I find myself thinking *Can I really do this? Is this too soon?*

Not helpful. I *am* doing this.

Giddily – spacily – I ask one last question.

'The witness protection programme. Why that? What was the threat? Why did all that blow up again?'

He shrugs. 'Don't know. Nobody bothered to tell me.'

'You must have asked.'

'"A credible, specific threat." That's what they told me. A credible, specific threat, now fuck off out of your life. You can take your dog.'

I push away at the same question, but Glyn is done with me now. Angry at me, as he's angry at everything else. His crazy wife. His dead dog. The criminals who forced him out of one life. The intelligence services who forced him out of another.

I think again of this hilltop setting. This natural castle.

I wonder if that's why Glyn ended up here. A sense of protection. Self-defence.

I say, 'The River Avon. English people say that, don't they?'

Glyn doesn't respond.

I stand up. Leave him a card with my mobile number. 'If you want to tell me anything else. I want to know.'

Glyn watches me with sorrowful eyes. Doesn't get up. Doesn't take my card.

Then, 'I don't. I never say that.'

No Welshman would. Avon – or *afon* – simply means *river*. When the English speak of the River Avon, they're saying

River River. Saxons too lazy to learn the language of the conquered.

Fuck 'em.

Malmesbury was our town before it was theirs. Our river, our hill, our castle.

Eilmer was, I think, a bad codename for Glyn. Eilmer might have been an idiot, but he was a romantic one. One who, for one furlong, some two hundred airborne metres, did what no human before him had done. Escaped gravity. Flew like a bird. Adventured out on the impossible.

Glyn is the opposite of all that. If his life had worked out the way he'd wanted it, he'd be finishing up his career in the Cardiff Planning Department, living in the same house, married to the same woman, doing the same things in the same way until arthritis stiffened him, cataracts dimmed him, muscles failed and cancers ate him.

Eilmer limped for want of a tail. Glyn limps for want of a backbone.

Fuck 'em all. Eilmer, Glyn, everyone.

I leave.

Drive far enough to get Glyn's sadness out of my hair, the corners of my eyes. Get to the motorway, but pull off at the first service station, Leigh Delamere.

Smoothie. IPad. Google.

Tina Jewell. Community activist. Tiger Bay. Died mid-eighties.

I try the search different ways. Get nothing, or nothing much.

I find a million Tina Jewells – PR people in London, hairdressers in Alabama, a drag queen in Berlin – but none who's dead enough and Welsh enough for my taste. I'm still doing OK. Despite my momentary tremor while I was with Glyn, I think I'm doing OK.

Then I try a different search string. The twentieth I've tried.

Google offers some answers, but asks, Did you mean: *Gina Jewell reported dead 1985*

Yes, Google, I've a feeling I did.

A feeling that's like I've opened my front door – some ordinary errand, buying some milk, posting a letter – and finding that there is nothing but pale sky below me. The planet curved and distant beneath my feet.

I click through, away from the drag queens and the hairdressers, and step out into that empty sky. I'm twenty thousand feet up and there is no sound at all.

Gina Jewell. Campaigning for local residents' rights. One of those old, redoubtable Tiger Bay tigresses. Welsh blood, Jamaican blood, Norwegian, God knows what. A fierce campaign, ended by her death.

Her death wasn't murder or, rather, it wasn't reported that way. A road accident, outside the Pewter Tankard, a poor man's boozer in the rough end of town. Neck broken, died en route to hospital.

*Your dad provided the muscle.*

Twenty thousand feet up and the same whispering silence that there was in the barn. Light dying. A girl taped to a chair, wondering what lies ahead.

I drive home, slowly. Blurrily.

I must recross the Severn Bridge at some point, but if so, I don't notice. No pale green arch. No Duffy. No seagulls.

And when I get to the door of my house, a funny thing. I find that I'm barefoot. Tights yes, shoes no.

Going back to the car, I find one shoe – coffee-coloured suede, dark red trim, quite nice – rolling around in the footwell. Of its coffee-coloured sister, no sign at all.

And Gina Jewell dead.

# 45

I'm not sensible.

Or rather: I don't know what sensible looks like. What it would look like for me.

Here's what I know:

- Two weeks ago I was tortured. I still can't think about the episode, not in any detail. My mind leaps from it, like a finger withdrawing from a hotplate's searing touch. Thanks to Lev and the dope and the romcoms, I haven't yet collapsed, but I still don't trust myself. My walls are paper and I can feel the coming storm.
- We haven't found the Stonemonkey.
- I can't get Watkins interested in ships, even though this whole damn case will stand or fall on our ability to get on board the right damn boat at the right damn time and with the right level of scary-as-shit police resources.
- I'm not right in my head.
- Watkins and Jackson can both see that I'm not right. They want me to see this psychologist in London. Take time off, sort myself out.
- And Glyn. What he said about Gina Jewell. The chronicle of a death foretold.

All those things, plus this: I keep losing my shoes.

A couple of times, I lost them at home. No big deal, just I noticed that shoes that had once been on my feet were now somewhere else. On the stairs, on a sofa, kicking around the kitchen floor.

Then, on the Saturday after my trip to Malmesbury, I decide to go into the office. Part of my rehab, knowing that work is one of the things that grounds me.

I spend the morning doing good things, useful things. Think I'm doing OK. Then I go out to get some lunch and happen to meet Bev in the lobby – she'd left a bag here, was coming in to pick it up.

We greet each other warmly – all that female bonding in the swimming lanes – but she adds, 'Interesting fashion choice there, Fi.'

I look at what I'm wearing. Dark trousers. Pale top. Jacket. It isn't interesting at all. Why I chose it.

I must look puzzled, I suppose, because Bev adds, 'The bare feet look.'

I look down, more attentive this time. Stockinged toes where black leather pumps were meant to be. I say something, I don't know what, but Bev doesn't care anyway, knowing me for a muddle-headed idiot at the best of times.

She continues on her merry Bevian way. I chase back upstairs and scurry round after my shoes. Find one under my desk. Another in the kitchenette, propped up on the counter under a little handwritten Post-It that says, *Help Me!*

I put the shoe on. Take the Post-It.

Sit down on the floor, in the mostly empty office, trying to feel my body, count my breaths, do any of those things that normally centre me.

No good.

Give up.

Go home.

Breathe. *In*-two-three-four-five. *Out*-two-three-four-five.

It doesn't help, or doesn't help much.

Remotely check Cesca Lockwood's computer. Her emails. Facebook.

I know already that on Saturdays she, and a group of friends, often meet up for sushi and beers, before an evening out on the town. From what I can tell, today seems no exception. I wish I could hack into her phone, but although hacking those things is quite easy, I would need temporary possession of her phone to do it.

Ah well. That there are limits to my dark powers: a sad, regrettable truth.

Time passes. I'm not sure what happens in it. But at some stage the little green digits of the oven clock in the kitchen tells me it's time to go.

Bag, keys, phone, coat.

Check my shoes – still there – and drive east.

# 46

King's Cross.

Back streets. That yellow-brown London brick. Dug from pits in Haringey, baked in Middlesex. A Victorian London built on the labour of Victorian children.

Houses, offices, railway stations.

Those things and restaurants. Some glitzy. Aluminium tables and chairs grouped under green awnings. Plate glass windows opening onto clean linens and murmuring waiters.

My place isn't like that. No awnings. No whispering glass.

I shove my car into a parking space. Try to read the signs, the ones that tell me whether it's legal to park here or not.

I can't work them out. They speak in some black and yellow language of their own. There's a parking machine you can put coins in, though, so I put some coins in. The machine beeps. I wait a bit, but it doesn't say anything else, so I go to the restaurant.

Sushi. Tempura.

I've never had either.

Cesca Lockwood is already there. With friends. It's a warm evening. Lockwood is wearing a knitted cotton top. Loose weave. Nice. Dark hair, gathered at the back. She looks cool, the sort of cool that doesn't have to try too hard.

Also, I notice, the kind of cool that isn't dressed for a big evening of partying. Which is good. I didn't want that.

I sit down at a table close to her. A Japanese waitress comes to me with a menu and asks me what I want.

I don't know. The menu is full of things I don't understand. I point at something. The waitress says something, speaking rapidly, communicating I don't know what, but she finishes with smiles and nods, so I finish the same way too.

She goes.

Lockwood is staring at me. Maybe I'm staring at her.

I look away.

Lockwood's gaze goes back to her friends. There's a kind of intensity in the way she buries herself in their company. A digging in.

My food comes. A plastic tray with things on.

When I'm scattered like this, I can usually ground myself by spending time with dead people. Summoning their quiet presences and letting them calm my unruly one.

But which dead people? There are so many. I've liked my time with Moon and Livesey on this investigation, but now there's Gina Jewell too, a woman whose face in death I haven't seen, not even in photos.

And not just her, but me too. That woman sitting in an empty barn. That woman thinking, *Guys, I'm already freaked enough. Really very, very freaked.* The ragged little puppet who keeps falling apart and keeps being put back together, as her attentive torturer prepares the next little spritz of brine.

Those four – Moon, Livesey, Jewell and me – circle round. A corpse quadrille.

I'm not sure where to put my attention and it keeps sidling back to Lockwood, who sees me watching her.

I eat prawns with my fingers.

I think I look odd. I'm definitely feeling odd. I realise that Lockwood – Cesca – has a confusing presence, like she's almost part of my little company of corpses.

I stare too much, too long, too obviously.

Some of her friends get up to go. Not her. She gets her bag, walks over to my table.

'And you are?' she says.

'I'm Fiona. Fi.'

'Do I know you?'

'No. Not really.'

A pause. If you can call it a pause when she's this busy assessing me.

'You're being really weird.'

'Sorry. It's my fault.' I get out my warrant card. Show it. Meaning actually properly show-it-so-she-can-read-it, not just flash a wallet at her. Once she's had a chance to look, I say, 'I worked on the break-in down at your mother's house, Plas Du. I was one of the people who charged your father with perverting the course of justice. The main one, in a way. I mean, I'm very junior but it was me who pushed the whole thing.'

One of her friends is lingering by the door. Wanting to go, but checking that Cesca is OK with the weirdo. There's an exchange of glances, which ends up with the friend leaving.

Cesca sits opposite me.

'You're the one who's sending my dad to jail?'

'Not me, the courts. But, yes, basically.'

'And you've come here to do what?'

'Um. See you. Talk.' Pause. 'Look, I know you don't get on with your dad. I know you don't see him.'

Her face pushes a question at me. I tell her that I can track her car and his and that they've never been in the same place. 'And I know you changed your name. And your brother, Ollie, told me he is a bit of a dick.'

'He's a total dick, not a bit of one.'

'I also know that your dad gives you four thousand pounds a month and that you give it away. Every month.'

Cesca looks furious, but also upset. It's a face we see a lot when interrogating people. It's like the first sight of prison bars: a dawning understanding that life, sometimes, has hard limits.

I like that face usually. The sign of an interrogation going well. But it's not something I can handle now. That face feels too like my face. My face as it was on that chair, in that barn.

I try – clumsily – to soften things.

'No one else knows. I mean, it wasn't a police thing.'

'If it wasn't police, what was it?'

'Cesca, can we go back to your flat? I'll tell you everything. You can choose what to tell me. If you want, you can tell me nothing at all.'

My warrant card is still sitting on the table. She picks it up again and studies it. Trying to see if it's a forgery, I think.

I say, 'I *am* police. I'm not all that normal in my head, so if I come across as a bit strange right now, that's because I am. You wanted to know how I knew about the money. The answer is that I burgled your flat. Not physically me, but a friend.'

'That time in the café? At college?'

'Yes.'

'You were there, like, watching me?'

'Yes. While my friend burgled your flat.'

'I could have you fired.' There are tears in her eyes. Angry ones.

'You could have me prosecuted. Fired, prosecuted, jailed. You'd be well within your rights.'

'You want to talk?'

'Yes.'

That angry flare again. But something decisive too. A rapid movement of the chin. 'And you'll leave if I tell you to?'

'Yes.'

She turns for the door. I know I have to pay, but I don't know how much. I just show my money to the waitress, and let her take what she needs.

Cesca and I walk to the Tube station.

Get a train heading north to Seven Sisters. Light alternating with darkness. Stations and tunnels. Adverts telling me about the thousand different selves I could be. Prettier, taller, saner, cooler.

Livesey, Moon, Jewell and that girl in the barn gallop through the tunnels with us. Skittering on the rails. Chattering in the cables. Howling in the dark space between carriages.

Cesca and I try talking but it doesn't really work, so she just plays with her silver jewellery and I watch for corpses in the flashing window reflections. In my bag, I still have the yellow Post-It that says *Help Me!* I keep my bag half-open on my lap, so I can see the note.

The train gets us to wherever we need to be.

We get out. Start ascending an escalator. From the bowels beneath us, a warm wind blows.

Cesca says, 'Where are your shoes?'

I stare at her. Then at my feet.

Tights yes. Shoes no.

I say I don't know where they are. When I lost them.

Whisper, 'Sorry.'

Sorry for being a crazy policewoman. Sorry for losing my shoes and burgling her flat. Sorry, sorry, sorry.

We get to her place. Her flatmate isn't there. Cesca makes herbal tea.

Her bedroom feels darker, more intimate than it did from Penry's photos. There's an overhead light, but Cesca turns on only a single heavily shaded sidelamp. A double bed, a small one. A long aubergine dress hangs from the side of a wardrobe. Art posters. A corkboard with photos and postcards. From a dressing table, the glitter of jewellery and make-up.

I put my hand to her desk drawer. Say, 'Do you mind if we smoke?'

She says, 'Smoke?'

I get out her hippy-dippy Indian box. 'I should have brought my own. Sorry.'

I start a roll-up.

She covers her hand with her mouth as she watches. Then goes into her kitchen and calls someone from there. I think she's speaking to her mother. Trying to see if I really am a police officer. Something her mother says persuades her that I am.

She rings off. Comes back in to the room, sits on the bed. Accepts a puff or two from the joint. Sips her tea.

Starts laughing. Not mostly because of the dope. I think she's partly laughing at me, partly just a release of nervous tension.

I smile back.

The dope is settling me a bit. Either that, or somehow my corpses and me are coming into line. Like the place they are and the place I am start to fit together better.

'This thing with my dad. Is he really going to go to jail?'

'I think so, yes. If his lawyers are smart, they'll look at the evidence, persuade him to plead guilty, and I'd say he'll probably get a year, no more. Serve a few months. Open prison.'

'So not that bad then?'

'Not bad enough.' I smoke more. Finish the joint. 'Look. He's your dad. And I meant what I said. If you ask me to leave, I will. I won't enter your flat or your life again. Won't get someone else to do it. I'll be good as gold.'

'OK.'

'And I don't know how much of the detail you know. But basically your dad lied to cover up an insurance scam – a scam where he wasn't the perpetrator. On the other hand, it was a big scam and a persistent lie. He deserves punishment, no question, but he'll tell the world he didn't do anything wrong. That he was just trying to prevent a crime.'

'And you don't believe that.'

She didn't really say that like a question. More a prompt. She hasn't, I notice, given me any real steer on where she stands in relation to her father. He's a 'total dick', yes, but that phrase could conceal anything from weary disdain to cold, hard fury.

I say, 'No, no, I don't. I think he's up to much worse things. I think he's capable of extreme violence.'

Extreme violence: I certainly suspect Evans of ordering the Livesey and Moon murders, but that's not really what I had in mind. Evans spoke of Idris Gawr as an investment fund run 'by a small group of us, quite active.' I think Evans is the front man. The Voice is one of his close associates. Whichever one of them ordered the torture on me, Evans was as complicit as if he himself had been holding the picana.

My fingers are rolling another joint. I apologise yet again. 'Sorry. I've had a really hard time recently. I'm off work.'

I light up again but, oddly, simply acknowledging the violence has helped to settle me. As though it's better to have the stink of those electrical burns in the room than hovering just outside.

'Our evidence is pretty scanty,' I continue. 'Nothing we could place in front of a court. But I saw evidence – real data, legitimately gathered – suggesting that you and your dad didn't get on, so I came to have a look.'

Cesca speaks at last, her mind made up about something. 'I don't know anything about violence. Not the sort you mean, anyway.'

'But . . .?'

'He screwed a friend of mine. She was fifteen, quite messed up. I mean, she was messed up beforehand. Afterwards . . .' She shrugs.

'Go on.'

'Jazz MacClure. That was her name. Jacinta, Jazz. She got into a thing with my dad. Totally consensual, except for the fact that she was underage and there was a thirty-five-year age gap.'

I nod. We'd never take action against a seventeen-year-old boy having sex with a fifteen-year-old girl, but we'd never ignore underage sex when there was such a massive disparity between the ages.

Cesca says, 'My dad did his stuff. Money. Private jets. Fancy parties. I mean, when he wants to be nice to people, he can really turn it on.'

'I know. He tried with me, sort of.'

'He's compulsive. He thinks it's some proof of manliness, the younger they are. Anyway, there came a point where Jazz wanted out. She'd somehow persuaded herself that this was a love thing, the real deal, then found he wasn't even being faithful to her.'

'Surprise, surprise.'

'She started to talk to friends again. Realised she'd been exploited. Sent a few angry texts or emails, whatever, to him, accusing him of stuff. Talked about going to the police. Not that she would have done. It was just venting.'

'She *should* have done, you know. We treat those things better than we used to.'

Cesca lets my remark go. I shouldn't have said anything. She was on a roll. She finds her train of thought again and says, 'He came to the school. Said he'd been friends with this girl, yes, but no sex, nothing like that. Then realised she'd become infatuated. Angry and vengeful when he tried to step away. Told the school she had a drug problem, which she *totally* didn't. I mean . . .'

'Dope yes, harder stuff no. And the dope under control,' I suggest. 'If that's a drug problem, then I've got a bad one.'

Cesca laughs. 'Actually . . .' she says, and laughs at me. I laugh too and wiggle my toes in my tights.

'They looked in her room. Found some coke. Also a tiny bit of heroin. Some drugs and needles that had been nicked from the school matron's office. A bundle of cash whose presence she couldn't explain. They expelled her. She had problems at home anyway and things got worse.'

'Yes?'

'A few months later, she attempted suicide. A year and a bit later, she actually did it. I mean, my dad wasn't there. He didn't make her do it. It *was* her choice and she *was* messed up, but still. Fucker.'

'Yes.'

Cesca gets up. Goes over to the corkboard, and its mess of photos and postcards. She picks a photo off the board and hands it over. Jazz MacClure, with a wineglass in her hand, laughing at someone or something out of sight. Long, dark-blond hair. A maroon top with a beaded collar. Pretty, in a windswept way. A picture overshadowed by the knowledge of what came after.

'Dad gives an allowance to me and Ollie. Ollie takes it. I don't. I'm fine with Ollie taking it. I mean, the money is just money, isn't it?'

'Yes.'

Cesca takes the photo off me and looks at it. Kisses her finger and touches it to the dead girl's face. Pins the picture back where it came from.

'I don't think I've helped you, have I?'

'We can't prosecute the crime, no. Not without Jazz. Not without a whole heap more evidence.'

Cesca looks at me. The first time she's done so properly, the mistress of her own apartment. Her assessment of me is confident, adult.

'Why did you come here?'

'Cesca, I think your dad is a criminal on a grand scale. One who will kill, if need be. I think he works in collaboration with others. Those others probably don't look like criminals. They probably look like legitimate businessmen. Probably *are* legitimate businessmen, except that that's not all they are.'

'I don't know about any of that. I'm not saying you're wrong. Just I don't know.'

'That's fine. Look, do you know what I mean if I distinguish between evidence and intelligence?'

Her answer: sort of, not really.

'OK. Evidence is anything we've acquired according to specific rules, which we can produce in court, which will make a material difference to the verdict. Intelligence is much looser than that. It's for our benefit, not the court's. It might be hearsay in a pub. Or an accusation left anonymously on a Crimestoppers line. Or something that a daughter says, strictly off the record, about her father.

'We can't mention those things in court. But we also don't have to reveal them to the defence team. Don't have to prove they're true. But most of our cases, most of our bigger ones anyway, start off with scraps of intelligence. The intelligence shows us what kind of evidence we need to gather. We build the case from there.'

'OK.'

Cesca has her bracelet off and she's fiddling with it. Long fingers, dark nails. She's barefoot too now, like me, except that her shoes are neatly placed at the end of the bed and she hasn't trodden holes into the soles of her tights.

'You know your father. You know who he sees and what his relationships are. You have insights that we don't have and can't gather. We can't even intercept his communications because we don't have enough evidence to secure permission.'

'You want me to – to grass on him?'

Her voice puts inverted commas round the word. This isn't

a world she normally lives in. Not a world she ever wanted to be part of.

'I do, yes. But that's me. What *I* want. You have to do what *you* want. What feels right.'

'I don't *know* anything.'

'Except maybe you do. Things that might seem irrelevant to you might seem very significant to us.'

Her face is naturally mobile, expressive, but it's got a stillness to it now.

'And if you're right . . .?'

'If your intelligence helps us direct our inquiries in the right direction, we'll be investigating your father on a charge of murder. If we can make that stick, he'll get a life sentence and most likely die in jail. You might not want that. Even if you're no longer in touch with him, even if you don't approve of him, you might not want that. And no one says you should. You *are* his daughter. It *is* your decision.'

Cesca's face flicks from me, the corkboard, and some place out in the hallway, a pool of dark shadows where her father stares back at her.

I realise I'm doing a Gareth Glyn. Telling a girl I've never met that I suspect her father of being a murderer. And the worst sort of murderer at that: one who kills for greed.

I couldn't handle it when Glyn told me that, no matter that I hardly believed my father to be any kind of saint. Cesca, I think, is handling the revelation better. But then, in her mind, her father was already some kind of killer. The man who wrecked young Jacinta's life, who drove it onto the rocks of suicide.

Plus, of course, Cesca handles *everything* better than me. I'm a fuck-up. She isn't.

'Will he know? Will you need to name me?'

'No. Never.'

'I can't believe it. That you burgled this place. But you did, you really did. When you wanted to smoke, you went straight to that drawer.'

'I did, yes. The person I used was a former police officer. Totally discreet. And, as I say, you'd be well within your rights to have me fired and prosecuted. If you want to do that, I'll tell you who to call and what to say.'

'That's all right.' That look again. An examination which concludes with, 'You are really odd, though. Like *really*.'

We laugh. She's right. We both know it.

'It's your call,' I say. 'It's whatever you want.'

She stares into space. The darkness in the hall, the picture on the corkboard.

I think of Nellie Bentley. The silk gown and the children's heads. That repetitive movement, to and fro.

The picture wins.

Cesca says, 'OK.' Just that. Whispered.

She throws her bracelet on the bed. Unties her hair, combs it out with her fingers, then re-clips it, loosely.

'OK.'

I turn her computer on.

I say, 'I'll show you some pictures and some names. You tell me anything you know. Anything you sense or suspect or wonder about. Intelligence, not evidence. I won't record anything. I won't take notes. It's just you and me, talking. What happens after that is up to me and my colleagues. I will never involve you in any way.'

She laughs. A laugh that takes in her hippy-dippy ganja box, my holey tights, my burglarous tendencies. She says, 'You couldn't really, could you? Involve me, I mean.'

'It might be a wee bit difficult.'

The computer lights up.

Blue and open. The light of twenty thousand feet above ground.

Four corpses in the room, plus Jazz MacClure. Five. And

one of them a raggedy little puppet who keeps falling off her chair and who isn't really dead.

I'm still feeling strange, but it's a good strange now. *My* strange.

I call up some photos and we start to work.

# 47

Work long, work hard.

Mostly, we just go through my long-standing list of names. My targets.

Ivor Harris. MP and slimeball.

Trevor Yergin. Technology and finance.

Brendan Rattigan. A dead man, but still a bastard.

Idris Prothero. A man who once tried to kill me and who I once, unsuccessfully, sought to jail.

Huw Allsop. A man about whom I still know little. Who may, in fact, be a perfectly nice guy.

Ben Rossiter. Close friends with Prothero and Rattigan.

David Marr-Phillips. A man I met once, glancingly, and don't trust.

Joe Johnson.

Owain Owen.

A dozen more.

I gathered those names following my first big case. One that delved into the peculiarly nasty crimes of the late and unlamented Brendan Rattigan. I put together a list of the people he seemed closest to, both socially and in business terms. I had reason to believe that many of those people either knew about Rattigan's habits or indulged in the same thing themselves. Either way, I felt they needed to be brought to justice.

Since then, my campaign has morphed a little. Become uncertain of its centre.

Prothero, I know, dealt in illegal weapons and consorted with professional contract killers. Almost certainly, tried to have me killed. David Marr-Philips is a business associate of Prothero's and presumably knew about the arms dealing, if not necessarily the itsy-bitsy murders that ran alongside. Cesca's father, Galton Evans, was on my original list of guys-not-to-like and has now promoted himself to suspect-in-chief for the Livesey and Moon murders. And then there's the Voice too, whoever he is. Also a man I saw only once, a dark shape on a distant hill. A man who had recently ordered my death and who was the mastermind of a criminal enterprise that would end up netting him personally some thirty-four million quid.

I don't know if the Voice and that dark shape are already on my list, or if they're people I haven't yet identified, or what.

I don't know how real the connections between these people are.

But one by one I summon the photos of the men I'm interested in. Hear what she has to say about them.

Many of them she doesn't recognise at all. Some she does, but has little to say about them. A small handful of others – Harris, Rattigan, Prothero, Rossiter – she saw with her father on a fair number of occasions. Family things. Business things. She tells me what she knows, but doesn't know much.

I'm not really surprised. Cesca is now twenty. She stopped seeing her father when she was seventeen and had issues with him for several years before that. And, in any case, how much does the average disenchanted teen know about their father's business activities? How much did *I* know about my father's illegitimate activity? How much do I know now, even?

But – one of my slogans – not all harvests look the same or ripen quickly. You don't always know what you've gained.

And among the litter, a jewel.

A pearl, a ruby, a sapphire, a diamond.

Without much hope, I show her a photo of Ned Davison. Start to ask if she knows anything about him.

She interrupts.

'Creep. Horrible little guy.'

Her voice says 'creep'. Her face says, 'fucker'.

I raise my eyebrows.

She says, 'Standard issue pervert. Fondled me when I was about fifteen. One of those accidental-deliberate things when he ended up with his hand on my breast. Yeugh.'

So far, so *meh*. I don't like older guys who fondle teenagers – I once burst the testicle of a man who fondled *me* – but I'm on the hunt for bigger prey.

Cesca says, 'I've got a photo somewhere. He was with us in France.'

She fishes around on the cloud, her Instagram account.

It's not there, I want to tell her. I've already looked.

I make tea. Peppermint for me, vanilla chai for her.

I taste her chai. It's nice.

Bring the mugs back to the room. Look at Cesca from behind.

She's pretty, maybe beautiful. When I was at Cambridge and didn't really know the first thing about myself, I confused thinking-someone-was-pretty with being-attracted-to-them. I had a brief lesbian phase, which didn't work out too well, because however much I liked a girl, she always lacked the one piece of kit I really needed her to have.

But now, seeing Cesca, I think I understand that old confusion. I'm such a mess myself that when I see an attractive, intelligent woman who has her life vaguely together, I think, *I want that quality. I want to be that person.* From that thought to kissing someone – well, it doesn't sound logical, but it made a kind of sense at the time.

I don't share these thoughts with Cesca. Don't risk a cheeky kiss.

Just sit back next to her, give her her tea. Do that, in time to hear a quiet *aha!* of triumph.

'Not my account,' she says. 'My mum's.'

She flips through her mother's account. Brings up the picture she's thinking of.

A table in the south of France, or somewhere like that. A shaded terrace. Vineyards in the background, blue hills beyond. Marianna Lockwood, Ollie, Cesca, her father. Plus five other men.

Prothero.

Marr-Philips.

Owen.

Rattigan.

Davison.

'I was about sixteen,' she says. 'Our last family holiday. I mean, mostly, it was just the normal crap. Mum and Dad sniping at each other. Me and Ollie trying to avoid them. Both of them using their money to get us on their side.'

She grimaces. The experience of every child in a collapsing marriage.

'But Dad could *never* let business drop. Not for Mum. Not for us. And this holiday was a classic. He was on the phone for a couple of hours every day. The computer too. And then, people would just *arrive*. Like this thing. I mean, having friends over for lunch, OK. But this was a takeover. There was a maid at this villa, Marie I think, whose job was to cook and clean, but then all these guys arrive, and me, Mum and Marie are running around to get things ready. Serve up. No thank yous, or not really. Stupid conversation, with these freaks like Davison and Rattigan making everything feel seedy. My dad too, of course. He was the worst, even. Then we finish pudding, and Mum and I are waiting for these guys to go away, so we can have our house back, and we're basically pushed out. "Look, Marianna, why don't you and the children go shopping?" Like I was ten years old and still went shopping with my mum. Like that's what Ollie wanted to do. But Dad made us go. "We've got a meeting." Called it something stupid. The Cardiff Rotarians, I don't know. But that's what it was: a business meeting. All these guys – who live in South Wales, for God's sake – have to fly to France to invade our holiday. And this guy Davison taking notes and acting like some creepy super-secretary guy. Like he's the linchpin that everything else depends on. And I just thought, have your frigging meetings in Cardiff and leave us to our crappy miserable holiday.'

She finishes.

I leave a little moat of silence round her words. Jazz and the others press a little closer in.

I am sitting in the gap between my various worlds.

A shady terrace in Provence.

A student flat off the Seven Sisters Road.

An empty barn in the hills above Rhayader.

I try to pull myself into the world I know to be real. Real now, real here. Put my hand out to the hanging aubergine dress. Feel the fabric.

I hear myself saying, 'Yes, but the British police can intercept communications in Cardiff. Place bugs. Get video. Arrange any kind of surveillance. We can do what we want, assuming we have the permissions.'

Cesca stares at me.

I continue. 'So you have your meetings abroad. Invade a holiday. The British police can't and the French police won't try to bug you. Even if they try, you're not using the phone and you're sitting outside, where conversations are harder to record. The principals – your dad, Prothero, the others – they can sort out the big stuff face to face. Then, when details need to be managed and you don't want to jump on another plane, you turn to your fixer, your creepy Davison character.

He's an accountant and a consultant, so he's got every reason to buzz about between guys like these. He's never been on our radar, not really, so we'd have a hard time justifying any active surveillance. And bingo, you have a conspiracy. Or not a conspiracy, even. Just a network of businessmen, where it so happens that the business concerned is totally illegal.'

Cesca doesn't answer immediately.

Jazz and the others sit tight, sit quiet.

I find myself holding the hem of the dress to my right. Like the fabric is the only thing that anchors me here, in this room, this reality.

Cesca says, 'It's just one photo. It's hardly proof of anything, is it?'

'It proves nothing. Intelligence, not evidence. But it *is* odd, isn't it? Why meet in France, when you all live in Wales? Why make sure that you and Ollie and your mother were out of the house? Why push you out, if they had nothing to hide?'

I don't mention it, but I'm also certain that Evans, Prothero, Marr-Philips, Owen and Rattigan had no legitimate business interests in common. There are lines joining one or two of them – Marr-Philips has a minority stake in Prothero's engineering company, Evans and Rattigan sat on a couple of boards together – but nothing that joins all five.

I ask to see other photos from the holiday, anything she has.

She's happy to let me see them, but there's nothing much.

Just one shot intrigues me. A shot from an upstairs window. One that was, I think, meant to capture her brother diving into the swimming pool, but which inadvertently grazed the edge of a gravelled parking area. And in that parking area, a pale blue car, a BMW, I guess. And beside it: a man, hand raised – in greeting? against the sun? because he's glimpsed the camera? The man is tallish. Lean. Youngish, perhaps about the age I am now. Tanned. Thinning hair and – or am I making this up? – blue, intelligent eyes.

'Do you have other shots of this guy?' I ask.

Cesca looks, but without much enthusiasm – she's tired now – and in any event she's got nothing.

'Do you remember him at all? Did you spend any time with him?'

Kind of. Not really. Just a guy who arrived as part of the invading army. Didn't stay for lunch. Didn't hang around. Not creepy, the way Davison was.

I call up a photo of my own.

One that shows a man. Mid-thirties. Lean. Tanned. Thinning hair and intelligent eyes, with two colours of blue in them. Rain-cloud grey and cobalt blue.

'Is this him?' I ask.

My voice is a husk. An empty shell.

Cesca looks at the man. Vic Henderson. A man I kissed with passion once. A man who would have liked to take me away on holiday, his very own brown-legged Caribbean boat-girl. I said no to that idea and – long story – he tried to kill me instead. That plan didn't work out so well and Henderson is now shuffling round a prison hospital, relearning how to walk, speak, feed and pee.

Cesca doesn't know that story and I'm not about to tell her. She just looks at the photo. Says, 'Don't know. Maybe. I don't really remember. Sorry.'

I want to push her, but don't. The harder you push at an unreliable memory, the less reliable it becomes.

I tell her fine. Tell her we're done.

Say thanks, and mean it.

I expect Cesca to push back from the computer with relief, but she doesn't, or not immediately.

Instead she puts a long forefinger to the screen and says, 'It's what you came for, isn't it? These pictures. This conspiracy idea.'

'I didn't know exactly. I just knew that you had better access than I did. But yes, I suppose, it was this.'

'Do you want them?' She means the photos.

I nod. 'Yes. Yes, I do. But it's your call. If you give them to me, I'll share them with my boss and with someone I know at SOCA, the organised crime agency. None of us are going to go shouting about any intelligence we've collected. But it's your call. It's totally your call.'

'I'll think about it.'

Cesca looks at me. Yawns. Laughs.

She picks up my ankle. Looks at the mess I've made of my tights, my dirty foot.

'Let me guess, you don't have anywhere to sleep tonight.'

I admit it.

She drags a bedroll from under the bed. 'For when people stay over. Or when boyfriends start kicking in their sleep.'

We clean up, pee, go to bed.

Evans, Rattigan, Owen, Prothero, Marr-Philips, Davison.

All in one place at one time, and wanting to talk about things so secret that Evans's own family was banished from the house.

Fruit from the golden tree. Fruit I've been seeking for years now.

But in that happy knowledge, a brown worm turns. Marr-Philips made his money from property, much of it during the decade of upheaval that rebuilt Cardiff from the late-eighties onwards. Gareth Glyn accused my dad of killing the people who stood in the way of that redevelopment. If there's a conspiracy here, I've no reason to think my father isn't a part of it.

For all I know, I'm not investigating Evans and the rest of them. I'm investigating my father. I'm investigating *me.*

*People never really reinvent themselves. They migrate back to whatever they truly were.*

And what was my father, if not the go-to man for violence in South Wales? That's the thought I can't handle. More than anything that happened in that barn near Rhayader, it's the thing that is making me lose my mind and scatter my shoes.

In the bed above me, Cesca murmurs, 'Fiona? Fi?'

'Yes?'

'Never fucking burgle me again, OK?'

I tell her OK. Tell her goodnight.

Tell her those things and try to sleep.

My father: provider of muscle.

And Gina Jewell dead.

# 48

I don't immediately share my discovery. Partly, it's Sunday, and even Watkins doesn't work every day and hour of the week. Partly, I'm not yet sure the best way to introduce my find. But partly too because when I go to pick up my car from its little parking place, I discover that it has outstayed its welcome and has been hauled off to the police pound. Rescuing it will cost me £200, which is bad enough, but it also costs me a trip by train to Cardiff to collect the stupid, stupid bits of documentation which the boring, boring enforcement people demand before they'll give me my car back.

So: by train to Cardiff Central.

Taxi home.

The car waits outside, while I find my stupid insurance details, some stupid photo ID, and a stupid, stupid, pointless, pointless utility bill.

Those things, plus also a pair of shoes, so I can return the pair I borrowed from Cesca this morning. I play it safe. Avoid anything slip-on, because those are the sort most likely to go walkabout. Instead, choose a pair of lace-ups, which I tie with a double knot, in the theory that that way it'll be harder for me to remove them without noticing.

Then back in the taxi.

Back on the train.

Once settled again, and the rhythm of the rails trotting in my ear, I vent some of my crossness by buying a whole set of fake identity documents from a Russian website, *buypassportsfake.cc*. I don't know if I even need to really. Just, when I see a barrier saying Do Not Cross, I have an almost overwhelming impulse to cross it.

Anyway. I buy a fake passport, a fake drivers' licence, and a set of fake utility bills. It costs me a thousand euros to get them all, and I have to set up a special account with Western Union to make the down payment because – as the website regretfully states – *Unfortunately, due to the nature of our business it has been difficult to obtain credit card or Paypal facilities.*

The site promises me the documents in five days. I doubt if the papers would get me safely across borders, but they should be workable for most other purposes. And they're the sort of thing I like to have.

As we leave Swindon, I get a text from Penry. GOT PHOTOS. NOT DEAD. SUPPER? I text back, GOOD. GOOD. YOU BET.

I use the rest of the journey to check if there's been any progress on the Stonemonkey. There hasn't, but Watkins has managed to swivel the inquiry in a remarkably short time so that it's now focusing on any remarkably able British climbers active in southern Europe. She has – sensibly, I think – decided to use some of Nat Brown's counterparts in France and Spain to help with the search. The decision increases the risk of information leaking, but it also vastly increases our chances of success.

The team, I notice, now includes three analysts from SOCA in London, which makes sense as they'll have more international experience than we do.

I'm pleased Watkins is in control of all this. Dunthinking would have cocked things up by now.

London.

Paddington station.

Iron columns and pigeons. A flutter of wings beneath the glass.

I have an odd time-shift moment, when I can't quite figure out what century I'm in. I keep looking up at that glassed Victorian roof, wondering why I can't see clouds of steam and speckles of soot. It genuinely troubles me that the station floor isn't a-scurry with gents in frock coats and women in gloves and bustles.

But the moment passes. Our own tiresomely attired century bumps at me until the scene in front of me and the one in my head line up, at least approximately.

I realise I'm feeling better again. Still a bit nuts, but somehow clarified. Hardened.

Made stronger by Cesca's example.

When Gareth Glyn told me he thought my father was a murderer, I started to fall apart. To collapse in a way that even those Rhayader morons hadn't managed to bring about. Faced with the same information, Cesca just said coolly that she'd help out. Nail her own father, because justice required it.

I'll do the same, I realise. Pursue my investigation wherever it leads. Accept its consequences, no matter what.

What's more, my recent discoveries have simplified things. I thought, originally, that I had two extra-curricular projects. One of those was investigating the mysteries of my own past. The second was bringing to justice those friends-of-Rattigan whom I suspected of being accomplices, or worse, in his crimes. But those accomplices now look like business associates of my father's. My past and their crimes seem inextricably entangled.

One mystery and one solution.

And one battered little investigator to join the two.

A battered little investigator who now takes another stupid taxi to the stupid car pound, where she hands over stupid documents to a stupid person along with a stupid amount of money and all to get a car which was in no one's way and which had stuffed the stupid, stupid parking machine with gold and silver until the damn thing belched in repletion.

My car is released from captivity. It blinks in the sunlight and promises to be good.

My shoes are still lashed firmly to my feet.

Drive to Central Saint Martins. Leave Cesca's shoes for her, with a note saying thanks.

Thanks for the shoes. Thanks for the bed. Thanks for the ganja. Thanks for the photo.

Thanks for being nice about the burglary: not phoning Watkins, not ending my career, not sending me to jail.

Thanks, most of all, for showing me the woman I need to be. A daughter with steel. A woman with backbone.

When, finally, I point my car's nose to the west, when we shake ourselves free of London-cluttering traffic, I press the accelerator down until we're doing ninety miles an hour. Racing onward to the land of the Celts. Leaving the city of the Romans, the Angles, the Jutes and the Saxons far behind.

One mystery.

One investigation.

One solution.

# 49

Penry did well.

Worked sensibly, worked safely.

He bought a wristwatch from a place in London for fifty quid. A thing that looks and functions just like a regular watch, but one that shoots photos and videos in 1280 by 960 pixel resolution.

At the docks, he strolled ship to ship, getting into conversations, asking for work. The *Isobel Baker* wasn't the first ship he stopped at, nor was it the last.

'Getting pictures of the stern was easy. I just walked along the dockside and shot video. Getting a view of the deck fixings was harder. They stopped me on the gangway, about halfway up, but I did what I could. I don't think it's too bad.'

We spend the evening at his house, eating his version of spaghetti bolognese and examining his booty. We clip the best stills, delete any junk footage, send the good stuff over to Lowe.

Penry asks me about Watkins. Whether our data will give her enough to act.

I shrug. I don't know.

He says, 'There's a bed and breakfast place on Lower Hill Street. It's got rooms.'

I look at the place on Google Maps.

Lower Hill Street: a road with a perfect view of the docks. A long telephoto distance from the *Isobel Baker*. The B&B in question has net curtains on its windows and, because of what and where it is, there'll be people coming and going all day long. One strange face more or less will never attract notice.

I say, 'Perfect. Yes. Thank you.'

Show him the e-fit picture of the guy who gave Buzz a thumping. The guy who, almost certainly, was the second of the two goons in the barn. The one who smashed his buddy's skull in. 'If you see this guy, you might want to tell someone. He's wanted for murder.'

'OK. I've got a night-vision scope, but I'll need a camera. A proper stake-out thing.'

'Fine. Get it.'

'I will, if you promise me to do this thing properly. You know, *properly*: as in actual police action with actual legal authority.'

'I will. Yes. I've always said that if I can, I will.'

'"If I can, I will." That's not the same as "yes". Look, these guys are dangerous, you said it yourself. You can't take them on alone.'

I stare at him. I don't know what makes Penry think he has the right to come over all parental with me. Maybe it's an older guy thing. Maybe he just can't help it.

I say, softly, 'I returned, and saw under the sun, that the race is not to the swift, nor the battle to the strong, neither yet bread to the wise, nor yet riches to men of understanding.'

Penry does a small double-take, but he's a Welsh boy and knows his Ecclesiastes.

'There's not a lot of sunshine in Milford Haven, if we're honest,' he says. 'And the swift tend to win their races, what with being swift and all.'

'This ship. The *Isobel Baker*. How many crew members does she have?'

'How many *crew* members?'

'Brian, is it the kind of boat that needs a cook?'

Penry says, 'Fuck.' Says he won't help. Says he doesn't want to be part of this.

But he does. And he will. And before the evening is over, he promises to find out.

# 50

Monday. The first day of July.

Atlantic Cables have hooked up their line. This week and next: onshore testing. Thereafter: full line tests. Brean to Long Island. London to New York. Finding out if the line is clean. If it's fast. I remember Whillans's rule of thumb: that, for a largeish hedge fund, a one millisecond speed advantage is worth a hundred million dollars a year.

Slivers of time. Oceans of money.

I'm working hard on Stonemonkey stuff, when Jackson comes by my desk.

'Fiona.'

'Sir.'

He thumps his knuckles down on my desktop, watching them whiten. I watch them too. We both watch.

Then he says, 'That van.'

'*My* van.'

'Your van, yes. We took a look at it. Bridgend, I mean, the forensics people. They found sodium hydroxide. The whole vehicle had been washed in the stuff.' Sodium hydroxide: caustic soda. A way to destroy DNA. As effective as it gets. 'You never quite know, though, do you? I mean, we might find something in a fabric seam. A tear in the floor. That kind of thing.'

I nod. Yes. We get ever better at that kind of thing. As Kyle Bransby knows. Which means he'd probably be very careful with seams, and tears, and that kind of thing.

'We also asked Kirsty Emmett about smells. She couldn't remember anything. Nothing at all. Only then – and this was planned – Mervyn Rogers pops some aniseed gum into his mouth. Starts chewing. Emmett started crying. Sobbing. So much we had to end the interview while Victim Support did their stuff.'

Mervyn Rogers. I don't know who chose him as an interrogator – he's not usually skilled at the nicey-nicey stuff – but he's a fair physical fit for Bransby, give or take a ten year age gap.

A neat trick.

A neat trick, but a victim crying at aniseed gum isn't the kind of evidence which will secure a conviction.

'We set up an old-fashioned identity parade. Our girl picked out Bransby, but she wasn't sure. Kept apologising.'

Those apologies will need to be handed to the defence team. The ordinary human reactions of an ordinary woman plunged into nightmare will play badly in court.

Jackson continues. 'We've pulled in Bransby for questioning. He's downstairs now. We're going to play it long, hard and nasty.'

Long, hard and nasty: except that Bransby will know his rights. Know that he just has to tough it out a day or two and he'll walk away without a stain on his loathsome rapist's character.

Jackson says, 'He's a little shit. He won't confess.'

I agree unhappily, but Jackson's face wrinkles in an expression I can't read.

A wrinkle that widens and widens, until he says, 'Thing is, though, we also got a search warrant on his house. I've just had a call from the search team. Pair of female knickers, torn and stained. Located in a shoebox in the attic. Description of the garment matches the item worn by Emmett on the day of the attack.' He laughs now. That open, broad, overdue laugh.

'The silly fucking fucker, eh? You do all that and you keep a trophy. You're a professional fucking SOCO and you keep a trophy.'

The joy of conviction washes over us. Conviction: not in the bloodless sense of philosophical certainty, but that most happy policeish one of knowing that your bad guy will be put away. The banging gavel, the guilty verdict. Handcuffs and the prison gates.

Closure. Literal and metaphorical.

I grin. 'Have you told Bransby yet?'

'Nope. Not going to tell him until one minute before we have to charge him or release him. We'll get the CPS lads to push for the maximum of the bloody maximum. Probably get it too.'

We share the joy. A police officer who turns to crime – nasty crime, at that – is just about the lowest of the low. For any decent copper, putting those guys behind bars is a particular delight.

Then Jackson says, 'That other crime you mentioned. I presume if you had any firm evidence, you'd share it?'

'Wouldn't just share it, sir. I'd give it to you on a tray lined with rose petals and kitten fur.'

'Thought so.'

'I mean, Dunthinking is a useless idiot, but he's not *that* useless. I've never seen him that useless.'

'No. Me neither.'

'And those hospital swabs would have closed the case.'

'Yes.'

Jackson thumps the desk again. Partly a 'need to think about this' gesture. Partly a 'good work, Constable' one. Mostly though, he's just a big Welshman and their hormones go funny unless they hit something now and again.

He leaves. I work.

If I think about Rhayader, then I do. If I think about Gina

Jewell, then I do. Neither thought appears to make me fall apart, go crazy or discard perfectly good shoes.

Progress. My version of it.

Then, at about eleven, Watkins marches in. Short hair. White shirt. Battle-grey suit. Her range-finders lock on to me and she trundles over.

'Fiona.'

'Good morning.'

'You're . . . you're . . .?'

'I'm OK. Yes, thanks. I'm fine.'

She scours my face, not quite believing my answer. Then, 'Listen, we've got news from London. Do you know where Haston is? He's not answering his phone.'

Mike has a theory that most calls are boring, so he often leaves his phone where he can't hear it.

I say no.

'He's not at work,' she says, disapprovingly.

'At home?' I offer. 'The climbing wall? The climbing club place?'

Watkins says, 'Would you mind going to look for him? We could really use him here.'

I say I'd be happy to.

Try his flat, a shared two-bedroom thing in Splott. No answer there. Try the climbing club place. Nada. As I'm leaving the car park, my phone buzzes.

Watkins.

She's texted through a link to a Spanish video sharing site and the words, TAKE A LOOK! THIS IS WHY WE NEED HASTON.

I open the video, which has an upload date of January 2009: exactly when our boy would have been gearing up for his insurance scam. The video starts. No title, no intro. Just somebody starting off up a climb.

Sunshine. Golden limestone. Thorn-dotted Mediterranean hills.

The little film is a real amateur affair. There's some messing about with rope. People chatting in Spanish. A climber climbing. No particular urgency or interest.

For a minute and a half, I watch, not sure what I'm watching or why. It just seems like a deeply boring climbing video.

Then something changes. Shouting from further along the crag. People running.

The videographer, whoever he is, pulls away from the guy who's been climbing and there's a moment or two of confused framing and bad focus.

Then the camera finds its target. A man picking his way up a cliff. The video zooms in to the limit of its range, perhaps fifty or a hundred metres distant.

It's hard to see much detail, but the climber involved has the muscled leanness of his breed. Red trousers, no top.

Also: a harness, but no rope.

The climber is maybe eighty feet up and there is nothing at all to stop him falling.

The guy continues upwards. Cautious, but never static. It's hard to figure out the angles from the view I have, but the cliff looks overhanging. An arch of stone that steepens as it rises.

The hubbub at the base of the crag continues, but it's too distant for the microphone to pick up any detail. There are people holding out some kind of groundsheet, an improvised safety net.

The camera steadies. The climber climbs.

At one point, he pauses. Shakes out his right arm, shifting the lactic acid, restoring the blood flow. Chalks up.

Dark hair, worn short. A glimpse of face, a scatter of pixels.

Then nothing. He continues to climb, out of frame, out of sight.

The videographer and his half-forgotten climbing buddy,

now dangling from an anchor halfway up the cliff, start talking excitedly in Spanish.

The video closes.

I don't know what I've just witnessed.

Drive on to the climbing wall, where I find a super-excited Mike. He's just bothered to look at his phone. Seen the same video. Spoken to the London analyst who found the clip.

Mike is fizzing with excitement. Starts to splurge as soon as he sees me, but I stop him.

'Not here. Somewhere private.'

There's not much privacy to be had – the place is heaving with schoolchildren – but Mike negotiates with the person on the door and we end up in some kind of internal kit room. Shelves, and ropes, and helmets, and boots. Cardboard and faded sweat. Mike thumps the door shut.

'It's him. It's him. It's him. I'd bet a million pounds. Look, that climb? It was 8b, an 8-bloody-b. I know that doesn't mean anything to you, but it's a seriously, *seriously* hard climb. And no ropes! Jesus. The guy just unclipped from his rope, Fi.'

I make him slow down. The story comes out in pieces – and backwards – but it all makes sense in the end.

The lead came to our team in London, via a climbing journalist, José Bereziartu, who's based in Barcelona and does much the same sort of job for his magazine that Nat Brown does here. Bereziartu was notified of the story by the local grapevine, tracked down a couple of witnesses and ended up writing a short diary piece entitled simply '*Sensación Británica*'. A piece evenly divided between admiration for the unknown climber's feat and fierce reproof for the bloodbath that could have resulted.

The story was this. A British climber, known only as John, was drifting round a crag near Rodellar, looking for partners to climb with. A strong local climber agreed to hook up with him, and they blitzed their way through various hard but not impossible routes. They then agreed to start working on the jewel of the crag, the route I was looking at in the video.

Both climbers were tested. The British guy was a fair bit stronger than his local partner, but even he kept falling when it came to the crux.

'And bear in mind, Fi, the crux is at more than thirty metres. And the route is desperately overhanging, so if you fall, you won't even bounce before you hit the ground. I mean, that's a death-fall, no two ways about it.'

'But you say he was roped,' I complain. 'The guy in the video was unroped.'

'Exactly. This guy, John, was pissed off that he kept on falling. I mean, that's already crazy. It's like Usain Bolt being pissed off that he's not breaking ten seconds in some routine training session. But anyway, this John guy is back on the route, trying again, when he just says, "Fuck this" and unclips. Just drops the damn rope. It's like he's telling himself, "You climb it or you die." The video shows you what happens next.'

Mike's excitement, I think, is mostly because of the athletic achievement of what he just witnessed. Mine is because this story is Nat Brown's prediction coming true. *You know 'em when you see 'em.*

'Names? Identities?' I ask.

Mike shakes his head. 'The guy gets to the top of the cliff and just walks away. Everyone was waiting for him to come down. He'd have been a frigging hero. The story would have been on every single climbing mag in Europe. But he just walked away. Vanished.'

He says that in a sombre voice – or as sombre as he can get, given his excitement – because he thinks he's relaying bad news. But he isn't. The opposite. Any normal person would have descended that cliff, to receive the adulation of his peers or simply to collect his gear. But not our boy. He preferred to walk away. Leave his equipment, his never-again moment of fame.

Who would do that except someone with an intense and specific desire for privacy?

I tell Mike this. *I'm* excited now. I want to get him straight over to the office to deliver him to Watkins, but it turns out that the kit-room door doesn't work properly from the inside, and we have to bang and thump to get someone to let us out.

The banging and thumping brings us close together. Physically close, I mean. Mike had been on the wall climbing most of the morning and he's lightly oiled with perspiration. But fresh-smelling. A clean, light smell. And even just thumping at the door, and laughing, and dancing back so that I can thump it too, he has a loose, muscular grace.

I realise, to my surprise, that I am strongly attracted to him. Strongly enough that I can see myself pulling off his horrible bit of hair elastic and spinning him round, my face upturned to receive his kisses.

I want to do that. Ache to do it.

Ache to, but go right on aching.

Partly because Jess, the person who gave us the kit room to conspire in, turns up again to let us out. And partly too, because I'm not the queen of spontaneity. Deliberately so. I avoid doing things on impulse, because I've learned that my feelings are too unreliable to trust.

So nothing happens. Jess opens the door. I walk out to the car park feeling Mike's presence, hot and limber, trotting beside me. I am slightly breathless. Unsteady. Unsettled by gusts of almost teenaged desire.

We walk over to my car. I blip it unlocked, but don't open the door, because I think I'll fumble it, or drop my keys, or do something that betrays me as the hopelessly infatuated, teen-at-a-Justin-Bieber-concert girl that I have suddenly become.

He looks down at me, smiling.

There's probably a technique somewhere for deciphering what that smile means, or if it means anything at all. But if there is, I don't possess it.

We stand there in the sunshine, me leaning against the warm metal wall of my Alfa Romeo.

He jingles his car keys at me, reminding me he has a car here too.

'Meet at your office, yes?' he says.

'Yes.'

'It *is* exciting.'

'Yes.'

I don't move.

He gets into his car. Drives off with a wave.

I don't move. Let the sunshine wash over me.

Text Watkins. FOUND HIM. WE'RE ON OUR WAY.

Why did Watkins assume I would know where to find Mike? Why did Nat Brown make the assumption that Mike and I were together? Maybe the whole world has been seeing something that I've been too dippily slow to understand. Maybe I've been half in lust with Mike all this time and it's taken me this long to notice.

I don't know. I don't know how physical attraction works for most people. Whether it's a thing that leaps out on them with a roar of surprise, or if ordinary people just know these things, the way they see a tomato and know that it's red, bish bosh, just like that.

I wonder about that. If there's someone I could ask.

Then my attention moves on. Rocks and seawater. The two halves of Zorro's tangled equation. We have the Stonemonkey in our sights now. His arrest will solve one half of the equation. And the other? The *Isobel Baker*?

I realise I need to get Watkins down to Milford Haven as soon as possible. Our window for effective is closing fast. Too fast. If I'm to close this case police-style, it's now or never.

With care, and aflutter with feelings I can't describe, I turn slowly onto the Newport Road, heading for work.

# 51

Milford Haven. The Heart of Oak, Lower Hill Street.

We're in Penry's room. A perfectly nice room which he's already managed to turn halfway into a shithole. Dirty clothes, including underwear, strewn on the bed and floor. A damp towel coiled on the only spare chair. Scattered between bed and window sill: three empty beer cans, two dirty coffee cups, some fast-food wrappers and a half-eaten Pot Noodle. The room smells of male sweat, of yeast extract and monosodium glutamate, of whatever damp towel smells of after incubating for two or three days.

Watkins stops in the doorway. Eyes revolving.

She takes in not only Penry's carefully staged shittery, but also the net curtain on the window. The tripod holding a camera and four hundred quids' worth of newly acquired zoom lens. The laptop on the bed. The spare battery pack for the camera, plus charger, red lamp glowing. The notebook with chewed biro. The night-vision monocular.

Penry is at his post in the window. Without properly looking round, he says, 'Hey, Rhiannon. All right?'

The two of them have met only once before, when Penry was in hospital, having been attacked in prison. He acted the prick with Watkins then, for no reason except that he can't help himself, and Watkins – rigorous, severe, female, uptight – brings out the worst in him.

'Brian,' she says, tautly.

No one says anything to that. Penry doesn't move. Doesn't even shift his feet from the window sill or make more than the most cursory of efforts to turn his head to the door.

I do nothing. I was the one who brought Watkins here, but I can't see that it's my job to look after two adults, each of whom is old enough to be my parent, so I just scoop some of Penry's clothes off the bed and sit on it.

Watkins says, 'That's the boat over there?'

'Ship,' says Penry. 'It's a ship. The *Isobel Baker*.'

Watkins navigates the floor over to the window. Penry – melodramatic sigh – heaves himself out of his chair, gives Watkins access to the viewfinder.

She stares out over two hundred yards or so of flat water to the dockside opposite.

Water the colour of stone, of a wet twilight.

Water the colour of storms and fish bellies.

Watkins takes her time to examine the ship. The lens is long enough that, on maximum zoom, you can't get the whole craft into the viewfinder at once, and it takes time to learn just how much you need to adjust the angle to get the part you want to look at.

Watkins sits, tight-faced, managing the camera.

It's a view I've seen a couple of times now. Familiar.

The white-painted gantry, flaking with rust beneath the arch. Trawl winches. Steel cable. Blue hull. Hoists for handling catch. The blocky white bridge in the ship's bow.

Steel and rust and paint and seawater.

A ship that seems only half at place here, in these silent waters. It needs Atlantic waves, a fierce wind, a bawl of men. Those things, and a sodden net streaming with water. Bulging with its black and silver catch.

I let Watkins sit with the camera till she's had enough.

'Photos on there?' she asks, nodding at the laptop.

Penry says nothing, but jiggles the thing awake. Pushes it over.

'Personnel?'

Penry says, 'Folder marked *People*. Three hundred and some photos so far.'

To me, she says: 'You've seen these?'

'Most of them, yes. We think we've got a crew of six. Multiple shots of each. A lot of the shots are crap, but Brydon's guy isn't there.'

Watkins wants to look at the e-fit which Buzz created, but feels uncomfortable doing that with Penry – a former prisoner, not retained by the inquiry, not bound by any written confidentiality undertaking – in the room.

I cut through her reservations. 'Brydon's guy is here.' Bring up the e-fit.

Watkins fires through the photos, comparing them against Brydon's image.

Penry smirks at me. He isn't actually as much of a slob as this room makes him appear. The look was carefully designed to provoke Watkins, who would have gone ballistic had any of her officers presented themselves in this way. Watkins is a shrewd detective, but she can't tell that Penry is deliberately riling her, which means she's even more riled.

I kick Penry's legs and say, 'We've driven from Cardiff and I'm thirsty.'

He's about to make a smart-arse response, but he's on my payroll, I haven't yet paid him for the lens and my face is wearing a 'Don't be a dick' warning. So he fills the room's little kettle from the bathroom sink and flicks it on, grinning all the while to reassure himself that his penis hasn't fallen off.

Peppermint tea for me: I carry spare in my bag. The ordinary stuff for Watkins and Penry.

Penry is physiologically incapable of simply making nice so instead he takes the piss by fussing absurdly over Watkins's tea. 'How strong? That about right? I didn't ask if you liked milk in first. It's OK this way, is it? I can get more milk if you need. Sugar? There's brown and white. Or sweetener if you prefer? That's all right, is it? That's OK?'

Watkins takes her cup. Finishes with the photos, the e-fit image.

'He's not there,' she says. 'Not unless he's keeping himself hidden.'

'Or if the ship isn't yet fully crewed,' I say.

She stares at me.

I don't, in fact, think that Brydon's guy – the second Rhayader goon, the one who ended up beating his buddy's head in – will show up anywhere close to the *Isobel Baker*. He'd risk his own safety and that of the ship. Far better to lie low and let others handle this next phase.

I say something to that effect.

'Do we have any names?' Watkins asks, meaning the crew members.

I shake my head. I could probably have got the names, if I was acting entirely solo, but the whole point of this venture was always to create something I could pass over. So I've done nothing illegal, nothing I couldn't take to Watkins.

I say, 'The Harbourmaster will have them.'

'OK.'

She takes a document from her case. A copy of Lowe's email, which I received on Monday night and forwarded. Some semi-formal blah-blah about the nature of my request. Then the meat:

> Gantry
> The gantry is of sufficient height and width to launch/retrieve a Remote Operated Vehicle (ROV) but, as originally configured, the gantry's positioning would have risked collisions between any ROV and the existing

stern ramp, thereby potentially damaging ROV. Gantry has been visibly adapted to locate suitable handling equipment farther aft, including an A-frame style pulley system which is not required for ordinary fishing purposes. Note also cabling to stern winch mounting, implying possible existence of a tether management system (TMS) which would not be required by a stern trawler of this type. Fixings on cable joints are 'clean', with little or no at-sea use visible. In addition . . .

Four more pages in the same vein, plus eighteen photo attachments with red arrows highlighting features that Lowe regards as suspect or non-standard.

His report also notes:

Days in port
This consultant is not highly familiar with the UK fishing industry, but I note that the *Isobel Baker* is of a size and specification to manage significant spells at sea. Her skipper and crew would typically expect a 3–4 day stopover in port, to allow for unloading, maintenance, cleaning, refueling and restocking, in addition to rest and family time for the crew. In this instance, however, the *Isobel Baker* docked on June 25 and has not yet shown any signs of putting out to sea. No major maintenance works have been reported. It is suggested that the length of the stopover would be uneconomical for an ordinary fishing vessel.

Lowe also includes his CV. I don't understand most of the things he's listed, except it's clearly one of those fuck-off-don't-doubt-me things we use in court to establish the quality of expert witnesses.

Watkins returns to the camera and looks from ship to email and back again, trying to establish Lowe's points for herself.

I've tried to do the same. A few of his observations are easy to check. Some are just baffling. Others might be obvious, if only we had a clearer view. In any case, though, I don't know what the *Isobel Baker* ought to look like, what equipment ships of her type normally need. Watkins the same.

She spends twenty minutes with the camera and document. Reaches for Penry's notebook – the place where he's logged and dated any on-ship movements or activity. Reads through that, then straightens. Drinks her tea, which is now cold.

Rubs her face.

'This is a lot of work. You've done a good job.'

That sort of thing would elicit a prim little 'thank you, ma'am,' if it had been aimed at me. But it was Penry's gift mostly, and he accepts it with a little shrug.

To me: 'You've been paying Mr Penry?'

'Yes. Daily rate, accommodation, petrol.'

'And the equipment?'

'Some he had. Some I bought.'

'From your own pocket, yes?'

'Yes.'

Then to Penry: 'You need to make out a proper invoice. Send it to me. I'll get it paid, then I need you to repay DC Griffiths. This' – she waves at the room, the Penrian shitheap – 'is not the right way to do things.'

True, but since Watkins herself refused to authorise the necessary surveillance resources, it was all we had.

Watkins turns to me. She doesn't say anything and her expression rides at anchor, immobile as the *Isobel Baker*.

I say, 'We need to research the crew. Names. Background. Records. Any intelligence from any database. Coastguard and Border Agency, Dyfed-Powys, everything.'

'Yes.'

I say, 'Organise surveillance. This isn't a one-man job and our equipment isn't up to scratch. We've got more than enough already to persuade Dyfed-Powys to spend some money. Plus there's a killing on their turf, which is linked to all this.'

'Yes.'

I think that, for perhaps the first time in this whole investigation, Watkins is with me. Seeing things as I see them.

But there's something wrong. Her gaze travels out of the window, slanting out sideways. Beyond the docks, the marina. Beyond the slope of the hill and the arm of the quay.

Watkins speaks again, and her voice is gravel.

'Before I came out this morning. I contacted Lloyds. Their shipping *Register*.'

I did that when we first located the ship as being our possible target. The *Register* had nothing of interest, not unless I was missing something big.

Watkins continues, 'The *Isobel Baker* has just been reflagged. Forty-eight hours ago. She was British, but she's a Cyprus vessel now. European, so it can fish in these waters, but . . .'

She trails off, but I know what she's thinking.

The Royal Navy can forcibly board any British-flagged ship, whether it's sailing in home seas or international waters. But doing the same thing to a foreign vessel? And one sailing outside the twelve mile national limits? That's not law-enforcement. It's piracy. An act of war.

Watkins says, 'I'll speak to the relevant agencies. Or get Dennis to do it. Use his seniority.'

I nod. My lips move, but nothing much comes out.

Watkins says, 'The timing. Do we have any guesses . . .?'

I tell her what Whillans told me. Him and Warren.

It's the 4th July today. The basic line tests are still expected to be complete by 19th July, which means that our guys might attack any time after the 22nd.

Watkins says, 'We might have enough time. Maybe.'

I say whatever needs to be said. Yes, ma'am. Great, ma'am. Happy to help, ma'am.

But a Cyprus-flagged vessel sailing in European waters? A vessel that looks like a fishing trawler? That *is* a damn trawler, crewed, from the look of it, by a bunch of honest-to-God fishermen. That's not a ship you can seize by force unless you have some very, *very* damn powerful evidence to back you up – and even then, usually only with the consent of the foreign country involved.

And what have we got? Penry's pictures. Lowe's email. My own dark suspicions. Plus we're talking *Cyprus*. A place awash with Russian cash. A known centre for money-laundering. The sort of place where the right sort of help could be bought for an envelope stuffed with euros.

It won't be Watkins who makes the decision whether to board the vessel or not. Not even Jackson, or the chief constable, or the Cardiff CPS.

The decision will be made by some maritime lawyer up in London. A moron in a suit. A moron who never once sat in a barn near Rhayader, trying their best to protect a live investigation, while some ski-masked arsehole shot fifty thousand volts into her collapsing body.

I feel funny.

I'm not always quick to work it out, when my feelings go strange. I usually figure it out in the end, but not always before I've done something regrettable or comment-inducing or just plain weird. On this occasion, though, I think I get there pretty much straight away.

I'm feeling funny.

Giddy. Spaced out. Dissociating.

Penry looks at me, a don't-do-it glitter in his eye.

Watkins looks at me too.

I can't read her expression, but what she says is, 'Fiona, are you all right?'

'I'm fine.'

'You don't look well.'

'I'm not well.'

'Look, if you need—'

'That guy in London. The psychologist. I can't see him.'

'I know. You've said that. But if you want a break. Take some time away . . .'

'Yes.'

'Yes?'

'Yes. I need a break. Some time away.'

'OK. Take as much as you need. Get a change of scene. Relax.'

I say something.

Other people say things.

I don't hear it, not really. Or hear it, but don't feel it.

All I do know is that Penry bends down to my ear, low down. Says – his angry voice – 'You are a fucking idiot.'

I say, 'Change of scene. Do me good. Fresh air, a spot of cooking.'

# 52

Albarracin, Spain.

Time away. A change of scene.

I'm here with Mike. Not holiday, exactly, but halfway there.

The Spanish police were hellishly fast.

Following *that* video and the story from Bereziartu, our team in London – the SOCA analysts – dug up five other possible sightings, all in Spain, of the Stonemonkey, *la sensación Británica*. Some of those sightings yielded actual photos, better quality than the one in the video.

Putting together what they had, SOCA were able to construct a reasonably precise likeness of the man, whom we still know only as John. His image and description was distributed internationally via Interpol, but it was the Guardia Civil in Spain who led the charge. Watkins, with SOCA's murmurs of support, presented the Stonemonkey as a wanted terrorist. (Torture, murder, bomb threats.) No police agency loves anything more than a hunt for a terrorist, particularly if the person involved is most unlikely to detonate a bomb. I think they also wanted to show off, to show us what they could do.

And in the end, it wasn't that hard. Officers fanned out across Spain's leading climbing areas, discreetly harvesting the local knowledge, the local rumours. A tip in Rodellar led to a climber near El Chorro, who claimed to have spent a week or so bouldering with a phenomenally able Brit, 'John', here in Albarracin. Said that John claimed to live in the area, albeit travelling often.

The Guardia Civil did their stuff. They've located the guy: his house, his car, his climbing haunts. The man goes by the name of John Wilson – a sturdily fake identity, if you ask me, and not one that sounds any particular alarms on our databases.

I've come out in order to confirm, on behalf of the South Wales Police, that Wilson is indeed the man we want arrested. I've got no more information than the Spanish, but they want to ensure that any consequences of a wrongful arrest flow to us, not them.

Mike and I flew to Madrid. Drove three hours on heat-whitened roads to Albarracin. Mike – thrilled to be here – headed straight for the pine forest that surrounds the village. The forest is full of red sandstone boulders, pebbles scattered by a giant. It's high season now, and warm, so most climbers have headed for cooler climes. But Mike and a few others perform their strange, unattainable gymnastics in the silence amongst these rocks, beneath these whispering trees.

Aragonese deer step out of the shadows, stare at us, then vanish with a flourish of dusty heels.

I sit with my back to a pine tree, eating peaches and cherries from a warm paper bag, watching Mike climb. I run my eye over the width of his shoulders, his narrow waist, the changing muscles of his back. Between climbs, he bounds over to me like a springer spaniel, shakes blood into his arms, steals bites from my peach and tries to persuade me to attempt one of the easier climbs.

I smile and say no.

I decide that I fancied him when I first met him. At the wall, yes, but especially at Plas Du. Rhod was clearly the better climber of the two, but there was something simpler, friendlier, cleaner about Mike. An easy grace.

I don't know why I didn't see it then. I don't know how it works for other people.

We don't see anyone who looks like our John Wilson, or climbs like him. The only cars in the little car park look ordinary, dusty, local.

We drive to the place we're staying: a little whitewashed cottage just outside Teruel.

We have supper outside on a little clay-tile patio shaded by an extravagantly flowered bougainvillea. We eat warm tomatoes and black olives. Bread and tinned sardines and ewe's milk cheese. We open a bottle of red wine and I drink the teeniest weeniest smidge, feeling brave.

When Mike wipes his mouth and pushes his plate back, I do the same.

Say, 'So, tonight. Were you thinking we would sleep together?'

# 53

We do sleep together, yes, and very nice it is too. It's like I've been thirsty for months and only now that I drink do I realise how thirsty I was.

We make love in a big white bed, with the windows open and a loose white cotton curtain stirring in the breeze. We have a bath together afterwards. Lukewarm water and a huge yellow sponge. Nibble at each other as we get ready for bed.

Mike has this honourable scamp thing going. He's anxious for me to understand that he's not really the settling down type, not yet, not until he's climbed more, travelled more, done more. Needed all that clarified before he would head for the bedroom. I tell him I hadn't thought of him as the settling down type. That a bit of happy shagging would do me fine.

We make love again in the morning. Eat fruit and bread and yogurt in the sun. Albarracin is a thousand metres above sea-level but even so, by the time we've cleared breakfast, the clay tiles of the patio are too hot to walk on.

I break a few twigs of bougainvillea and put them in a vase, while Mike traces the line of my spine through my sundress.

We walk back to the forest and its field of boulders. This time, in the car park, we find a yellow Lotus Elan with Spanish plates. HU: Huesca, a local car.

Mike and I exchange looks, say nothing.

He climbs. I sit and watch, puddled in my own contented lust.

At eleven thirty, we go to refill water bottles from a tap in the car park. There's a guy there. Spanish. Mid-forties. Jeans and old shirt.

He murmurs his name as we fill our bottles. Teniente Estefan Marin, a lieutenant. The rank sounds odd to my ears, but the Guardia Civil is technically part of the Spanish armed services and their ranks, unlike ours, are military.

I say my name, but without the rank. He nods, but barely. We don't shake hands.

Marin indicates the Lotus with a look. Says, in English, 'This man, Wilson, climbs usually till *mediodía*, middle of the day. We can make a little picnic, and we will see.'

We make a little picnic at the wooden table which Marin indicates. He's well-prepared – in surveillance terms, I mean, although the preparation translates into food too. Ham. A thick slab of cold Spanish omelette in foil. More peaches. A little camping stove, at which Marin brews espresso in a silver pot.

Mike wears flip-flops and leaves his boots and chalk on the ground behind him. Marin has come equipped with the same props, and wears tape on a couple of his fingers: something I've seen climbers do – to protect finger tendons, I think. We drink, talk, pick at the omelette.

I ask Marin if he's a climber. He says no. *El windsurf* is more his thing. Mike's done a bit of windsurfing and they talk about it a bit. I happen to mention that a friend of mine, Ed Saunders, is a windsurfing nut and, to my surprise, Mike says, 'Ed? Ed the Wildman?'

I say I don't think my Ed is much of a wildman, but it turns out we are talking about the same guy. There was some rock and wave weekend in Gower, where Cardiff's climbers showed their sport to the windsurfers and vice versa. Ed, who's part of some surfing club, was there, as was Mike, the president of his. Ed, apparently, placed third in the windsurfing race they had on the Sunday afternoon, and on the rocks the day before he was 'basically mental. I mean, he was attempting these DWS routes – deep water solos – where he didn't stand a chance of getting to the top. He just liked seeing how far he could get before he dropped. *Brilliant* guy.'

I can't quite square that image of Ed with the one I know. The collar-and-tie wearing psychologist. The only man I know who makes his own tagliatelli and who wanted my help to locate the broad and steady waters of his Forever Married Life.

But a few cross-checks prove that his Ed is definitely also mine. And it shouldn't surprise me really. I mean, detective work repeatedly proves that we only ever know the face that turns towards us, not the face that turns away. As detectives, we know our targets as killers, rapists, thieves. But those same people's mothers know them as children, who turn up for Sunday dinner, unblock drains and help get the lawnmower started. How often has *he can't have* turned into *he did*?

The conversation moves on.

At about midday, a guy walks out of the forest.

The guy in the video. The guy whose image is now with Interpol. The guy who unclipped his rope on a climb whose difficulty made Mike breathless with admiration.

I look long enough that I can be sure that it's him, then look away. Mike gives a little hello-style nod. Marin doesn't do much at all.

And that's it. The guy gets into his Lotus and drives away, a kettle drum of exhausts as it pulls from the car park dirt to the tarmacked road. The forest echoes briefly, then falls silent.

I call Watkins. 'It's him': the gist of my call.

She asks to speak to Marin and I put the phone on speaker. He says they're planning to make the arrest that evening. The

Guardia will come in force. Surround the house. All officers will be armed. 'Also dogs,' says Marin. 'Also, I don't know how you say, *helicóptero*,' moving his fingers round in a circle to help with the translation.

Watkins, I can tell, is stressed because she doesn't like an important arrest happening in a place and via a force she can't control, but Marin doesn't strike me as anyone's fool and the Guardia were more than slick enough in finding their man in the first place. And the truth is, this should be easy enough. 'Wilson' is a dangerous man, for sure, but he's not a terrorist, not really. We've no reason to think he has any particular skill or interest in weaponry.

Marin says that he'll come to collect us at six. The raid will be made later that evening.

Mike goes back to his beloved rocks. I go back to the house.

Read a book. The *Meditations* of Marcus Aurelius, a second-century Roman emperor and a notable Stoic philosopher.

*Whatever happens to you has been waiting to happen since the beginning of time*, he tells me. *The twining strands of fate wove these two together: your own existence and all that befalls you.*

That's not necessarily true, in fact. As the Scottish philosopher, David Hume, pointed out, there are two logical possibilities. One is that everything is preordained, à la Marcus Aurelius. The other is that there is an element of pure randomness – quantum chance, as we'd now think of it, unknown and unknowable.

But as Hume also made clear, those two things look much the same when you get down to it. It's somehow comforting to think that all we do and say and think and choose is akin to the movement of a cork bobbing on a current. Perhaps preordained, or perhaps the outcome of cosmic chance, but on neither model would we blame the cork for its final position.

Me. My father. Gareth Glyn.

Buzz. Watkins. Jackson.

John Wilson, the Stonemonkey. A cork whose course – whoops-a-daisy – happened to bump up against the rocks marked Theft, Murder, Torture. Whose course, I hope and trust, will soon be swept up in the little circular eddy called Category A Prison, an eddy whose motion repeats and repeats until the cork itself dips beneath the waters, never to return.

*You have the power . . . to consider time everlasting, to think of the swift change in the parts of each thing, of how brief is the span from birth until dissolution, and how the void before birth and the void beyond dissolution are equally infinite.*

I call my sister. She's coming to meet me in Portugal after all this. A long holiday, my treat. We chat, then hang up.

Time passes.

I watch the violet shade of the bougainvillea. Watch a chain of tiny sand-coloured ants busying itself with some fallen cherry stones.

Run a bath of cold water – as cold as it gets here – and sit on the edge, shaving my legs.

Light moves across the wall.

Mike said he'd be back at three. He arrives well after four.

He's breathless and apologetic and has a mouthful of explanations.

I shrug. Say, 'You were climbing.'

He says, 'You didn't mind?'

'No.'

'Is that *no*, as in actual-no? Or *no* as in I'm-secretly-very-pissed-off-but-you're-going-to-have-to-guess-how-to-put-it-right-no?'

'The first of those. Actual-no.'

He bites my shoulder and I pull his T-shirt off and he gets in the bath and submerges himself. His long hair floats in the water, Ophelia Neanderthalensis.

When he's emerged, washed and dressed and as civilised

as he ever gets, he says, 'You seem very simple. For a girl, I mean.'

I laugh at that. Tell him I'm the least simple girl he's ever met. That I have to keep some bits simple, because otherwise even I lose track.

He doesn't know what I'm talking about, but I don't care.

We drink gazpacho – which we bought in cartons and kept in the fridge – outside in the shade.

Marin arrives at six, looking grim. He's in plain clothes, but has a radio, black and crackling, in his hand. A gun is holstered at his waist.

They've lost Wilson.

He went into Teruel to shop. Parked his Lotus outside a shopping centre, went inside. Nothing out of the usual.

The Guardia, leaving nothing to chance, had a tracking device on his car. Didn't want to maintain visual contact with Wilson beyond a point, for fear of being burned. Kept a loose watch on exits, but mostly just waited for Wilson to return to his vehicle.

He never came back. The Lotus is still there, empty, in an emptying car park. Guardia officers – first plain clothes, then also uniformed – combed the shopping centre without joy. 'We are looking at cameras also,' says Marin, 'but . . .'

But CCTV is always less helpful than you want it to be and Spain, for some strange reason, hasn't decided to cover the country in cameras the way we've done, presumably out of some bizarre concern for the privacy and civil liberties of its citizens.

Marin is expecting me to be angry, I think, but I've spent the afternoon with a Roman emperor.

*A cucumber is bitter. Throw it away. There are briars in the road. Turn aside from them. This is enough. Do not add, 'And why were such things made in the world?'*

I say this to Marin, not those exact words maybe, but he gets the drift.

We go to Wilson's house.

No dogs, no helicopters.

Any police vehicles are kept well back and unmarked, in case Wilson decides to return.

Six officers inside, however. All armed. Checking for occupants first, then gathering in the cool tiled hall to determine priorities.

They look at me as though I might know. I don't.

I explore the house with Marin at my side. It's big, rich, well-maintained. My sandals – cute, strappy, holiday things – sound a little frivolous on these tiled floors, between these echoing walls.

A living room with a big fireplace. Sofas in pale leather.

Climbing paraphernalia everywhere. Not just ropes and harnesses, but photos. Some arty stuff too. Badly painted canvases of sunlight on rock. Alpine sunsets.

Perhaps it's just my mood, but I sense a kind of loneliness here. When Wilson chose to burgle his way to riches, he gained something material, but he lost something too. The climbers I've met – Mike and Rhod, Nat Brown and his little world, even the press of schoolchildren down at the wall – have something that binds them together. A passion hot enough that it causes a little melt of community wherever it touches.

If Wilson had chosen to use his talents in a more ordinary way, he'd have had all that. The friendships. The rivalries. The competitions. The expeditions.

As it is, he has this huge, grand, echoey house, with wistful prints of Alpine sunsets, and climbing buddies that never last longer than a week, because he can't afford to let his profile rise too high.

We search on.

No computers. No phones, except the landline.

Not much personal stuff, either. I mean clothes and that kind of thing, yes. Shorts and trousers. Some old T-shirts. One – *Plas-y-Brenin, The National Mountain Centre* – looks like a memento from the long-ago past. At any rate, it's two sizes smaller than everything else.

But that's it. No personal photos. No family letters. No postcards. No board by the fridge with lists of important numbers and a reminder to ring Auntie Joan.

I drift around. Remind Marin that we want any climbing boots, to see if we can match them against the rubber we found both at the lighthouse and at Bristol. We do find some boots but, better still, we find an indoor training wall. A slab of overhanging plywood studded with holds – and bootmarks. I tell Marin we'll want to forensicate the whole damn wall.

Call Watkins. Break the news. She's grim, but not, I think, utterly surprised. 'He must have an informant in the Guardia,' she says.

'Or in South Wales,' I say. 'Or Bristol. Or SOCA. Or Interpol. And it might not even be him, it might be the gang he works for.'

I don't mention the Voice, because I haven't discussed any of that side of thing with Watkins or anyone else, but it strikes me that my friend, Mr Voice, would be more than likely to take precautions along those lines.

Watkins says she'll be on the first flight out. She'll bring the officer in charge of the Bristol crime scene analysis. She says other stuff too.

I don't listen.

*I'm on holiday*, I think. Eating gazpacho and wearing sandals and having that no-strings-attached holiday sex which is meant to be really nice and is, in fact, as nice as it's meant to be.

Watkins asks if I'm planning to hang around. I say no,

probably not, that Mike and I are moving on to Portugal. That's not what we had arranged, but I don't want to see her. Don't feel like standing next to her bristling, angry, effective energy.

Marin drops me back at our little cottage.

Mike has 'cooked' dinner, which means he's taken things out of the fridge and put them on plates.

He says, 'Did you kick down some doors and make people cry?'

I say no. Tell him what happened.

He's disappointed.

I am too, I suppose, but I don't feel like we've lost. Not yet. Wilson's house will yield further clues as to his identity. It'll give us DNA. And now that Wilson knows we're on his trail, we can go public in our requests for information and help. If Wilson goes some place we can't extradite him, we might lose. If he doesn't, I still think we'll get him.

But I don't want to talk about that, and don't.

We finish eating. Mike wants to go straight through to the bedroom, but I say I want to go into the forest. See what it feels like by starlight.

So we go. A silvery kingdom. The boulders seem even stranger by night than they do by day, as if we're on tiptoe through a fairy tale. When an owl breaks from a branch and flaps away through the shadows with heavy wingbeats, it feels as though we've just witnessed a griffin, or a unicorn, or a centaur.

We make love under one of Mike's beloved boulders. Naked on a picnic blanket in the cool dark. Lean up against the stone afterwards, feeling its heat. I sit nested up against Mike's body, his arm spread over me

I'm lucky to have this, I realise. The sincere affection of a good man. This curled-up intimacy. Skin to skin and mingled breath.

I play with Mike's hair and pull his shirt over me when I get cold.

I also notice, without quite paying direct attention, that the Rhayader barn has receded yet further. An injury starting to heal over.

My hand, I notice, is exploring the little pebbled hillocks around my right ankle. Little white fibroids, each of them nursing an old shotgun pellet. Remembrances of things past.

I make an announcement: '"Before long, all things will be transformed. They will rise like smoke or be scattered in fragments."'

Mike stays holding me, says nothing.

I say, '"To do what needs doing. Because dying too is one of our tasks in life."'

Rhayader, it seems, was one of my tasks in life. My little cork happening to bump up against that particular rock. Bumping up, moving on.

Marcus Aurelius watches the path of my little cork and murmurs, 'Do the right thing. The rest doesn't matter.'

Good advice, that. The only advice there is, in a way.

Mike says, 'Is any of that meant to mean anything?'

I say, 'I think I need to go to Portugal tomorrow. Sorry.'

Mike's upset. Not big-bad upset. Just not-wanting-to-let-go-of-sexy-naked-girl upset. Or maybe, not-wanting-to-let-go-of-sexy-naked-girl-who-seems-quite-up-for-a-lot-of-sex-and-isn't-too-fussed-when-her-mister-comes-back-an-hour-and-a-half-later-than-he-said upset.

I tell him that it's nothing to do with him. That I've had a lovely time. Say there's stuff I have to do.

We kiss. Proper, nice, best-buddy kisses.

Snuggle a little longer, then tiptoe back through our fairy tale to something that approaches real life.

# 54

Portugal.

The Algarve.

Sun and wind. People and beaches.

Whitewashed towns dazzling beneath the pressing light.

And my sister, Kay. Skinny, leggy, self-possessed, chic. Already ensconced in the villa I've rented for the next few weeks. Pleased to see me, but in that way of hers that always holds something back. Something which always retains her own independence of being.

The villa has a small plunge pool and I'm happy to plunge. Soak off the travel. Kay brings me a glass of orange juice, clinking with ice, and sits with her feet in the pool.

I tell her about my bank card. Explain what I need. Tell her how to use it: where, and how often, and how much.

Give her my phone. The same thing there.

Then we do some work.

Take a suitcase of clothes and a camera. Flit about various local sites and attractions. Take photos. Get other people to take pictures of the two of us together. Then change outfits, move on, repeat.

All that afternoon and evening. Some more first thing in the morning.

Then I'm done.

I kiss her. Say, 'Have a *fab* time.'

'I will.'

And she will, of course. She has friends coming out, one of whom is a boy whose name makes her laugh and look coy and change the subject. I've not met the guy – Cai – but I hope he's nice.

She takes me to the bus station. She assumes I'm doing something very illegal, which I'm actually not. I say as much but Kay, I can tell, doesn't believe me. Our father's daughter.

Bus to Seville.

Train to Madrid.

Another train to Santander.

Arrive late. Spend the night in a perfectly OK station hotel. I don't sleep much, but that's my fault, not the hotel's.

A ferry leaves for Portsmouth at eleven in the morning. I use the time beforehand to scout about. Find a chandlery with a small second-hand clothing section. Buy waterproofs, thermals. The clothes are my size, in theory, but when I try them on in front of a mirror, I look like a small animal trying to escape from a laundry basket.

The same chandlery sells cooking equipment and I buy pots and pans. Not the biggest ones, the ones where you can boil ten kilos of potatoes at a go. It's not that I can't lift ten kilos – I can, of course – but then there's the water too, and every possible combination of roll, pitch, shudder and yaw. So I pick the mid-sized pots. Ones I reckon I could handle, even with heavy seas.

I wish I wasn't completely bloody useless in the kitchen.

I wish I knew if I got seasick.

The chandlery sells me a big black bag with a shoulder strap that will hold my cookware and still leave a bit of room for my clothes. It's big and clumsy, but just about manageable.

I buy a *pain au chocolat* still warm from the baker's oven and eat it.

Then I board the ferry, a foot passenger only. I have to present my passport, of course, but anyone wanting to trace my movements would have to work pretty damn hard to jump from my flight to Lisbon and my holiday villa in Faro to a foot-passenger-only ticket from Santander to Portsmouth.

The ferry leaves Iberia's sunny shores.

Heads for Britannica's cloudy ones.

Marcus Aurelius watches his Spanish colonies vanish below that golden horizon and says, 'Do not think upon the many and various troubles which have afflicted you in the past and which will come again in times to come. Instead, with regard to every present difficulty, ask yourself: "What is there here that is unbearable and beyond endurance?"'

He's right. I stop worrying and go below on a hunt for peppermint tea.

# 55

Milford Haven.

Stone and twilight. Storms and fish bellies.

The same as last time, except that now I'm on the deck of the *Isobel Baker*. My big black bag at my feet. A tall Scotsman, the ship's captain, Alexander Honnold, gazing down at me.

It's not dark, but almost. Lights glimmering across the harbour.

'You have experience, you say?'

'Yes.'

'Would that be the sort of experience that comes with references?'

'Yes.'

I worked on a case once that brought me into contact with a shipping company. I've spoken to one of the guys there – Andy Watson – and asked him to provide a reference for me in case anyone phones. I let him think that I'd be on regular police business and he was happy enough to say yes.

And anyway, I *am* on regular police business. It just so happens that no one in the regular police knows anything about it.

Honnold asks for details. I give them. Honnold strides away, long legs covering restless yards. Lights, yellow and blue, on the inkily violet waters beyond. He talks to Watson, who presumably says what he needs to say.

Honnold returns.

'Bulk carriers?'

'Yes.'

'No trawlers?'

'No.'

'Ye might have a more bumpy ride than you're used to.'

I shrug. Don't care. 'I might have to serve cold for a day or two, if the sea's high.'

He nods.

My answer was the right one. My 'experience' as cook on bulk carriers won't necessarily have given me the kind of sea legs you need to stay upright on a trawler, but a ship's cook job is to provide food, come what may.

'There'll be cleaning up as well, not just the galley.'

'I don't mind working hard.'

We talk about pay. I ask for one-fifty a day. He offers one-twenty. I grumble, but say yes.

He looks sceptical about my ability to manage large quantities of food in high seas. Physically manage, that is. I tell him I have my own pots. That I cook in batches I can manage.

I ask about the length of the trip.

'Depends on the catch. Anywhere from ten days to four weeks. We've got supplies for four.'

He doesn't like having a woman on board. Doesn't like it for superstitious reasons, but for practical ones too. Trawlers are mostly all-male preserves. Men alone with the dangerous intimacy of the sea. Throw a woman into that environment and you add a combustible element to what is already the country's most frequently lethal profession.

Honnold looks at me, not liking it. 'It's risky,' he tells me, 'and I hate risk.'

But since Brian Penry managed, using big splodges of my cash, to buy off Honnold's existing cook, and since – as Honnold told that cook, yelling down the phone with anger

– the *Isobel Baker* now needs to sail within twelve hours, and since I'd been drifting around the docks for the past few days, seeking a position as cook, or cleaner, or skivvy, he didn't have a whole heap of options.

So Honnold nods. Holds out a lean hand. Says, 'Welcome aboard,' and shows me brusquely to my tiny berth below decks.

I stow my bag. Take my pots and pans to the galley. Get used to the clamps that hold the cooking equipment stable. Go down to the holds. The giant freezers which will store the catch as it comes in. The ice-maker, which will make as much ice as those fish, and those freezers, need. The room-sized freezer compartment which holds food for the voyage. Boxloads of it, mostly heat and serve.

'This is a trawler,' Honnold told me. 'I don't know what you cooked on your other ships, but here we keep it simple. Serve it hot. Serve it big. And serve it on time. OK?'

As I start to inventory what's there, I meet a couple of my crewmates – men I already know from their photos, Doug Pearson, Stuart MacHaffie. They nod, offer a handshake, but they're busy and move off.

Steel corridors. Yellow guards over the bulkhead lights. The thrumming of an engine.

Boxes of food.

Man food. Simple, fatty, cheap. The kind of stuff that even I might be able to cook without ballsing it all up.

I figure out what I'll cook for the next couple of meals, then leave it.

Go to my berth.

Working with Dyfed-Powys, Watkins secured a warrant allowing her to intercept communications to and from the ship. She was able to track the names and backgrounds of all six men on board, including Ted Huber, the cook whom Penry nobbled. All the six were fishermen with long track records at sea. None of them with any meaningful criminal record.

A more professional surveillance campaign, conducted by Dyfed-Powys in close liaison with Cardiff, has yielded better images of the *Isobel Baker*. Those images were scrutinised by marine experts in Scotland, and Lowe's basic conclusions were emphatically vindicated. The *Isobel Baker* has been adapted to handle an ROV. But she isn't carrying an ROV.

In London, Atlantic Cables has finished its basic line tests without problems.

The ship is still Cyprus-registered. Watkins has not obtained permission to board it at sea. She's still trying.

I haven't spoken to Watkins – who assumes I'm in Portugal with my sister – but I follow every detail of the inquiry from whatever internet connection I can find.

When the dark has settled further, I go out on deck.

Stand looking out to sea, my back to any cameras that Dyfed-Powys may still have trained on the ship. When I came on board, I was wearing a fleece with a hood. Hardly a perfect disguise, but enough that no one, watching from behind, will be able to identify me with certainty. And anyway, Dyfed-Powys doesn't know me.

We're in harbour, but the engines are operating at low power and a thrum runs through the hull. A breeze ruffles the waters. Somewhere, unseen, a wire clacks against metal.

The deck isn't moving, but the ship still feels mobile, impatient, alive.

She wants to be gone, and so do I.

# 56

The sun rises at five, but we're under way before four.

A rattle of anchor chain and the deep bass of the ship's diesel. Honnold on the bridge and navigation lamps showing.

Blue water to port and starboard.

Water, and two huge oil refineries. Towers, pipes, tanks. Brightening silver in the dull light.

Dyfed-Powys can't see me now and I stand on deck, watching the land slide past.

This waterway forms one of the deepest natural harbours in the world. A *ria*. A valley formed in the last Ice Age, then drowned as the seas rose and the land sank.

A submergent coastline.

I go below and get ready for breakfast.

A trayful of sausages. A vat of beans. A spadeful of egg. Toast. Take butter out of the fridge so it'll be easier to spread.

Don't burn the sausages.

Don't burn the beans, or not much.

Because I'm anxious to be ready on time, I start the eggs way too early, so they go a bit funny. Pale yellow and somehow leathery. But I think they'll be OK. I don't do more anyway.

I forget all about tea to start with, because I'm worried about the food, but then I remember and put the urn on to heat. A ten litre thing, bolted to the wall.

Milk.

HP sauce. Ketchup.

Vinegar. Do you need vinegar if you don't have chips? I don't know. Put vinegar out anyway.

It's ten to six and I don't think I've fucked up.

Beneath my feet, the deck has started to move. When I use the sink – a big stainless steel affair, vaguely reminiscent of mortuary equipment – water heaves moodily from side to side. I stare at it. It stares back, malevolently, at me before, finally, draining with a subterranean gargle.

I wonder about seasickness, but think I feel much as I normally do. A bit spacey. A bit disconnected. But not particularly likely to vomit or turn green.

Good enough.

I serve up.

The galley backs straight onto the dining room. A long pine table, two benches, a caged ceiling lamp. The plates are acrylic, unbreakable.

The men enter.

Honnold, the captain. Lean, Scottish, vigilant.

He takes a plate of food and carries it out. Up to the bridge, I think.

The others follow. Jonah Buys, Honnold's first mate. Swarthy. Bushily moustached. Disconcerting somehow, I don't know why.

Then Doug Pearson, Stuart MacHaffie, Sean Coxsey. Sailors. Trawlermen, who look like what they are. Faces that have seen weather. Danger. Hauled nets and braved gales.

The men, both those who haven't met me and those who already have, greet me with a little caution. A little reserve.

A woman on a boat: I'm not meant to be here, I realise that.

I hand out food. The sausages are a bit more burned than I'd realised, but it's all OK. The guys take their food, but don't start eating. MacHaffie has to jog me: 'Cutlery?'

I give them cutlery.

Tea. Toast.

Keep the tea and the toast and the milk and the sugar coming, till no one asks me for anything more.

Take tea – milk, two sugars – up to Honnold on the bridge.

The land has vanished. We are travelling on sea the colour of wet rock. Of light falling on slate. Waves trouble the surface and a steady breeze rakes ripples into the broader swell. Our trail is marked out in a white that vanishes as you watch.

My gaze keeps reaching for the world's rim. Looking for a glimpse of land, an anchor.

Doesn't find it.

Honnold tells me what he wants from me.

Serve a mountain of food at six in the morning, midday and six in the evening. 'Midnight as well, if the factory deck is busy.' Keep the galley and bathrooms clean. Keep the processing room 'vaguely clean, if you can.' The processing room: the place where the fish are gutted under greenish lamps, before being cleaned in cold water and sent on down to the freezers.

'Don't take any shit from the men. Don't give them any shit. If you have a problem with anyone, you tell me first. Is that clear?'

'Yes.'

Honnold doesn't say anything else for a moment. The ship's engines are grinding away, but there's no sign that we're actually moving. A gleam of sunlight to port says we're heading roughly south-west. Ireland a hundred miles to the north and west of us. Devon or Cornwall a hundred miles to the south and east. Wales, already out of sight, slips ever further from us.

The bridge is closed to the weather, but the doors to port and starboard hang open, bang loose in the wind.

Steel doors.

Waterproof seals in thick rubber.

A metal door-sweep three inches high.

And all the glass so thick, that fifty tons of water could crash over it and leave it unscathed. *Has* crashed over it, indeed. The *Isobel Baker* is twenty years old and more, and her elderly frame will have seen every sea, every wind.

Outside, to port and starboard, there are two orange buoys, holstered in plastic, some electronic gadgetry on top. I recognise these, from my research in port, as being marine EPIRBs – Emergency Position-Indicating Radio Beacons. Inactive now, but they'll operate automatically if the ship founders or if they're manually activated.

I say, 'I don't know what we're fishing for.'

'Nephrops. Plaice. Whiting. Sole. Turbot. Anything that gets into the nets, as long as we're allowed to keep it and sell it.'

My face doesn't know what nephrops are and presumably looks it.

Honnold says, 'Lobsters, wee ones. You eat them as scampi.'

I nod, in an *ah yes, of course* way.

Honnold, who doesn't believe my nod, watches me for a few moments, then says, 'We'll take a few men on board later. Four of them. You'll be serving for ten.'

'Ten? Today, you mean?'

'No. Later. I'll tell you when.'

I don't say anything to that. My face probably does an 'Is that normal in fishing?' thing, but if it does, Honnold doesn't react.

We stand for a few moments in silence.

I say, 'I'll need one fifty. If there are more men.'

Honnold half laughs. 'OK. Do a good job of work, and ye can have it.'

Then there's nothing else to say.

The sea is empty.

We're heading for who knows where.

Nephrops. Baby lobsters. Scampi.

Somewhere in the waters beneath us, a telecoms cable links London and New York. A cable that has killed two. That would have killed me, if I hadn't escaped its lethal touch.

I leave Honnold and go below. Clean the kitchen, the dining room, the toilets. Get ready for the midday meal.

# 57

I work hard. I'm a good cleaner, accurate and fast, and I like the strictly utilitarian approach of the on-board fittings. Their boltedness. Their unbreakability.

The kitchen work is harder. I think that's because it's hard to cook unless you have some feel, however basic, for what you're cooking. I lack that feel, but even I am mostly capable of tipping a two-and-a-half litre can of macaroni cheese into a saucepan and putting the thing on to heat. I don't know what you're meant to serve with macaroni cheese – the tin doesn't tell me – but I open some tinned pilchards and heat those too. Then I'm worried that macaroni cheese and pilchards doesn't seem like much of a meal, so I get a huge block of cheddar cheese and grate a mountain of that.

Make toast, because everyone likes toast.

My plan was to avoid much interaction with the men. A simple way to obey Honnold's 'don't give or take shit' injunction. But we're not at the fishing grounds yet. The ship has already, on its long stopover in harbour, had any maintenance work it needs. Net repairs, oil changes. So the pace of work seems easy. Not the six hours on/three hours off rhythm that'll be ours in due course.

Coxsey and Pearson are on deck, doing some electrical work – possibly connected with the tether management system that Lowe is expecting to see. MacHaffie's not involved in that. He's theoretically got some job down in the fish-holds.

Servicing the refrigeration system, I think. But whatever his task is, he keeps bobbing up in the dining room, begging a cup of tea.

He gets his tea. I try to stay largely silent with just a sprinkling of surly aloofness, but my efforts don't last long.

MacHaffie is maybe fifty. From Orkney, he tells me, born and bred. Didn't set foot on the mainland – of Orkney, that is, not Scotland – till he was fifteen. Twenty-five before he saw Scotland itself. Over thirty before he saw England.

He's got a twinkly charm to him, a lightness. As though he's saying, in his heavily accented Orcadian, 'Ah cin tale thoo're a peedie lass wantin tae dae thee best, but we baith ken thoo'd ower blether wi' me than wipe yon teeble again.'

So I do the jobs I have to do, but also blether wi' Caff, as he tells me to call him.

Honnold, he tells me, is a good skipper. That is, if I understand right, one who runs a safe ship and can be relied upon to find fish. Of Coxsey and Pearson, he says, 'I'm nae flought the baoot wi' thaim lang, bit they seem hard-workin' enaw. Guid fishermen.'

Buys, the mustachioed mate, he doesn't know. 'First time oan th' baoot, the lenth o' ah ken.'

Which doesn't necessarily mean much, since people come and go.

At midday, I serve up my pilchards and pasta, and those things together with the cheese and the toast turn out to be culinary successes and I feel stupidly proud of myself. Two meals done, and neither of them fuck-ups.

I clean up. Figure out a strategy for supper. Check the bathrooms. Give them a quick wipe over.

Go up on deck.

I like the way you can actually see the weather here. Watch the wind moving the water. See where a rain shower thickens the light. Where a cloud-window expands to allow a spill of golden light to widen across the unsteady sea.

The evening passes.

The days.

The *Isobel Baker* is Honnold's own boat. Heavily mortgaged, of course, but the title is still his. He'll earn the major share from this catch, but – after diesel and food costs are deducted – the crew will share what's left and I can sense their fluttering hope for 'fair winds and stowed oot nets.'

We get to our station, which turns out to be the edge of the continental shelf, where the seabed drops to the deep Atlantic floor. We are, in effect, on the final edge of Europe, its outermost boundary. Our beat ranges from the Porcupine Bank at its top edge to the Goban Spur on its lower one. We're a hundred, a hundred and fifty miles west of Ireland. The area we're patrolling is a strip of sea perhaps sixty miles long, by thirty or forty wide.

A strip of sea, through which any Anglo-American cable has to pass. Through which the Atlantic Cables line *does* pass.

A cable, and also plenty of fish, as our nets attest.

As we hit the fishing grounds, Caff's 'hard-working enaw' alters, in my mind at least, to insanely hard-working.

The work never stops. The nets keep dropping, their maws always gaping. Caff's faith in Honnold – 'he kens hoo tae fin' the fish' – seems amply justified. Catch after catch is hauled over the stern ramp, black and flapping. In the processing room, a pair of men – whoever's on duty – stand with knives, expertly selecting, gutting, filleting, discarding. Plastic buckets fill with guts and livers. With fish too strange, too unknown, to eat or sell. Heads, eyes, fins, tails. The silver slime of fresh fish scale.

My days and nights blur into one single unit of time, crazed by sleeplessness. The men sleep when their legs buckle. Wake six hours before they're ready.

Without even being asked, I serve a full meal at midnight, in addition to the other three. My portion sizes increase too. I cook enough food to feed double the number of people who will actually sit to eat it, and nothing much goes to waste.

If I'm not cooking, I'm cleaning.

If I'm not cleaning, I'm hauling food out of the holds, ready to start the next meal. Or changing the propane cylinders that fire the cooker. Or trying to dispose of a bucket of slops without falling over in these rising Atlantic seas.

I do my best in the processing room too.

Honnold asked me to keep the room 'vaguely clean, if you can,' and I understand now why he was so provisional in his request. The room is awash. With sea water tramped in from outside. With the fresh water used to clean blood from the gutted fish. With guts and slime.

I use a plastic broom to sweep the mess into a corner. Try to slide a shovel under the slippery pile before the moving deck heaves it aside and away from my bucket, a thing the size of a laundry basket. One time, the pile includes an eel – or something like that, a sea serpent, I want to say, a python of the deep – and the damn thing evades my shovel every time I try to lift it. Slithering away as if still alive. A six foot cord of black and glistening muscle, ending in a mouth large enough to swallow itself.

Buys and Coxsey are on processing duty, and Buys watches my efforts with a bloodshot eye.

He says nothing. The ship is, in any event, by now so noisy – with the engines, the clatter of processing machinery, the pumps and compressors, the unceasing assault of waves against the hull – that we don't talk except when we need to. And when we need to, we shout, mouth to ear. Gestures big, emphatic and repeated. Swearwords falling like seaspray.

Another attempt with the shovel, another failure.

I've been awake twenty-one hours now – Honnold gave me

three hours off, but I couldn't sleep, couldn't even lie down really – and I don't know what to do. Don't know how to get the fucking eel into the fucking bucket. Keep trying, keep failing, as the ship bucks and the greenish light clots the air.

Buys drops his filleting knife. Those things are so fearsomely sharp that they snick through a fish as long as a man's forearm with only a whisper of effort. The knife rattles around the steel fish tray, as though in search of its next victim.

Buys approaches. Demented as I am, as he is, I think, *He's going to hit me. I can't get the eel into the bucket and Jonah Buys is going to hit me.* I sort of accept it, too. There's an internal logic in my head which says, *That's only fair. Your job was to get the eel in the bucket and you were given a fair old try at it. You've no reason to complain.*

But Buys doesn't hit me. Just takes the shovel from my hand, and with three or four smashing blows splits the eel into rags. Doesn't divide it cleanly, by any means, but leaves the thing in a series of bloody stumps, connected by tatters of skin and the white threads of exposed nerves.

Buys fixes me with that bloodshot eye, nods, goes back to his knifework. My shovel has no problem now heaving the mass into my bucket. It feels as though the world has become more orderly. *Ah yes, that's how you clean a room. You smash any once-living creature into fist- and foot-sized fragments, then just shovel it away.* I carry my bucket over to the trash chute, where our discards go, and send the eel, and all its fishy co-travellers, to the next stop on their black roads.

Take the clean-water hose and spray enough cold water on the floor that I can sweep up most of the slime and offal too small to shovel. The movement of the ship and the encouragement of my broom pushes the water out to the scuppers, and away.

The room is for a short moment almost clean. Clean that is, given that this is a world in which the fish guts hanging from the wall-mounted fire extinguisher, the blood and slime staining even the ceiling fixtures don't strike anyone as something that needs to be removed or dealt with. There's a bucket of fish guts in between Buys and Coxsey, but I don't feel like moving it and I don't think they do either.

I stow my broom, shovel and bucket back into the wall-clips next to the mallet used to budge the sorting flaps when they stick. Nod at Buys and Coxsey. Go on to the next thing.

The sea, which was well behaved when we were in Ireland's sheltering embrace, is rougher now. Unbound. Honnold tells me that the wind isn't particularly high – force six, approximately, a 'strong breeze' – but my sea legs don't really manage the waves that result. I don't get sick, but I do – often – lose my footing and find myself slammed against an iron wall, a wooden bulkhead. In the kitchen, after I scald myself twice, I get better at using the steel clamps for the cookware. Learn to fill pots to no more than one-third their level.

We fish.

We work.

We survive.

And on our fifth day out at sea, Honnold tells me, 'There'll be four more mouths for lunch. And ye can please check their cabin.'

Tells me this, as I'm up on the bridge, bringing him a hot drink. The mugs we use have lids and drinking spouts, but even so I've managed to scald my hand for the I-don't-know-how-manyth time that day.

I nod. Offer a thumbs up, because that's easier than screaming through the noise.

Honnold waves for me to go, then has a second thought and summons me back.

He jabs down at the computer screen in front of him, some kind of automated chart-plotter. Clicks some buttons. Brings up a weather map overlay. Blue lines deepening into black.

'Weather's coming in a bit,' he shouts.

I don't know what that means. Not really. I offer an omnipurpose shruggy-nod, intended to indicate a general OK-ness with whatever it is he means.

Honnold changes the scale on his chart. Zooms out to maximum extension. He places a long finger on the centre of a whorl of black-blue lines. The whorl is two thousand miles distant, somewhere in the tropical waters east of the Caribbean.

'They're having a fair auld blow there,' he comments. 'We'll pick up whatever's left over. A proper storm, I expect.'

The view from the bridge shows a sea with larger waves starting to rise among the many smaller peaks and ridges. And all of them, the big waves and the small, crested with white. The bridge windows are wet with blowing spray.

But the weather that concerns Honnold is nothing we can see. It's what lies over that bucking horizon. The dangers incubating in those dark clouds, those tangled winds.

'Ye might want to cook cold for a wee while. Only if it gets difficult, mind.'

Nod.

'And get some cot boards up in the spare cabin.'

Nod.

Cot boards: things to stop you rolling out of your bed in heavy seas. I've already got mine up. I thought these seas *were* heavy.

I don't say anything further. Nor does Honnold. So I go below, to the one empty bunkroom and its four beds. Get the cot boards in place, with difficulty. Place a magnetic voice-recorder on the underside of the lower aft bunk. I've no idea if the damn thing will pick up anything useful in the racket, but there's nothing to do but try.

I think, *This is it. All this is about to finish.*

In my sleeplessness, my friends move about me in silence.

Derek Moon, who died with his skull cracked open and the blue light of Swansea Bay in his eyes.

Ian Livesey, who hung in the clear light above a city he didn't know. Whose beloved cried salt tears at his going.

Jazz MacClure, with her maroon top and beaded collar. Who isn't a part of this story, and yet who accompanies me still.

And Gina Jewell? Does she belong here? I don't know. I don't know her face. Never saw her in death or life. Gina Jewell, whose photos are blurry, old, newsprint things. Prints which don't tell me about the person she was, the corpse she's become.

But these echoing walls, these shrieking waters are no place for complex thought.

I do my work.

We catch our fish.

The endgame nears.

# 58

They arrive in a small vessel, the *Kate of St Ives.* A fishing boat, yes, but one far smaller than our own.

Four men. None of them, I'm relieved to see, look anything like Buzz's e-fit. The guy who was in the barn with me, the one who walked away. If that guy had been present, I'd simply have declared my true identity to Honnold.

Identified myself as a police officer, the newcomer as a murder suspect. We'd have radioed for help and the Royal Navy, or any navy, could have boarded us with perfect legitimacy.

But the guy isn't here and I don't want to declare my true identity. Don't know if I'd still have a job, if I did that.

The new arrivals: four men and an ROV.

A Remote Operated Vehicle. Yellow buoyancy tanks on top. A machine about my height. Four feet wide. Nine feet long.

Thrusters. Lamps. Cameras. Cutting and coring tools. Pump.

A set of connection points to supply power. To send and receive data.

The machine comes up over the stern ramp. Hauled over the lip by the A-frame extension to the gantry which Lowe noted.

Buys and Pearson are on deck, with some cabling. Bolting a drum winch to the superstructure, making use of fixings that Lowe had noted in his report as being non-standard for a vessel of this class. As being of recent vintage. As being suitable for a tether management system.

The four new arrivals aren't introduced to me.

Two of them, it looks like, come with the ROV. They're the ones checking how it's stowed. Directing Buys and Pearson on their cabling work. I suspect those two are simply men doing a job, technicians provided by whichever company hired out the ROV.

Then there's a computer guy. Glasses. Skinny. No more comfortable in oilskins than I am. No more natural on this moving deck. He's needed up here because some of the connectivity issues require his input, but basically he can't wait to get out of the cold and spray.

The last guy is the boss. The one all the others defer to. Even Honnold takes orders from him. When there was some difficulty arising, because waves kept on rising over the level of the stern ramp, the boss guy summoned Honnold with a click of his fingers and, with a gesture, asked him to spin the ship through ninety degrees, so that waves would hit broadside on and leave the stern ramp clearer of water.

As it happened, Honnold refused that request. I can't hear what he said, but I think his gestures were indicating that the ship wouldn't be properly stable at that angle. And, in any event, neither Pearson nor Buys, nor the two ROV specialists, care about the waves. When a wave comes in at knee-height, or thigh-height, they just let the thing come and let the thing go, then get on with whatever it was they were doing. The four men all wear harnesses and safety lines and aren't troubled by the ship's movement.

Once the *Kate of St Ives* has unloaded her cargo, her captain gives a quick thumbs up to Honnold, bridge to bridge, then sails off to the south-east. It doesn't take long before her little bulk is lost in the larger masses surrounding her. It's almost as though she was never here. A winking bubble, a butterfly's dream.

I watch for a while, but I've got work to do, so don't watch for long.

Go below.

Clean the bathrooms. Go to the galley. I've brought some one-kilo tins of chilli con carne up from the hold. Open six of them, put the stuff on to heat. Add some Tabasco, to make the stuff chilli-ish, then realise that the tins probably came with chilli already added.

Oh well. I probably shouldn't have added salt either.

I try tasting the slop in the pan, but can't really tell whether it tastes right or not. To be on the safe side, I water it down with another couple of cans.

Rice.

I know you have to have rice with chilli, but I'm not very good at it. I put two kilos of rice, plus plenty of water in a pan, and put it on to heat.

I know you're meant to put salt in rice, but I think I've oversalted the chilli, so I compromise by not adding any now.

Things cook.

My evolving technique is to wait till something is bubbling on top, but only just beginning to burn on the bottom. There are probably better ways to manage things, but this way works for me. And if the seas get any higher, I'll just make sandwiches.

The chilli looks OK. The rice looks a bit funny.

People troop in to eat. Not Caff, because he's off duty. Probably asleep. Not Buys, because he's on the bridge and someone takes food up to him.

The two ROV guys take their food and introduce themselves. Ryan and Eddie. English accents. Friendly.

My guess is that the pair of them are contractors who mostly work for the offshore oil industry. North Sea. Perhaps the seas west of Shetland and the Hebrides. They have a bluff, nomadic confidence. Something open.

The computer guy comes in, looking pale. Looks at the food. Says, 'Ah Christ!' and walks straight out again. Ryan and Eddie laugh. Mime throwing up. Grin at me.

The boss guy, Connor, takes his food. Sits next to Ryan and Eddie. Doesn't talk either to them, or anyone else. Eats rapidly, with quick darts of his fork. At one point, he gazes up from his plate. Fixes me with dark eyes. Scrutinises me, as though adding me to some collection of specimens in his mental catalogue. Once my data is inputted, recorded and checked, his eyes flick back to his plate, the small, female cook no longer of interest.

How I like to be.

People want tea. I give them tea.

Caff gives me his plate. Breathes out through his mouth, miming 'hot'. Laughs.

There's quite a lot of leftover rice, I notice. Glistening snowballs. Hillocks and caves.

The fishing stops.

The men are angry. Coxsey and Pearson, when they're not on deck, are down in the dining room, drinking tea and muttering.

'We're in the fucking fish,' says Pearson, 'and we're not fucking fishing.'

It's his money he's thinking of. His lost earnings.

I've seen Honnold talking to Pearson and Caff. Promising them cash, I'd guess, but the mood is still ugly. Once I'm in the corridor leading down to the processing room and I see Buys squaring up to Connor. I don't know what the argument is, but there's flame in the two men's eyes. Physical aggression flickers in the space between them.

They see me, separate, let me pass. My mop and bucket like a letter of passage. A herald's flag.

Buys has the legs of a sailor, legs that move him with the ship. Connor is OK – he's better than me – but he's not a mariner. Even as he was glowering at Buys, Connor had his hand on a bulkhead support, keeping his balance.

Connor would be dangerous in a fight, but Buys would be worse. And Buys knows how to use a knife.

The ROV is readied.

The machine is prepared. The winch. The tether. The data cable.

Ryan and Eddie have set up a control room in a little cabin beneath the bridge. Monitors that show what the ROV is 'seeing'. Keyboard and joystick-style controls to send commands. The computer guy – 'Wee Philly', as the men are now calling him, though I'm not sure that he's even called Philip – helps a bit with that, but he's still pale green and has the manner, willowy and surrendered, of a bride reluctant before her wedding night. I'd be the same, I think, except that the sea was calm when we first sailed and my adjustment has been gradual. Any case, Wee Philly's suffering doesn't matter much to anyone. His hour of glory is yet to come.

And still the seas rise.

The waves heap up.

Foam from breaking crests is blown in streaks down the wave-fronts, like snow lying on a rocky mountaintop. The valley between each successive peak is fifteen feet deep, I guess, though it's hard to tell. The spray is constant now and the wind strong enough that I avoid going on deck. If I do go up to look at the weather, I keep a grip of a handrail. Stay on the lee side of the wind.

Force seven, Caff guesses with a shrug. Force seven and rising.

# 59

Evening.

I serve the lunchtime rice, plus the leftover chilli, stirred up with some tins of tomatoes and some frankfurters that I found at the back of the freezer. All that, with cheese on top and plenty of toast.

Most of the guys seem happy with that, but Wee Philly is still on hunger-strike. After I've cleaned up, I go to his bunkroom with a mug of tea.

He's alone in there. Lying out on one of the lower cots, jammed fetally between the cot board and the bulkhead.

I give him the tea and say, 'You should try to drink,' not because I care whether he does or not, but because that's what people like me are meant to say to people like him.

He takes the mug.

I say, 'It's a bit blowy, isn't it?'

He looks at me with eyes of hatred.

I say, 'What are you all doing here? I know the boys want to get on and fish.'

Wee Philly, with an effort of will, says, 'Seismic monitoring. Listening out for sub-sea quakes. There's a whole system.' He waves his hand in a kind of ring, a network of sensors. 'It's a maintenance thing.'

'Oh, I used to work on a seismic survey vessel. Part of the European Major Disaster Prevention and Analysis Project. Are you with that?'

He nods, but says nothing.

'So you'll know Terry Cooper and all those guys? That Italian guy, Matteo Thingummy, with the missing fingers?'

He nods, but watchful. Uncommitted.

It's a strange conversation. Neither of us are simply speaking, for one thing. We're shouting over the metallic beating, that's now omnipresent. Tons of water crashing at the hull. The booming sound as it strikes. The moan and slip of release. A thousand fathoms of ocean beating for admittance. Midnight-green. Lethal.

But it's the lies too. He's lying. I'm lying. We both strongly suspect the other knows our lies for what they are.

I listen to the sound of the sea. Try to guess whether my crappy little voice recorder will pick up anything audible through this din.

I'm guessing not.

Ty to guess how long its crappy batteries will last.

I'm guessing not long.

Down in the freezer area, where Buys and Pearson are discontentedly repacking fish, I recount my conversation. Conclude: 'I just made it up. Terry Cooper and all that crap. These guys aren't seismologists. I don't know what the fuck they *are* doing, but it's not what they're saying.'

Pearson spits. Not on the fish exactly, but not far away from them either.

'We were right in the fish. We were right in the fucking fish.'

Buys says nothing, not right away. Just pulls a bit of liver from a badly gutted skate. Throws the fish down in an ice-nestled plastic box. Stares at Pearson. Stares at me.

Then, 'You need to check the bathroom. Wee Philly's been redecorating.'

I do my job. Clean up in the bathroom, which is indeed disgusting. Wear my oilskins and rubber boots to do it because, as the ship is moving so violently, I can't help but be tumbled against the walls as I work.

That done, I go up to the darkening deck. Let the rain and sea spray clean me off. Caff comes in from the bow, harness clinking at his waist. Shouts, 'This is whit his ahll aboot, is it no? A grand peedie tirl.'

A grand peedie tirl, indeed.

There are lamps at the stern. The ROV's yellow tanks shine luridly under their glare, but the rest is emptiness. A waste of wind-torn water, nothing else.

As I understand it, the ROV is loaded, readied, connected, tested. Work begins tomorrow, and will go ahead no matter what the seas.

I remember Lowe telling me that one of his ships boasted automatic movement compensation. That it could launch and retrieve ROVs in any sea state. The *Isobel Baker* is a simple trawler and not a particularly new one at that but, I realise, Connor doesn't care particularly about being able to retrieve the ROV in one piece. If he can, great. If not, he'll just pay the hire company whatever compensation they need.

I go into the little control room.

There's no one present. The monitors are powered off. The console that controls the ROV is powered up, but not active. Clamps secure it to the metal table which is itself bolted to the floor. There's a smaller control gadget for the winch that runs through to the A-frame on the gantry. I inspect it to see if there's an easy way to cause it damage, but the answer is no, not without pulling it apart.

In the past, I've seen one of those military-style laptops kicking around here too. One of those rugged extreme-environment machines. But it's not here now. There are a couple of computer cables, though. Things running from the console to where the laptop was.

I clean the room. Basic wipe and tidy, nothing special.

The room has two doors. One internal, leading to the companionway down. The other external, leading to the main deck itself. The external door is stiff and hard to work. I open the door, and turn the handle till the latch is fully retracted. I push the tip of my knife as far as it'll go into the gap between the latch and the backplate. Then bend the knife till the tip snaps off. The latch isn't totally jammed, but nor does it want to go about its ordinary latchy work. I make an attempt to close the door, but it doesn't really hold. Bangs about a bit in the frame, then springs open when the ship kicks.

I take both cables out of the console. Throw one on the floor under the desk. Have the other one knotted in my hand as I step outside. Either Ryan or Eddie is on deck, fussing around the gantry under the lamps. He waves to me. I wave to him. As I wave, the knotted cable slips from my grasp. It's picked from my hand and flies out to sea in the darkness. I let my broken knife follow it out.

I don't like being out here, not even in the shelter of the superstructure. I have one hand on the handrail the whole time. Both hands when I'm walking and especially if the waves are breaking over the deck.

I hurry below. I'm already on the ladder down, before I notice Buys below, wanting to come up. He stands aside for me, and I say, 'Thanks,' and continue. He says nothing. Doesn't even set foot on the ladder, just stares after me till I'm gone and out of sight.

*A dangerous man*, I think. Brooding and dangerous.

I don't serve food at midnight. Make sandwiches for anyone who wants one, but we're not fishing now and the crazy pressure of the nets and the processing room has lifted for now.

Honnold and his men, not the newcomers, are all down in the galley with a bottle of whisky, supplied by Honnold from his own cabin, I think. They invite me to join them, but

I don't, not really. Just wipe up, get a few bits ready for the morning.

As I'm doing that, Connor pokes his nose in, looking for either Ryan or Eddie.

Pearson says, 'Hey, mate, you found any earthquakes yet, or are you still looking?'

Connor says nothing. Honnold moves his lips but says nothing.

Connor goes.

I go. As I do so, Caff winks at me. Raises eight fingers and grins.

I don't know what that means, but smile back.

Bed.

Brush my teeth, but don't get undressed. There's a sticky salt dampness that permeates everything. A chill that's entered the bone and won't leave till I'm somewhere warm, dry and stable.

Get into my cot, but the ship is bucking now like a crazy thing. Twenty-foot falls between each wave, and the pause between each rise and fall is a juddering, heaving, uncertain gap of time. An unsteady thing that lengthens, shortens or pauses as it chooses. That never lets you find a rhythm.

I don't sleep, not really. Each plunge is sickening. Each rise frightening. Every now and then we're struck on the side by some rogue wave, some chance combination of waters that causes a sudden roll or yaw, quite different from the now-regular pitching. Each time that happens, I jolt awake in terror, convinced the boat has foundered and is about to sink.

The night is a roaring nightmare. Walls of water that strike and strike and strike again.

Like that Rhayader barn. Different, but also the same.

At four in the morning, I stagger out to the bathroom for a pee. Find Wee Philly there, clutching the stainless steel bowl of the toilet. He's exhausted and haggard. Too pale even to be green. His eyes are red, bloodied. I think he's been crying.

I say nothing. He says nothing.

I pee in the next door cubicle, rinse my hands, go back to my cabin.

Caff's eight fingers.

He was giving me the windforce, I realise. Force eight, gale force.

Honnold told me he expected a 'proper storm' in due course and he, I think now, was being more precise than I'd understood. To a sailor, a force eight or nine wind is a gale all right, but you don't call it a full storm until you hit force ten.

We haven't yet encountered the full fury of what's coming and I don't know if I can handle what we already have. I don't know how long it'll take Connor and Wee Philly to do what needs to be done. Or even if they can do it in these sea conditions.

I climb back into my cot, and endure the heaving ship. A few minutes before five, I get up, put on boots and go down to the galley to prepare breakfast.

A trayful of sausages. A spadeful of egg. And a ship whose howling metal hull is our only world, our only safety.

# 60

Connor is openly furious.

'The door's totally unsecured. The fucking control room has spent the whole fucking night underwater.'

Honnold – sitting next to Coxsey, eating my egg and sausage – stays studiedly calm.

'It's *your* control room. You should have secured the door.'

'I *did* secure the fucking door.'

Honnold raises his eyebrows, quietly drawing attention to Connor's inconsistency. All he says is, 'Is your equipment OK?'

'*Our* equipment is polar grade expedition quality. The equipment is completely fucking fine. But there was stuff in that room – cables and stuff – that's gone outside for a midnight fucking swim. And the winch controls are totally fucking fucked.'

Honnold nods gravely, as though considering the health benefits of a salt sea swim. 'So ye're not able to launch?'

'We have to fucking launch.'

Honnold shrugs. 'Then launch.'

Connor approaches. Inspects the breakfast options. Pokes the egg. Says, 'Christ!' Takes a couple of sausages, which he starts eating standing up.

Then, his mouth still full, says, 'Let's do it.'

Easier said than accomplished.

The first thing is turning the ship.

At the moment, as I understand it, we're facing away from the wind, running with the waves, not against them. That's more comfortable, because the gaps between the waves are greater and because we can surf down the wave fronts rather than butting into them.

But if we're to operate an ROV, we have to remain – however approximately – above the damn vehicle. And that in turn means we have to head into the wind, letting the waves pass beneath us as we remain roughly stationary over the seafloor.

That sounds straightforward enough but Caff, who explains all this, is clearly anxious about the manoeuvre. 'Thoo dohnt wahnt tae be skelp while turning,' he says, as his hands show a big wave hitting the ship side-on as it turns. 'If tha' happens, we'll hae oor bahookie in th' sky in twa shakes o' a hoor's fud.'

Honnold's on the bridge. Buys assisting.

They make the turn.

We're not skelped. And our bahookie, whatever that is, remains wherever it's supposed to be.

As Caff predicted, our motion instantly feels worse.

The waves come faster, steeper, harder. The ship doesn't even maintain a constant direction. As Caff says, 'If a wave's cresting, ye dohn't wantae be under th' crest.' So we slalom through the inferno. Picking our route through the flying water. Two men on the bridge at all times. One steering. One wave-spotting.

Even the men, experienced and strong as they are, don't keep their footing very well in these conditions. The men on the bridge wear body harnesses to keep them in their seats. As for me, I'm not even close to managing. I'm simply flung around. A cat in a tin box. I hold on to anything that's fixed down. If I have work to do, I do it one-handed or – swiftly –

in the few seconds of peace between one breathtaking descent and the next terrifying rise.

But the next part, the hardest part, I want to watch and I do.

Buys and Honnold, on the bridge, keep the ship's bows pointed into the storm. The waves are massive now. Thirty-foot cliff faces, lined and pitted with flying foam, hurtling towards us. Smashing into and over the ship. The sickening fall of release, followed by the next blow, and the next, and the next.

It might or might not be raining. I can't tell. There's so much airborne spray, the air is already thick. There's nothing dry or quiet in the whole ship. Fear howls in the wires. It moans in the wind. I'm scared to stand on deck. Scared to lurk in the ship's iron bowels, hearing nothing but the tug of water against steel, the grind of engines.

And yet, for all that, the vehicle is launched.

Connor is in the sodden control room. As I understand it, the winch can still raise and lower the ROV. What they can't do, any longer, is sway the A-frame out from the gantry to give the vehicle a clear drop over open sea. I'd hoped my little act of sabotage would have been enough to wreck their plans, but apparently not.

*Tant pis.*

The monitors are on and working. The data connection is on and working. The game seems very much on, alas. I think the loss of the computer cables has caused some kind of problem, but just what that might be, I don't yet know.

Ryan and Eddie, assisted by Pearson and Coxsey, stand at the stern.

The gantry lights are still blazing, even though it is notionally full day.

Oilskins, lifejackets, harnesses, safety lines.

Ryan and Eddie have long grappling poles laced into the

frame of the ROV. Pearson and Coxsey, I think, are wrestling with the bolts that have kept the machine fixed to the deck.

The ship herself keeps the stern relatively sheltered from the storm, but 'relative' is not much of a protection out here. There are times when the entire stern disappears beneath the swell. Moments when we lose sight of all four men, only for them to re-emerge, struggling figures in yellow and orange, tugging on their safety lines, seeking to re-establish their grip on our little steel world.

And bit by bit, they do it. Unloose the ROV. Proffer a thumbs up to Connor, who sways the machine up from the gantry, so it hovers like a giant insect above their heads. This will be the tricky bit now. To bring the vehicle down cleanly into the water. Without simply ripping an arm or head or torso from one of the men there. Without crashing it too violently against the hull. Without wrecking the equipment, fierce yet delicate, that's mounted within the ROV's spidery frame.

Ryan and Eddie stand with their poles, swaying with the ship's motion. Pearson co-ordinates. Coxsey positions himself so he can see both the control room and the stern ramp, no matter what the sea is doing.

The men wait as the ship heaves and surges. The ROV sways above them. A weight that would kill them if it fell.

One particularly violent wave throws me off my feet. Water sweeping over the main deck. Surging round the superstructure, the bridge, so that it alone remains castled above the foam.

I'm wearing a harness myself: Caff, knowing I wanted to see the launch, set me up with the harness and a safety line that gives me no more than a foot or two of free movement.

And when I find my feet again, figure out which way up is vertical and how to get there – the ROV is gone. Vanished beneath the waves.

Ryan is clutching his arm. Eddie seems to be leaning in to Pearson. Kissing him, it looks like. The men start back along the deck. Holding themselves steady when the deck forms an abrupt upward slope. Making ground, as the tilt reverses and they can half walk, half slide downhill.

Ryan's arm seems bad, and there's something wrong with Pearson.

I can't tell what and am not left to watch alone in peace.

Honnold – immune to the ship's movement – approaches. Yells at me to get down to the galley. 'Hot water, clean towels, OK?'

I nod. OK. But can't unclip from my safety line and have to wait as Honnold does it for me. He handles me the way he'd handle a crate of fish, a pallet of stores.

His grip doesn't even relent when my line is unclipped. With one hand on my harness, he half walks, half carries me to the ladder down. Doesn't release me entirely until I have hands and feet on the metal treads.

I clamber down to the galley. Put water on to heat. Fetch clean towels from the storeroom. Last night's whisky bottle, still a third full, stands next to the tea and ketchup, secured by an elastic strap that keeps everything more or less in place.

From the bathroom, I fetch a stack of paper towels.

Ryan comes in, escorted by Eddie. Pearson too, escorted by Coxsey.

Pearson's head is badly gashed. Now that's he's out of the spray and wind, the blood, no longer diluted, seems startlingly red. Abundant. He seems baffled at finding himself here, his vision crimsoned.

I start snipping hair from his scalp with a pair of kitchen scissors, but I'm not the most adept in this pitching surgery. Tell Coxsey to get the scalp cleared. When Honnold materialises, I shout at him to get a razor. I can't read his face but, once he's understood my request, he nods.

Shouts, 'D'ye know anything about first aid?'

I shout back, 'Yes.' Which is true. It's part of every copper's basic training. I'd guess that someone on board has a notional responsibility for first aid, but Honnold seems relieved that I'm willing to put myself forward. He gives me a thumbs up. Shoves a white first aid box into my hands.

As Coxsey works on Pearson, I turn to Ryan. He's got his oilskin off, but is struggling to get undressed further. Pushing Eddie away, I run a kitchen knife down Ryan's sleeve, till his clothes, including his thermal innerwear, falls open from the elbow. The arm is visibly broken, but the skin's only bruised, not punctured, and the break might be a clean one. I give Ryan's good hand the whisky bottle, tell him to drink. Tell Eddie to hold the guy steady – a near-impossible request – but Eddie grips Ryan's torso and upper arm in a wrestler's grip.

I manipulate the broken forearm, till I can feel the break. Sense the way the bones ought to lie. Straighten the arm till it looks right. Ryan swears, but in the kind of repetitive bloodyfuckingshittingsodding incantatory way that's as much pain-relief as actual swearing. Eddie's burly arm keeps his buddy more or less fixed in place. His spare arm holds me too, keeps me in place.

I bind the arm, tightly. Two splints from the first aid box. Tie off the bandage the way I was taught on the first aid course at Hendon, the knot flat against the skin.

'Done,' I say.

'Jesus, thanks, love,' Ryan says, giving me a kiss, that's as wet and scratchy and oceany as if a giant spiny sponge from the Atlantic floor had chosen to rear up and kiss me through the spines.

I turn to Pearson, whose head is now reasonably shaved, but still spilling an alarming amount of blood. Pearson wants the whisky off Ryan and Coxsey wants to give it to him, but I tell them he can't touch it. Alcohol thins the blood and that's the last thing we need.

I clean the wound. It's not that dirty, in truth, and the ocean environment is a clean one, but you don't know what's been living in Pearson's hair and, anyway, you clean the wound first. That's just the rule.

Warm water. No soap. Towels that redden as I use them.

The first aid box has some packets of QuikClot, a dressing that forms a gel in contact with blood. Those things have slashed battlefield mortality rates. Deaths from road accidents too: our ambulance teams use them all the time.

I get Pearson's scalp dressed and bandaged.

Blood still trickles down the crevices of his face, but not fast now. His fingers keep creeping to the wound, but they move gingerly and withdraw quickly.

He manages a faint grin.

'Thanks, pet. Fucking brilliant.'

It seems that the ROV was launched cleanly enough, but Ryan's grappling pole was snared and as the ship bucked and the ROV descended, the pole screamed through the air, managing to break Ryan's arm and half kill Pearson on the way.

Eddie says, 'We don't have a spare. If the weather stays bad, the ROV stays down there.'

He doesn't seem to mind much, but these boys are deep-sea specialists. If they can't retrieve the ROV now, they'll just come back for it later. Connor is in the room now as well. He's equally unperturbed by the machine's loss.

I say, 'It *is* staying down there. This man needs a hospital.'

This man, meaning Pearson.

I'm speaking to the room, but really my words are for Honnold, who's leaning up against the wall, watching everything.

He doesn't say anything, but his look tells me to go on.

I say, 'The first issue was blood loss, which is now solved. Unless those dressings fail, the wound itself will be fine. But we don't know if there's a skull fracture. I can't risk looking for a fracture by palpation, because that risks brain damage or death. And even if the skull is OK, a blow like that is exactly the sort of thing to bring on a subdural haematoma. Blood between the skull and the brain. That kind of thing is virtually symptom-free, until you keel over from it. And it can be – often is – lethal.'

Connor hears my little speech with impatience. Before I've even finished, he interrupts.

'The guy looks fine. Doug, you're a strong man. You're fine, aren't you?'

Pearson – Doug – moves his head in the light. His gaze is visibly blurry, confused.

'I'll be OK,' he says. 'Just need to lie down.'

'Don't be fucking stupid,' I snap. 'He's got no idea if he's fine or not. He needs a hospital and a brain scan. I'm not a doctor, but I used to live with a paramedic, and that man needs a hospital. Oh, and Ryan's arm needs setting by someone who knows what they're doing. He needs an X-ray, a doctor, a cast, and a proper damn hospital.'

Honnold has seen enough.

Turns to leave. 'I'll radio Cork,' he says. 'We'll turn aboot.'

Connor says to Pearson. 'You're fine, aren't you? You look fine.'

Says that, his words at odds with the fury in his face. Then leaves.

Coxsey says, 'Fucker.'

Stares at Ryan and Eddie with something like hostility.

Eddie spreads his hands. 'He's not with us, mate. We're just here on a job.'

Ryan agrees, saying, 'Doug, mate, if you need a hospital, then you do.'

The nascent alliance cements itself with all four men telling me I did an incredible job. Competing with each other to praise me, as a way to affirm their common membership of the Pearson-to-hospital camp.

I'm not sure I'm a good fit for the angel of mercy role, but I know how to make tea, so I make tea.

Coxsey says, 'Wee Philly says you guys are seismologists. Some kind of monitoring thing.'

Eddie shrugs. 'No idea. Ryan and me, we're with Gullich Glowacz. Sub-sea construction, basically. We go all over. Do whatever people pay us to do. All I know is that we've rigged the vehicle for cable work. Cable lifting. Cable cutting. Cable repair. Could be seismology. Could be anything.'

I say, 'It's not seismology.'

Ryan and Eddie discuss that. Eddie goes into a story I can't quite follow about a seismology project they did for some oil company. 'They did it properly. I mean, no offence, but this ship isn't right for the job. Got the wrong hoists. No stabilisation. That control room, I mean, it's basically a piece of shit. And working like this, in seas like this – I mean, it's not right, is it? If you've got to use the wrong vessel, then wait till the weather's not so crazy.'

I hand out teas, generously sugared. Paracetamol for the injured men.

But it's Coxsey who notices first.

The bucking of the boat, the screaming of the metal, the thundering waters. It hasn't changed. None of it. Not the rhythm, speed or pitch.

'We're not turning,' he says. 'We're not going about.'

And that's when the fear really starts. It's not just me now, it's everyone. The wrong ship, in the wrong sea, doing the wrong job, for a man that nobody knows and nobody likes and nobody trusts.

Then the door opens. Caff enters. Face white, or as white as that weathered face could ever go.

'They've murdurred th' cap'n. They've murdurred th' fookin' cap'n.'

# 61

They haven't, in fact, murdered the fucking captain, but there has been a mutiny, all right. Calmly planned, efficiently executed.

I don't know what happened up on the bridge, in that place of flying foam and screaming wind. What I do know is this. That Caff saw Honnold being dragged – face-bloodied, only part conscious – to his cabin.

That Buys and Connor have both sprouted guns. Semi-automatic pistols worn at the hip.

That we are now prisoners.

As Coxsey is sent up to take the bridge, the rest of us – barring only Wee Philly – are gathered in the dining room.

It's Buys, not Connor, who addresses us.

'We've spoken to Cork,' he says. 'They want us to watch the pair of you' – he means Pearson and Ryan – 'keep you away from anything too physical, but they say to rest up, look after yourselves, and you should be just fine.'

That said, with a last glittering eye on me. An eye of warning.

'As for the reason we're here. Our little assignment. Connor's organisation has paid us well to do a job and we're going to do it. You'll all share in the income. You'll all make more money than you would by dropping nets and pulling the guts out of fish.

'And this job is urgent. Time-critical. We've not been lucky with the weather and we've lost some items from the control room. Those things are going to slow us down. And if we fannied about, taking good strong men to hospital, we'd miss the chance we have to do this job. Which means missing a hatful of cash. For all of you.'

Pearson: 'Where's the captain?'

Buys: 'In his cabin. He fell on the companionway and hurt himself. He'll be fine.'

Caff: 'Whit's this joab wur daein, anywae?'

Buys: 'That doesn't concern you. Just do as you're told and you'll get your money.'

Caff says something to that, but in an Orcadian so thick that none of us follow it.

The mood among the men is an angry acquiescence. Angry, because no one likes what's happening here. Honnold was a respected captain, Buys neither particularly known nor particularly liked. Connor was outright unpopular, almost from the first.

But – those pistols. Those pistols and that promise of cash.

The men start bargaining. What work? How long? How much is a hatful of cash? When can Pearson and Ryan get medical help?

I'm part of the bargain too. A counter shuffled across the board in this game of evil consequences.

Pearson insists that I be allowed to go to the captain. Work my medical magic on him. Buys and Connor exchange nods. Buys escorts me, as Connor turns to the business of finding out just how much cash will buy off rebellion.

We clamber and slip down these skidding metal tunnels. Buys's more practised legs have little difficulty with the shifts of angle, with the occasional sideways yaw, when we've been rammed by a rogue wave. I have to keep both hands on the handrail. Scuttling forwards when the slope is downward or approximately flat, then hanging on for dear life as the world inverts.

But we get there. To Honnold's cabin.

Buys has his hand on the door handle. His other arm is full of medical stuff – the first aid box, towels, a flask of warm water.

I think he's about to let us in, but he doesn't, or not at once. Instead, he leans forward. Puts his mouth so close to my ear that I can feel his breath steamy on my skin.

'I don't trust you,' he says. 'Just so you know, I don't fucking trust you.'

I remember that it was Buys who stood aside for me as I came down from the companionway after sabotaging the door of the control room. Remember that brooding stare following me as I walked away.

I say, '*You* don't trust *me*? I'm not the one who half killed the fucking captain.'

I let my eye fall on the blood that smears the grip of Buys's pistol. Put my finger out to the butt. Bring it away red.

Buys lets me touch the gun, but grabs my hand as it pulls away. Yanks my hand back over my wrist, till I gasp in pain. He holds me there, extending the moment, till he releases me with a final, vicious yank.

'I. Don't. Trust. You.' His final breathy word in my ear.

That's our beautiful moment over, I think, but if I were Buys, I'd be thinking the same thoughts. The Honnold-Pearson-Coxsey-MacHaffie team was fairly well-established on the *Isobel Baker*. There were only two newcomers. One, Buys himself, a guy placed there by Connor. The inside man.

The other, me.

Who replaces the existing guy at zero notice. Whose 'references' amount to one single phone call, made on a twilit deck. Who was the last person to leave the control room, the night the door failed. Who led the men into wanting a return to harbour.

A ship's cook who can't cook. A sailor with no sea legs. A little woman in a big man's world.

Buys gives me a last, malevolent stare, then opens the door.

Honnold is there. Blood on his scalp and face. Bruises already inking his eye. One hand cuffed to an iron handrail.

I say, 'I'll need more water. And the razor.'

Settle down to work.

Cleaning the face and scalp of blood. Cutting away hair. Starting to shave around the wound.

Honnold sucks in when I hurt him, but remains steady. The truth is, the cuts all look worse than they really are. All headwounds bleed easily, but the injuries here are nothing compared with Pearson's.

Buys returns with the extras. Watches as I work.

I put up with that for a while, then turn and say, 'Yes?'

He shrugs. Leaves.

Honnold says, 'It's my fault. I shouldn't have taken the assignment in the first place.'

'Why shouldn't you? I assume they didn't come to you and say, "We're a bunch of semi-homicidal gangsters and we're planning to club you unconscious and leave your men dangerously injured and without medical help." If they did say that, then I'd have to agree you were a fuckwit.'

He grins. Lopsidedly. The left side of his face won't be great for a while.

I carry on doing what I'm doing.

He says, 'Who are you? I mean, really?'

'I'm me. I'm a cook.'

He doesn't say anything to that. I'm at the stage where I can squish one of the QuikClot dressings on his head. Get him bandaged up.

It's overkill, really. The wounds just aren't that awful. But it won't hurt for Buys and Connor to think that Honnold is a mess.

I say, 'The clamps in the galley are getting stuck. Is there a toolkit anywhere?'

Honnold stares at me. One eye as clear and blue as an arctic morning. The other purple and crushed and grapey and sore.

'There are tools in the engine room. Caff can show you where.'

I nod. Finish. Pack up.

Honnold says, 'And it *is* my fault. This is a fishing boat, and we didnae need any other type of work. You can tell the boys, I'm sorry.'

'Tell 'em yourself.'

I don't see why, just because I'm the ship's skivvy, I should have to do every little thing.

I go.

Not sure what to do next. But if in doubt: work. I start to make sandwiches for lunch. Egg and sausage. Cheese. Ham and mustard.

The sea is all but impossible now.

The noise is the worst thing, I think. An indescribable howling. A noise that makes you realise that, every second of every minute, the boat is being assaulted by thousands of tons of water. A furious energy hurtling against the hull. And beyond that hull, only a green-black emptiness, a chilling cold.

Death's howling army. An underworld populated by sea-monsters.

Coxsey, briefly swapping his duties on the bridge with Caff, so he can get a hot drink and a bathroom visit, pops into the galley to give me a status report. Winds of sixty miles an hour, and gusting higher. Waves well over thirty feet. Probably nearer forty. A 'proper storm'. Force ten, a full gale.

I ask him if the ship will be all right.

'This old girl? Yes, she'll be fine.' He shows me with his

hands that if the ship keeps her nose into the wind, she'll be able to ride the waves, no problem. If the man on the bridge dozes off, even for a few moments, and allows the ship to turn sideways on to the waves, 'she'd be under in no time. And of course, when the big waves are cresting, you don't want to get under the crest, in case the bows dig in. But we should be all right, as long as we don't hit a killer wave, one of those once in a lifetime whoppers. But you never know. These waters throw up some big 'uns.'

He tells me that the largest waves ever recorded were found in the Rockall Trough, a few miles north of where we're currently cruising. As 'you'll be fine' speeches go, I feel that one was lacking a certain something.

I ask about the life-raft. If it could manage in these waters.

Coxsey laughs. 'Bloody well hope so, love. I bloody well hope so.'

He gets his drink. Goes back to the bridge.

I go to find Caff coming down. Ask him about the toolkit.

He throws me a sharp look, but takes me down to the engine room to find it.

Caged ceiling lights. Red metal anti-slip floor. An engine, painted green and dirty cream, pounding away. The engine is huge. Perhaps not quite the width of an ordinary family car, but one and a half times as long. An auxiliary engine, a spare in case of failure. Cooling system. Pumps. Boilers. Electronics control panel.

None of it looks very high-tech. None of it *is* all that high-tech. But the only technology that matters in these waters is one of reliability. The screw has to keep turning. The pumps have to keep pounding.

Caff finds the toolkit. A dirty white metal box, stowed against the wall.

He opens it up.

I take out a hacksaw and a hammer.

Try to get the hacksaw blade out of the grip, but can't figure out how to do it, so Caff does it for me.

Tape the blade to my leg with surgical tape. Same thing with the hammer.

Caff watches. Helps. Re-stows the toolkit when I'm done.

When we're out of the engine room din, he says to me with a grin, 'Whitna raffle wur geen and gottin wursels intae noo, eh? A right roo o' shite.'

I don't know what that means, but he sounds friendly and 'roo o' shite' sounds accurate enough, so I nod in agreement.

Caff goes on to tell me that he, Coxsey and Pearson are more or less prisoners. They're each to do four hours on the bridge. Four hours on, eight off. The spare men are to handle any maintenance and repair tasks necessary, and to assist Buys and Connor, if required to do so. Aside from that, 'we're tae bade in oor room, lik a pair o' peedie buoys.'

Which means that, assuming Eddie and Ryan remain, however approximately, loyal to Connor, the only person with some freedom of movement is me.

Which is good, since my To Do list is already long and getting longer..

I shout, 'Captain Honnold isn't badly hurt. And this is his ship.'

'Aye, shay is that. An' the ither lads wid lik tae see th' cap'n back.'

'Well then,' I say, with a let's-not-stand-here-blethering shrug.

Caff punches my shoulder, not hard, and says, 'Ye'r a guid peedie lassie. Th' wurst damn cook a'm ever seen, but a guid lassie fur a' that.'

We go back to the galley, via the refrigeration hold, so Caff can carry a food box up for me – cover for our trip.

Connor is there at the dining room door. Stance rolling with the ship. Left hand on the rail. Gun hand free.

He glares, but sees the box of food, and nods to let us pass. Sees Caff back to his bunkroom. Returns to watch me in the galley. Does nothing to help. Just watches me, flung between stove and countertops like a rat in a bucket.

I'm bruised everywhere, but that's hardly the worst of it. The fear and the noise is worse. The way that all thought is torn apart. The fear of a big wave hitting hard.

Connor tells me to feed the men on the bridge first, then the control room, then Honnold, then the men in the bunkroom. Serve hot drinks in the same order after that. I nod.

He leaves.

I assemble a plateful of sandwiches, double wrap it in foil, and clamber up to the bridge.

I thought it was worse in the ship's bowels, because I couldn't see the waves about to strike, but it's worse up here. Seeing the waves, their endlessness. A grey-black violence that never ends.

Buys and Coxsey take their food, without looking at me. The bridge doors are firmly shut. The glow of electronics underlights the two men's faces. Buys steering. Coxsey reading the waves, offering course corrections with his hands as much as his voice. And I understand, from the two men's concentration, just what a task is being performed up here. If one of these cresting waves, these forty footers, is allowed to break right over the bows, there's a risk that the bows dig in, effectively braking the ship. If that happens, there's a risk that the ship pivots round, propeller thrashing empty air, leaving the ship exposed broadside to the waves.

And we wouldn't survive that. Even I, landlubber as I am, can see that.

I go down.

Another plate of sandwiches, painfully assembled. Another bruising journey upwards to the control room.

The door partly fixed, but not entirely. The room still sodden. Salt water curling around the metal floor, like a prey animal constantly seeking an exit.

Connor there. Eddie too, but not Wee Philly. Not yet.

Connor's on his feet. Eddie's seated, wearing a full harness, like the men on the bridge.

The monitors are turned on now. Images beamed up from the ROV two hundred metres beneath the waves. Images of the seabed. Dim grey and green and yellow. Artificially brightened by the ROV's halogen lamps.

Rock, sea, sand.

Those things and a black cable, snaking left to right across the field of vision.

Those things, and a pronged grappling device extended from the ROV itself. A device which is even now being teased under the cable. Which will snap round it, gripping it firmly as soon as it gets purchase.

Connor – less practised at this – is darting Eddie sharp looks. Looks that say, 'Do it now!'

Eddie shakes his head. Says, 'You get no sense of depth on these things' – he means the monitors. 'You've got to get the grapple right under the line and out the other side.'

He moves his controls. The response from below isn't instant – it feels like there's a half-second gap – and the movements from below are jerky and as much under the influence of deep ocean currents as anything sent down from above. But Eddie knows what he's doing. Pokes the grappling tool right under the cable. Sends the signal that gets the tool to close over the line.

'Good lad,' says Connor.

But Eddie's gaze is still fixed to the screen. He uses the grappling tool to lift the cable. Just a few inches, but a few inches is all he needs.

And in that slo-mo world, another tool slowly creeps into

view. No mistaking what this one is. It has a pincer grip and steel fangs.

Eddie brings the cutting tool to meet the cable. Manoeuvres it until the tool has the cable in its jaws.

Eddie looks across at Connor.

'Yes?'

'Yes.'

'Bam'

Eddie hits a button on the control panel. Almost instantly this time, nothing slo-mo about it, the jaws of the cutting tool snap shut.

The cable spasms and falls. One end is secured by the grappling tool, the other end lies loose.

Connor says, 'Let's bring her up.' And to me, 'Don't you have work to do?'

He's right. I do.

# 62

Work that starts with Honnold.

Give him sandwiches. Bread, sausage and egg, smished together with plenty of butter and tomato ketchup. It's a messy job, but the sandwiches, I think, are proper manly affairs. Huge and thick and oozing with fat and dead animal and sugar and vinegar. The sort of thing it takes two hands to eat and makes a mess even so.

Give him his sandwiches and the hacksaw blade and the hammer.

Tell him that Caff and the others will be on his side if he chooses to retake the ship. 'I don't think Connor's guys will fight for him. I mean, Buys, yes. But Ryan and Eddie are just hired hands. I don't think they care one way or another. And Wee Philly . . .' I shrug.

Honnold laughs.

Wee Philly is the least of our worries.

Honnold taps the hacksaw blade against the iron rail that chains him. 'Thanks for this.'

'Nae worries,' I say, in a loose version of his accent. 'And take care with that,' I add, indicating the hammer. 'It could cause a nasty injury.'

Honnold grins.

'I'm hoping so.'

Connor asked me to tell him how Honnold was, so I go to tell him: fine, sleeping.

They've winched the cut end of the cable up now. Pulled it out of the sea, like the head of the world's longest sea-snake. Eddie, working with Caff, is sent to retrieve it from the stern gantry.

Oilskins, harnesses, lifejackets, safety lines.

The full works. Thirty minutes spent doing a job which would take two minutes in ordinary conditions. I'm wearing oilskins and a harness myself, because I don't even like the minuscule trip from the top of the companionway to the door of the control room. I'll only do it after attaching a sling from my harness to the steel rail that runs along it.

'Tough work, seismology,' I say.

Connor gives me a look which says, 'Fuck off.'

Feed Wee Philly, who's pale but ready for food. Feed Ryan, Caff and Pearson.

Then teas for the bridge. Caff swapping with Coxsey. Pearson seems OK, but the risk of concussion or mental fatigue means he won't be putting in a shift until he's clearly better or until the winds have subsided.

Stick my nose in on Honnold. He's still wearing a metal bracelet, but that bracelet is no longer chained to anything.

'Ready?' I say.

'Ready.'

I bring teas to the control room. They've got the cable end into the dry now, or what passes for dry on this ship. Eddie is trimming the end. Getting ready to splice it, I imagine. There's a roll of identical cable – a few hundred yards of it, perhaps – lashed to the deck outside.

I hand out the teas. Tell Connor that Honnold is lying on his face. Didn't wake when I called him.

Connor says, 'Fuck,' but doesn't seem particularly bothered. Goes to look anyway.

Eddie – soaked, tired, but still going – looks up from his cable.

Says, 'What a fucking job, eh? What a fucking job.'

I agree with him. What a fucking job.

Go down again. To Wee Philly's cabin. Ready to finish this thing.

# 63

'Hey Phil,' I say. 'You're wanted upstairs. Your hour of glory.'

He nods.

Looks awful, but you don't have to look beautiful to do what he needs to do.

Sits up on his bunk, feet on the floor, getting used to the ship's motion in this new posture.

He's wearing thick clothes, including thermals, but no boots, no oilskin. I tell him the control room is awash. Tell him he'll need to suit up.

He nods. Stands. Gropes for his waterproofs, bright yellow, hanging from a hook in the door.

I sit on the bunk where he was. Hands holding the steel rail behind me.

A few breaths. Centring myself. Getting ready.

Wee Philly opts to go with the trousers first. Good move. Well-advised. The trousers are harder to put on if you have the skirts of the coat to contend with. The fishermen on board have all-in-ones. Jumpsuit-type affairs that are way better.

Still. Trousers, jumpsuits. It's no biggie.

I wait till the computer man has one leg in his trousers, the other one poking around for the left trouser thigh.

That's when I kick him.

Hard, really hard, in the back. Both legs lashing him just under the fall of his shoulder blades.

He flies forward. Head smacks hard into the iron wall.

Hard enough that even with these shrieking seas, I can hear the impact.

He stumbles half-round, tottering one-legged. Blood falls from a cut in his forehead. I think he's not sure what's happened. Assumes – as I would have done – that some terrible thing has happened to the ship.

I arrange my face in a 'Did you see that terrible thing that just happened to the ship?' way. Then kick him in the crotch. Again in the face as he falls.

He lies on the floor, moaning. I stamp on his hands, until they retract, curled under his body like some lumpen sea-creature half emerged from its yellow rind.

'Don't fucking move,' I tell him, 'or I will fucking kill you.'

He nods.

'That counts as moving,' I say, and stamp on his ankles.

I go through his stuff.

He doesn't have much. None of us do here. A good-sized gym bag, nothing more.

And in amongst his stuff: that army-style laptop. That thing and a little black box. A box with space for two cable connections, an in and an out. A box that looks like it's been designed to be waterproof, even at depth.

A box that has killed two people. That took me to a barn near Rhayader. That has killed three people, indeed, if you include the Rhayader goon.

I take the laptop and the box.

'Move, and I fucking kill you. Leave the room, and I fucking kill you. Do anything I don't like, and I fucking kill you. OK?'

I don't know why these interchanges have to feature the word 'fucking' so prominently, but they kind of do. They'd feel bare without it.

Outside in the corridor, I meet Honnold. Hammer in one hand, Connor's gun in the other.

He says, 'You've got blood on your face.'

'Not mine. Wee Philly's.'

I show him my booty.

He stares in puzzlement. 'That's what this thing is all about, eh?'

'I assume so.'

'You know what those things are for?'

'No,' I say, 'but I assume that someone in law enforcement will be able to tell us.'

'Aye, I'd say so.'

He stares some more. Wants to take the trophies off me – he's the captain, I'm the temporary cook – but I don't yield them, and he doesn't force the issue.

He tells me about Connor. 'He's hurt, but alive. I've bound him up for the noo. He might get out of his bindings, but he's no got a gun, and his right hand won't be holding much for a wee while.'

Good enough.

Honnold looks at me.

I look at him.

'Are ye making a brew? I could fair use a cup o' tea.'

# 64

We assemble in the dining room, the urn heating in the galley.

Me, Honnold, Pearson, Coxsey.

Also, Eddie and Ryan. Not Honnold's men, but both clearly relieved to see him back in command. Both quick to evince their loyalty to the new-old regime.

Coxsey and Pearson go to tie Connor properly. Proper seamen's rope. Proper seamen's knots.

They leave him in Honnold's cabin, lashed to the cot.

I've hidden Wee Philly's computer stuff down in the fish-hold. Honnold knows, at least approximately where it is, but no one else.

Honnold phones the bridge. Speaks to Buys.

'Jonah? This is the captain. I'm back in command of the ship. Your man Connor has been subdued. I've got his weapon. The man himself is secured and will remain that way till we can release him to the authorities.

'I'm asking ye noo to hand your gun to MacHaffie, then I want ye to come down to the mess, with yer hands where I can see them. Is that clear?'

Silence on the line.

No answer.

'Jonah?'

'Fuck you, Honnold. Fuck you.'

Honnold wasn't expecting the resistance, but nor is he much perturbed by it.

'Suit yerself. But it'll be thirsty work up there before too long. And ye'll want a peck to eat.'

Stalemate, kind of, but the sort of stalemate which can only run in our favour.

Buys can't do anything except keep the ship afloat. Can't run anywhere except to a port in Europe, where he'll be arrested as soon as he steps foot on shore. There are, conceivably, places in Latin America, or Russia, or elsewhere, that might take a more lenient view of Western wrongdoers, but Honnold is right: hunger and thirst will force Buys off the bridge long before the ship can get any place like that.

Tea.

There's a cake in one of my boxes. Frozen, but I whack it into the microwave, till it's sizzling on the outside, albeit still icy within.

'Like baked Alaska,' I say, serving it.

Honnold gathers a harvest of congratulation. Me too. We all do.

Good old us. The team that beat the bad guys.

Mouthfuls of cake and lashings of tea.

And that's when Wee Philly arrives at the door. A wild look on his eyes. A machine pistol in his hands.

# 65

The pistol subdues us, but so too does the look in Wee Philly's eyes.

His gun can fire at ten times – fifty times? – the rate of Honnold's but, just as significant, we none of us think that he'll be able to maintain control of his weapon. Once Wee Philly's finger closes around that trigger, there'll be a spray of bullets which could go anywhere, hit anyone, kill who knows how many.

Wee Philly orders me to go and untie Connor.

I say, 'I'm no good at knots. Sorry. Oh, and coming in here? That counts as moving.'

There is, for a brief moment, another kind of stalemate. An armed and dangerous one. Precarious. Enemy patrols facing off over a contested border.

At first, I think Honnold will win this one. His nerve is steadier, his support firmer.

But then the ship lurches and Wee Philly's gun leaps in his hand, describing an arc that would have sliced most of us in half. And I realise that Wee Philly's unsteadiness will win this one for him. The old nuclear age theory of mutually assured destruction relied on both parties being at least vaguely rational. When you get a genuine wacko – a North Korea, a Kim Jong Crazy – everyone else backs off because they have to.

Another lurch. Another terrifying sweep of the gun.

Honnold's first duty is to protect his men. Law enforcement is not his concern. The fate of some screwed-up deep-sea cable project is not his business.

To me he says, 'Fiona, please go and untie Connor. Cut the ropes if you have to.'

To Wee Philly, he says, 'I'm not going to ask you to put your gun down, but I do ask that you lower it and keep it pointed at the floor.'

Moving slowly and carefully, he removes the magazine from his gun. Removes the chambered bullet. Drops bullet and magazine on the floor. With the gun pointed up at the ceiling, he 'fires' a couple of time, letting the hammer click on emptiness. Drops the gun on the floor too.

I get a knife. Go to untie Connor.

Find him in Honnold's cabin. He's a bit smashed about and his right hand is badly broken, but he's in much better shape than he deserves to be.

I cut his bindings. Tell him there's cake in the galley.

Me, I go downstairs. Retrieve the computer junk. Take them up on deck, where there's a big orange plastic box containing lifejackets. Most of its contents are already in use. Not actually being worn – not downstairs anyway – but hanging on pegs ready for anyone setting foot on deck.

I take out the remaining kit. Throw it down the companionway. Put my computer junk in the big orange box. Close it. Close the mechanism which keeps everything sealed and watertight. Then cut the bindings which keep the box fixed to the superstructure wall.

The box starts to move instantly. Rides a sluice of bubbles across the desk. Hits the port handrail and bounces off. But the stern ramp is unprotected. If anything bounces around this deck for long enough, it will wash off the back, if a big wave doesn't snatch it first.

I go downstairs.

The fish processing room. A big bucket of fish guts still there. Scales, fins, heads, livers, guts, eyes, anything. The last person on processing duty should have shoved the lot down the discards chute, but they didn't. Unless it was meant to be my job, perhaps.

Anyway. I take the bucket.

Go down to the engine room.

Engine. Auxiliary engine.

Pumps. Boiler. Cooling system. Whatever.

I find the cap that lets you refill the cooling system. Wrestle it off. It's hard to do, and I gash my left hand, but I get it done. My hand looks nasty, but it's only a cut.

Shove the fish guts into the cooling system. Not all of them, but most of them.

Go over to the auxiliary engine.

Do the same there, using all the fish guts that remain.

Nothing happens. Nothing good, nothing bad, just the engines hammering away exactly the way they did before.

I wish I knew more about engines.

Sit down.

I'm feeling tired and hungry, I realise. One of those *doh!* moments when I understand the feeling that's been nagging at me for hours now. It's like it was always there, that feeling, and only when I turn my attention squarely to it, do I notice it.

Anyway. Stupid. Me being a cook, working in the galley all day and still forgetting to eat.

Stupid and typical.

The ship judders. It's been juddering all the time, of course, but this one was different. A mechanical judder. Like the *ting* of a knife on a wineglass, only a *ting* loud enough to jolt a trawler.

*No spark plugs with a diesel*, Iestyn told me. *You compress your mixture, your fuel and air, compress it so hard that the temperature rises and – bang! ignition. It's a good system, but it gets very hot. If you don't cool it, you'll wreck your engine.*

Stupid that. Wrecking an engine. Especially a nice big one like the *Isobel Baker*'s. One that's worked perfectly fine for twenty years and more.

I wonder if I've thought it through, this plan of mine.

Don't think so.

Hope Coxsey's right about the damn life-raft, though.

I drag myself back to the galley.

Now that I notice my tiredness, I can't help but notice it all the time. Heavy legs. Aching muscles. I just want to lie down, in a bed that doesn't move, in a room that doesn't shriek.

My damn hand hurts a lot as well. Drips blood, in this boat that has already seen enough.

Never mind.

Get to the dining room.

Buys in command. Wee Philly relieved of his machine pistol. Buys wielding it.

Connor and Pearson not present, but I assume they must be on the bridge.

Buys is talking. Something about who's going to do what when.

Maybe he's saying something to me. I don't know.

I sit down. My harness jingles metallically on the bench. Nick a bit of cake, using my good hand.

The ship judders again, more unmistakably this time.

I say, 'The ship is sinking. I think someone's put fish guts in the cooling system.'

That causes a rumpus.

There's a bit of a who-would-be-fool-enough-to-do-a-thing-like-that, but since it's fairly obvious that the fool in question is me, that particular phase of things doesn't last long. There's also the question of whether I'm telling the truth. No one quite believes that I know my way round an engine well enough to sabotage it, but the jolts and shudders are coming continuously now, and the men on the bridge are phoning down to ask what the fucking hell is going on.

Honnold, calm beneath the gaze of Buys's guns, witnesses the commotion with a quiet smile. A regretful one. When another bad shudder hits the ship, and when we can feel the ship's rhythm start to sag – to become the plaything of the waves not the master of them – he stands up. Says, 'Abandon ship. All hands to the life-raft.'

He heads for the door. Brushes the barrel of Buys's machine pistol on the way out. 'Jonah, ye can put that damn stupid thing away. Unless ye plan to row with it.'

We abandon ship.

Caff and Coxsey are master of ceremonies. The life-raft is packed in a big fibreglass container, like a tin of beans. It's swooshed off the side and self-inflates. In theory, it should be possible just to step off the ship and into the raft. But the conditions are so fierce, the raft sometimes higher than the side of the ship and sometimes as many as four metres lower, that even the process of saving our lives seems fraught with peril. I only manage the manoeuvre at all, because Coxsey more or less throws me off the ship, with Caff catching from below.

The raft is circular, designed for twelve, and there are loops of nylon tape round the circumference where you can wind your arms in, to prevent yourself from being thrown around.

The others join me. The broken-armed Ryan. The head-bandaged Pearson.

Wee Philly, who enters the raft with as little dignity as I did, throws me a look of pure loathing.

Buys and Connor don't look at me with much loving kindness either. I don't think either of them is carrying a gun – them, or anyone else – but even if they were, Honnold was right. If you can't row with it, eat it, or drink it, a gun's no use here.

Honnold, whose ship I've destroyed, looks at me, and laughs, and shakes his head, but it's a friendly shake, I'm pretty sure. Eddie, Caff and Coxsey all seem in good spirits. Joking and bright.

Coxsey does whatever you have to do to in order to free the raft from the davit that had suspended it. He closes the zip that seals off the outside.

We're two things now. The ship and the raft. Nothing keeps us together and the winds and waters, I assume, whirl us apart.

We don't hear the ship sinking. Don't even know if it sinks or not. Hear nothing beyond the storm.

No conversation, not really. Each man lost in his own thoughts. The only talk that does go on is bellowed between Honnold and his guys as they inventory the raft's equipment.

Hand-operated pumps? Check. Fully operative? Check.

Food and water? Yes, but not much. A day's supply.

Flares? Yes.

A mini-EPIRB, yes, which Honnold activates, though the two EPIRBs on board the *Isobel* would have activated automatically if she has indeed foundered.

The floor of our pod is semi-rigid. The walls and ceiling not at all. When big waves break around us, we feel the surge everywhere. Our little roof flattens over our heads like an oystershell closing.

And that's what it's like, this raft in this storm. Like we have our own little oystershell kingdom – orange, nylon, flexible, evasive. We slip under and round and through the waves, at one with them in a way that the poor old *Isobel* never was.

I'm still tired. Very tired, probably. I can feel that quite clearly now. It's easier without that damn engine always chuntering in my ear. But something else too. I think happiness. Or maybe its softer cousin, contentment. Like happiness but quieter. Sunlight softened by mist.

I say, 'This is nice, isn't it? I should have brought the cake, though. It would have been better with cake.'

# 66

It's the French navy which finds us.

The first we know of it is the beat of a helicopter overhead, followed by the sound of a boat outside. The seas are still high, but subsiding. Honnold untents our entrance flap.

Blue light invades the orange.

A boat bumps up against the raft. French voices, speaking English.

Strong hands and friendly faces.

The grey bulk of a destroyer, the *Edlinger*, looms above us to windward. This smaller boat, a rubber speedboat thing, will take us from here to there.

The light is astonishing. Clear skies. The ocean turbulent, yes, but blue. Puffs of white foam almost dazzling in the sunshine.

As for the sea itself – it's completely empty. No *Isobel Baker*. No orange box. Just us. The grey destroyer. And this troop of handsome, helpful, smiling French *matelots*.

# 67

We're taken to Brest.

Not where any of us wanted to go, but that's one of the inconveniences of travel. Snow at Heathrow? You'll be set down in Birmingham. Lose your ship off Ireland? Find yourself in France.

*En route*, the ship's doctor bandages my hand and flirts with me, but nicely. Nicely enough that he goes straight into my top ten Sexiest French Sailors list which, given the quality of raw material around, takes some doing.

Honnold, who was treated before me, sticks around to chat.

I ask him if his ship was insured. He says yes. I say sorry for sinking it. He says, *de nada*, the Scottish version anyway. 'At least I dinnae have to eat another one o' yer meals.'

I tell him about the orange box with the computer junk inside. He grins. Says he'll tell someone.

I say would he mind not mentioning my part in all that. Just that I'd rather not get too involved with the police.

He looks sharply at me, but says fine. I think he wonders just how uninvolved I'm likely to be after all this.

After my hand has been seen to, I'm given a cabin with one of only a handful of women on board, Alizée, an aircraft handler. Alizée, who's quite glam, lets me use her make-up, and I choose Noir-Rouge for my lips. Dark eyeliner. Mascara. Eyeshadow.

I still don't look as glam as Alizée, but it's nice playing.

She gives me a cap with the name of the ship on it.

As we enter port, I go into the women's shower room and take my bandage off. Put it on my other hand, the right one.

In Brest, we're handed over to the Police Nationale, but no one quite knows what to do with us. With Connor, Buys and Wee Philly it's fairly clear. There are allegations of piracy, hostage taking and illegal firearms, and those men are taken straight into custody. With Pearson, Ryan and Honnold, things are less clear. All three men are visibly hurt, but it's not clear that they've committed any offence, nor is anyone alleging that they have. I assume that Watkins and colleagues will be screaming their interest in talking to these people – but a foreign police force's interest in talking to someone is not sufficient reason for holding them against their will. In any event, hospital seems a higher priority than custody, and all three men need medical care, so that's where they go.

I go with them, so my hand can be looked at. We sit in a blue police van with two gendarmes.

When we get to hospital – the Hôpital d'Instruction des Armées – I go off in search of the Ladies, but once I'm out of sight of our chaperones, I simply walk away. Out onto the street, down the Avenue Georges Clemenceau to the railway station, where I buy a ticket and get on the first train to Paris.

Don't go all the way, of course. Slim as the risk is, I don't want to be welcomed at Montparnasse by a bevy of policemen, so I get off at Rennes, then hitchhike down to Nantes. Travel most of the way with a lorry driver who tells me all about chicken farming and Gascony.

At Nantes, I think I've covered my tracks enough, so I buy a rail ticket that will zoom me from here to Bordeaux, from Bordeaux to San Sebastian, and from there, via Madrid, to Lisbon, and Faro.

Meet up with my sister again. We spend a few days together. Beach days, pool days. A happy time. My skin is of the tan-resistant Welsh variety, but my sister does good things with fake tan and I work hard on supplementing that with the real thing.

I get a haircut. Shave my legs. My sister does my nails, including my toes, which I don't normally do, but which do look nice, bright red toenails in strappy leather sandals.

We eat fried fish and salad and my sister tells me about a Portuguese guy who she's sort of dating, 'only not really. Don't tell Dad.' She doesn't tell me what happened to Cai, but I don't ask. I turn myself under the sun's hot lamp and read a lot.

I don't think about work. Nothing I can do about it now anyway.

And after four days, I'm done. Book a flight back. Email the office telling them that my holiday is over.

Holiday over, and time to see what sweet fruits my colleagues gathered in my absence.

# 68

'You look well.' Jackson's comment on the post-Portugal me.

'Am well, sir. In the pink. Fine fettle and mint condition.'

'I'm pleased to hear that,' says Jackson gravely.

I nod. Want to ask about Zorro, except I don't want to ask, I want Jackson to tell me.

He says, 'Did you go online while you were on holiday?'

'Sometimes, but not really. Not work stuff.'

'So you don't know what happened?'

'What did happen?'

A long pause. Jackson's eyes heavy on me.

Then: 'The *Isobel Baker* left Milford Haven.'

'Yes?'

'She was a fishing boat. She went fishing.'

'Scampi,' I say. 'That's made out of little baby lobsters. Did you know that?'

'No. No, I didn't know that.'

Another pause.

My fault this one. I shouldn't have got Jackson thinking about scampi.

I wait until Jackson gets back on track and when he does, he says, 'After a few days out at sea, four men joined the ship, bringing with them a Remote Operated Vehicle, of exactly the sort you said we should be expecting.'

'Yes.'

'The men proceeded to locate the Atlantic Cables line. They cut it. Lifted it. And they were about to install this little item before splicing everything together again.'

From a drawer, he pulls Wee Philly's little black box. The one I kicked the crap out of him to acquire. The one I put out to sea in a bright orange waterproof container.

Jackson's face examines mine.

My face hears itself say, 'This case started with a man hanging in an inaccessible room, with nothing stolen, nothing missing. Except the room *had* been accessed, the man *had* been murdered and something *was* missing – namely, the company's data.

'Now why would anyone steal data? I mean yes, if you were planning a $300 million cable of your own, it might be interesting to see your competitor's route map, but we knew no one was planning such a line. Perhaps you might want to *destroy* a particular cable and maybe there are ways of gaining a commercial advantage if you did that. But not for long. Those things are easily repaired. And in any event, if you did something to wreck an expensive piece of infrastructure, you'd have a massive international police inquiry coming after you right away. So that doesn't seem especially clever.'

Jackson falls into my rhythm. He murmurs, 'So as you've been saying all along, sabotage must have seemed like a better route. But *subtle* sabotage. A sabotage that would never be noticed.'

'The thing is,' I say, 'there's so much money swooshing down those lines – or rather, so much financial trading activity depending on the data which those lines transmit – you only need to interfere a teeny-tiny bit to give yourself an advantage. One millisecond is worth a hundred million quid, remember.'

I stop. Remember that this is meant to be about Jackson giving me information, not the other way round. So I shut up.

'Yes.' Jackson turns the little black box, retaining its secrets for another few moments yet. 'Work is still ongoing, of course.'

'Of course.'

'This here is just the case. The innards are at some lab in Cheltenham.'

'Good.'

'Rhiannon's in London, working with our friends and colleagues in the Serious Fraud Office.'

Friends and colleagues: idiots in suits might be more accurate, but a wrinkling of Jackson's mouth is as close as he'll get to acknowledging that.

'I'm sure she'll be enjoying that,' I say.

Jackson nods. 'Computer work. Complicated stuff.'

I nod. Maybe say something. I'm not sure.

Then Jackson divulges, 'At the moment, as far as we can tell right now, this box had one simple job. It was there to put a tiny pause on the line. Three milliseconds. No more than that. The Atlantic Cables line would still have been the fastest one out there, just a tiny bit less fast than their boffins would have had been expecting.'

I say, 'A tiny pause on the line, but not on *all* of the line, maybe. Maybe it wouldn't have interrupted *all* of the data.'

'No. Quite right. There was one bit of the line that wasn't going to get paused.'

'The bit of the line being rented by Idris Gawr. Galton Evans's "investment fund".'

'Correct. Absolutely correct.'

Since Jackson has now shut up and doesn't look like he wants to continue, I tell the story for him.

'Basically, Galton Evans's crowd would get to see its data those three milliseconds ahead of everyone else. The big investment banks. The big hedge funds. Everyone. Mostly, betting on the financial markets is just betting. Speculation.

But if you know that the biggest players in the market are seeing old information, and if you know what the real information is, you have an unbeatable advantage. You can rip off the big boys at their own game. You literally can't lose.'

Jackson nods. 'And it's even better than that. The big boys never know someone's stealing from them. I mean, yes, they might notice the occasional trade going wrong, but those guys just play the odds anyway. A few bad trades wouldn't give them a moment's pause.'

'Like *The Sting*, sir. Have you seen that film?'

Jackson nods, but I don't really know what his nod means. In the movie, Paul Newman and Robert Redford set up a complicated con that involved getting access to horse-race results before they were made public. Galton Evans was trying to pull the same scam, except that he was targeting the world's primary financial axis – and adding a few noughts to his potential for gain.

'Have we made arrests?'

Jackson nods. 'Galton Evans. Conspiracy to murder. Application for bail denied. As for the four men who boarded the *Isobel Baker*, we've brought charges against two of them. Jack Longland, a computer specialist, the guy who was going to install and test this thing. And a nasty piece of work called Connor Houlding, who seemed to be in charge of things. Also, one of the crew members. Jonah Buys. Boarded the ship as a regular fisherman, but was part of Houlding's gang.'

'Evidence?' I ask.

'We've got plenty and we're getting more. This little black box links directly to Idris Gawr, so we can demonstrate that Idris Gawr was set up specifically for the purpose of this fraud. And since there were two murders aimed at enabling that fraud, we have a very strong case to put before a jury. We'll probably offer to go soft on Jack Longland if he tells us everything, and the lad's basically shitting himself so I think he'll go with it. Any case, one way or another, we'll get the verdict we want.'

'And the Stonemonkey?' I say.

'Yes. The Stonemonkey.'

It seems like one of us ought to speak but I've done my share so I stay shtum. Wait for the spirit to move Jackson.

When he is so moved, he says, 'Fiona, when I told you to take a look at the Plas Du burglary, I thought, just possibly, you might find a thief. If you had done, I'd have been impressed. Cold case. No new evidence. Nothing much to go on. And instead – all this. And it's like you knew the whole damn thing all from the start.'

'Not from the start, sir. No.'

'Go on.'

'Well, look. It's just logic. When those artworks vanished then reappeared, that was odd. When Galton Evans lied to us, that was odder. Those things led me to investigate further. When I found out that the members of a particular insurance committee had all been targeted, I realised there had to be some kind of insurance scam at the heart of this. A threat levelled against the insurance industry itself.

'Now that could have been that. Perhaps this was just the way the Stonemonkey chose to profit from his skills. Except that the story *wasn't* over. Derek Moon's death looked rock-climbery, but any old climber could have arranged that murder as neatly. Only then we got the Livesey killing. A murder carried out by an elite-level athlete. The kind of climber who pulled that insurance stunt.

'And again, it's just logic. Yes, you could in theory have two equally able climbers, one of whom carries out an insurance scam and the other one of whom enjoys a bit of murder. But the odds are overwhelmingly in favour of the perpetrator being a single individual. And that's curious for two reasons. One, because if you've just made ten million quid from a successful insurance fraud, it's going to take a lot of money – like a *lot* – to get you involved in murder. And two, because any fraud that involves high-speed telecoms cables and the financial markets doesn't sound like an operation which any climber will know much about.

'So I needed to find an individual who knew about the Stonemonkey's special attributes, and who had the cash and other resources to put in place the kind of telecoms scam we've just uncovered. In theory, that person could have been any member of that insurance committee. Except, not really. For one thing, that committee was mostly full of ordinary corporate executives, people like Nellie Bentley. Well-paid, but a long way short of the resources you'd need to set this scam up. The only person with the cash to do it properly was Galton Evans. And then, for another thing, the silly bugger was stupid enough to call his investment company after one of the climbs on the cliff where Derek Moon was found dead.'

Jackson: 'So basically, you reckon that Galton Evans had the idea for this telecoms scam. Needed to steal a route map so accurate that he could find the cable, even far out at sea. To do that, and do it secretly, he needed to be able to kill someone in a way that didn't even look like murder. And as he's wondering how to do that, it occurs to him that the Stonemonkey would be the ideal person. Someone able to achieve the impossible.'

'It's neat, isn't it?' I say. 'Galton Evans thought so too and got in touch. He had the Stonemonkey's Hotmail address. Knew how to make contact. Presumably said "I've got cash and I need your help with something massively illegal. Please give me a call." Said enough to persuade the Stonemonkey to take it seriously.'

Jackson nods. 'Yes. We're getting the computer people to see if they can trace anything.'

'But you're still calling him the Stonemonkey.'

'Yes. We've not found him yet. We're still looking. The Guardia are looking. Everyone's looking. We've got a load more data now.' Jackson pushes a thick file over the desk at me. 'But nothing concrete, not yet.'

I take the file. Sit with it on my lap.

I'm still half in holiday mode, so I'm wearing stuff more summery, more playful than I'd usually wear to the office. A sleeveless dress in sky blue and sandals that show off my red toes.

Jackson nods at my hand. It's much better now, but I still have a dressing on it.

'You hurt your hand,' he says, exhibiting the observational prowess of a seasoned officer.

'Yes, sir. I splidged myself in a car door.'

'Did you now?'

'Sir? That stuff in Rhayader. You and DI Watkins. I want to say that I really appreciate the way you handled that. I couldn't have managed it if we'd gone down official routes. So thank you. You really helped.'

'You're more than welcome.'

He watches my face carefully, but I am OK. I really feel OK.

'That abduction,' he says carefully. 'Tell me about it. I mean, I don't need you to tell me what happened. I want to understand their logic. Why do it? Why abduct a police officer?'

'It's because we were on to them. They assumed the Livesey murder would be treated as suicide, which indeed it was. Then DI Findlay decided to share everything we had with the coroner.' I make my I-didn't-like-that-at-the-time face, but continue, 'And that meant the Idris Gawr mob needed to know how far our suspicions ran. I mean, if it was just the Livesey murder, they didn't have much to worry about. But when they saw South Wales was involved, they realised we must have connected the Livesey killing to the Moon one, and then they were seriously worried. Had we understood their whole plan? Had we identified the *Isobel Baker*? Did we have the ship under surveillance?

'If they'd been able to access our systems, they'd probably have poked around and left it at that. But DI Watkins did an extremely effective job at blocking access, which meant they needed an actual human target. That target just so happened to be me.

'As it happens, we were both lucky and unlucky in their choice of target. Unlucky, because I was about the only officer who had very strong suspicions of what these people were up to. If I'd said all I suspected, I assume they'd have taken some extremely strong measures to protect themselves. Fortunately, I managed to keep my mouth shut for long enough.'

'That was the lucky part?' Jackson's face is grave. Fatherly.

'No.' I give him a twisted smile. 'I meant that not everyone would have been able to escape. I was lucky that I could.'

'Yes.'

Jackson studies me. I think I've lost the little bit of weight I gained during my junk-foodathon with Lev. I'm back to my normal not-very-sturdy me.

Jackson is, I guess, wondering, not for the first time, how the skinny bare-armed girl in front of him manages to get herself out of the situations she finds herself in. But if so, he doesn't ask.

'But then you got away, and that gave them a problem. According to your answers, our inquiry basically had nothing. No surveillance. No interest in the *Isobel Baker*. No interest in shipping. But then you escaped. And we'd have been asking ourselves what that whole interrogation had been for. So their abduction effort might have ended up making us ask questions which hadn't previously occurred to us.'

'Exactly.'

‘They must have discussed what to do. I mean, they must have thought about abandoning the entire plan.’

‘Yes.’

‘But they didn’t.’

‘No.’

Partly, of course, Evans and his gang would have made a considerable investment by then, one that would have been hard to walk away from. And then as well, my answers under interrogation implied that we knew and understood almost nothing. Perhaps they figured that they had nothing to fear, even if my abduction did put our inquiry on red alert.

I say something to that effect, and Jackson nods in agreement, but there’s one further conjecture, which I don’t choose to share.

That conjecture is this. Evans was certainly the figurehead, the public face, of Idris Gawr, but that didn’t necessarily mean he was in ultimate command of the operation. Perhaps the Voice was the real leader, the one calling the shots. And his own financial interests were carefully kept behind many walls of secrecy in the Caymans and elsewhere: walls we’ve been unable to surmount.

Simply put, if the operation succeeded, the Voice would make a fortune. And if it failed – well, hell, it would be Galton Evans paying the price, not him.

‘Any case,’ says Jackson. ‘They decided to proceed as planned, but with a bit of extra protection. They re-registered the *Isobel Baker* as a Cypriot ship. Made sure that the ROV only came on board well out at sea. Same thing with the underwater specialists. All those things only came together at the last possible moment and only when the ship was far out in international waters.’

‘Yes.’

And there it is, I think. The whole story. The picture of this case from beginning to end.

*And Galton Evans on a charge of murder.* We'll have to make that stick, of course, but from what Jackson has said so far, I can't foresee too many difficulties.

The corpses I've lived with for so long – Moon, Livesey, Jazz MacClure – start to release themselves. Unstick from me. I'll be sorry to see them go, but it's what I do. Justice is the gift I bring them, in exchange for the peace they bring me.

As I'm thinking those thoughts, Jackson is pausing and I realise he's not yet done.

'Fiona, you haven't asked me what happened to the *Isobel Baker*.'

'Oh. What happened to the *Isobel Baker*, sir?'

'It sank.'

'Oh.'

'No loss of life, fortunately.'

'That's good.'

'Nine men rescued. One woman.'

'Oh.'

'This woman.'

He throws a photograph at me. CCTV from the Police Nationale station in Brest. They didn't take a formal photo, because I wasn't suspected of any crime. Jackson pushes some other pictures towards me. Some taken at Milford Haven, when I boarded the ship. Other stills from the station in Brest. None of them are much good. The Milford Haven ones show almost nothing, because I had my back to the cameras and was wearing a hood. And CCTV is never all that good. You can rule people out – men, anyone with dark skin, anyone of obviously the wrong height, weight or age – but after that you just don't really know. Alizée's fancy make-up and baseball cap don't amount to a disguise exactly, but they do confuse any identification.

The woman in the photos could be me or could be someone else.

I say, 'Do we know this person?'

'I don't know. Do we?' Jackson flicks the photo that best shows my bandaged hand. 'Remind me, Fiona. You "splidged" your hand?'

'In a car door, sir. I know "splidge" isn't a real word.'

'Odd though. The same injury.'

'*Not* the same injury. She's hurt her right hand. *My* right hand is just fine.'

I hold out my right hand, wiggling it to demonstrate its just fineness.

Jackson doesn't say anything, ask anything, do anything.

I wonder if this was his interrogation technique when he was a mere DI. Take that man down to the cells and hit him with two hours of silence. If he survives that, give him another two, and another two after that. Stay silent and do nothing till he begs for mercy.

I sit with Jackson, doing and saying nothing in a companionable way. Then, when I think we've done enough, I say, 'May I borrow your computer, sir?'

He nods. Revolves the screen. Pushes the keyboard towards me.

I go to my bank's website. Log on.

Pull up a list of recent transactions. All of them Portuguese. Restaurants. Supermercados. Bars. A couple of clothes shops.

Swivel the screen back.

Jackson scrutinises the list. Rubs his face.

'Must have been nice. Pretty place, the Algarve.'

'Yes, my first time. I loved it.'

'Take any pictures?'

I get out my phone. Tap through to my photos. I'm no expert on these things, but I've done enough to remove any obvious time-and-date stamps on the files.

Jackson is still less of an expert. He flips through photos.

Sees lots of pictures. Me. My sister. Me and my sister. Different outfits, different places, different times of day.

'How do I get a call log on this thing?'

I show him, sulkily.

He pokes around till he gets what he needs. Phone calls from Portugal to Wales and back again. He doesn't give me my phone back though. Doesn't close the screen with my banking records.

He says, 'The *Isobel Baker*. Its captain seems to be just a regular fisherman. Alexander Honnold. Scottish. Experienced trawlerman.'

I shrug. I don't know where Jackson is going with this, but I wish he'd give me back my phone.

'I had a good chat with Honnold. A long debriefing session.'

I nod.

'The guy owned his own vessel. A good skipper. Respected. This guy, Connor, comes to him wanting to charter his boat for a construction project. The money's good. Fishing isn't exactly a brilliant business. Honnold would quite like to dig the boat out from under a giant mortgage, so he says yes. In retrospect, that wasn't a particularly smart move, but there's nothing illegal about being dumb.'

'Just as well, sir, really.'

'Anyway. At the last minute, his cook gets ill or, I don't know, has a dying aunt. Some bollocks like that. He skips off the boat. This woman' – pointing to the photos – 'gets on it. Everything's fine, give or take the quality of food. Pilchard macaroni, I don't know. Then Connor and his damn ROV come on board. There's a storm. All kinds of shenanigans. Then this woman, allegedly, pours fish guts into the engine cooling system. The engine starts to fail. The boat can't keep its nose into the waves and is about to sink. So everyone piles into a life-raft and awaits rescue.'

I say, in a tone as even as I can manage, 'Is this woman facing charges? I mean, sinking ships is probably against some law or other.'

'No. No, she wouldn't be facing any charge. Not from me anyway. The situation on that boat had turned pretty ugly. It seems like her actions were aimed at bringing about an end to hostilities.'

'Well, then. Good for her.'

'Yes, good for her. Unless she happened to be an officer of mine. In which case, she still hasn't done anything illegal, but she has interfered in an operation under my command without my knowledge or permission.'

Jackson beats my phone thoughtfully against the ball of his hand. Those Welsh hormones again: they just have to hit things.

If Jackson chose to send my phone into the electronics lab at Bridgend, it would take them all of a few minutes to determine that the photos had been taken within one scant eighteen-hour period. It would take a fair bit of work, but doable work, to place me on that ferry from Santander. And of course Honnold and the rest of them could easily confirm that I was on that damn boat.

I'm scared, actually. I think Jackson means his implicit threat. If he really believed I was on that boat, he'd chuck me out of CID.

I say, sulkily, 'Right. But as you've just verified, I was in Portugal. On holiday. In accordance with the strongly expressed wishes of both you and DI Watkins.'

Jackson thinks another few moments.

Then: 'Sorry, Fiona.'

His voice is very soft. Gentle. And he's never gentle with me.

He clicks around on his computer. Brings up Skype. Not a program he's all that familiar with, as he's slow to click his way through to where he needs to be. But there's only one name on his call list anyway. Ahonnold62. He clicks the name, makes the call.

That annoying ringing noise.

Two rings, three. Then Honnold answers.

My mouth is dry. This thing has been prearranged, I realise: Honnold is no more part of the Skype generation than Jackson is. I watch and wait as two fifty-something men fiddle with their webcams, their volume controls.

Watch and wait, as the executioner's cart rumbles clumsily into place. As the blade is sharpened, the rope knotted.

I feel a physical tightening in my throat. Sounds come to me from a long way off.

Jackson, a million miles away, says, 'Captain, I have a young woman with me here. She's not facing any charges, nor will she face any, no matter what you may have to tell me now. I just need to know if this woman is the same one who sailed with you on the *Isobel Baker* recently. A simple yes/no answer will be fine. Is that clear?'

From where I'm sitting, I can't properly see Honnold's face, but I hear his dry Scots, 'Aye, Inspector, that's clear enough.'

Jackson vacates his seat. One of those big, black leather and chrome affairs.. Fitted for Jackson's height and weight. His head-of-Major-Crimes seniority. The chair rocks back on its springs.

Jackson waves a hand.

At me, at the chair, at the end of my career.

I stand up, of course. There's nothing else to do. Move towards my doom, but – a funny thing – have this almost literal sense of getting smaller as I approach. A kind of *Alice in Wonderland* experience, in which I find myself shrinking until, by the time I have somehow clambered onto that evilly rocking seat, I feel myself no bigger than a tiny white mouse, nibbling, and twitching, and combing my whiskers.

I face the screen.

Honnold's face, but I'm so spacey, so gluey with apprehension, that I can read nothing at all in his expression, his tone, his smile.

Somewhere beyond the orbit of Pluto, I hear Jackson say, 'Can you see all right, Captain?' Jackson adjusts the webcam at our end and rolls my chair forward. The little rectangle, lower right, that gives the view that Honnold sees, fills with my face.

'Aye, that's fine.'

'And? Is this the woman?'

There's a pause.

I'm good with pauses usually. Can pause with the best of them. Keep pace with Jackson's marathon silences.

But not now. Not this time.

I feel the silence fill with the bones of a thousand winters, the death of galaxies. My limbs are lead. My mouth is glue.

I'm in a state so altered that, although I hear Honnold's words – 'No. No, Inspector, that's not her.' – it takes me several seconds to make sense of them. There's a shift in his expression, a twitch in his left eye – a wink? – but I'm already sliding off the seat, away from the screen, making good on this miraculous reprieve.

The two men sign off.

I try to look normal. Find my tongue. Retrieve my scattered wits, the use of my limbs.

Jackson closes the Skype app.

'Sorry, Fiona. But I needed to know.'

'Holiday,' I say, aggrievedly. 'What do you want from me? I was on holiday.'

'OK. Good. I'm pleased you enjoyed it. You're looking very well.'

I nod. A kind of thank-you thing, though whether that's how Jackson interprets it, I don't know. He doesn't say.

'Hope the hand's OK.'

'It's fine.'

We're back in pause mode again, but this is one I can handle. No galaxies burning out, just the gentle rock of a little boat against some sunny harbour wall.

Jackson: 'That other crime. On Chicago.'

'Yes?'

'We didn't manage to gather enough evidence to justify charges. Sorry.'

'No. I thought, probably . . .'

'But you may be interested to learn that I had a heart to heart chat with DI Dunwoody, at the conclusion of which he decided he would prefer to pursue a career outside the police service.'

'Did he?'

'He did.'

'Did you actually tear his head off, sir? I always think you'll tear off mine.'

'No, his head remained on his shoulders. But' – a flickering smile – 'there were moments. There were certainly moments . . .'

I sigh. I wish I could have seen it. I'll have to seek out Amrita, the queen of office gossip, to see what I can glean from her. Add some merry fuel to that fire. Some highly coloured truths, a few believable lies.

Jackson gives me my moment of sweet delight, then says with a we're-done-now exhalation, 'Check in with Rhiannon when she's back from London. Take a look at that file, the Stonemonkey one. Let me know if anything occurs to you.'

'Yes, sir.'

I stand. It's nice, actually, wearing a dress to the office now and again. It's easy to get all policey in here. Sometimes it's good to be a bit girly too.

So I stand, smooth my dress, admire my red toes, but don't quite leave.

Jackson, his rumbly voice: 'Fiona?'

'Two things, sir. First, the Spanish police found a T-shirt at the Stonemonkey's house. A Plas-y-Brenin one. From a climbing centre in North Wales.'

'Yes?'

'Is there any chance I could take a look at it, please?'

He nods. 'I don't know where that evidence is being held. Rhiannon will know. I'm sure she'll be happy for you to take a look.'

'Thank you.'

I don't say anything further and Jackson has to nudge.

'Two things, you said.'

'I've got some data I'd like to share. With you. With DI Watkins. And ideally with Adrian Brattenbury too. I think you'll be interested.'

Adrian Brattenbury: my old sort-of boss from the Serious Organised Crime Agency. A good investigator and one who mostly likes me.

'I'll give Adrian a call. Should I tell him what it's regarding?'

I nod. Yes.

Jackson raises his eyebrows. Big shaggy affairs that take some lifting. 'Well?'

'What it's always about, sir. It's about nailing the fuckers.'

Jackson grins. Says he'll call. Says something else nice, to make up for the whole Honnold thing.

I leave. Walk down the corridor to the lifts.

Red toes, clacky sandals. Tanned arms, sleeveless dress.

And Galton Evans in jail.

And Galton Evans in jail.

# 69

Life is good.

I go swimming with Bev. She admires my tan. I say the right things about her thighs and arms. We drink vegetable smoothies and laugh a lot.

I eat sensibly, remember to sleep. See my family. See friends.

See Lev, even, who drops by for a weekend of dope-smoking and pilchard macaroni, which has become something of a culinary standby for me. He mentions my whole post-Rhayader convalescence only once, asking, 'You are OK now?'

'Yes.'

'No dreams? No bad ones?'

'No. I mean, not really. Not worse than usual.'

'These panics?'

He means, I think, panic attacks, but I don't get those and say as much. He stares at me with those deep brown eyes of his. Then puts on some Russian music and changes the subject. Doesn't bring it up again. Probably never will.

See Mike. We sleep together a few more times. Have a nice time. Not as magical as our sex in that kingdom of unicorns, but most things aren't. The relationship doesn't really feel right here, though. It's not true me and isn't true him, so we stop sleeping together but still see each other, off and on. We're friends, I think, and always will be.

Ed too. See him. Mike's wildman of the rocks and waves.

It's odd learning that new thing about this person I thought I knew. A corrective. A guard against error.

I eat Ed's food – butterflied lamb, cooked on the barbecue, with herbs, lemon and chilli – and try to see Mike's Ed in the one I know. Trying to fit my suit-and-tied psychologist into the sun-stubbled windsurfer who climbs impossible rocks just for the pleasure of falling into the chattering sea.

I don't think I connect the two all that well, but even the effort is helpful.

Ed tells me that he's started meeting people, having dates. 'No one amazing yet, but it feels good to get out there.'

That makes me feel twingey, I think. Not in a bad way. Just – other people moving on with their lives. Finding partners, settling down. Heading for Forever Married, those broad waters.

Waters whose sunny surface I'm not sure I'll ever see.

I tell Ed about my time with Mike. Not that it matters really, but I'd rather that if Ed heard it from anyone, he heard it from me.

We eat. Talk. Yawn.

Another evening, I see Penry. Sort out money stuff: him paying me back, because Watkins has settled his fees and expenses directly.

I say thanks. For the money, yes, but more for the help.

He *de nada*s me. Tells me Watkins has given him a stellar reference. That various security jobs are opening up for him. 'Boring as fuck, to be honest, but proper jobs. Ones I can do without messing up. I'll be OK.'

Nor do I forget Honnold, the man whose ship I sank and who nevertheless chose to save me when a hundred others wouldn't. I send him flowers. Send him three bottles of single malt whisky, ones not available through regular shops, but direct from the distillery. Send him also a catering size tin of macaroni cheese plus a six-pack of tinned pilchards, the cheapest brand I can find.

I cannot repay his kindness, but I can make him drunk and I can make him smile. And smiles are precious.

The dead, they matter too. They ask for my attention and I am happy to give it.

I go out to Gower. Moon's churchyard. Lay flowers there. Don't see the girl. Don't feel Moon, not really. He's gone from me now. I miss him, but it's a good sort of missing. Sad and sweet like the end of a romantic weepie.

Fly to Virginia again. To Livesey's memorial service, held in a little white church, under a flagpole, looking out over those wide American seas.

Lowe is there. I give him a short summary of what happened. Thank him for his help. 'Proud I could be of service,' he says and is clearly happy that his assessment of the *Isobel Baker* was proved sound. 'But why did she sink? I don't see why a ship like that would sink.'

I don't enlighten him.

Carolyn Sharma is busy, of course. She, together with Livesey's mother and brother, is at the centre of these solemn proceedings. But we still have time for a private word.

I don't tell her most of what transpired. She doesn't need to know. Doesn't want to, even. But I tell her the bit she does need. The thing that lets her little ship move on, to whatever seas await her next.

In the subdued light of the church porch, a light softened by the God within, the sea without, I tell her, 'We got the sonsofbitches, Carolyn. The main man and half his people too. We haven't yet got the others, but we will. The case isn't closed. It's still active. And we'll get them all.'

'The main man. Your British courts. I don't know . . .?'

I laugh. 'We don't really go in for your kind of sentencing. No death penalties. No life plus ninety-nine years. But a crime like this one? Two murders. Highly premeditated. Plenty of aggravating factors. You're looking at a forty year minimum term, I'd say, before he can even think of applying for parole. He's mid-fifties now and prison isn't kind.'

Sharma plucks at the shoulder of the black suit she's wearing. A hot thing to wear in this Virginian summer.

'Thank you. I don't know why it matters really. But thank you.'

'It doesn't matter. That's the truth. It makes no difference, but we still have to do it.'

People are drifting from the church to a hotel over the road, where I can see waitresses move on a shaded terrace. Awnings and white linen.

Sharma gives me one of her shoulder punches. 'Officer Griffiths, I think I'm going to go get hammered.' And we walk together to the hotel.

# 70

Nailing the fuckers.

Because of holidays and the like, it takes time to get everyone in the same place at the same time. That suits me. I've a lot to prepare and I'm enjoying just being me. Living my life.

And I know that I don't always do things professionally. Sometimes I mess things up that I could get right. Sometimes piss off my colleagues for no reason at all. Sometimes go missing, show up late, go off-piste, ignore instructions, swear.

I can't see that I'm about to stop doing all those terrible things. I don't have that much control over who I am. Perhaps none of us do: corks on a current. But Marcus Aurelius, who thought he *was* a cork floating on a current, a cork whose path had been predetermined since the beginning of time, still enjoined us to, *Do the right thing. The rest doesn't matter.*

So I take the man's advice. Just for once, I do my spick-and-span professional best.

Compile charts. Timelines. Data.

Draw my material up into the best policeish form. The sort of thing that has executive summaries, and indexes, and sources that are listed and checkable. Drawing on my time down in Ifor's dungeon, I get my stuff printed and bound. Colour-coded covers, straight edges. The smell of warm toner and good material prepared.

I do all this, but don't obsess. Don't work beyond six.

Don't ignore my other duties. Don't omit to put in overtime claims the way we're meant to.

Once, Jackson happened to walk past my desk as I was hard at work. 'Good girl, Fiona,' he said, tapping my desk with his big paw. 'Good girl.'

The big day comes. The last working day of August, a Friday. It's been a nice month. Warm. Not much rain. Bute Park has felt like a big city park should. Ice creamy. Green. The sort of place where small girls run and dogs go bounding through long grass.

Our conference room overlooks the waving green. Nods at Cardiff Castle across the way.

Present today: Me. Jackson. Watkins. Brattenbury.

Also – my one concession to my own nuttiness – a modified version of my photo wall. Up on a board behind me, I have 4" x 6" images of my corpses.

Janet Mancini. April Mancini. Stacey Edwards.

Mary Langton. Ali Al-Khalifi. Mark Mortimer.

Hayley Morgan. Saj Kureishi. Nia Lewis.

Derek Moon. Ian Livesey.

Jazz MacClure, Gina Jewell.

A gallery of friends. Their gazes warm, even in death.

No one really comments on the photos. Jackson and Watkins have already said whatever they wanted to say. Brattenbury doesn't really know what to do with them, so says nothing.

Teas. Coffees. A garnish of small talk.

When everyone's ready, Jackson says, 'Fiona,' and I start.

Quickly rehearse the broad lines of three recent major cases.

One, Operation Lohan, an ugly little sex-trafficking case, with a rich man – a dead one – at its heart.

Two, Operation Abacus, universally known as Stirfry. An arms-dealing case, where the central perpetrator was never prosecuted, though we all knew he was as guilty as fuck.

Three, Operation Tinker. A sophisticated payroll fraud,

where we rounded up most of the foot-soldiers, but never so much as got a name for its commander-in-chief.

Mention too, the broad outlines of Zorro. An astonishingly audacious effort to subvert the world's major financial trading axis. An effort that would, but for a few handfuls of fishguts, have succeeded.

Jackson and Watkins know most of this already, but it doesn't hurt to lay it out again. And Brattenbury, who is London-based, doesn't know much about the first two cases, nor a whole heap about the last.

I say, 'Four cases. Complex, ambitious crimes. In three of them, we know the identity of the perpetrators. Successful, well-connected men. Local men. Welsh. Not outsiders.

'Numerous common elements between these crimes. Remarkable commercial sophistication. A highly unusual degree of security awareness. Communications. Data. False identities. Use of offshore financial vehicles. Willingness to invest. Long time horizons.'

I push copies of the first of my documents across the table.

*Common Elements in Four Recent Crimes: Lohan, Abacus, Tinker, Zorro.*

A lengthy, remorseless analysis of operating practices in each of the four conspiracies. Factual. Objective. And, I hope, compelling.

We start to go through it. Not only me talking now. The others too. Comparing notes. Discussing my analysis.

We run for about an hour. The discussion isn't finished. Isn't really started. But everyone wants to know what comes next.

I tell them.

'Brendan Rattigan. Idris Prothero. Galton Evans. Men we know to be behind three of these crimes. I want to add three further names to that list. David Marr-Philips. We don't know if he's involved but he did own a twenty per cent stake in Prothero's little enterprise. Didn't seem particularly concerned by its criminality. Also Ned Davison. Not wealthy on the scale of these other men, but one whose name came up in connection with Project Tinker. And finally Owain Owen. A successful businessman, with no police record and no intelligence suggesting criminal activity. You'll just have to bear with me on that name for now.'

I produce my next document.

*Known Links Between Rattigan, Prothero, Evans, Marr-Philips, Davison and Owen.*

Push it across the desk. Start to talk it through.

Common investment projects. Gold club memberships. Yacht clubs. Dining societies. Kids' schools. Anything.

Talk for ten minutes before Jackson interrupts.

'Fiona. This is good stuff, but look. These are rich guys. Of course they know each other. This isn't London. Out here, it's a small group you're talking about.'

I nod.

'Yes. Yes it is. And if you found these men did, for example, meet for dinner on a social basis, you wouldn't be surprised.

'But here.' I unfold a chart that depicts their various activities – business, financial, recreational, social, educational, philanthropic. 'There's nothing that connects them all. You find things that connect any two or three of them. Maybe even four of them. But not all. Not that we know.'

Jackson nods. Doesn't say anything. But the room feels on the brink of something now. My moment to deliver.

I hand out the photo that Cesca gave me.

Prothero.

Marr-Philips.

Owen.

Rattigan.

Davison.

All five men, seated at Galton Evans's table in the south of France.

I say, 'I obtained this photograph from a source in the course of Operation Zorro. The photograph was given to me on the basis of total confidentiality. I can't and won't reveal the source's name. At the end of our meeting here, I will collect these prints back again and destroy them. I will not answer questions on how they came to be in my hands. Nor will I allow the picture to appear in any court proceedings.

'What I will tell you, however, is that this photograph was taken in France. And the other occupants of this villa were ordered to leave so that these men could talk in privacy.

'And one more thing. This photograph was taken on the same day. The figure of possible interest is the one in the little parking area, next to the blue BMW.'

I hand out Cesca's photo. The one that might or might not show Vic Henderson.

The picture means nothing to Watkins, who wasn't involved in Tinker.

Jackson is slow to make the identification, but when he does his eyes dart across to Brattenbury, who led that project.

'Adrian?' says Jackson.

Brattenbury nods. 'Yes. Yes. I think it's him.'

Three pairs of eyes stare back at me. I didn't just know Henderson, I kissed him. Stood naked in front of him. Was almost killed by him.

Gravel-voiced, I say, 'Yes. I think so too. But I would. I'm looking for evidence of this kind. I'm not a reliable judge.'

Brattenbury: 'I'll get this analysed. Can I do that?'

I nod. I asked Cesca and she said OK. But even the best analysts in the world need better material to work with and in the end Brattenbury's analysts will just offer us a more jargon-filled version of 'yeah, could be, definitely possible.'

Watkins says, 'Just to be clear, Fiona: what precisely are you suggesting?'

Jackson likes the question, but he holds a hand up, stopping me.

Reaches for the conference room phone. Dials a number.

'Hey, June. It's Dennis here. Is the chief around? . . . Oh, is he? Good. Excellent. Can you give him a bell? Tell him I want to see him right now if possible. Twenty minutes, that's all.' He waits for me to remind him which conference room we're in, then tells June Whoever where we are, then hangs up.

The chief: the Chief Constable of South Wales. Works in the Bridgend HQ, but is apparently in town right now.

In town, and heading for my little show and tell.

We pause, as we await the great man's arrival.

Brattenbury, making chit-chat, says to me, 'You're a sergeant now, are you? Do I need to congratulate you?'

'No.'

Jackson says, 'Oh bollocks. OSPRE II. That damn stupid role-playing day happened while you were away. I don't think they've got another date this year. I totally forgot.'

Watkins says, 'They sometimes make extra dates available in the autumn. I can ask if . . .'

Jackson: 'No. Sod that. Adrian, would you say this young lady needs to do some bullshit roleplay thing to prove her professional fitness?'

Brattenbury laughs. 'No.'

'Rhiannon?'

Watkins doesn't like the idea of circumventing rules, but she twists her face up and says, 'No.'

'OK. I'll just phone 'em up and tell 'em I've got Fiona employed on actual police work. Can't spare her. See what they say to that.' His face changes a bit, and he adds, 'Any case, it's true. Fiona's the only capable exhibits officer we've got right now.'

Brattenbury: 'Fiona? An exhibits officer?'

'That's right. Can't spare her.'

I know Jackson is messing with me, but I don't know what he's on about and even the mention of that job sends a shiver through me the way that the Rhayader barn now couldn't.

I say, anxiously, 'Sir?'

He's about to continue his thing, whatever it is, but sees my face and stops short. 'Our guys are all at some big exhibits meet-up in central London. A conference of exhibits officers, eh? Just imagine the hi-jinks. But' – this bit to me – 'don't worry, you're more useful up here anyway.'

Ifor Dawes is back now, part time only, three mornings a week, but the doctors say he's mending well. As for the conference itself, we laugh about that. What do exhibits officers get up to when they're feeling frolicsome? Go over long columns of figures? Correct each other's location references?

I think, *I have a job. Friends. The respect of my colleagues. I am lucky to be a part of this world. Lucky at all that I have.*

I allow my thoughts to travel to the barn again. Not stopping at the walls, but going all the way.

Think of myself taped to that chair under the bulb. As the light dwindled and time died.

Think of the questions, the sleeplessness, the interrogation, the threats.

Think of the jab of that thing. The picana. Its explosive touch.

Remember all that. Feel it all.

*Feel* it. The fear, yes, and the pain, but also my awareness that I'm still here, in one piece, happy. I think, *I survived that. Not just bodily, but mentally too. Here I am, on Planet Normal, having a laugh with my colleagues.*

I think that I have never been as well as this. As intact. My Cotard's has never been more distant.

These thoughts are interrupted by the door opening. The

chief enters. Jackson introduces him to me – strictly speaking, reintroduces him, as the chief has already met me once – and to Brattenbury.

Jackson says, 'Fiona, from the top please. Give us a ten minute recap.'

I do as he asks.

'Good. Now Rhiannon's question. What exactly is your theory here?'

I say, 'I believe these men – Evans, Prothero, Marr-Philips, Owen, Rattigan – are or were some of the principals in a large scale conspiracy.

'Each of those men has some totally legitimate business interests. No funny stuff. No nothing. But I believe they also share – in Rattigan's case, shared – an interest in originating, funding and operating a variety of criminal enterprises.

'Those enterprises are typically very audacious. Very well planned and organised. They reflect exceptional levels of investment and expertise. The execution is completely ruthless. Murder, and worse, are simply the incidental by-products.

'I have no idea how the conspiracy is organised in detail. For example, do they all contribute equally to each project? How are the risks and rewards shared out? For what it's worth my guess would be that they follow a fairly regular business model. That is, the principals all have the right, but not the obligation, to participate in a given scheme. That if, let's say, three of the five were interested, and two of the five wanted to pass, then the three would go it alone.

'But that part is speculative. What we do know is that these schemes have been highly commercially ambitious. We successfully disrupted the group behind Tinker, but even so, they stole more than thirty million pounds. The potential gain on Zorro was even larger. Perhaps an order of magnitude larger.

'I have very little evidence to support these conjectures.

In the end, it comes down to three things. One, the extreme unlikelihood that completely unrelated schemes of this type should be proliferating in South Wales. Two, the degree of operational similarity, as documented in my *Common Elements* booklet. Three, the photographs that I've placed in front of you today.'

I've said what I need to say. Don't know what to do next. So I sit down. The chief gets a good view of my corpses for the first time.

Corpses, meet the chief.

Chief, corpses.

He doesn't smile, doesn't blanch.

Questions fly.

I've excluded Davison from the list of principals. Why?

'I think he's part of their operational staff. Perhaps something like the chief operating officer type. Or a core part of the way they communicate. But I can't be sure. This is all still speculative.'

Do I think the five businessmen I've identified constitute the entire group?

'I'm not sure. But no, we've no reason to think that.'

I have another booklet with me and hand it out.

*Known Associates of the Hypothetical Principals.* A list that includes the names of my long-standing targets: Ivor Harris. Trevor Yergin. Huw Allsop. Ben Rossiter. Joe Johnson. A dozen others. Many of those names – probably most – will prove to be completely innocent. But it's a list of the people with the densest links, social and professional, with our five principals. The booklet contains data on each one. Forty-five close-typed pages of research.

Further questions.

Further answers.

These are intelligent officers whose training inclines them to distrust wild speculation.

After ten minutes, the chief looks at his watch for the fourth time.

'I'm sorry.' Standing up. 'I've got a thing I'm already late for.'

Jackson holds up a restraining finger. 'Adrian, you're the organised crime expert. What do you make of this?'

Brattenbury hefts my booklets in his hands. Looks at Cesca's photos again.

'Needs work, of course. But gut instinct? At this stage? I'd have to say yes. Yes definitely.'

'Rhiannon?'

'I can only really speak for Abacus and Zorro. But yes. Do the cases have the same feel? The same organisational flavour? Yes, I think they do.'

'Chief?'

The chief doesn't answer. Not directly. To me, he says, 'Good work.' Tries to remember my name. Can't. Says, 'Good work,' again to make up.

Then turns to Jackson's enquiring face.

Breathes out. A long exhalation.

Then, 'Tell me what you need, Dennis. Just tell me what you need.'

# 71

Boughrood. A small village on the turn of the Wye. A row of white cottages on one side. Some modern things, whitewashed and angular, on the other.

A village shop. A bridge. Green hills rising all around.

It's very quiet. It's Christmas Day.

I'm in an unmarked van with DCI Jackson. It's not really his job to be here. This is Watkins's case. But Watkins wanted the day at home with Cal – her fiancée, as she is now – while Jackson's wife is away on a three week visit to Oz, seeing her sister, and Jackson didn't want to sit around getting pissed with his daughter and her 'terrible' boyfriend.

Jackson has his seat shoved back as far as it'll go.

'Imagine it. Growing up here. A place like this. You swim in the river. Go messing about on the hills. Do whatever kids do. How do you get from all that to this?'

This: he means the last twist of Operation Zorro.

Plas-y-Brenin is the biggest climbing centre in Wales. Loads of kids have passed through its doors, been introduced to rock for the first time.

And, because kids like souvenirs, the centre produced T-shirts with the corporate logo. Each year, a slightly different design.

We traced the design of the Stonemonkey's T-shirt to a specific year, 1997. Then obtained lists of all those who had used the centre's services that year – literally thousands of names. But also got records of staff members. The climbing instructors, an itinerant bunch.

We tracked them down. Asked them about any kids who made a big impression on them in the course of that year.

Not everyone had an answer. Those that did, didn't always give the kind of answer that was helpful: mentioning, for example, a partially sighted girl, whose grace and courage had impressed everyone at the centre.

But one name cropped up more than once. Dylan MacLeod. Scottish father, Welsh mother. Eleven years old, something like that. And extraordinary. Clearly, even at that age, extraordinary.

'I mean, he was just about competition level for his age group by the time he left the centre. Balance like you've never seen. Totally without fear. Really calm. This kind of laserlike focus. And strong, you know. Climbing strength normally takes time to build. We used to see older teenagers who came out of some city gym, all bulging with muscles, only to discover that they couldn't actually climb squat. This kid had never been on a crag before, and he was pulling moves that no one else in his group could even think about.'

The guy who told us that – a genial outdoorsman, Roy Fawcett, now employed as a PE teacher in a village school outside Sheffield – said that it had been impossible to integrate MacLeod into the group of novices he'd arrived with. The two of them – Fawcett and MacLeod – ended up climbing together all that week.

'We started on the normal kid stuff. By the end of the week, we were climbing E1, E2. I mean, except that MacLeod didn't yet have a long reach, and his fitness wasn't there yet, he wasn't so far off climbing at my level, and I thought I was pretty much OK. At the end of the week, he said to me, "This is what I'm going to do with my life. I'm going to get rich and be the world's best rock climber." I mean' – and here Fawcett's tone acquired a gritty, schoolmaster's edge – 'I didn't *like* those ambitions. Neither of them. Good climbers climb for the sake of it, not for anything else. But he did have talent, no question.'

We investigated MacLeod's subsequent career, as far as we could trace it.

It showed the kind of trajectory we'd been seeking. A kid obsessed. Talented. A child who started skipping school so he could hitchhike up to North Wales or the Peak District to climb. Sometimes with friends. Just as often, it seems, on unroped solos.

He wasn't close to his father, who left home in 1999 and never returned. He was, kind of, close to his mother, except that his trips away climbing became ever longer, his stays at home ever shorter. From 2008 onwards, he was hardly ever seen in the village of his birth. The last time he came, he drove a yellow Lotus Elan, only rented, but still.

These discoveries enabled us to intercept all communications into that little Boughrood cottage. The authorities don't normally like handing out warrants letting us bug Person A in the hope of getting at Person B, but the circumstances here were compelling.

And – a strange, unhappy piece of luck – Mrs MacLeod, Bethan, a long-term lupus sufferer, may be dying. Poor diet, a lack of exercise and a mild smoking habit have combined to give her a nasty case of chronic obstructive pulmonary disease. She's on bottled oxygen ten hours a day. Her doctors are not optimistic.

Two days ago, the twenty-third, we intercepted a call.

Under the rules attached to our interception warrant, we have just fifteen seconds to determine if the caller is our target. On this call, however, we needed only about three of those fifteen seconds. The caller began, 'Hi, Mum . . .'

Our guy, Dylan MacLeod, the Stonemonkey, was coming home. A last, sad farewell.

We have twelve officers in the village now, including six firearms officers. Further resources available on call from Brecon. Audio and video feeds in Bethan MacLeod's cottage. The back of our van now has three monitors, speakers, radio equipment.

As Jackson talks, a six-year-old on a new bike wobbles precariously down the road towards the bridge, chased by a laughing father.

A bike with a wobbly six-year-old going one way. A silver Lotus coming from the other.

Jackson and I look at each other.

'Merry Christmas, Dylan MacLeod,' he says.

We do nothing. The plan is to let Macleod enter the cottage, because we don't know if he's armed and static arrests are more easily controlled than ones where the suspect has any chance to run or drive.

MacLeod parks. Enters the cottage.

Jackson and I, moving through to the back of the van, watch as MacLeod greets his mother. Affection and love and sadness and goodbyes.

We watch for a bit, then Jackson reaches for the radio.

I say, 'Boss?'

He stares at me. 'Really?' But he shakes his head, and when he clicks his Talk button, he says, 'All officers, Fiona Griffiths here wants to let our guy have Christmas lunch with his mum. Now I don't care, because I don't have any place I particularly want to be right now. But you lot do. It's your call. Let them have their last lunch together or go in and pick him up now?'

There are three other units. One round the corner in Beeches Park. Another on the hill out of the village. A third at the back of the little row of cottages, guarding the exit to the river.

One by one the three units discuss the matter, then report back.

'OK with us, boss.'

'Yeah, let's give 'em their lunch.'

'Fair enough. It's Christmas.'

'OK. He's got till three o'clock. Don't switch off.'

Jackson clicks the radio off. Looks at me. Laughs.

'Did you bring sandwiches?'

'No.'

'Me neither.'

We stay in the van's dark back looking at the monitor.

A bottle of wine. Something in the oven. Bethan MacLeod's laboured breathing. Her son, a killer, tender and sad.

'Wonder what they're having,' says Jackson. 'Can't be turkey. Not for two of them.'

It's uncomfortable in the back and Jackson finds a way to rip the monitor from its fixing and trails the wires forward, so we can sit in the front and watch the quiet street, while the monitor burbles.

Dylan MacLeod opens wine, peels carrots.

The six-year-old cyclist comes back.

Bethan MacLeod checks the oven. Says, 'Five minutes.'

The carrots go on to boil.

'Chicken, could be,' says Jackson. 'Roast chicken. My wife does it with lemon and some kind of herbs. Really moist. Tangy.'

The back of our van starts to be gently agitated.

I look out. A big black Staffordshire terrier is gnawing our tyre.

'Sir, what's the correct operating procedure if a big black dog is trying to eat our van?'

'You explain that he's committing an offence and you require him to cease and desist.'

I get out. The dog's name tag says he's called Tuggy and a much-chewed green toy lies at his feet.

I say, 'DCI Jackson says you're committing an offence and you're to cease and desist.'

He ceases, but it's a bit early to tell whether he's planning to desist. I try throwing the toy, but he has no interest in it. He licks my hand.

A man – grey-hair, old flannel shirt – approaches. Says, 'Not the most sociable day for a stake-out.'

Before I can tell him that this definitely isn't a stake-out, he opens his wallet and shows me his Police Federation card. 'Traffic officer for twenty years. Then ran the Brecon custody suite.'

I let Jackson deal with the guy. Jackson admits that there's a police presence in the village, but says we're keeping it quiet.

'Not like the lad in the Lotus, eh?'

Jackson laughs and says nothing.

The man leaves.

I don't know what's happened to the dog, but he's no longer eating our van.

I get back inside.

'Chicken, but from a packet,' says Jackson, disappointed. 'That's not right, is it?'

Since the mother is dying of obstructive lung disease and the son is on the run from multiple police forces, I think that packet chicken is the least of their worries.

We sit in the van and watch the road and I listen to Jackson talking about food.

It's a peaceful place. Nicer than Cardiff, I think. And Jackson is right: what makes a kid from here want to do what MacLeod did? I don't know.

The Police Federation guy approaches with a woman, his wife I assume, following on behind. Jackson winds down the window. The woman has two plates of food – turkey, roast potatoes, gravy, veg, stuffing, cranberry sauce. Knives and forks. Paper napkins.

'I hope this is OK,' she says. 'We just thought you couldn't sit there and go without. You can have a drink if you want it . . .'

'Oh, Lord, this looks all right. No, no drinks for us. Stuffing as well! What's your name? Sian? Sian, this looks amazing. A Queen's Police Medal for you, I reckon.'

They go. We eat. I don't eat much. Pick at my food until Jackson says, 'Oh for God's sake,' and takes the plate from my hands. Finishes everything on it.

I say, 'I was saving that.'

Time creeps forward.

Bethan asks her son about his year. He ducks the bigger issues – murder, torture, fleeing from justice – and talks about climbing.

Those Alpine sunsets.

Jackson jabs a knife at the screen. 'He sounds OK, really. I mean, you listen to him here, you wouldn't think he's done what he's done.'

Christmas angels remove our plates. Bring pudding and cream and mince pies.

We keep pace, more or less, with the MacLeods. On the radio, the boys in the other vans are grumbling at their foodlessness. Jackson and I say nothing.

I don't eat any Christmas pudding but keep Jackson away from my mince pie with the point of my fork.

'No wonder you're tiny. You don't eat anything,' he complains.

'You sound like my mam.'

Three o'clock approaches. The MacLeods are on coffee now.

Jackson reaches for the radio. Speaks to the officers behind the cottage. Tells them to 'Get close, get tight. Safeties on, please, gents. We are *not* expecting resistance.'

A video feed from the unit shows us what they're seeing. A steep embankment. Some closeboard fencing. Then the French windows at the back of the cottage. The MacLeods within.

Jackson calls the other units into position. The street, so empty for so long, is suddenly thickened by our presence. Black jackets. Fluorescent strips. Weapons pointed at the ground, but still visible.

Jackson is about to order the final approach, when something alerts Dylan MacLeod to our presence. Perhaps a flash from the garden. Perhaps a reflection from the street outside.

In any case, he goes to the French windows. Stares out.

'OK, boys. Show yourselves,' says Jackson. 'You can show your weapons, but don't point them.'

MacLeod stands at the window long enough to see all he needs. Moves to the other side of the small cottage, sees our presence.

Dense. Inescapable. Final.

A climb without exit.

He looks at the living room wall, suddenly wondering, too late, about surveillance. Speaking to the wall, he whispers, 'Give me a moment.' He chooses the wrong wall as it happens, but we catch the echo.

He goes to his mum.

Hugs her long and wordlessly.

'I've got to go, Mum.'

'Already? I thought . . .'

'Yeah, so did I. But something's come up. I love you, Mum. Thanks for absolutely everything.'

Pulls away.

The radio in the house is playing something slow and sad.

Like one of the slower, sadder bits of *Rhapsody in Blue*. Prison blue.

A pale, golden sunshine gilds the street.

MacLeod gets his coat. Reaches for his car keys, but then – rueful smile – realises he doesn't need them. Takes them anyway.

Leaves the living room. Steps into the front hall, heading for the door.

Jackson turns to me. 'Well?'

'Sir?'

'Well, Sergeant, I believe I asked you to arrest Peter Pan.'

So I get out of the van, and do just that.

# Afterword

Books, sometimes, arrive backwards. This one certainly did: my first really clear idea about this novel was that the denouement would come at sea, in a storm. I also knew, very early on, that Fiona would end up sinking the ship and would do so by tipping a bucket of fishguts into the engine.

But an ending isn't a story and the biggest question I had to answer was what on earth Fiona was doing at sea anyway. What crime could bring her out into an Atlantic storm? I mulled over lots of possibilities (shipping? fishing? something to do with oil? smuggling?), but then it came to me in a flash. Oxwich Bay is the launching point for some big international cables and those things trail out, under the sea, invisible and mostly unthought of. What if someone were attempting to sabotage one of those cables? That insight gave me, more or less, the story you've just read: an old-fashioned fraud, remade for the Internet age.

And that – give or take plenty of hard work – was that. Except that as I was in the course of writing, reality came jogging to catch up.

Atlantic Cables is a completely fictional outfit, of course, but it has real-life analogues which do much the same thing and for much the same client base: hedge funds, investment banks and anyone else with an interest in high-speed trading. Because the sums at stake are so huge, the investments are also huge. The high-speed trading community has spent billions of dollars, probably tens of billions, on fancy telecoms, fancy computers, and lots and lots of program code.

And so what, you might think? Who the hell cares?

The answer is simple. *You* should care because, it turns out that, those people are stealing *your* money. Let's say, for example, that the outfit which manages your pension money decides it wants to sell some of its stocks. Your pension manager will place a 'sell' order, which will work its way through to the exchange to be settled. Unfortunately for you, it turns out that those high-speed traders are able to 'see' that sell order before it's executed, so they can nip in ahead of you to make their trades, confident in the knowledge that they know what's coming. On the buy side, the same thing. It's like a guy who adds a penny to the price of tomatoes every time you enter the store. A guy who knocks prices down any time you have anything to sell. You get a worse deal; he gets to profit from the difference.

Because this is the financial industry, it works on a massive scale, ripping off everyone except those with no savings at all. Unless you are yourself a high-speed financial trader, you will find that your savings are lower, your pension crappier and your children poorer than they ought to be. It's theft, and one that operates on an almighty scale. If that seems improbable to you – surely not even bankers could behave like that? surely the authorities couldn't be so comatose as to allow it? – then it's worth reading a book, a superb exposé of the scam, which was published about the time I was nudging Fiona Griffiths into a barn near Rhayader.

That book is *Flash Boys*, by Michael Lewis. And it's like this book, except that the villains are real, the proceeds of theft much greater – and there's no Fiona Griffiths storming in to put things right.

**Harry Bingham**

## The Stonemonkey's challenge

Some readers will have noticed that I've had a little game with the character names in this book. Indeed, if you put aside names belonging to series characters, my game extends to pretty much everyone else. You've probably figured it out already, but if you haven't, then try playing around a bit on a search engine: I don't think it'll take you long.

I'm aware, however, that crime readers are a redoubtable breed and puzzles that can be solved by a little gentle Googling are hardly mysteries worthy of the name. So I've put together, below, a more challenging quiz, consisting of seven short questions. Just email me the answers via HarryBingham.com and, if you're the first person to get everything right, I'll send you a signed copy of every book so far. I'll also publish the winning entry on my website, so you can see the answers for yourself.

Oh, and if *your* name has found its way into this book, please don't think that the character concerned is a portrait of you. It isn't: this is a work of fiction. But since (to put it mildly) it's quite hard to meet the criteria for inclusion in this game of mine, I hope you enjoy being part of it. Truly, you walk among heroes.

1. Describe what happened on the First Date.
2. 'A face etched with the realisation of the final act in her

lover's biography'. Where might you find that realisation? Or, indeed, biography?

3. The lighthouse at Linton Hill stands on 'a kind of nose or headland'. What remarkable nose springs to mind?
4. When Fiona escaped from the barn near Rhayader, did she do so with a bang or a whimper? Please explain.
5. Rank the following: the Bellavista clinic, the *Isobel Baker* and her successful spells, the *Kate of St Ives* and her butterfly's dream, Jose Bereziatu's bloodbath.
6. Jackson mutters about the hi-jinks that his exhibits officers got up to in Central London. Just how high were those jinks? Answers in feet or metres, please.
7. Where is Mr Ondra?

# A note on Cotard's Syndrome

Cotard's syndrome is a rare but perfectly genuine condition, and an exceptionally serious one besides. Its core ingredients are depression and psychosis, which together bring about an extreme form of depersonalisation. Or, to put the same thing in plainer language: sufferers believe themselves to be dead. Patients frequently report 'seeing' their flesh decompose and crawl with maggots. Early childhood trauma is implicated in pretty much every well-documented case of the syndrome. Full recovery is uncommon, death by suicide all too frequent.

Fiona Griffiths's own state of mind is, of course, a fictional representation of a complex illness and I have not sought to achieve clinical precision. Nevertheless, the broad strokes of her condition would be familiar to anyone unfortunate enough to be acquainted with it.

## Stay in touch

About once a year, I send out an email alerting readers when I'm about to release a new book. If you would like to join my mailing list you can do so via HarryBingham.com. I promise not to clog your inbox with rubbish. I won't sell your details to the good folk who sell Viagra. And if you ever want to unsubscribe from my mailings, it'll be incredibly easy to do so.

I'd be thrilled if you did want to stay informed. Books need readers, and Fiona and I are blessed with an unusually committed and intelligent bunch. We're both mightily grateful.

**HB**

## About the Author

Harry Bingham is an author of fiction and non-fiction. He also runs The Writers' Workshop, an editorial consultancy, and Agent Hunter, a service which helps connect writers with literary agents. When he isn't working, he's probably looking after not one but two sets of twins, but can still just about remember a time when he found time for rock-climbing and wild-swimming. He is married and lives in Oxfordshire.